Desmond Bagley was born in 1923 in Kendal, Westmorland, and brought up in Blackpool. He began his working life, aged 14, in the printing industry, and then did a variety of jobs until going into an aircraft factory at the start of the Second World War.

When the war ended he decided to travel to southern Africa, going overland through Europe and the Sahara. He worked en route, reaching South Africa in 1951.

He became a freelance journalist in Johannesburg and wrote his first published novel, *The Golden Keel*, in 1962. In 1964 he returned to England and lived in Totnes for twelve years. He and his wife then moved to Guernsey in the Channel Islands. Here he found the ideal place for combining his writing with his other interests, which included computers, mathematics, military history, and entertaining friends from all over the world.

Desmond Bagley died in April 1983. Two previously unpublished Bagley novels have since been published: the first *Night of Error*, was published in 1984, the second, *Juggernaut*, in 1985. Both were on the bestseller lists for many weeks.

DESMOND BAGLEY

The Snow Tiger

FONTANA/Collins

To Joan, on her birthday
I said I would, and I did

First published by William Collins Sons & Co. Ltd 1975
First issued in Fontana Paperbacks 1976
Fifteenth impression November 1990

Printed and bound in Great Britain by
William Collins Sons & Co. Ltd, Glasgow

Snow is not a wolf in sheep's clothing
– it is a tiger in lamb's clothing.
Matthias Zdarsky

Absence of body is preferable to
presence of mind.

Anon.

This book is a work of fiction with its roots deeply embedded in fact. Many of the organizations mentioned exist, but it is not my intention to denigrate them in any way, and if I am thought to do so, I apologize.

The book would have been impossible to write without the help of many men and their expertise. My thanks go to Ken Parnell, one-time mountain guide in the Mount Cook National Park; Bob Waterhouse and Philip Brewer, both of the Cold Regions Research and Engineering Laboratory of the US Army Terrestrial Sciences Centre; Dr Barrie Murphy, MD; Lt-Comdr F. A. Prehn and Lt-Comdr Thomas Orr, both of Antarctic Development Squadron Six (VXE-6), Operation Deep Freeze.

My thanks also go to the staff of William Collins (New Zealand) Ltd, and the Librarian and staff of New Zealand House, London, for incredible patience in the face of a barrage of questions. I asked many stupid questions but never once got a stupid answer.

PROLOGUE

It was not a big avalanche, but then, it did not need to be very big to kill a man, and it was only because of Mike McGill's insistence on the Oertel cord that Ballard survived. Just as a man may survive in an ocean with the proper equipment and yet drown in a foot of water, so Ballard may have perished in a minor slippage that would have gone unrecorded even in avalanche-conscious Switzerland.

McGill was a good skier, as might be expected considering his profession, and he had taken the novice under his wing.

They had met in the ski lodge during an après-ski session and had taken an immediate liking to each other. Although they were the same age McGill appeared to be the older man, possibly because of his more varied life, but he became interested because Ballard had much to teach of areas other than snow and ice. They complemented each other, which is not an uncommon basis for friendship among men.

One morning McGill proposed something new. 'We've got to get you off the piste,' he said. 'And on to soft snow. There's nothing like cutting a first track.'

'Isn't it more difficult than on the piste?' queried Ballard.

McGill shook his head decisively. 'A beginner's myth. Turning is not quite as easy, but traversing is a cinch. You'll like it. Let's look at the map.'

They went up by the chair-lift, but instead of going down by the piste they struck off to the south, crossing a level plateau. After half an hour they arrived at the top of the clear slope which McGill had chosen, following local advice. He stopped, resting on his sticks, while he surveyed the slope. 'It looks all right, but we won't take chances. Here's where we put our tails on.'

He unzipped a pocket of his anorak and produced a bundle of red cord which he separated into two coils, one of which he handed to Ballard. 'Tie one end round your waist.'

'What for?'

'It's an Oertel cord – a simple device which has saved a hell of a lot of lives. If there's an avalanche and you get buried there'll be a bit of that red cord showing on the surface to show where you are so you can be dug out fast.'

Ballard looked down the slope. 'Is there likely to be an avalanche?'

'Not that I know of,' said McGill cheerfully, knotting the cord around his waist.

'I've never seen anyone else wearing these.'

'You've only been on the piste.' McGill noted Ballard's hesitancy. 'A lot of guys don't wear cords because they think it makes them look damn fools. Who wants to go down a slope wearing a red tail? they say. To my mind they're damn fools for not wearing them.'

'But avalanches!' said Ballard.

'Look,' said McGill patiently, and pointed down the slope. 'If I thought there was a serious avalanche risk down there we wouldn't be going down at all. I checked on the snow reports before we left and it's probably as safe as the nursery slopes. But *any* snow on *any* slope can be dangerous – and it doesn't have to be in Switzerland; people have been caught in avalanches on the South Downs in England. The cord is just a precaution, that's all.'

Ballard shrugged and began to tie the cord. McGill said, 'We'd better continue your education. Do you know what to do if the snow does slide?'

'Start praying?'

McGill grinned. 'You can do better than that. If it goes at all it will go under you skis or just behind you. It doesn't go in a rush so you have time to think about what to do – not much time, mind you. If it goes underfoot you might have time to jump higher up the slope, in which case you'll be out of it. If it starts sliding behind you and into you remember just one thing – you can't ski out of it. I might be able to, but not you.'

'So what do I do?'

'The first thing is to get your wrists out of the loops of the sticks. Throw the sticks away, then snap off the quick release fastenings on your skis. They're supposed to release automatically in a fall but don't trust them. When the snow hits you start swimming upstream and try to head up to the surface. Hold your breath and don't get bunged up with snow. When you feel yourself slowing bring one arm in front of your face, but not too close – that will give you an air space to

8

breathe, and maybe you can shout so that someone can hear you.' He laughed at the expression on Ballard's face, and said lightly, 'Don't worry, it may never happen. Let's go. I'll go first, not too fast, and you follow and do what I do.'

He launched himself down the slope and Ballard followed and had the most exhilarating ride of his life. As McGill had said, turning was not as easy in the soft snow and his ankles began to ache, but schussing was a joy. The cold wind stung his cheeks and whistled past his ears with a keening sound but, apart from that, the only sound was the hiss of his skis as they bit into the virgin snow.

Ahead of him, at the bottom of the slope, he saw McGill execute a stop christiania and come to a halt. As he drew alongside he said enthusiastically, 'That was great! Let's do it again.'

McGill laughed and pointed. 'We have a way to go to get back to the chair-lift; it's around the spur of the mountain. Maybe we'll have another crack at it this afternoon.'

At about three in the afternoon they arrived at the top of the chosen slope and McGill pointed to the two sets of tracks. 'There's been no one here but us chickens. That's what I like about this – it's not as crowded as the piste.' He handed an Oertel cord to Ballard. 'You go first this time; I want to watch your technique on the way down.'

As he knotted the cord he studied the slope. The late afternoon winter's sun was already sending long shadows creeping across the snow. McGill said, 'Keep to the centre of the slope in the sunlight; don't go into the shadowed areas.'

As he spoke Ballard took off, and McGill followed leisurely, keeping an eye on the less experienced skier and noting any faults for future instruction. All went well until he noted that Ballard was swinging to the left and towards slightly steeper ground where shadows lay. He increased speed, calling out as he did so, 'Keep to the right, Ian. Keep to the main slope.'

Even as he shouted he saw Ballard apparently trip, a slight hesitation in the smooth downward movement. Then the whole slope started to slide taking Ballard with it. McGill skidded to a halt, his face pale, and kept his eyes on Ballard who was now plunging out of control. He saw him throw away his right stick and then Ballard was hidden in a swirl of powder snow. A rumble filled the air with the noise of soft thunder.

Ballard had got rid of his sticks but found himself in a world of mad instability. He managed to release his right ski but then found himself upside down and rotating violently. He struck out vigorously with his arms, sternly repressing the rising tide of panic within him, and tried to remember McGill's instructions. Suddenly he felt an excruciating pain in his left thigh; his foot was being twisted outwards inexorably until it felt as though his leg was being unscrewed from the hip.

He nearly passed out from the pain but, after a sharp intensification, the pain eased a little. The tumbling motion ceased and he remembered what McGill had said about making an air space about his mouth, so he brought up his left hand across his face. Then all motion stopped and Ballard was unconscious.

All that had taken a little over ten seconds and Ballard had been carried not much over a hundred feet.

McGill waited until there was no further snow movement and then skied to the edge of the disturbed scar of tumbled snow. He scanned it quickly then, jabbing his sticks into the snow, he removed his skis. Carrying one stick and one ski he walked carefully into the avalanche area and began to quarter it. He knew from experience that now time was of the utmost importance; in his mind he could see the graph he had been shown a few days earlier at the local Parsenndienst Station – the length of time buried plotted against the chance of survival.

It took him half an hour to explore the area and he found nothing but snow. If he did not find Ballard he would have to begin probing with little chance of success. One man could not probe that area in the time available and the best bet was to go to find expert help – including an avalanche dog.

He reached the lower edge of the slide and looked up indecisively, then he squared his shoulders and began to climb upwards again through the centre of the slide. He would make one quick five-minute pass and if he did not find anything by the time he reached the top he would head back to the ski lodge.

He went upwards slowly, his eyes flickering from side to side, and then he saw it – a tiny fleck of blood red in the shadow of a clod of snow. It was less than the size of his little fingernail but it was enough. He dropped on one knee and scrabbled at the snow and came up with a length of red cord in his hand. He hauled on one end which came free, so he tackled the other.

The cord, tearing free from the snow, led him twenty feet

down the slope until, when he pulled, he came up against resistance and the cord was vertical. He started to dig with his hands. The snow was soft and powdery and was easy to clear, and he came across Ballard at a little more than three feet deep.

Carefully he cleared the snow from around Ballard's head, making sure first that he was breathing and second that he could continue to breathe. He was pleased to see that Ballard had followed instructions and had his arm across his face. When he cleared the lower half of Ballard's body he knew that the leg, from its impossible position, was broken – and he knew why. Ballard had not been able to release his left ski and, by the churning action of the snow, the leverage of the ski had *twisted* Ballard's leg broken.

He decided against trying to move Ballard, judging that he might do more harm than good, so he took off his anorak and tucked it closely around Ballard's body to keep him warm. Then he retrieved his skis and set off down to the road below where he was lucky enough to stop a passing car.

Less than two hours later Ballard was in hospital.

Six weeks later Ballard was still bed-ridden and bored. His broken leg was a long time in healing, not so much because of the broken bone but because the muscles had been torn and needed time to knit together. He had been flown to London on a stretcher, whereupon his mother had swooped on him and carried him to her home. Normally, when in London, he lived in his own small mews flat, but even he saw the force of her arguments and succumbed to her ministrations. So he was bed-ridden and bored in his mother's house and hating every minute of it.

One morning, after a gloom-laden visit from his doctor who prophesied further weeks of bed-rest, he heard voices raised in argument coming from the floor below. The lighter tones were those of his mother but he could not identify the deeper voice. The distant voices rose and fell in cadences of antagonism, continuing for a quarter of an hour, and then became louder as the running fight ascended the stairs.

The door opened and his mother came into the room, lips pursed and stormy in the brow. 'Your grandfather insists on seeing you,' she said curtly. 'I told him you're not well but he still insists – he's as unreasonable as ever. My advice is not to listen to him, Ian. But, of course, it's up to you – you've always

11

done as you pleased.'

'There's nothing wrong with me besides a bad leg.' He regarded his mother and wished, not for the first time, that she would show more sign of dress sense and not be so dowdy. 'Does he give me any option?'

'He says if you don't want to see him he'll go away.'

'Does he, by God? He must have been touched by an angel's wing. I'm almost inclined to test this improbability.' Sending Ben Ballard from a closed door was fit for inclusion in the *Guinness Book of Records.* Ian sighed. 'You'd better show him in.'

'I wish you wouldn't.'

'Bring him in, Mother; there's nothing wrong with me.'

'You're as pig-headed as he is,' she grumbled, but went to the door.

Ian had not seen old Ben for a year and a half and he was shocked at the transformation in the man. His grandfather had always been dynamic and bristling with energy but now he looked every day of his eighty-seven years. He came into the room slowly, leaning heavily upon a blackthorn stick; his cheeks were hollow and his eyes sunk deep into his head so that his normally saturnine expression was rendered skull-like. But there was still a faint crackle of authority as he turned his head and said snappily, 'Get me a chair, Harriet.'

A small snort escaped her but she placed a chair next to the bed and stood by it. Ben lowered himself into it creakily, planted the stick between his knees and leaned on it with both hands. He surveyed Ian, his eyes sweeping the length of the bed from head to foot and then back to the head. A sardonic grin appeared. 'A playboy, hey! One of the jet-set! I suppose you were at Gstaad.'

Ian refused to be drawn: he knew the old man's methods. 'Nothing so grand.'

Ben grinned widely like a shark. 'Don't tell me you went on a package tour.' One of his fingers lifted to point to the leg. It trembled slightly. 'Is it bad, boy?'

'It could have been worse – it could have been taken off.'

'Must you say such things?' Harriet's voice was pained.

Ben chuckled softly, and then his voice hardened. 'So you went skiing and you couldn't even do that right. Was it on company time?'

'No,' said Ian equably. 'And you know it. It was my first

holiday for nearly three years.'

'Humph! But you're lying in that bed on company time.'
Ian's mother was outraged. 'You're heartless!'

'Shut up, Harriet,' said the old man without, turning his
head. 'And go away. Don't forget to close the door behind
you.'

'I'll not be bullied in my own home.'

'You'll do as I say, woman. I have to talk business with this
man.'

Ian Ballard caught his mother's eye and nodded slightly. She
made a spitting sound and stormed out of the room. The door
slammed behind her. 'Your manners haven't improved,' Ian
said flatly.

Ben's shoulders shook as he wheezed with laughter. 'That's
why I like you, boy; no one else would have said that to my
face.'

'It's been said often enough behind your back.'

'What do I care about what's said? It's what a man does that
matters.' Ben's hands tightened momentarily upon his stick.
'I didn't mean what I said about you lying in bed on company
time – because you're not. We couldn't wait until you're up
and about. You've been replaced.'

'Fired!'

'In a manner of speaking. There'll be a job for you when
you're fit enough. I think it's a better job, but I doubt if you
will.'

'That depends on what it is,' said Ian cautiously.

'Nearly four years ago we opened a mine in New Zealand –
gold. Now that the price of gold has gone up it's beginning to
pay its way and the prospects are good. The managing director
is an old idiot called Fisher who was brought in for local
reasons, but he's retiring next month.' The stick thumped on
the floor. 'The man is senile at sixty-five – can you imagine
that?'

Ian Ballard was cautious when the Greeks came bearing
gifts. 'So?'

'So do you want the job?'

There had to be a catch. 'I might. When do I have to be out
there?'

'As soon as possible. I suggest you go by sea. You can rest
your leg as well on board a ship as here.'

'Would I have sole responsibilty?'

'The managing director is responsible to the Board – you know that.'

'Yes, and I know the Ballard set-up. The Board dances on strings pulled from London. I have no wish to be office boy to my revered uncles. I don't know why you let them get away with what they're doing.'

The old man's hands whitened as he clutched the knob on top of the blackthorn. 'You know I have no say in Ballard Holdings any more. When I set up the Trust I relinquished control. What your uncles do is their business now.'

'And yet you have a managing directorship in your gift?'

Ben offered his sharklike grin. 'Your uncles are not the only ones who can pull strings from time to time. Mind you, I can't do it too often.'

Ian thought about it. 'Where is the mine?'

'South Island.' Ben's voice was studiedly casual. 'Place called Hukahoronui.'

'*No!*' It was torn from Ian involuntarily.

'What's the matter? Scared to go back? Ben's upper lip drew back showing his teeth. 'If you are then you're no good blood of mine.'

Ian took a deep breath. 'Do you know what it means? To go back? You know how I loathe the place.'

'So you were unhappy there – that was a long time ago.' Ben leaned forward, bearing down heavily on the stick. 'If you turn down this offer you'll never be happy again – I can guarantee it. And it won't be because of anything I'll do, for there'll be no recriminations on my part. It's what you'll have to live with inside yourself that'll do the trick. For the rest of your life you'll wonder about it.'

Ian stared at him. 'You're an old devil.'

The old man chuckled deep in his throat. 'That's as may be. Young Ian, now listen you to me. I had four sons and three of them aren't worth the powder to blow 'em to hell. They're conniving, they're unscrupulous and they're crooked, and they're making Ballard Holdings into a stink in the City of London.' Ben drew himself up. 'God knows I was no angel in my time. I was rough and tough, I drove a hard bargain and maybe I cut a corner when it was needed, but that was in the nature of the times. But nobody ever accused Ben Ballard of being dishonest and nobody ever knew me to go back on my word. With me it was a word and a handshake, and that was recognized in the City as an iron-clad contract. But nobody will take your uncles' words – not any more. Anyone dealing with them must hire a regiment of lawyers to scrutinize the fine print.'

He shrugged. 'But there it is. They run Ballard Holdings now. I'm an old man and they've taken over. It's in the nature of things, Ian.' His voice became milder. 'But I had a fourth son and I hoped for a lot from him, but he was ruined by a woman, just as she damned near ruined you before I had the wit to jerk you out of that valley in New Zealand.'

Ian's voice was tight. 'Let's leave my mother out of this.'

Ben held up his hand placatingly. 'I like your loyalty, Ian, even though I think it's misplaced. You're not a bad son of your father just as he wasn't a bad son of mine – not really. The trouble was I handled the matter badly at the time.' He looked blindly into the past, then shook his head irritably. 'But that's gone by. It's enough that I got you out of Hukahoronui. Did I do right there?'

Ian's voice was low. 'I've never thanked you for that. I've never thanked you for that or for anything else.'

'Oh, you got your degree and you went to the Johannesburg School of Mines and from there to Colorado; and after that the Harvard Business School. You have a good brain and I didn't like to see it wasted.' He chuckled. 'Bread cast on the waters, boy; bread cast on the waters.' He leaned forward. 'You see, lad; I've come for repayment.'

Ian felt his throat constrict. 'What do you mean?'

'You'll please an old man by taking this job in Hukahoronui. Mind, you don't have to take it – you're a free agent. But I'd be pleased if you did.'

'Do I have to make up my mind now?'

Ben's voice was sardonic. 'Do you want to talk it over with your mother?'

'You've never liked her, have you?'

'She was a whining, puling schoolmarm, afraid of the world, who dragged a good man down to her crawling level. Now she's a whining, puling woman, old before her time because she's always been afraid of the world and of living, and she's trying to do the same to another man.' Ben was harsh. 'Why do you think I call you "boy" and "lad" when you're a grown man of thirty-five? Because that's all you are yet. For Christ's sake, make a decision of your own for once in your life.'

Ian was silent. At last he said, 'All right, I'll go to Huka-horonui.'

'Alone – without her?'

'Alone.'

Ben did not appear to be elated; he merely nodded his head gravely. He said, 'There's quite a town there now. I doubt if you'd recognize it, it's grown so much. I was there a couple of years ago before my damned doctor said I shouldn't travel any more. The place even has a mayor. The first mayor's name was John Peterson. Quite a power in the community the Petersons are.'

'Oh Jesus!' said Ian. 'Are they still there?'

'What would you expect? Of course they're still there. John, Eric and Charles – they're still there.'

'But not Alec.' Ian appeared to be addressing the back of his hands.

'No – not Alec,' Ben agreed.

Ian looked up. 'You're really asking for something, aren't you? What the hell do you expect of me? You know damned well that putting a Ballard into Huka is like putting a detonator into a stick of dynamite.'

Ben's eyebrows rose. 'The Petersons being the dynamite, I presume.' He leaned forward. 'I'll tell you what I want. I want you to run that bloody mine better than it's been run up to now. It's a tough job I've handed you. That old fool, Fisher, couldn't keep control – that's one thing. For another, Dobbs, the mine manager, is a chronic fence-sitter – and, for number three – Cameron, the engineer, is a worn-out American has-been who is holding on with his fingertips because he knows it's the last job he'll ever have and he's scared witless that he'll lose it. You have to put some backbone into that lot.'

Ben leaned back in his chair. 'Of course,' he said musingly, 'the Petersons won't welcome you with open arms. It's not likely, is it, when it's a family tradition of theirs that they were robbed of the mine? A lot of poppycock, of course, but that's what they believe – and, Ian, always remember that men are not governed by facts but by what they believe.' He nodded. 'Yes, I can see you might have trouble with the Petersons.'

'You can stop needling,' said Ian Ballard. 'I said I'd go.'

The old man made as if to rise, then paused. 'There is one thing. If anything serious should happen – to Ballard Holdings or to me – get in touch with Bill Stenning.' He thought awhile. 'On second thoughts, don't bother. Bill will get in touch with you fast enough.'

'What's this about?'

'Don't worry; it may never happen.' Ben got slowly to his feet and made his way to the door. He stopped halfway across the room and held up his blackthorn. 'I doubt if I'll want this any more. I'll send it to you tomorrow. You'll need it. When you've finished with it don't send it back – throw it away.'

He paused outside the door and raised his voice. 'You can come in now, Harriet. No need to listen at the keyhole.'

GOVERNMENT OF NEW ZEALAND

The Hearing of the Commission of Inquiry into the Disaster at Hukahoronui

CHAIRMAN: Dr H. A. Harrison

ASSESSORS: Prof. J. W. Rolandson
Mr F. G. French

SECRETARY: Mr J. Reed

in the Canterbury Provincial Chamber
CHRISTCHURCH, SOUTH ISLAND

CHAPTER ONE

The great hall was unexpectedly and floridly magnificent. Built in the mid-nineteenth century at the height of the Gothic Revival and designed by an architect who was, equally unexpectedly, a direct descendant of Simon de Montfort, it brought medieval England to the Southern Hemisphere and to that more-than-English city, Christchurch. Lofty, with an arched ceiling, painted and carved, it abounded in corbels, pillars, lancets and wood panelling, and every surface that could possibly be carved was carved to a fare-thee-well. There was also a lot of stained glass.

Dan Edwards, doyen of the Press of Christchurch, was blind to the incongruity of the scene; he had seen it too often before. He was more concerned about the floor which creaked abominably as the ushers walked beneath the Press gallery setting out note-pads and pencils. 'The acoustics are lousy,' he said. 'And that bloody kauri floor doesn't make things better.'

'Can't they oil it or something?' asked Dalwood, who was from Auckland.

'They've tried everything but nothing seems to work. I'll tell you what – let's do a pool. If I miss anything I'll take it from you – and vice versa.'

Dalwood shrugged. 'Okay.' He looked over the edge of the Press gallery to the dais immediately beneath. Three high-backed chairs were set behind the rostrum, and before each chair was a new foolscap note-pad with two ball-point pens to the left and three newly sharpened pencils to the right. Together with the water carafes and the glasses, the whole looked remarkably like place settings at a dining table.

Edwards followed his glance and then nodded towards the public gallery, already full, at the north end of the hall. 'They're going to make a meal of this.'

Dalwood nudged him and indicated the door beneath the public gallery. 'There's young Ballard. He's brought a legal army with him.'

Edwards studied the young man who walked at the head of a

phalanx of older, soberly dressed men. He pursed his lips. 'The question is whether they're representing him or the company. If I were Ballard I'd be keeping a tight sphincter.'

'A sacrificial lamb?'

'A lamb to the slaughter,' agreed Edwards. He looked down at the rostrum. 'Things are happening.'

The hum of conversation died as three men took their places at the chairs behind the rostrum. One of the two stenographers looked up and held his hands poised expectantly over the keys of his machine. There was a rustle as everyone arose.

The three men sat down and a fourth came forward and sat at the desk in front of the rostrum. He laid a sheaf of papers before him and consulted the uppermost document. The man above him, in the centre of the rostrum, was elderly with a shock of white hair and deeply lined face. He looked down at the virgin pad in front of him and pushed it away. When he spoke he spoke quietly and in an even voice.

'In the winter of the year, on the eighteenth of July, a disaster occurred in the township of Hukahoronui on the South Island of New Zealand in which fifty-four people lost their lives. The New Zealand Government has appointed a Commission of Inquiry, of which I am Chairman. My name is Arthur Harrison and I am Rector of Canterbury University.'

He moved his hands apart. 'With me are two assessors, both well qualified by their knowledge and experience to sit on this Commission. On my left we have Professor J. W. Rolandson of the Department of Scientific and Industrial Research.' Harrison paused. 'In the interests of brevity his department will, in future, be referred to as the DSIR.'

Rolandson smiled and nodded.

'On my right sits Mr F. G. French of the New Zealand Mines Department. The gentleman immediately below me is Mr John Reed, barrister-at-law; he is Secretary to the Commission.' Harrison surveyed the tables in the hall. 'There are several interested parties present. Perhaps they would identify themselves, beginning from the right.'

The well-fed, middle-aged man seated next to Ballard rose to his feet. 'John Rickman, barrister, representing the Hukahoronui Mining Company, Proprietary, Limited.'

There was a long pause before the man at the next table got to his feet, and Edwards whispered, 'Ballard has no personal representation.'

'Michael Gunn, barrister, representing the General Miners'

Union of New Zealand and the relatives of its members who lost their lives in the disaster.'

'Alfred Smithers, barrister, representing the Ministry of Civil Defence.'

'Peter Lyall, barrister, representing Charles Stewart Peterson and Eric Parnell Peterson.'

There was a sound of surprise in the room, a compound of sudden involuntary movement and indrawn breath. Edwards looked up from his notes. 'Why should they think they need legal help? This sounds promising.'

Harrison waited until the stir died away. 'I see we are greatly endowed with legal aid. I must therefore warn the legal gentlemen present that this is not a Court of Law. It is a Commission of Inquiry which is empowered to make its own rules of procedure. Evidence will be heard here which would not necessarily be admissable before a Court of Law. The object of this Commission is to find the truth of what happened during the events which led up to the avalanche at Hukahoronui, during the avalanche itself, and what happened afterwards.'

He leaned back in his chair. 'Adversary tactics, such as are common in law courts, will be frowned upon here. We wish to find the truth unimpeded by legal technicalities, and the reason we wish to find the truth is to make certain that such a disaster does not happen again. The force of this consideration is so great that the Commission hereby rules that any evidence given here may not be used in any future legal action other than criminal which may eventuate as a result of the avalanche at Hukahoronui. The protection of lives in the future is of more importance than the punishment of those who may be felt to be guilty of acts of omission or commission arising out of the disaster. The Commission is legally empowered to make such a ruling and I hereby do so.'

Gunn hastily rose to his feet. 'Mr Chairman; do you not think that is an arbitrary decision? There will be matters of compensation arising. If interested parties are denied the use of evidence in a future legal action, surely an injustice will be done.'

'Mr Gunn, I have no doubt that the government will appoint an arbitrator who will study the findings of this Commission and make the necessary dispositions. Does that satisfy you?'

Gunn bobbed his head, a pleased expression on his face. 'Indeed it does, Mr Chairman.'

Dalwood murmured to Edwards, 'No wonder he's pleased.

23

It's all going to happen here – a bloody drumhead court-martial with no holds barred.'

Edwards grunted. 'He'll not get much past old Harrison.'

'And now we come to the question of witnesses. Some citizens have come forward voluntarily to give evidence here, others have been subpoena'd by one or more of the interested parties.' Harrison frowned. 'I, and my fellow members on the Commission, have been much exercised as to how the evidence should be taken, and we have decided that it shall be taken in chronological order, insofar as that is possible. Because of this, any person giving evidence may be asked to step down before his evidence is wholly completed if we find it necessary to do some filling in. It follows, then, that all witnesses should hold themselves in readiness at all times during the sitting of the Commission.'

'Mr Chairman!'

Rickman was on his feet. Harrison said, 'Yes, Mr Rickman?'

'Such a condition is likely to be onerous on certain of the witnesses. Some of them are busy men with duties which lie outside this room. This is likely to be a long inquiry and I do not feel that such a condition is entirely fair.'

'When you refer to certain of the witnesses can I take it that you refer to Mr Ballard?' asked Harrison drily.

'Mr Ballard is one such witness,' conceded Rickman. 'Out of consideration for him it would be better if he could give his evidence and retire.'

'Is Mr Ballard a citizen of New Zealand?'

'No, Mr Chairman; he is a United Kingdom subject.'

'And would his retirement from this hall be as far away as England?'

Rickman bent down and spoke quietly to Ballard who replied in equally low tones. Rickman straightened. 'It is true that there are certain matters in the United Kingdom which urgently require Mr Ballard's attention.'

Harrison's voice was cold. 'If I thought it was Mr Ballard's intention to leave New Zealand during the sitting of this Commission I would ask the relevant authority to relieve him of his passport. This inquiry is a serious matter, Mr Rickman.'

'I am sure it is not Mr Ballard's intention to flout the authority of the Commissioners,' said Rickman hastily. He bent down again and spoke to Ballard, then he rose and said, 'Mr

Ballard has no intention of leaving New Zealand at the present time.'

'I would prefer to hear that from Mr Ballard.' Harrison leaned forward. 'Is that correct, Mr Ballard?'

Ballard stood, and said in a low voice. 'That is correct, sir. My time is at the disposal of the Commissioners.'

'In that case you will have no objection to attending this inquiry with the rest of the witnesses. Thank you.'

In the Press gallery Edwards said, 'My God! Whoever Rickman is representing, he's not representing Ballard. He set him up just to knock him down.'

Harrison said, 'This inquiry will not have the formality of a law court, but neither will it be a free-for-all. Representatives of the interested parties may address the witnesses at the discretion of the Chairman. It will not be necessary to disturb the sacro-iliac by standing each time – a mere raising of the hand will suffice. The assessors may question the witnesses in their respective fields of expertise.'

He put his hands together. 'Since we are gathering information in chronological order it becomes necessary to decide at which point of time to begin. From depositions laid before the Commission I gather that it was the appearance of Mr Ballard in Hukahoronui which led to a series of events which may – or may not – have relevance to the disaster which took place some weeks later. That is for this inquiry to decide. Be that as it may, I think the first witness should be Mr Ballard.'

Reed, the secretary, said, 'Will you come forward, Mr Ballard, and sit down there?' He indicated an ornately carved chair a little to the right of the rostrum. He waited until Ballard was seated, then said, 'Your name is Ian Dacre Ballard?'

'Yes, sir.'

'And you are managing director of the Hukahoronui Mining Company, Proprietary, Limited?'

'No, sir.'

A hum as of a disturbed hive of bees filled the air. Harrison waited until it had died away, then said quietly, 'All present will be silent during the questioning of witnesses.' He leaned forward. 'Thank you, Mr Reed; I'll take it from here. Mr Ballard, at the time of the avalanche were you managing director of the company?'

'Yes, sir.'

'Can you give me a reason why you are no longer in that position?'

Ballard's voice was colourless. 'I was suspended from my duties a fortnight after the disaster.'

'I see.' Harrison's eyes flicked sideways as he saw a hand raised. 'Yes, Mr Gunn?'

'Can the witness tell us who owns the Hukahoronui Mining Company?'

Harrison nodded to Ballard, who said, 'It's a wholly-owned subsidiary of New Zealand Mineral Holdings, Limited.'

'And that company is just a shell instituted for legal and financial reasons, is it not? Who owns it?'

'It is owned substantially by the International Mining Investment Corporation.'

'And who has the controlling interest in the International Mining Investment Corporation?'

'Mr Chairman!' Rickman said sharply. 'Is there provision in your procedure for objections?'

'Of course, Mr Rickman. What is your objection?'

'I cannot see what this line of questioning has to do with an avalanche on a hillside.'

'Neither can I,' said Harrison. 'But no doubt Mr Gunn can make it clear.'

'I think the answer to my last question will make it quite clear,' said Gunn. 'I asked who owns the controlling interest in the International Mining Investment Corporation.'

Ballard raised his head and said clearly, 'Ballard Holdings, Limited, registered in the City of London.'

Gunn smiled. 'Thank you.'

'Well, well!' said Edwards, scribbling rapidly. 'So he's one of those Ballards.'

Dalwood chuckled. 'And Gunn is gunning for Rickman. Up the workers and down with international capital. He smells money.'

Harrison tapped lightly with his gavel and the hall became quiet again. 'Mr Ballard, do you own shares – or any interest whatever – in Ballard Holdings? Or in any of the companies mentioned?'

'No, sir.'

'Does any of your family own any such interest?'

'Yes; my three uncles and some of my cousins.'

'Not your father?'

'He is dead.'

'How did you come to be appointed managing director of the Hukahoronui Mining Company?'

Ballard shrugged. 'The company is an old family concern and I suppose that . . .'

'Can the witness describe his qualifications for the position?'

Harrison jerked his head around to identify the source of the interruption. 'You will oblige me by not calling out in this hall, Mr Lyall. Further, you must not interrupt a witness.' In a milder voice he said, 'However, the question is relevant and the witness will answer.'

'I have a degree in mining engineering from Birmingham University. I have done post-graduate studies in South Africa and the United States.'

Lyall had his arm firmly in the air by this time. 'But no *practical* experience as a mining engineer?'

Pink spots glowed in Ballard's cheeks but he appeared to be in control as he said to Harrison, 'May I finish answering Mr Lyall's *first* question?'

'Of course.' Harrison looked at Lyall. 'Mr Lyall: you will *not* interrupt the witness, and you *will* address your questions through me unless I indicate otherwise. Go on, Mr Ballard.'

'I was about to say that, apart from the engineering studies, I attended the Harvard Business School for two years. As for practical experience as a mining engineer, that would be called for if I professed to be a mining engineer, but as managing director my field was rather that of business administrator.'

'A valid point,' said Harrison. 'A managing director need not have the technical expertise of the men he directs. If it were so a large number of our managing directors would be immediately unemployed – and possibly unemployable.'

He waited until the laughter died away, then said, 'I do not see the point in further questioning along those lines, Mr Lyall.' As Lyall's hand remained obstinately raised, he said, 'Do you have a further – and different – question?'

'Yes, Mr Chairman. I am reliably informed that when Mr Ballard appeared in Hukahoronui he was unable to walk except with the aid of a stick. Is this correct?'

'Is this relevant, Mr Lyall?'

'I believe so, sir.'

'Witness will answer the question.'

'It is correct.'

Lyall, his hand up, remained punctiliously silent until Harrison nodded at him curtly. 'Can you tell us why?'

'I broke my leg in a skiing accident in Switzerland.'

'Thank you, Mr Ballard.'

'I can't say that I see the relevance,' observed Harrison. 'But no doubt it will appear in time.'

'It was in an avalanche,' said Ballard.

There was dead silence in the hall.

CHAPTER TWO

Harrison looked across at Lyall. 'The significance still escapes me,' he said. 'And since Mr Lyall does not see fit to pursue the subject I think we should carry on. Mr Ballard, when did you arrive in Hukahoronui?'

'On the sixth of June – six weeks before the avalanche.'

'So you had not been there very long. Was Hukahoronui what you expected?'

Ballard frowned in thought. 'The thing that struck me most was how much it had changed.'

Harrison's eyebrows rose. 'Changed! Then you had been here before?'

'I lived there for fifteen years – from infancy until just after my sixteenth birthday.'

Harrison made a note. 'Go on, Mr Ballard. How had Hukahoronui changed?'

'It was bigger. The mine was new, of course, but there were more houses – a lot more houses.' He paused. 'There was a lot more snow than I seem to remember from my childhood.'

Professor Rolandson of the DSIR said, 'It is a matter of record that the snow precipitation in the Southern Alps was exceptionally high this past winter.'

Ballard had been depressed as he drove west from Christchurch in a company Land-Rover. He was going back to his origins, to Hukahoronui which lies in an outrider of the Two Thumbs Range, and which he had never expected to see again.

Hukahoronui.

A deep valley in the mountains entered by a narrow rock-split gap and graced with stands of tall trees on the valley slopes. A river runs through, cold from the ice water of the high peaks, and there is a scattering of houses up the valley, loosely centred about a church, a general store and a village school. His mother had once been the schoolteacher.

He hated the place.

It was a bad place to get to in thick snow. There had been heavy snowfalls and even with snow tyres and four-wheel drive Ballard found the going tricky. As far as he could remember there had not been a snow like that in those parts since 1943, but of that his memory was understandably hazy – he had been four years old at the time. But he had particular reasons for remembering the heavy snow of that year.

After a lot of low gear work he eventually reached the Gap and he pulled off the road on to a piece of level ground overlooking the river gorge where he contemplated Hukahoronui.

It had certainly changed, just as old Ben said it had. In the distance was a little township where no township had been. On one side, under the western slope of the valley, was a cluster of industrial buildings, presumably the milling works and refinery belonging to the mine. A streamer of black smoke coming from a tall chimney was like a stain against the white hillside beyond.

The township spread along the valley floor with most of the houses to the west of the river which had been bridged. The valley people had talked inconclusively for years about putting a bridge across the river, and now it had been done at last under the prodding thrust of an affluent economy. That was probably to be chalked up on the credit side; you had to pay the price of the mine to get the bridge.

Beyond the township there did not seem to be much change. In the far distance Ballard saw Turi's house beneath the great rock called Kamakamaru. He wondered if the old man was still alive or whether the smoke coming from that distant chimney rose from the fireside of another. Turi had been an old man even when Ballard left the valley, although age in a Maori is difficult to estimate, especially for a youth of sixteen. At sixteen anyone over forty is verging on decrepitude.

But there was something else about the valley that was strange and Ballard was puzzled to determine what it was. A change had occurred which had nothing to do with the mine or the new town and he tried to match up sixteen-year-old memories with the actuality before him. It was nothing to do with the river; that still ran the same course, or seemed to.

And then he found the change. The hill slope on the western side was now almost completely treeless. Gone were the stands of tall white pine and cedar, of kahikatea and kohekohe – the hillside had been stripped almost completely bare. Ballard looked up at the higher slopes of the mountain to where the snows stretched right up to the base of the crags in one smooth and beautiful sweep. It looked good for skiing.

He switched on the engine and went on down into the new town. As he approached he was impressed by the way it had been laid out. Although much detail was blanketed by snow he could see the areas which, in summer, would be pleasant open gardens and there was a children's playground, the swings and slides, the seesaws and the jungle gym, now white-mantled and stalactited with icicles and out of use.

Although the house roofs were heavily laden with snow the road was quite clear and had apparently been swept recently. Coming into the town centre he came across a bulldozer clearing the road with dropped blade. There was a name on its side: HUKAHORONUI MINING CO. (PTY) LTD. It seemed as though the mine management took an interest in municipal affairs. He approved.

There were houses built along the bluff that projected into the river; when Ballard was a child that was called the Big Bend and that was where they had their swimming hole. Peterson's store used to be at the base of the bluff, and so it still was, although it took him a long time to recognize it. In his day it had been single-storey with a corrugated iron roof, a low building with spreading eaves which protected against the summer sun. There used to be chairs on the veranda and it was a favourite place for gossip. Now it was two-storey with a false façade to make it look even larger, and there were big plate-glass windows brightly lit. The veranda had gone.

He pulled the Land-Rover into a designated parking place and sourly wondered when parking meters would be installed. The sun was setting behind the western slopes of the valley and already the long shadows were creeping across the town. That was one of the drawbacks of Hukahoronui; in a narrow valley set north and south nightfall comes early.

Across the street was a still-raw building of unmellowed concrete calling itself the Hotel D'Archiac – a name stolen from a mountain. The street was reasonably busy; private cars and industrial trucks passed by regularly, and women with shopping bags hurried before the shops closed. At one time Peterson's had been the only store, but from where he sat in the car Ballard could see three more shops, and there was a service station on the corner. Lights glowed in the windows of the old school which had sprouted two new wings.

Ballard reached for the blackthorn stick which was on the back seat and then got out of the car. He crossed the road towards the hotel leaning heavily on the stick because he still could not bear to put too much weight on his left leg. He supposed that Dobbs, the mine manager, would have accommodated him, but it was late in the day and he did not want to cause undue disturbance so he was quite prepared to spend a night in the hotel and introduce himself to the mine staff the following morning.

As he approached the hotel entrance a man came out walking quickly and bumped his shoulder. The man made a mutter of annoyance – not an apology – and strode across the pavement to a parked car. Ballard recognized him – Eric Peterson, the second of the three Peterson brothers. The last time he had seen Eric he had been nineteen years old, tall and gangling; now he had filled out into a broad-shouldered brawny man. Apparently the years had not improved his manners much.

Ballard turned to go into the hotel only to encounter an elderly woman who looked at him with recognition slowly dawning in her eyes. 'Why, it's Ian Ballard,' she said, adding uncertainly, 'It *is* Ian, isn't it?'

He hunted through his memories to find a face to match hers. And a name to put to the face. Simpson? No – it wasn't that. 'Hello, Mrs Samson,' he said.

'Ian Ballard,' she said in wonder. 'Well, now; what are you doing here – and how's your mother?'

'My mother's fine,' he said, and lied bravely. 'She asked to be remembered to you.' He believed white lies to be the social oil that allows the machinery of society to work smoothly.

'That's good of her,' said Mrs Samson warmly. She waved her arm. 'And what do you think of Huka now? It's changed a lot since you were here.'

'I never thought I'd see civilization come to the Two Thumbs.'

'It's the mine, of course,' said Mrs Samson. 'The mine brought the prosperity. Do you know, we even have a town council now.'

'Indeed,' he said politely. He looked out of the corner of his eye and saw Eric Peterson frozen in the act of unlocking his car and staring at him.

'Yes, indeed,' said Mrs Samson. 'And I'm a councillor, imagine that! Whoever would have thought it. But whatever are you doing here, Ian?'

'Right now I'm going into the hotel to book a room.' He was sharply aware that Eric Peterson was walking towards him.

'Ian Ballard.' Peterson's voice was flat and expressionless.

Ballard turned, and Mrs Samson said, 'Do you two know each other? This is Eric Peters . . .' Her voice tailed away and a wary look came into her eyes, the look of one who has almost committed a social gaffe. 'But of course you know each other,' she said slowly.

'Hello, Eric.'

There was little humour in Peterson's thin smile. 'And what are you doing here?'

There was no point in avoiding the issue. Ballard said, 'I'm the new managing director of the mining company.'

Something sparked in Peterson's eyes. 'Well, well!' he said in tones of synthetic wonder. 'So the Ballards are coming out of hiding. What's the matter, Ian? Have you run out of phoney company names?'

'Not really,' said Ballard. 'We've got a computer that makes them up for us. How are you doing, Eric?'

Peterson looked down at the stick on which Ballard was leaning. 'A lot better than you, apparently. Hurt your leg? Nothing trivial, I hope.'

Mrs Samson suddenly discovered reasons for not being there, reasons which she explained volubly and at length. 'But if you're staying I'll certainly see you again,' she said.

Peterson watched her go. 'Silly old bat! She's a hell of a nuisance on the council.'

'You a member, too?'

Peterson nodded abstractly – his thought processes were almost visible. 'Did I hear you say you are booking a room in the hotel?'

'That's right.'

Peterson took Ballard's arm. 'Then let me introduce you to the manager.' As they went into the lobby he said, 'Johnnie and I own half of this place, so we can certainly find room for an old friend like you.'

'You're doing well for yourself.'

Peterson grinned crookedly. 'We're getting something out of the mine, even if it isn't raw gold.' He stopped at the reception desk. 'Jeff, this is Ian Ballard, an old friend. You would say we were friends, wouldn't you, Ian?' He drove over any reply that

Ballard might have made. 'Jeff Weston is manager here and owns the other half of the hotel. We have long arguments over which half he owns; he claims the half with the bar and that's a matter for dispute.'

'Glad to meet you, Mr Ballard,' said Weston.

'I'm sure you can find a good room for Mr Ballard.'

Weston shrugged. 'No difficulty.'

'Good,' said Peterson jovially. 'Give Mr Ballard a room – the best we have.' His eyes suddenly went flinty and his voice hardened. 'For twenty-four hours. After that we're full. I wouldn't want you to get the wrong idea of your welcome here, Ballard. Don't be fooled by Mrs Samson.'

He turned on his heel and strode away, leaving Weston open-mouthed. Ballard said lightly, 'Eric always was a joker. Do I sign the register, Mr Weston?'

That night Ballard wrote a letter to Mike McGill. In it, among other things, was the following passage:

I remember you telling me that you'd be in New Zealand this year. Why don't you come out earlier as my guest? I'm in a place called Hukahoronui in South Island; there's a hell of a lot of snow and the skiing looks great. The place has changed a bit since I was here last; civilization has struck and there are great developments. But it's not too bad really and the mountains are still untouched. Let me know what you think of the idea – I'd like to meet your plane in Auckland.

CHAPTER THREE

Harrison sipped water from a glass and set it down. 'Mr Ballard, at what point did you become aware of danger by avalanche?'

'Only a few days before the disaster. My attention was drawn to the danger by a friend, Mike McGill, who came to visit me.'

Harrison consulted a document. 'I see that Dr McGill has voluntarily consented to appear as a witness. I think it would be better if we heard his evidence from his own lips. You may step down, Mr Ballard, on the understanding that you may be called again.'

'Yes, sir.' Ballard returned to his seat.

Reed said, 'Will Dr McGill please come forward?'

McGill walked towards the rostrum carrying a slim leather satchel under his arm. He sat down, and Reed said, 'Your name is Michael Howard McGill?'

'Yes, sir; it is.'

Harrison caught the transatlantic twang in McGill's voice. 'Are you an American, Dr McGill?'

'No, sir; I'm a Canadian citizen.'

'I see. It is very public-spirited of you to volunteer to stay and give evidence.'

McGill smiled. 'No trouble at all, sir. I have to be here in Christchurch in any case. I leave for the Antarctic next month. As you may know, the Operation Deep Freeze flights leave from here.'

Professor Rolandson stirred. 'You're going to the Antarctic and your name is McGill! Would you be the Dr McGill who wrote a paper on stress and deformation in snow slopes which appeared in the last issue of the *Antarctic Journal*?'

'Yes, sir.'

Rolandson turned to Harrison. 'I think we are fortunate in having Dr McGill with us. I have read many of his papers and his qualifications as an expert witness are unimpeachable.'

'Yes, indeed.' Harrison waggled an eyebrow. 'But I think his qualifications should be read into the record. Will you tell us something about yourself, Dr McGill?'

'I'd be glad to.' McGill paused, marshalling his thoughts. 'I took a B.Sc. in physics at the University of Vancouver and then spent two years with the Canadian DSIR in British Columbia. From there I went to the United States – M.Sc. in meteorology at Columbia University and D.Sc. in glaciology at the California Institute of Technology. As to practical experience, I have spent two seasons in the Antarctic, a year in Greenland at Camp Century, two years in Alaska and I have just completed a year's sabbatical in Switzerland doing theoretical studies. At present I work as a civilian scientist in the Cold Regions Research and Engineering Laboratory of the United States Army Terrestrial Sciences Centre.'

There was a silence which was broken by Harrison. He gave a nervous cough. 'Yes, indeed. For simplicity's sake, how would you describe your employment at present?'

McGill grinned. 'I have been described as a snowman.' A ripple of laughter swept across the hall, and Rolandson's lips twitched. 'I should say that I am engaged on practical and theoretical studies of snow and ice which will give a better understanding of the movement of those materials, particularly in relation to avalanches.'

'I agree with Professor Rolandson,' said Harrison. 'We are very fortunate to have such a qualified witness who can give an account of the events before, during and after the disaster. What took you to Hukahoronui, Dr McGill?'

'I met Ian Ballard in Switzerland and we got on very well together. When he came to New Zealand he invited me to visit him. He knew that I was coming to New Zealand on my way to the Antarctic and suggested that I arrive a little earlier than I had originally intended. He met me at the airport in Auckland and then we both went down to Hukahoronui.'

Lyall held up his hand, and Harrison nodded to him. 'How long did the witness know Mr Ballard in Switzerland?'

'Two weeks.'

'Two weeks!' repeated Lyall. 'Did it not seem strange to you on such a casual acquaintanceship that Mr Ballard should undertake such a long journey involving an air flight from South Island to North Island to meet you at the airport?'

Harrison opened his mouth as though to object, but McGill, his face hardened, beat him to it. 'I don't understand the import of the question, but I'll answer it. Mr Ballard had to attend a board meeting of his company in Auckland with which my arrival coincided.'

'I didn't understand the tenor of that question, either, Mr Lyall,' said Harrison grimly. 'Does the answer satisfy you?'

'Yes, sir.'

'It will speed this inquiry if irrelevant questions are kept to a minimum,' said Harrison coldly. 'Go on, Dr McGill.'

In the Press gallery Dan Edwards said, 'There was some sort of malice behind that. I wonder what instructions the Petersons have given Lyall.'

McGill said, 'There was a lot of snow on the way to Hukahoronui . . .'

Fifteen miles from Hukahoronui they came across a Volkswagen stuck in a drift, the skis strapped on the top proclaiming its purpose. It contained two Americans helplessly beleaguered by the snow. Ballard and McGill helped to haul the car free and received effusive thanks from the two men who were called Miller and Newman. McGill looked at the Volkswagen, and commented, 'Not the best car for the conditions.'

'You can say that again,' said Newman. 'There's more snow here than in Montana. I didn't expect it to be like this.'

'It's an exceptional season,' said McGill, who had studied the reports.

Miller said, 'How far is it to Huka . . .' He stumbled over the word but finally got it out by spacing the syllables. 'Huka-horo-nui?'

'About fifteen miles,' said Ballard. He smiled. 'You can't miss it – this road goes nowhere else.'

'We're going for the skiing,' said Newman. He grinned as he saw Ballard's eye wander to the skis strapped on top of the car. 'But I guess that's evident.'

'You're going to get stuck again,' said Ballard. 'That's inevitable. You'd better go on ahead and I'll follow, ready to pull you out.'

'Say, that's good of you,' said Miller. 'We'll take you up on that offer. You've got more beef than we have.'

They hauled the Volkswagen out of trouble five times before they reached Hukahoronui. On the fifth occasion Newman said, 'It's real good of you guys to go to all this trouble.'

Ballard smiled. 'You'd do the same, I'm sure, if the position were reversed.' He pointed. 'That's the Gap – the entrance to the valley. Once you're through there you're home and dry.'

They followed the Volkswagen as far as the Gap and watched it descend into the valley, then Ballard pulled off the road. 'Well, there it is.'

McGill surveyed the scene with a professional eye. Instinctively he looked first at the white sweep of the western slope and frowned slightly, then he said, 'Is that your mine down at the bottom there?'

'That's it.'

'You know something? I haven't asked what you get out of there.'

'Gold,' said Ballard. 'Gold in small quantities.' He took a packet of cigarettes and offered one to McGill. 'We've known the gold was there for a long time – my father was the first to pick up the traces – but there wasn't enough to take a chance on investment, not while the gold price was fixed at thirty-five dollars an ounce. But when the price was freed the company

36

risked a couple of million pounds sterling in establishing the plant you see down there. At present we're just breaking even; the gold we're getting out is just servicing the capital investment. But the pickings are getting richer as we follow the reef and we have hopes.'

McGill nodded abstractedly. He was peering through the side window at the rock walls on either side of the Gap. 'Do you have much trouble in keeping the road clear just here?'

'We didn't seem to have trouble years ago when I used to live here. But we're having a fair amount now. The town has got some of the company's earth-moving machinery on more-or-less permanent loan.'

'It'll get worse,' said McGill. 'Maybe a lot worse. I did a check on meteorological conditions; there's a lot of precipitation this year and the forecast is for more.'

'Good for skiers,' said Ballard. 'Bad for mining. We're having trouble getting equipment in.' He put the car in gear. 'Let's get down there.'

He drove through the town and then to the mine office. 'Come in and meet the senior staff,' he said, then hesitated. 'Look, I'm going to be a bit busy for maybe an hour.' He grinned. 'Finding out if they've made a fortune while I've been away. I'll get someone to take you to the house.'

'That'll be fine,' said McGill.

They went into the office building and Ballard opened a door. 'Hello, Betty. Is Mr Dobbs in?'

Betty jerked her thumb. 'Inside with Mr Cameron.'

'Fine. Come on, Mike.' He led the way to an inner office where two men were discussing a plan laid on a desk. 'Hello, Mr Dobbs; hello, Joe. I'd like you to meet a friend who'll be staying in Huka for a while – Mike McGill. This is Harry Dobbs, the mine manager, and Joe Cameron, the mine engineer.'

Dobbs was a thin-faced New Zealander with a dyspeptic expression who looked as though his wife's cooking did not agree with him. Cameron was a broad-shouldered American pushing sixty but not admitting it. They shook hands, and Ballard said, 'Everything okay?'

Cameron looked at Dobbs and Dobbs looked at Cameron. Dobbs said in a thin voice, 'The situation is deteriorating at the same rate.'

Cameron chuckled. 'What he means is that we're still having trouble with this goddam snow. We had a truck stuck in the

Gap yesterday; took two 'dozers to get it out.'

'If we can't keep up essential supplies then output is going to be restricted,' said Dobbs.

'I don't think we'll make a profit this half year,' said Ballard.

'Mike, here, says things will get worse, and he ought to know – he's a snow expert.'

'Don't take that as gospel,' protested McGill. 'I've been known to be wrong.' He looked through the window. 'Is that the mine entrance?'

Cameron followed his gaze. 'Yes, that's the portal. Most people think of a mine as having a vertical shaft, but we just drove an adit into the mountainside. It slopes down inside, of course, as we follow the reef.'

'It reminds me of a place in British Columbia called Granduc.' McGill slanted his eyes at Cameron. 'Know it?'

Cameron shook his head. 'Never heard of it.'

McGill looked oddly disappointed.

Dobbs was saying, '. . . and Arthur's Pass was closed for twelve hours yesterday, and the Haast has been closed since Tuesday. I haven't heard about Lewis Pass.'

'What have those passes to do with us?' asked Ballard. 'Our supplies come from Christchurch and don't cross the mountains at all.'

'They're the main passes across the Southern Alps,' said Dobbs. 'If the government can't keep them open, then what chance do we have? They'll be using every machine they've got, and no one is going to send a snow plough to clear a way to Hukahoronui – it's a dead end.'

'We'll just have to do the best we can, Mr Dobbs.' Ballard jerked his head at McGill. 'Let's get you settled in, Mike.'

McGill nodded and said to the room at large, 'Nice to have met you.'

'We'll have to get together,' said Cameron. 'Come over to my place and have dinner some time. My daughter's a great cook.'

Dobbs said nothing.

They went into the outer office. 'Betty will show you where the house is. The bedroom on the left at the back is yours. I won't be more than an hour.'

'Take your time,' said McGill.

It was nearly three hours later when Ballard turned up and by that time McGill had unpacked, taken a walk around town which did not take long, and returned to the house to make an urgent telephone call.

When Ballard came into the house he looked tired and depressed. When he saw McGill he winced as recollection came back. 'Oh hell! I forgot to tell Mrs Evans we were coming back. There's no grub ready.'

'Relax,' said McGill. 'There's something in the oven – McGill's Antarctic Burgoo, as served in all the best restaurants south of latitude sixty. We'll eat well.'

Ballard sighed in relief. 'I thought we'd have to eat in the hotel. I'm not too popular there.'

McGill let that pass. 'There's just one thing I can't find – your booze.'

Ballard grinned. 'Come on.'

They went into the living-room, and McGill said, 'I used your phone. I hope you don't mind.'

'Be my guest.' Ballard opened a cupboard and took out a bottle and two glasses.

'You get your supplies from Christchurch. I know you're tight for space but is there a chance of getting a parcel in for me?'

'How big?' McGill made sketching motions with his hands, and Ballard said, 'Is that all? We can do that.' He checked his watch. 'That truck Cameron had trouble with is leaving Christchurch with a load. I might be able to catch it before it leaves.'

He crossed the room and picked up the telephone. 'Hello, Maureen. Ian Ballard here. Can you get me the Christchurch office?'

'I had a look round town,' said McGill. 'It looks mostly new.'

'It is. When I lived here it was a tenth of the size.'

'Nicely laid out, too. Is most of it mine property?'

'A lot of it. Houses for the married couples and single quarters and a club house for the bachelors. This is a mine house. My predecessor lived in one of the old houses but I prefer this one. I like to be on the spot.'

'How many mine employees?'

'At the last count it was a hundred and four – including office staff.'

'And the total population?'

'A bit over eight hundred, I'd say. The mine brought a fair amount of prosperity.'

'That's about what I figured,' said McGill.

An electronic voice crackled in Ballard's ear, and he said, 'This is Ballard at the mine. Has Sam Jeffries left yet? Put him on will you?' There was a pause. 'Sam, Dr McGill wants to talk to you – hold on.'

McGill took the telephone. 'McGill here. Do you know where Advanced Headquarters for Operation Deep Freeze is? Yes . . . near Harewood Airport. Go to the Headquarters Building and find Chief Petty Officer Finney . . . yes, finney as in fish . . . ask him to give you the parcel for me . . . McGill. Right.'

'What was all that about?' asked Ballard.

McGill took the drink which Ballard offered. 'I just thought I'd keep myself occupied while I'm here.' He changed the subject. 'What's with your Mr Dobbs? He looks as though he's swallowed a lemon.'

Ballard smiled wearily and sat down. 'He has a chip on his shoulder. He reckons he should have been put on the board of directors and have my job, instead of which he got me. To make it worse, my name is Ballard.'

'What's that got to do with anything?'

'Don't you know? If you trace things back far enough the whole mine is owned by the Ballard family.'

McGill spluttered into his drink. 'Well, I'll be goddamned! I've been hobnobbing with the plutocratic capitalists and never knew it. There's a name for that kind of thing – nepotism. No wonder Dobbs is acid.'

'If it's nepotism it isn't doing me any good,' said Ballard. There was a touch of savagery in his voice. 'I don't have a penny except my director's fees.'

'No shares in the company?'

'No shares in this or any other Ballard company – but tell that to Dobbs and he wouldn't believe you. I haven't even tried.'

McGill's voice was soft. 'What's the matter, Ian? Come from the wrong side of the family?'

'Not really.' Ballard got up to pour himself another drink. 'I have a grandfather who's an egotistical old monster and I had a father who wouldn't co-operate. Dad told the old boy to go to hell and he's never forgotten it.'

'The sins of the fathers are visited on the children,' said McGill thoughtfully. 'And yet you're employed by a Ballard company. There must be something there somewhere.'

'They don't pay me any more than I'm worth – they get value for money.' Ballard sighed. 'But God, I could run the company better than it's run now.' He waved his glass. 'I don't mean this mine, this is a piddling little affair.'

'You call a two million pound company a piddling affair!' said McGill in wonder.

'I once worked it out. The Ballards control companies with a capital value of two hundred and twenty million pounds. The Ballards' own shareholdings are about forty-two million pounds. That was a few years ago, though.'

'Jesus!' said McGill involuntarily.

'I have three rapacious old vultures who call themselves my uncles and half a dozen cousins who follow the breed. They're only interested in loot and between them they're running the show into the ground. They're great ones for merging and asset-stripping, and they squeeze every penny until it hurts. Take this mine. Up in Auckland I have a Comptroller of Accounts who reports to London, and I can't sign a cheque for more than a thousand dollars without his say-so. And I'm supposed to be in charge.'

He breathed heavily. 'When I came here I went underground and that night I prayed we wouldn't have a visit from the Inspector of Mines before I had time to straighten things out.'

'Had someone been cutting corners?'

Ballard shrugged. 'Fisher, the last managing director, was an old fool and not up to the job. I doubt any criminal intent, but negligence combined with parsimony has led to a situation in which the company could find itself in serious trouble. I have a mine manager who can't make decisions and wants his hand held all the time, and I have a mine engineer who is past it. Oh, Cameron's all right, I suppose, but he's old and he's running scared.'

'You've got yourself a packet of trouble,' said McGill.

Ballard snorted. 'You don't know the half of it. I haven't said anything about the unions yet, not to mention the attitude of some of the town people.'

'You sound as though you earn your pay. But why the hell stick to a Ballard company if you feel like this?'

'Oh, I don't know – some remnants of family loyalty, I suppose,' said Ballard tiredly. 'After all, my grandfather did pay for my education, and quite extensive it was. I suppose I owe him something for that.'

McGill noted Ballard's evident depression and tiredness and decided to change the subject. 'Let's eat, and I'll tell you about the ice worms in Alaska.' He plunged into an improbable story.

CHAPTER FOUR

The next morning was bright and sunny and the snow, which had been falling all night, had stopped, leaving the world freshly minted. When Ballard got up, heavy-eyed and unrested, he found Mrs Evans in the kitchen cooking breakfast. She scolded him. 'You should have let me know when you were coming back. I only learned by chance from Betty Hargreaves last night.'

'I'm sorry,' he said. 'I forgot. Are you cooking for three?' Mrs Evans usually ate breakfast with him; it was a democratic society.

'I am. Your friend has gone out already, but he'll be back for a late breakfast.'

Ballard consulted his watch to discover that he had overslept by more than an hour. 'Give me ten minutes.'

When he had showered and dressed he felt better and found McGill in the living-room unwrapping a large parcel. 'It came,' said McGill. 'Your truck got through.'

Ballard looked at what was revealed; it was a backpack which appeared to contain nothing but sections of aluminium tubing each nestling in an individual canvas pocket. 'What's that?'

'The tools of my trade,' said McGill. Mrs Evans called, and he added, 'Let's eat; I'm hungry.'

Ballard toyed with his breakfast while McGill wolfed down a plateful of bacon and eggs, and pleased Mrs Evans by asking for more. While she was out of the room he said, 'You asked me here for the skiing, and there's no time like the present. How's your leg?'

Ballard shook his head. 'The leg is all right, but sorry, Mike – not today. I'm a working man.'

'You'd better come.' Something in McGill's tone made Ballard look at him sharply. McGill's face was serious. 'You'd better come and see what I'm doing. I want an independent witness.'

'A witness to what?'

'To whatever it is I find.'

'And what will that be?'

'How do I know until I find it?' He stared at Ballard. 'I'm serious, Ian. You know what my job is. I'm going to make a professional investigation. You're the boss man of the mine and you couldn't make a better witness. You've got authority.'

'For God's sake!' said Ballard. 'Authority to do what?'

'To close down the mine if need be, but that depends on what I find, and I won't know that until I look, will I?' As Ballard's jaw dropped McGill said, 'I couldn't believe my eyes at what I saw yesterday. It looked like a recipe for instant disaster, and I spent a damned uneasy night. I won't be happy until I take a look.'

'Where?'

McGill got to his feet and walked to the window. 'Come here.' He pointed at the steep slope above the mine. 'Up there.'

Ballard looked at the long curve, blinding white in the sunlight. 'You think . . .' His voice tailed away.

'I think nothing until I get evidence one way or the other,' said McGill sharply. 'I'm a scientist, not a soothsayer.' He shook his head warningly as Mrs Evans came in with a fresh plate of bacon and eggs. 'Finish your breakfast.'

As they sat down he said, 'I suppose you can find me a pair of skis.'

Ballard nodded, his mind busy with the implications of what McGill had said – or had not said. McGill dug into his second plateful of breakfast. 'Then we go skiing,' he said lightly.

Two hours later they were nearly three thousand feet above the mine and half way up the slope. They had not talked much and when Ballard had tried McGill advised him to save his breath for climbing. But now they stopped and McGill unslung the backpack, dropping one of the straps over a ski-stick rammed firmly into the snow.

He took off his skis and stuck them vertically into the snow up-slope of where he was standing. 'Another safety measure,' he said conversationally. 'If there's a slide then the skis will tell someone that we've been swept away. And that's why you don't take off your Oertel cord.'

Ballard leaned on his sticks. 'The last time you talked about avalanches I was in one.'

McGill grinned. 'Don't fool yourself. You were in a little trickle – a mere hundred feet.' He pointed down the mountainside. 'If this lot goes it'll be quite different.'

Ballard felt uneasy. 'You're not really expecting an avalanche?'

McGill shook his head. 'Not right now.' He bent down to the backpack. 'I'm going to do a little gentle thumping and you can help me to do it. Take off your skis.'

He began to take aluminium tubing from the pack and to assemble it into some kind of a gadget. 'This is a penetrometer – an updating of the Haefeli design. It's a sort of pocket piledriver – it measures the resistance of the snow. It also gives us a core, and temperature readings at ten-centimetre intervals. All the data for a snow profile.'

Ballard helped him set it up although he suspected that McGill could have done the job just as handily without him. There was a sliding weight which dropped down a narrow rod a known distance before hitting the top of the aluminium tube and thus driving it into the snow. Each time the weight dropped McGill noted the distance of penetration and recorded it in a notebook.

They thumped with the weight, adding lengths of tubing as necessary, and hit bottom at 158 centimetres – about five feet.

'There's a bit of a hard layer somewhere in the middle,' said McGill, taking an electric plug from the pack. He made a connection in the top of the tubing and plugged the other end into a box with a dial on it. 'Make a note of these temperatures; there'll be fifteen readings.'

As Ballard took the last reading he said, 'How do we get it out?'

'We have a tripod and a miniature block and tackle.' McGill grinned. 'I think they pinched this bit from an oil rig.'

He erected the tripod and started to haul out the tube. As the first section came free he disconnected it carefully and then took a knife and sliced through the ice in the tube. The sections were two feet long and the three of them were soon out. McGill put the tubes back into the pack, complete with the snow cores they contained. 'We'll have a look at those back at the house.'

Ballard squatted on his heels and looked across the valley. 'What now?'

'Now we do another, and another, and another, and another

in a line diagonally down the slope. I'd like to do more but that's all the core tubing I have.'

They had just finished the fourth trial boring when McGill looked up the slope. 'We have company.'

Ballard turned his head to see three skiers traversing down towards them. The leader was moving fast and came around in a flashy stem christiania which sent the snow spraying before he stopped. When he lifted blue-tinted goggles Ballard recognized Charlie Peterson.

Peterson looked at Ballard with some astonishment. 'Oh, it's you! Eric told me you were back but I haven't seen you around.'

'Hello, Charlie.'

The two other skiers came up and stopped more sedately – they were the two Americans, Miller and Newman. Charlie said, 'How did you get here?'

Ballard and McGill looked at each other, and Ballard wordlessly pointed to the skis. Charlie snorted. 'You used to be afraid of falling off anything steeper than a billiard table.' He looked curiously at the dismantled penetrometer. 'What are you doing?'

McGill answered. 'Looking at snow.'

Charlie pointed a stick. 'What's that thing?'

'A gadget for testing snow strength.'

Charlie grinned at Ballard. 'Since when did you become interested in snow? Your Ma wouldn't let you out in it for fear you'd catch cold.'

Ballard said evenly, 'I've become interested in a lot of things since then, Charlie.'

He laughed loudly. 'Yes? I'll bet you're a hot one with the girls.'

Newman said abruptly, 'Let's go.'

'No, wait a minute,' said Charlie. 'I'm interested. What are you doing with that watchamacallit?'

McGill straightened. 'I'm testing the stresses on this snow slope.'

'This slope's all right.'

'When did you have this much snow before?'

'There's always snow in the winter.'

'Not this much.'

Charlie looked at Miller and Newman and grinned at them. 'All the better – it makes for good skiing.' He rubbed the side of his jaw. 'Why come here to look at snow?'

McGill bent down to buckle a strap. 'The usual reason.'

The grin left Charlie's face. 'What reason?' he asked blankly.

'Because it's here,' said McGill patiently.

'Funny!' said Charlie. 'Very funny! How long are you going to be here?'

'For as long as it takes.'

'That's no kind of answer.'

Ballard stepped forward. 'That's all the answer you're going to get, Charlie.'

Charlie grinned genially. 'Staying away for so long has made you bloody prickly. I don't remember you giving back-chat before.'

Ballard smiled. 'Maybe I've changed, Charlie.'

'I don't think so,' he said deliberately. 'People like you never change.'

'You're welcome to find out any time you like.'

Newman said, 'Cut it out, Charlie. I don't know what you have against this guy and I don't much care. All I know is he helped us yesterday. Anyway, this is no place to pick a fight.'

'I agree,' said Ballard.

Charlie turned to Newman. 'Hear that? He hasn't changed.' He swung around and pointed down the slope. 'All right. We go down in traverses – that way first. This is a good slope for practising stem turns.'

Miller said, 'It looks good.'

'Wait a minute,' said McGill sharply. 'I wouldn't do that.' Charlie turned his head. 'And why not, for Christ's sake?'

'It could be dangerous.'

'Crossing the road can be dangerous,' he said contemptuously. He jerked his head at Miller. 'Let's go.'

Miller pulled down his goggles. 'Sure.'

'Hold on,' said Newman. He looked down at the penetrometer. 'Maybe the guy's got something there.'

'The hell with him,' said Charlie, and pushed off. Miller followed without another word. Newman looked at Ballard for a moment, then shrugged expressively before he followed them.

McGill and Ballard watched them go down. Charlie, in the lead, skied showily with a lot of unnecessary flair; Miller was sloppy and Newman neat and economical in his movements. They watched them all the way to the bottom.

Nothing happened.

'Who's the jerk?' McGill asked.

'Charlie Peterson. He's set up as a ski instructor.'

'He seems to know you.' McGill glanced sideways. 'And your family.'

'Yes,' said Ballard expressionlessly.

'I keep forgetting you were brought up here.' McGill scratched his cheek reflectively. 'You know, you could be useful. I want to find someone in the valley who has lived here a long time, whose family has lived here a long time. I need information.'

Ballard thought for a moment and then smiled and pointed with his ski-stick. 'See that rock down there? That's Kamakamaru, and a man called Turi Buck lives in a house just on the other side. I should have seen him before now but I've been too bloody busy.'

McGill hung his backpack on a convenient post outside Turi Buck's house. 'Better not take that inside. The ice would melt.'

Ballard knocked on the door which was opend by a girl of about fourteen, a Maori girl with a cheerful smile. 'I'm looking for Turi Buck.'

'Wait a minute,' she said and disappeared, and he heard her voice raised. 'Grandpa, there's someone to see you.'

Presently Turi appeared. Ballard was a little shocked at what he saw; Turi's hair was a frizzled grey and his face was seamed and lined like a water-eroded hillside. There was no recognition in his brown eyes as he said, 'Anything I can do for you?'

'Not a great deal, Turi,' said Ballard. 'Don't you remember me?'

Turi stepped forward, coming out of the doorway and into the light. He frowned and said uncertainly, 'I don't . . . my eyesight's not as good as . . . Ian?'

'Your eyesight is not so bad,' said Ballard.

'Ian!' said Turi in delight. 'I heard you were back – you should have come to see me sooner. I thought you had forgotten.'

'Work, Turi; the work comes first – you taught me that. This is my friend, Mike McGill.'

Turi beamed at them. 'Well, come in; come in.'

He led them into the house and into a room familiar to Ballard. Over the great fieldstone fireplace was the wapiti head with its great spread of antlers, and a wood fire burned beneath it. On the walls were the wood carvings inlaid with paua shell shimmering iridescently. The greenstone *mere* – the Maori war axe – was still there and, in pride of place, Turi's *whakapapa* stick, his most prized possession, very intricately carved and which gave his ancestry.

Ballard looked around. 'Nothing has changed.'

'Not here,' said Turi.

Ballard nodded towards the window. 'A lot of change out there, though, I didn't recognize the valley.'

Turi sighed. 'Too much change – too quickly. But where have you *been*, Ian?'

'A lot of places. All over the world.'

'Sit down,' said Turi. 'Tell me about it.'

'Tell me about yourself first. Did that beautiful young lady call you "Grandpa"?'

'I am a grandfather five times now.' Turi's shoulders shook. 'My sons are men and all married. Both my daughters are mothers.'

'Tawhaki,' said Ballard. 'How is Tawhaki?' He had been Ballard's playmate as a child and a constant companion as he grew older.

'He does well,' said Turi. 'He went to the University of Otago and took a good degree.'

'In what?'

Turi laughed. 'In economics. Imagine a Maori knowing about economics. He has a post in the Department of Finance in Auckland. I don't see him often.'

'You must give me his address. I'll look him up when next I'm in Auckland.' Ballard saw Turi regarding McGill with interest. 'Mike, here, is very interested in snow. He's so interested he's going to Antarctica later in the year.'

Turi's seamed face broke into a grim smile. 'Then there's something for you here, Mike. We have a lot of snow; more than I can remember since 1943.'

'So I've seen.'

Ballard went to the window. On the other side of the valley the cedar branches drooped heavily under the weight of snow. He turned, and said, 'What happened to the trees on the west slope, Turi?'

'Above the mine?'

'Yes,' said Ballard. 'That slope has been stripped.'

McGill became alert. 'The slope used to be timbered?'

Turi nodded and then shrugged. 'When they put in the

mine they wanted props. *Kahikatea* make good mine props.' He looked up. 'The Petersons own that land; they made a good profit.'

'I bet they did,' said Ballard.

'Your mother shouldn't have sold it to them' Turi clasped his hands. 'Then they blasted out the stumps and put the land down to grass for hay. They run cattle on the river flats; Herefords for beef and a few dairy cows. That's also become profitable now the town has grown.'

Ballard said. 'Didn't anybody think of what would happen when the snow came?'

'Oh yes,' said Turi. 'I did.'

'Didn't you say anything? Didn't you object when they put up the mine building? When they built the township?'

'I objected. I objected very loudly. But the Petersons were louder. Who would listen to an old man?' His lips twisted. 'Especially one with a brown skin.'

Ballard snorted and looked at McGill who said slowly, 'The stupid bastards! The stupid, greedy bastards!' He looked about the room and then at Turi. 'When did you come to the valley, Mr Buck?'

'My name is Turi, and I was born here.' He smiled. 'New Year's Day, 1900. I'm as old as the century.'

'Who built the house?'

'My father built it in about 1880, I think. It was built on the site of my grandfather's house.'

'And when was that built?'

Turi shrugged. 'I don't know. My people have lived here a long time.'

McGill nodded. 'Did your father give any reason for building on the same site? Under this big rock?'

Turi answered obliquely. 'He said that anyone building in Hukahoronui must take precautions.'

'He knew what he was talking about.' McGill turned to Ballard. 'I'd like to test those samples pretty quickly. And I'd like to come back to talk to you, Turi, if I may?'

'You must both come back. Come to supper and meet a couple of my grandchildren.'

As Turi accompanied them to the door Ballard said, 'You don't think much of the mine, do you, Turi?'

'Too many changes,' he said, and shook his head wryly. 'We now have a supermarket,'

You know I'm in charge of the mine now – and I don't like it much, either. But I think my reasons are different. You're going to see more changes, Turi, but these I think you'll like.'

Turi thumped him gently on the arm. '*He tamariki koe?* You're a man now, Ian; a real man.'

'Yes,' said Ballard. 'I've grown up. Thanks, Turi.'

Turi watched them put on their skis and, as they traversed the slope which led away from the house, he waved and called, '*Haere ra!*'

Ballard looked back over his shoulder. '*Haere ra!*' They headed back to the mine.

CHAPTER FIVE

The late afternoon sun poured through the windows of the hall, rendered multi-coloured by the stained glass. Patches of colour lay across the tables; the carafe of water in front of Ballard looked as though it was filled with blood.

Dan Edwards loosened his tie and wished he could have a cold beer. 'They'll be adjourning pretty soon,' he said to Dalwood. 'I wish old Harrison would get a bloody move on. All this talk of snow doesn't make me feel any cooler.'

Harrison poured himself a glass of water and sipped. He set down the glass, and said, 'So you took samples of the snow cover on the western slope in the presence of Mr Ballard. What were your findings?'

McGill unzipped the leather satchel and took out a sheaf of papers. 'I have written an entire report on the events that occurred at Hukahoronui – from the technical side, of course. I submit the report to the Commission.' He gave the report to Reed who passed it up to Harrison. 'Part One consists of my findings on the first series of snow profiles which was submitted to the mine management and, later, to the municipal authorities of Hukahoronui.'

Harrison flipped through the pages and frowned, then he passed the papers to Professor Rolandson. They conferred for a moment in low voices, then Harrison said, 'This is all very well, Dr McGill; but your report appears to be highly technical and contains more mathematical formulae than the majority of us are accustomed to. After all, this is a *public* hearing. Could you not describe your findings in a language that can be understood by others apart from yourself and Professor Rolandson?'

'Of course,' said McGill. 'Indeed, I did so to the people in Hukahoronui.'

'You may proceed; and you may expect to be questioned – in the interests of clarity – by Professor Rolandson.'

McGill clasped his hands in front of him. 'Snow is not so much a substance as a process; it changes in time. It begins with a snowflake falling to earth and becoming part of the general snow cover. It is a six-sided crystal and not very stable, and sublimation begins – a sort of evaporation. Eventually the crystal becomes a small, rounded granule. This is called destructive metamorphism and results in a higher density because the air is squeezed out. At the same time, because of the evaporative process, there is water vapour in the snow mass and, due to the low temperature, the separate granules tend to bond together by freezing.'

'This bond is not particularly strong, is it?' asked Rolandson.

'The bond is not strong, when compared with other materials.' Rolandson nodded and McGill went on. 'The next thing to take into account is the temperature through the snow cover. It's not constant – it's warmer at the bottom than the top, thus forming a temperature gradient. If you look at Graph One you will find the temperature gradient of those first five samples.'

Rolandson flipped pages. 'Not a very steep gradient – not more than two degrees.'

'It's enough for the next stage in the process. There is still a lot of air in the snow cover and the relatively warm air at the bottom begins to rise carrying water vapour with it. The vapour precipitates on the colder granules above. There is now a building process at work which is called constructive metamorphism, and a new kind of crystal begins to form – a cup crystal.'

'Could you describe a cup crystal, Dr McGill?'

'It's a conical shape with a hollow in the blunt end – the cup.'

'And how large is a cup crystal?'

'A well-developed crystal may run to half an inch long, but you can take a quarter-inch as average.' McGill paused, and when Rolandson remained silent, he said, 'Graph Two shows the penetrometer readings – that is the resistance of the snow to stress.'

Rolandson studied it. 'This is the resistance in kilograms plotted against depth?'

'Yes, sir.'

'There's a discontinuity half way down on all five samples.'

'Yes, sir; that's a layer of surface hoar.'

Harrison interrupted. 'If it is not on the surface how can it be described as surface hoar?'

'It *was* on the surface. When the surface of the snow is colder than the air above it then there is more sublimation of water vapour – something like the condensation on the outside of a glass of cold beer.' (In the Press gallery Dan Edwards sighed in anguish and licked his lips.) 'In this case I should imagine it happened on a clear and cloudless night when there would be a lot of outgoing radiation. Then the hoar, or frost, would form on the surface producing flat plates of thin ice.'

Again Harrison brought up the objection. 'But this discontinuity, as Professor Rolandson calls it, is not on the surface.'

'No,' agreed McGill. 'Normally, when the sun hits it in the morning it disappears. In this case, I imagine that clouds came over before sunrise and it began to snow again quite heavily. The layer of hoar was covered and preserved.'

'With what significance?' queried Rolandson.

'Several things could happen. The layer is quite hard, as you can see from the penetrometer readings. It is also quite smooth and could form a sliding surface for the snow above it.' McGill extended a second finger. 'Secondly, a layer of hoar is formed of flat plates of ice fused together – that is, it is relatively impermeable to air. This means that the most likely place for cup crystals to form would be just under the hoar layer.'

'You emphasize cup crystals. In what way are they dangerous?'

'They are dangerous because of their rounded shape and because there is very little bonding between one crystal and another.' McGill tugged at his ear. 'As a very rough analogy I would suggest that it would be very difficult for a man to walk on a floor loosely packed with billiard balls. It's that kind of instability.'

'Was there any evidence of cup crystals forming at this time?'

'They had begun to form in sample one, the highest up the slope. I had reason to believe that the process would continue which would result in a marked decline in stability.'

'Go on, Dr McGill.'

McGill put up a third finger. 'Three, the weather forecast at the time indicated more snow – more weight – on that slope.' He dropped his hand. 'All things considered I came to the conclusion that the snow cover on the western slope of the valley of Hukahoronui was relatively unstable and thus formed a potential avalanche hazard. I so informed the mine management.'

'You mean Mr Ballard?' asked Harrison.

'Present at the meeting were Mr Ballard; Mr Dobbs, the mine manager; Mr Cameron, the mine engineer; Mr Quentin, the union representative.'

'And you were present during the whole of that meeting?'

'Yes, sir.'

'Then I think we can take your evidence as best evidence of what occurred at the meeting, subject to later appraisal. However, the time has come to adjourn for today. We will gather here at ten in the morning when you, Dr McGill, will again be a witness. The hearing is adjourned.'

CHAPTER SIX

The participants of the hearing flooded on to the pavement of Armagh Street and began to disperse. Dan Edwards, heading rapidly beerwards, stopped when Dalwood said, 'Who is the tall redhead talking to Ballard? The girl with the dog.'

Edwards craned his neck. 'Good God! Now what the hell goes on there?'

'Who is she?'

'Liz Peterson, the sister of Charlie and Eric.'

Dalwood watched Ballard pat the Alsatian and smile at the girl warmly. 'They seem on good terms.'

'Yes – bloody funny, isn't it? Charlie has got his knife so deep into Ballard that he's in blood up to his armpit. I wonder if he knows Liz is fraternizing with the enemy?'

'We'll soon know,' said Dalwood. 'Here come Charlie and Eric now.'

The two men came out of the building, unsmiling and exchanging monosyllables. Charlie looked up and his face became thunderous. He snapped something at his brother and quickened his pace, elbowing his way through the crowd on the pavement. At that moment a car drew up and Ballard got into it and when Charlie reached his sister Ballard had gone. Charlie spoke to his sister and an argument seemed to develop.

Edwards watched the by-play, and said, 'If he didn't know he does now. What's more, he doesn't like it.'

'And the dog doesn't like Charlie. Look at it.'

The Alsatian's upper lip was curled back in a snarl and Liz Peterson shortened her grip on the lead and spoke sharply to it.

Edwards sighed. 'Let's get that beer. The first one will hiss going down.'

Mike McGill was driving the car. He slanted an eye at Ballard and then returned his attention to the road. 'Well, what do you think?'

'Your evidence was good. Very concise.'

'Rolandson helped; he fed me some good lines. He makes a good straight man to my comedian. You didn't do too well, though.'

'I'm doing all right.'

'Wake up, Ian! That son of a bitch, Rickman, is going to deliver you bound and gagged if you don't stop him.'

'Save it, Mike,' said Ballard shortly. 'I'm too bloody tired.'

McGill bit his lip and lapsed into silence. After ten minutes he swung off the road and parked in the forecourt of their hotel. 'You'll feel better after a cold beer,' he said. 'It was goddam hot in that courthouse. Okay?'

'All right,' said Ballard listlessly.

They went into the hotel bar and McGill ordered two beers and took them to a discreet table. 'Here's mud in your eye.' He drank and gasped with pleasure. 'God, how I needed that!' He replenished his glass. 'That courthouse is sure some place. Who designed it – Edward the Confessor?'

'It's not a courthouse – it's a sort of provincial House of Parliament. Or it was.'

McGill grinned. 'The bit I like about it are those pious texts set in the stained glass windows. I wonder who thought those up?' In the same even tone he said, 'What did Liz Peterson want?'

'Just to wish me well.'

'Did she?' said McGill sardonically. 'If she really meant it she'd operate on that brother of hers with a sharp knife.' He watched the condensation form on the outside of his glass. 'Come to think of it, a blunt knife might be better. The Peterson lawyer was really sniping at you this morning.'

'I know.' Ballard took another draught. It seemed to do him good. 'It doesn't matter, Mike. You and I know the evidence is on our side.'

'You're wrong,' said McGill flatly. 'Evidence is how a lawyer puts it – and talking about lawyers, what about Rickman? You know what he did to you this morning, don't you? He made it look as though you were trying to renege. Hell, everyone in that hall thought you were trying to slip the country.'

Ballard rubbed his eyes. 'I said something to Rickman just before the hearing opened, and he got it wrong, that's all.'

'That's all? That's not all – not by a thousand miles. A smart guy like that doesn't get things wrong in a courtroom. If he got it wrong then he meant to get it wrong. What did you say to him, anyway?'

Ballard took out his wallet and extracted a piece of paper. 'I was leaving the hotel this morning when I got this.' He passed it to McGill. 'My grandfather's dead!'

McGill unfolded the cablegram and read it. 'Ian, I'm sorry; I really am.' He was silent for a moment. 'This Harriet – is she your mother?'

'Yes.'

'She wants you to go home.'

'She would,' said Ballard bitterly.

'And you showed this to Rickman?'

'Yes.'

'And he got up on his hind legs and, by inference, demonstrated that you are a coward. Hell, Ian; he's not representing you! He's representing the company.'

'Six of one and half a dozen of the other.'

McGill regarded Ballard and slowly shook his head. 'You really believe what the Chairman of the Commission said, don't you? That all they want is to get at the truth. Well, that may be what Harrison thinks but it's not what the public want. Fifty-four people died, Ian, and the public want a scapegoat. The President of your company knows . . .'

'Chairman.'

McGill waggled his hand. 'To hell with semantics. The Chairman of your company knows that, too, and he's making goddam sure the company isn't the goat. That's why he's employed a sharp cookie like Rickman, and if you think Rickman is acting for you then you're out of your mind. If the company can get out from under by sacrificing you then that's what they'll do.'

He thumped the table. 'I can write the scenario right now. "Mr Ballard is new to the company. Mr Ballard is young and inexperienced. It is only to be expected that so young a man should make unfortunate mistakes. Surely such errors of judgment may be excused in one so inexperienced."' McGill leaned back in his chair. 'By the time Rickman is finished with you he'll have everyone believing you *arranged* the goddam avalanche – and the Petersons and that snide lawyer of theirs will fall over themselves to help him.'

Ballard smiled slightly. 'You have great powers of imagination, Mike.'

'Oh, what the hell!' said McGill disgustedly. 'Let's have another beer.'

'My round.' Ballard got up and went to the bar. When he came back he said, 'So the old boy's dead.' He shook his head. 'You know, Mike, it hit me harder than I thought it would.'

McGill poured more beer. 'Judging by the way you talked about him, I'm surprised you feel anything at all.'

'Oh, he was a cantankerous old devil – stubborn and self-opinionated – but there was something about him . . .' Ballard shook his head. 'I don't know.'

'What happens to the parent corporation . . . what's it called?'

'Ballard Holdings.'

'What happens to Ballard Holdings now he's dead? Is it up for grabs?'

'I shouldn't think so. The old man established a trust or something like that. I never really got the hang of it because I knew I wouldn't figure in it. I imagine that things will remain pretty stable, with Uncle Bert and Uncle Steve and Uncle Ed running things pretty much as they are now. Which is to say badly.'

'I don't see why the shareholders put up with it.'

'The shareholders don't have a bloody thing to do with it. Let me tell you a fact of financial life, Mike. You don't really need fifty-one per cent of the shares of a company to control it. Thirty per cent is enough if the other shares are fragmented into small parcels and if your lawyers and accountants are smart enough.' Ballard shrugged. 'In any case, the share-holders aren't too unhappy; all the Ballard companies make profits, and the kind of people who are buying into Ballard companies these days aren't the type to inquire too closely into how the profits are made.'

'Yeah,' said McGill abstractedly. This was not really of interest to him. He leaned forward and said, 'Let's do some strategy planning.'

'What do you mean?'

'I've been figuring how Harrison's mind works. He's a very logical guy and that works in our favour. I'm going to give evidence tomorrow about the meeting with the mine manage-ment. Why me?'

'Harrison asked if you'd been present during the entire meeting – and you had. He picked you because you were already on the stand and it was quicker than calling another witness. That's what I think, anyway.'

McGill looked pleased. 'That's what I think, too. Harrison said he'd take evidence in chronological order, and he's doing just that. Now what happened after the mine meeting?'

'We had the meeting with the town council.'

'And what will Harrison ask me?'

'He'll ask if you were present during the whole of that meeting – and you'll have to say no, because you left half way through. So?'

'So I want to pick the next witness, and knowing how Harrison's mind works, I think I can swing it.'

'Who do you want for the next witness?'

'Turi Buck,' said McGill. 'I want to get on record the history of Hukahoronui just to ram things home. I want to get on record the sheer stupidity of that goddam town council.'

Ballard looked broodingly into his glass. 'I don't like doing that to Turi. It might hurt.'

'He wants to do it. He's already put himself forward as a voluntary witness. He's staying with his sister here in Christ-church; we'll pick him up tomorrow morning.'

'All right.'

'Now, look, Ian. Turi is an old man and may be likely to become confused under hostile cross-examination. We've got to make sure that the right questions are asked in the right order. We've got to cover the ground so thoroughly that no one – not Lyall nor Rickman – can find a loophole.'

'I'll make out a list of questions for Rickman,' said Ballard.

McGill rolled his eyes skyward. 'Can't you get it into your thick skull that if Rickman questions Turi it will be in a hostile manner.'

Ballard said sharply, 'Rickman is representing me and he'll follow my instructions.'

'And if he doesn't?'

'If he doesn't then I'll know you're right – and that will free me completely. We'll see.' He drained his glass. 'I feel sticky; I'm going to have a shower.'

As they left the bar McGill said, 'About that cablegram. You're not going back, are you?'

'You mean running home to Mamma?' Ballard grinned. 'Not while Harrison is Chairman of the Commission. I doubt if even my mother could win against Harrison.'

'Your mother isn't Jewish, is she?' asked McGill curiously.

'No. Why do you ask?'

'Oh, it's just that Jewish mothers are popularly supposed to be strong-willed. But I think that your mother could give a Jewish mother points and still win.'

'It's not a matter of a strong will,' said Ballard soberly. 'It's just straightforward moral blackmail.'

CHAPTER SEVEN

McGill and Ballard found Turi Buck waiting outside his sister's home at nine-thirty next morning. Although it was still early the weather showed signs of becoming oppressively hot. Ballard leaned over to open the back door of the car, and said, 'Jump in, Turi.'

'I'm past jumping anywhere, Ian,' said Turi wryly, 'But I'll endeavour to accommodate myself in this seat.'

Sometimes Turi's phrases had an oddly old-fashioned ring about them. Ballard knew he had never been formally educated but had read a lot, and he suspected that Sir Walter Scott was responsible for some of the more courtly expressions.

'It's good of you to come, Turi.'

'I had to come, Ian.'

In the Provincial Chamber, at precisely ten o'clock, Harrison tapped the top of the rostrum gently with his gavel, and said, 'We are now prepared to resume the inquiry into the avalanche disaster at Hukahoronui. Dr McGill was giving evidence. Will you please resume your seat?'

McGill walked to the witness chair and sat down. Harrison said, 'Yesterday you referred to a meeting of the mine management at which you presented a report. What happened at that meeting?'

McGill tugged at his ear thoughtfully. 'The problem was to explain the evidence and to get them to accept it. Mr Ballard had already accepted it. Mr Cameron wanted to go through the figures in detail, but he came around in the end. The others weren't as convinced. It went like this . . .'

It was Cameron, the engineer, who saw the true significance of the cup crystals. 'Could you draw a picture of one of those, Mike?'

'Sure.' McGill took a pencil from his pocket and made a drawing. 'As I said, it's conical in shape – like this – and it has this hollow in the blunt end. That's why it's called a cup crystal.'

'I'm not worried about the hollow.' Cameron stared at the drawing. 'What you've sketched here is a pretty good picture of a tapered roller bearing. You say these are likely to form under that layer of hard hoar frost?'

'Correct.'

'That's not good,' said Cameron. 'That's not good at all. If you get a lot of weight on top pushing downwards vertically by gravity then there'll be a resultant force sideways on the slope. The whole hillside could come down on ready-made bearings.'

Cameron passed the drawing to Dobbs who looked at it with Quentin, the union man, peering over his shoulder. 'Any of those cup things there now?'

'There are indications of them forming in one of the samples I took. I'd say the process is well under way.'

'Let's have a look at your stress figures.' Cameron grimaced as he began to go through the equations. 'I'm used to working with stronger stuff than snow.'

'The principle is the same,' said McGill.

Dobbs handed the drawing to Ballard. 'Are you seriously telling us that there'll be an avalanche which will fall on this mine?'

'Not exactly,' said McGill carefully. 'What I'm saying, at this moment, is that there is a potential hazard that must be watched. I don't think there is a present danger – it's not going to come down in the next hour or even today. A lot depends on future events.'

'Such as?' asked Ballard.

'The way the temperature goes. Future snow precipitation. An appreciable rise in wind speed wouldn't help much, either.'

'And the forecast is for more snow,' said Ballard.

McGill said, 'When you have a potential hazard like this you have to take precautions. Protecting the mine portal, for instance. There's a steel construction called Wonder Arch which comes in useful. It was developed at Camp Century in Greenland specifically for this type of application. It's used a lot in the Antarctic.'

'Is it expensive?' asked Dobbs. His voice was clouded with doubt.

McGill shrugged. 'It depends on how much money you put against lives on the balance sheet.' He turned to Cameron. 'Joe, remember me asking if you'd heard of Granduc in British Columbia?'

Cameron looked up from the figures. 'Yeah. I hadn't.'

'Granduc is remarkably like your mine here. They installed Wonder Arch – put in a covered way to the mine portal.' He rubbed the side of his jaw. 'It was like closing a stable door after the horse has gone; they put in the arch in 1966 after the avalanche of 1965 when twenty-six men died.'

There was a silence broken after a while by Cameron. 'You make your point very clearly.'

Ballard said, 'I'll put it to the Board of Directors.'

'That's not all,' said McGill. 'You got to look at the situation in the long term. That slope is dangerous mostly because it's been stripped of timber. It will have to be stabilized again, and that means building snow rakes. Good snow rakes cost sixty dollars a foot run – I doubt if you'd get away with under a million dollars.'

The sound of Dobbs's suddenly indrawn breath was harsh.

'Then there's the snow deflection walls at the bottom,' went on McGill inexorably. 'That's more – maybe even half a million. It's going to cost a packet.'

'The Board won't stand for it,' said Dobbs. He stared at Ballard. 'You know we're just paying our way now. They're not going to put in all that extra capital for no increase in production. It just isn't on.'

Quentin stirred. 'Would you want to close down the mine?'

'It's a possibility,' said Ballard. 'But it's not my decision.'

'My people would have something to say about that. There's a lot of jobs at stake.' Quentin looked at McGill hostilely and threw out his hand. 'And who's to say he's right? He comes busting in here with his tale of doom, but who the hell is he, anyway?'

Ballard straightened. 'Let's get one thing clear,' he said. 'As of yesterday Dr McGill became a professional consultant employed by this company to give us advice on certain problems. His qualifications satisfy me completely.'

'You didn't talk to me about this,' said Dobbs.

Ballard gave him a level stare. 'I wasn't aware I had to, Mr Dobbs. You are so informed now.'

'Does the Chairman know about this?'

'He'll know when I tell him, which will be very soon.'

Quentin was earnest. 'Look, Mr Ballard; I've been listening carefully. There's not been an avalanche, and your friend hasn't said there's going to be one. All he's been talking about are potentials. I think the Board is going to need a lot more than that before they spend a million and a half dollars. I don't think this mine is going to close – not on this kind of talk.'

'What do you want?' asked McGill. 'Avalanche first – and protection later?'

'I'm protecting the men's jobs,' said Quentin. 'That's what they put me in here for.'

'Dead men don't have jobs,' said McGill brutally. 'And while we're at it, let's get another thing quite clear. Mr Ballard has said that he has engaged me as a professional consultant, and that is quite true. But fundamentally I don't give one good goddamn about the mine.'

'The Chairman will be delighted to hear it,' said Dobbs acidly. He looked at Ballard. 'I don't think we need carry on with this any more.'

'Carry on, Mike,' said Ballard quietly. 'Tell them the rest. Tell them what's really worrying you.'

McGill said, 'I'm worried about the town.'

There was a silence for the space of ten heartbeats and then Cameron cleared his throat. 'It's snowing again,' he said, not altogether inconsequentially.

'That just about finished the meeting,' said McGill. 'It was decided that the mine management should consult with the town council that afternoon, if possible. Then Mr Ballard was to communicate by telephone with the Presi . . . Chairman of his company.'

Gunn had his hand up, and Harrison said, 'Yes, Mr Gunn?'

'May I question the witness, Mr Chairman?' Harrison inclined his head, and Gunn proceeded. 'Dr McGill, the meeting you have just described took place a long time ago, did it not?'

'The meeting took place on the sixteenth of July. On the Friday morning.'

'It is now December – nearly five months later. Would you say that you have a good memory, Dr McGill?'

'About average.'

'About average! I put it to you that you have a much better than average memory.'

'If you say so.'

'Indeed, I do say so. When I listened to your evidence – when you related the conversations of others *ad verbatim* – I was put in mind of a stage performance I saw quite recently in which a so-called memory man amazed an audience.'

'Mr Gunn,' interjected Harrison. 'Irony and sarcasm may, or may not, have their place in a law court; they have certainly no place here. Please refrain.'

'Yes, Mr Chairman.' Gunn did not seem put out; he was aware that he had made his point. 'Dr McGill, you have given evidence that Mr Quentin, the elected union leader at Huka-horonui mine, *seemed* – and I use the word advisedly – seemed to be more intent on filling the pockets of his comrades than in preserving their lives. Now, Mr Quentin is not here to defend himself – he was killed in the disaster at Hukahoronui – and since I represent the union I must defend Mr Quentin. I put it to you that your recollection of this meeting so long ago may be incorrect.'

'No, sir; it is not incorrect.'

'Come, Dr McGill; note that I said that your evidence *may* be incorrect. Surely there is no loss of face in admitting that you may be wrong?'

'My evidence was correct, sir.'

'To traduce a dead man when it is not necessary is not thought to be good manners, sir. No doubt you have heard the tag, *"De mortuis nil nisi bonum."* ' Gunn waved his arm largely. 'The good and wise men who caused this hall to be built saw fit to include cogent aphorisms in these windows to guide them in their deliberations. I draw your attention to the text in the windows just above your head, Dr McGill. It reads: "Be not a hypocrite in the sight of men, and talk good when thou speakest." '

McGill was silent, and Gunn said, 'Well, Dr McGill?'

'I was not aware that I had been asked a question,' said McGill quietly.

Harrison shifted uneasily on his seat and seemed about to interrupt, but Gunn waved his arm again. 'If it is your claim to have a memory so much better than other men then I must accept it, I suppose.'

'I have an average memory, sir. And I keep a diary.'

'Oh!' Gunn was wary. 'Regularly?'

'As regularly as need be. I am a scientist who investigates snow, which is an evanescent and ever-changing substance, so I am accustomed to taking notes on the spot.'

'Are you saying that while that very meeting was in progress you were actually taking written notes of what was said?'

'No, sir.'

'Ha! Then a period of time must have elapsed between the

meeting and when you wrote down your impressions. Is that not so?'

'Yes, sir. Half an hour. I wrote up my diary in my bedroom half an hour after the meeting ended. I consulted my diary this morning before I came to this hearing to refresh my memory.'

'And you still insist on your evidence as it relates to Mr Quentin?'

'I do.'

'Do you know how Mr Quentin died?'

'I know very well how Mr Quentin died.'

'No more questions,' said Gunn with an air of disgust. 'I am quite finished with this witness.'

McGill glanced at Harrison. 'May I add something?'

'If it has a bearing on what we are trying to investigate.'

'I think it has.' McGill looked up at the roof of the hall, and then his gaze swept down towards Gunn. 'I also have been studying the texts in the windows, Mr Gunn, and one, in particular, I have taken to heart. It is in a window quite close to you, and it reads: "Weigh thy words in a balance lest thou fall before him that lieth in wait."'

A roar of laughter broke the tension in the hall and even Harrison smiled, while Rolandson guffawed outright. Harrison thumped with his gavel and achieved a modicum of quiet.

McGill said, 'As for your Latin tag, Mr Gunn, I have never believed that latinity confers virtue on stupidity, and therefore I do not believe that one should never speak ill of the dead. I believe in the truth, and the truth is that the death roll in the Hukahoronui disaster was much higher than need be. The reason lies in the actions, reactions and inactions of many men who were confronted with an unprecedented situation beyond their understanding. Mr Quentin was one such man. I know that he died in the disaster, and I know that he died heroically. Nevertheless, the truth must be told so that other men, in the future, when faced with a similar situation will *know* the right things to do.'

'*Mr Chairman!*' Gunn was waving his arm, but Rickman had beaten him to it. He was on his feet, finger upraised. 'This is monstrous! Must a witness make speeches and lecture us to tell us our duty? Must . . .'

Harrison's gavel cracked down sharply, cutting off Rickman in mid-spate. 'Mr Rickman, may I again remind you that this is *not* a court of law and that procedure is at my sole discretion. Dr McGill has just restated the nature and intention of this Commission of Inquiry in words more well chosen and acute than I myself used yesterday during the opening proceedings. I have noted in counsel a regrettable tendency to adversary tactics, a practice against which I warned you. I will have no more of it.'

There was a dead silence.

Dan Edwards was busily scribbling. 'Boy, oh boy, oh boy! Good copy at last.' He tore off a sheet and handed it to a youth behind him. 'Get that back to the office as fast as you can.'

Harrison laid down his gavel. 'Dr McGill: you say that the mine management had a meeting with the Hukahoronui Town Council on the afternoon of Friday, the fifth of July.'

'No, sir. I said that was the arrangement at the meeting in the morning. In the event it proved to be impossible.'

'Why?'

'Three of the councillors were absent from town that day and it was impossible to find a quorum. The meeting was held next morning – the Saturday morning.'

'A delay of half a day.'

'Yes, sir.' McGill hesitated. 'Mr Ballard and I debated whether or not to approach the two councillors who remained in town and we decided against it. Our view was that such an important matter should be communicated to the council as a whole; we did not want to tell a complicated story twice.'

'So you met on the Saturday?'

'Yes, sir. There was one other person present at my request.'

'Oh, who was that?'

'Mr Turi Buck. I have to tell you that I was not present during the entire meeting. I left half way through.'

Harrison bent forward and said to Reed, 'Is Mr Buck present?'

'Yes, Mr Chairman.' Reed turned in his seat. 'Will you step forward, Mr Buck?'

Turi Buck came forward and stood before the rostrum. 'Were you present during the entire meeting under discussion, Mr Buck?' Harrison asked.

'Yes, sir; I was.' Turi's voice was strong.

'Then you will replace Dr McGill in the witness chair.'

McGill stepped down and went back to his place, winking at Ballard as he passed.

CHAPTER EIGHT

Harrison said, 'Mr Buck, would you be related to that illustrious member of your race, Sir Peter Buck?'

A ghost of a smile hovered on Turi's seamed face. 'No, sir.'

'I see.' Harrison drew his note-pad towards him. 'Can you tell us who was present at this meeting?'

'There was Ia . . . Mr Ballard and Mr Cameron from the mine. Dr McGill was there. And there was Mr Houghton, the mayor, and Mr Peterson – that's to say John Peterson – and Eric Peterson, Mr Warrick and Mrs Samson.'

'The last five were members of the council?'

'Yes, sir.'

Harrison consulted a list. 'Wasn't Mr Quentin present?'

'Oh yes; he was there. I forgot about him.'

'Well, Mr Buck, perhaps you can tell us what went on at the meeting.'

Turi frowned. 'It started off by Dr McGill telling of what he'd found. From what I've been hearing while I've been here I'd say it was just what he'd said at the meeting at the mine on the Friday. He told them there was a danger of avalanche and he told them why.'

'What was the general reaction?'

'They didn't believe him.'

Lyall put up his hand. 'Mr Chairman.'

'Yes, Mr Lyall?'

'It is incumbent on me to point out that of the ten people present at that meeting only four are able to be here at this inquiry. I ought to add that of the five council members only Mr Eric Peterson is able to be here.'

Harrison stared at him. 'Now that you have given me that information – of which, I might add, I was well aware – what am I supposed to do with it?'

'With respect, sir, one might think that Mr Eric Peterson is best qualified to give the reaction of the council.'

'Does Mr Peterson wish to be a witness?'

'He does.'

'Then he will have his chance later. At present we are hearing the evidence of Mr Buck.'

'Again with respect, Mr Chairman; may I point out that of the original mine management only Mr Ballard is here. Mr Dobbs and Mr Quentin are dead, and Mr Cameron is in hospital. It is well known in Hukahoronui that Mr Ballard and Mr Buck are friends of many years standing, and there has been evidence given here of the friendship between Mr Ballard and Dr McGill. It may be thought that the evidence given here is, shall we say, too one-sided.'

Harrison leaned back in his chair. 'It is evident, Mr Lyall, that you are doing at least one of two things. You are impugning the integrity of this Commission, or you are questioning the honesty of Mr Buck. Possibly you are doing both. Do I understand you correctly?'

'I do not question the integrity of the Commission, sir.'

Turi's face was stricken as he half rose from his chair. Ian Ballard wriggled in his seat. He dug his elbow into Rickman's ribs, and said, 'The bastard! the utter bastard! Intervene and get on with that line of questioning I gave you.'

Rickman shook his head. 'It would be most unwise. It wouldn't be in the interests of the company.' He twisted his head and looked at Lyall. 'See how he's stirring things up.'

'But, God damn it, he's making us into some sort of conspiracy.'

Rickman stared at him unwinkingly. 'But not involving the company,' he snapped.

Turi Buck lifted his hands helplessly. They were trembling as he said to Harrison, 'May I be excused from the witness chair, sir?'

'No, you may not, Mr Buck.' Harrison turned his head. 'Yes, Mr Ballard?'

Ballard lowered his hand. 'I would like to question Mr Buck.'

Harrison frowned. 'I thought you had representation, Mr Ballard. I gave warning at the beginning of this hearing that I would not allow it to be turned into a free-for-all.'

Ballard said, 'As of thirty seconds ago Mr Rickman ceased to represent me personally, He will, of course, continue to represent the company.'

A wave of noise washed across the hall. Amid the uproar Rickman said, 'You bloody young fool! What the devil do you thing you're doing?'

'You're fired,' said Ballard briefly.

Harrison wielded his gavel lustily and at last achieved relative quietness. 'If there is any more uproar I will have the public gallery cleared,' he announced. 'These proceedings will be conducted in an orderly manner.' He waited until there was utter silence, broken only by the creaking of the old wooden floor, before he addressed Ballard. 'Are you asking for an adjournment so that you may obtain a new legal adviser?'

'No, sir. For today, at least, I am content to represent myself. I do not wish to waste the time of the Commission.'

Harrison allowed himself a wintry smile. 'Very laudable. I wish the legal fraternity would follow your example. And you wish to interrogate Mr Buck?'

'Yes, sir.'

'I object,' said Rickman. 'Apart from the personal insult to me in being dismissed so cavalierly and in public, I consider this to be most irregular.'

Harrison sighed. 'Mr Rickman, you have been told many times that the procedure of this Commission is a matter for my discretion. Even in a law court it has not been unknown for a person to represent himself, choosing not to enlist the aid – or otherwise – of a lawyer. Therefore I will allow it.' He held up his hand. 'And I will entertain no argument about it. Proceed, Mr Ballard.'

Ballard smiled at Turi. 'I will not comment on any remarks that have been made here, but will go on from your last relevant statement. Mr Buck, you said that the councillors did not believe Dr McGill when he informed them of avalanche hazard. What were their reasons for disbelief?'

'They said there had never been avalanches in the valley.'

'Did they? Mr Chairman, is it possible to have a map of the valley on view?'

'Provision has been made. Mr Reed, will you see to it.'

Presently a large-scale map was set up on an easel behind the witness chair. Harrison said, 'Since this map is evidence of a sort we must be sure that it is the best evidence. Mr Reed, call your technical witness, please.'

'Call Mr Wheeler.'

Wheeler was new to Ballard, who regarded him with interest. He returned his gaze to the map, and his eyes narrowed suddenly. Reed said, 'What is your full name?'

'Harold Herbert Wheeler.'

Harrison said, 'There is no need for you to take the witness chair, Mr Wheeler. Your evidence is technical and will not take long. What is your occupation?'

'I am a cartographer employed by the Lands and Survey Department of the New Zealand Government.'

'And you have prepared this map especially for this Inquiry?'

'That is correct, sir.'

'What does the map represent?'

'It depicts the Hukahoronui Valley, including the township of Hukahoronui. The scale is one in two thousand, five hundred; that is twenty-five inches to the mile approximately.'

'Does it represent the valley before or after the disaster?'

'Before, sir. It is drawn according to the latest information available to the Topographical Office.'

'Thank you, Mr Wheeler. That will be all.'

Ballard said, 'Could Mr Wheeler hold himself available for possible further questions?'

Harrison wrinkled his brow. 'I suppose so, Mr Ballard. You will stay available, Mr Wheeler.'

Ballard studied the map. 'Mr Buck, I would like you, if you will, to point out on this map your own house.' Turi stood up and indicated a point on the map with his finger. 'And the Peterson store.' Turi's hand came up around in an arc and stopped. 'Now my house.' Again Turi pointed. 'And the mine portal.'

'I fail to see the point of this,' said Rickman.

'The point is to prove that Mr Buck can read a map as well as the next man,' said Ballard pleasantly. 'Mr Buck, at the meeting with the council was a map produced?'

'Yes, but not as big as this one.'

'And were you asked to point out various places on that map?'

'Yes, sir.'

'Now I want you to think very carefully. I don't want you to say anything here, because of my questioning, that was not said at the meeting with the council. Do you understand?'

'Yes.'

'Why did you attend the meeting?'

'Because Dr McGill asked me to go.'

'Do you know why he asked you to go?'

'He said I knew more about the history of Hukahoronui than anyone else he'd met.'

'You say the reaction of the council was that there had, hitherto, never been avalanches in the valley. Was that the reaction of *all* the councillors?'

'It was – at first.'

'So their views changed, then. Let us find out why. Mr Buck, you are of the Maori race. Do you understand the language?'

'Yes, sir.'

'Can you give us a translation – a free translation, if you like – of the name, Hukahoronui?'

'Yes sir; it means "The Great Snow Slide".'

There was a subdued murmur from behind Ballard. 'Would you point out your own house again, Mr Buck. There is a great rock between your house and the mountainside, is there not? What is the name of that rock?'

'Kamakamaru.'

'Kamakamaru,' repeated Ballard. 'Can you translate that into English?'

'It means "The Rock of Shelter".'

Again came that quickly suppressed sound in the hall. 'When was your house built, Mr Buck?'

'It was built by my father about 1880, but there was a house there before built by my grandfather.'

'Let us get one thing straight. Your family did not live in Hukahoronui before the incursion of the white settlers into New Zealand?'

'Before the Pakeha! No, sir, my family came from North Island.' Turi smiled. 'It was said that we came to South Island to escape the Pakeha.'

'Did your family name the valley and the rock?'

'No, they were already named. There were some of my people living close by. Not in the valley, but close by.'

'Did your father replace your grandfather's house because, let us say, it had been damaged by an avalanche?'

'No, sir. He replaced it because the house was in bad condition and because the family was growing larger.'

Ballard was silent for a moment as he consulted a paper. At last he raised his head and asked quietly, 'Mr Buck, do you, of your own knowledge, know any avalanches in the valley of Hukahoronui?'

'Yes, there was an avalanche in 1912 when I was a boy. A family called Bailey had built a house quite close to ours but not protected by Kamakamaru. My father warned the Baileys but they took no notice of him. There was an avalanche in the winter of 1912 and the Bailey house was swept away. The whole family died – all seven of them.' He looked at Ballard and said definitely, 'I was there – I helped dig out the bodies.'

'So the rock – Kamakamaru – acted as a splitting wedge. Is that it?'

'The snow flowed around Kamakamaru, and our house was safe.'

'But the Bailey house was destroyed. Any more avalanches?'

'There was one in 1918.' Turi hesitated. 'I was not there; I had joined the army. I had a letter from my father saying there had been an avalanche.'

'Again on the western slope?'

'Yes. There were no lives lost nor damage to property, but the snow blocked the flow of the river and there was flooding. The farmers lost a lot of stock by drowning.'

'A six-year gap. Any more?'

'There was the avalanche of 1943.'

'Did you see that avalanche actually fall?'

'No – but I remember it broke a lot of trees on the west slope. I used to collect firewood there afterwards.'

'Yes,' said Ballard. 'There was a lot of good firewood around there for two or three years. Were there any fatalities in the avalanche of 1943?'

Turi's eyes opened wide. 'Why, yes, Ian. Your father was killed.'

The hall had been quiet as Ballard led Turi through his evidence but now there was a gust of pent-up emotion let loose in a wave of sound. Harrison let it die away before he rapped gently with his gavel.

Ballard said, 'Could you point out on the map the place where my father was killed?'

Turi stretched out his hand. 'There,' he said. 'Just where the mine office is now.'

'How do you know it was there?'

'Because you showed me three days after it happened. You had seen it happen.'

'And how old was I then, Mr Buck?'

Turi considered. 'Maybe four years.'

'Mr Buck, you have given us a lot of information. Was the same information given to the councillors at the meeting?'

'Yes, it was.'

'Thank you, Mr Buck.'

Ballard leaned back and glanced sideways at Lyall who already had his hand up. 'I would like to ask Mr Buck one or two questions.'

Harrison nodded. 'Very well.'

'Was the avalanche of 1943 a very large one?'

Turi thought about it, then nodded his head vigorously. 'Very large – bigger than the one in 1912.'

Lyall looked pleased. 'I see. Could you say, perhaps by indicating on the map, just how far down the slope it came?'

'Just to the bottom. Mr Ballard's father was killed here. It didn't go much farther than that.'

'It didn't go as far as the Peterson Supermarket?'

'It didn't go anywhere near the Peterson store.'

'Remarkable. Now tell me, Mr Buck: if the Peterson Supermarket was not destroyed by a very big avalanche in 1943, why then was it destroyed this year?'

Turi looked blank, then said, 'The trees, of course.'

Ballard let out a long sigh and let Lyall dig his own pit. Lyall said, 'The trees! Oh, you mean that timbered area marked on the west slope?'

Turi turned to look at the map. He examined it for a moment, then said, 'But this is all wrong.'

Ballard put up his hand. 'Mr Chairman – on a point of evidence. I would like to have Mr Wheeler recalled briefly. It would seem that his map is not the best evidence.'

Harrison looked startled, then raised his eyebrows. 'Mr Lyall?'

Lyall frowned, but said, 'No objection.'

Wheeler was brought back and Ballard said, 'Look at the map, Mr Wheeler. Do you see that forested area on the western slope of the valley?'

'Yes, sir.'

'I can bring five hundred witnesses to swear that that area was not forested before the avalanche struck. What do you say to that?'

Wheeler did not know what to say to it. He twitched nervously for a while, then said, 'The information I put into that map comes from the latest sources available.'

'But not late enough, it would seem. In respect of a vital piece of evidence – the lack of timber on the western slope – this map is untrue. Is that correct?'

Wheeler shrugged. 'If you say so. I have never been to Hukahoronui myself.'

'It is not for me to say,' said Ballard. 'But let us ask Mr Buck. When were the trees cut?'

'They started cutting when the mine opened. The timber

went into the mine and for building houses.'

'That was four years ago?'

'Yes. The cutting went on for two years. By that time the slope was just about stripped.'

Rolandson stirred, and said, 'Mr Ballard, are we to understand that you regard the cutting of that timber as a contributory factor which led to the avalanche?'

Ballard hesitated. 'I am not an expert on avalanches, sir. I would prefer you to direct that question to Dr McGill.'

'I will,' growled Rolandson, and conferred for a few moments with Harrison. They both looked at Wheeler who shuffled his feet nervously. 'You have not been to Hukahoronui and yet you present this map as evidence,' said Harrison unbelievingly. 'That is what you said, isn't it?'

'Yes,' said Wheeler unhappily.

He was even more unhappy when Harrison had finished with him and sent him off. When Lyall was asked if he had further questions he warily said that he had none. Ballard raised his hand. 'I would like to ask Mr Buck one more question.'

'Very well.'

'Mr Buck, what was the immediate reaction of the councillors towards your revelations about the incidence of avalanches in Hukahoronui?'

Turi Buck froze. In a low voice he said, 'I would rather not say.'

'Mr Buck – I must ask you the question.'

Turi shook his head. 'I will not say.'

'You must answer the question, Mr Buck,' said Harrison, but Turi shook his head dumbly.

Harrison looked at Ballard blankly for a moment and Ballard shrugged. The hall was very quiet when someone said, 'I can answer that question.'

Harrison's head jerked. 'Dr McGill, this is most unseemly.'

McGill stepped forward. 'Mr Chairman, there are only four people who can answer the question. Mr Buck refuses for reasons I can understand. Mr Eric Peterson will not answer, again for reasons I can understand. In all propriety Mr Ballard cannot, because he is interrogating Mr Buck – he cannot be questioner and witness simultaneously. I am the only one left who was present at the meeting.'

Harrison sighed. 'Very well, you will answer the question. What was it, Mr Ballard?'

'What was the immediate reaction of the councillors to Mr Buck's evidence?'

McGill unzipped his satchel and drew forth a flat notebook. 'As is my habit, I took notes immediately after the meeting. I can read here exactly what was said.' He selected a page and stared at Eric Peterson where he sat next to Lyall. 'Mr Eric Peterson's exact words were, "Turi Buck is an ignorant old black man. He knows nothing – he never has and he never will".'

There was pandemonium in the Press gallery.

The hall errupted in a babble of noise and Harrison hammered in vain on the rostrum but the crash of his gavel was lost in the uproar. When, at last, he could make himself heard, he said in anger, 'This hearing is adjourned until further notice and until those present can control themselves.'

CHAPTER NINE

'Turi Buck is an ignorant old black man. He knows nothing – he never has and he never will.'

The words hung heavily in an embarrassed silence in the residents' lounge of the Hotel D'Archiac which did duty as a council chamber. At last Matthew Houghton coughed nervously, and said, 'There's no call for that sort of talk, Eric.'

Ballard was angry. 'I should bloody well think not.'

John Peterson, who was standing, put his hand on his brother's shoulder. 'Eric, if you can't talk sense you'd better keep your big mouth shut. You're starting to behave like Charlie.' He looked at Turi. 'My apologies.'

'Maybe you'd better let Eric make his own apologies,' said Ballard tightly.

Eric went red in the face but said nothing. John Peterson ignored Ballard and addressed himself to McGill. 'So you've come up with past avalanches, and now you say there's going to be another.'

'I have *not* said that.'

'Then what *are* you saying?' demanded Houghton.

McGill spread his hands. 'Who cares if a few thousand tons of snow falls off a mountain? It's happening all the time in the Southern Alps. But if someone is standing underneath at the time then it's downright dangerous. That's the position you're in. You have a potential hazard here.'

'Not an actual hazard?' queried John Peterson.

'I can tell you more after another series of tests. But I'll tell you this – the hazard isn't getting any less.'

Peterson said, 'It seems pretty flimsy to me. From the line you're shooting it seems to me that you want us to spend a lot of money because of something that may never happen.'

'There's something I don't understand,' said Houghton. 'If there have been avalanches in the past, why weren't the houses knocked down? My house was the second one built in the valley; my grandfather built it in 1850, two years after the Otago Settlement.'

Ballard said, 'Let's have a look at the map.' He pushed the map across the table to Houghton. 'Matt, I want you to cast your mind back, say, twenty years – before all the houses were built when the mine started. I want you to mark all the houses you can remember.' He handed Houghton a pen.

'Well, there's my house there, and Turi Buck's house – but we know why that's still there. And there's the Cunningham house, and the Pearman house . . .'

'. . . and the Jackson place and the old Fisher house,' said Mrs Samson.

Slowly Houghton marked them all and then leaned back. Ballard said, 'Don't forget the church and the school – and Peterson's store.'

Houghton scratched more crosses on the map, and Ballard said, 'Just look at it. All those buildings are well scattered and if you look at the terrain you'll see that every one of them is protected against falls from the western slope to a greater or lesser degree.' He picked up the pen. 'But we do know there was another building – the Bailey house.' He marked its position on the map. 'That's gone now.'

Mrs Samson said, 'What are you getting at?'

'When the settlers first came here, back in the middle of last century, they didn't bother overmuch about keeping records, so we don't know a lot about houses destroyed. We only know about the Bailey house because of Turi. My bet is that the houses Matt has just marked are the survivors.'

Phil Warrick said, 'That makes sense. If a man had a house knocked down he wouldn't rebuild in the same place. Not if he had any brains.'

'Or if he survived,' said McGill. 'The Baileys didn't.' He

put his hand flat on the map. 'Those houses survived because the builders were lucky or knew what they were about. But now you've got a whole township here – not just a few scattered houses. That's where the hazard comes in.'

'So what are you asking us to do?' asked John Peterson.

'I want you to accept the fact that avalanche hazard exists – that's the first step and all follows from that. So you'll have to take the necessary precautions, first in the short term and, later, in the long term. You must notify the appropriate authority outside the valley that a hazard exists. Then you must be ready for it if it comes. You must have rescue gear stored in safe places where it can be got at in case of disaster. And you'll have to have men trained to use that equipment. And you'll have to have contingency planning in case it becomes necessary to evacuate the town. I can help in advising on a lot of that.'

Eric Peterson said, 'My brother is right. It seems to me that you're asking us to spend a lot of money guarding against something which might never happen. If we have to train men we have to pay them; if we have to have equipment we have to pay for it. Where do we get the money?'

Quentin laughed bitterly. 'You haven't heard anything yet. Wait until you hear about the long-term precautions.' His finger stabbed out. 'If this man has his way the mine will shut down.'

'What the hell!' John Peterson stared at Ballard. 'What foolish talk is this?'

'Ask McGill how much it will cost to protect the mine,' said Quentin. 'At the last meeting we had they were talking in millions of dollars – and we all know the company won't stand for that.'

'Not to protect the mine,' snapped Ballard. 'To protect the town. In a case like this you'll get a government grant.'

Eric Peterson laughed shortly. 'Everyone knows that government grants don't cover everything – not by a long chalk. We learned that when we were extending the school. And you are talking in millions of dollars, not in thousands.' He looked up at his brother. 'Guess how much the town rates will be next year if this damn silly caper carries on.'

Ballard said, 'How much is your life worth, Eric?'

'That's a hell of a question! But I'll give you a short answer. My life is worth that of one of my brothers – that much and no more.'

'There's no call for that,' said Houghton quickly.

'Well, he brought it up,' said Eric. 'In any case, according to him, I'm safe.' He tapped the map. 'My place is one of the survivors.'

'Not any more,' said Ballard. 'Not since the trees were cut down on the west slope. Did you do that, Eric?'

'What the hell has that got to do with anything?'

'The only reason the store survived in 1943 was because of the trees. Now they're gone there's nothing between you and the snow. You made a bad bargain there.'

Eric stood up. 'Too right I made a bad bargain, or rather, my old man did. You know damned well that when your mother sold him the property she cheated him of the mineral rights. Oh, she was bloody clever, wasn't she? She even kept hold of that bit of land at the bottom where the mine is now – just enough land to put up the crushing mill to work the ore she gets out of *our* land.'

Ballard rubbed his eyes. 'That's not the way it was, Eric. It was my father who separated the mineral rights from the property. He did it in his will. Your father didn't buy the land for five years after that. 1948, wasn't it?'

'The hell with it!' said Eric. 'She still gets the gold.'

'No, she doesn't,' said Ballard. 'She doesn't hold the mineral rights.'

'Pull the other one,' scoffed Eric. 'You're all Ballards.'

Matt Houghton drummed his fingers on the table. 'We seem to have left the subject.' He glanced nervously at Eric.

'Yes,' said McGill. 'I don't know what this is all about but I don't think it has anything to do with snow on a hillside. But those missing trees do; there's nothing left to bind the snow.'

Eric shrugged and sat down again. 'It's a lousy piece of land, anyway. Too bloody steep for cattle, and I couldn't even get in the hay crop this year.'

McGill's head jerked up. 'What hay crop?' he said sharply. 'What do you care?'

'You'd better tell me. What happened to your hay crop?'

John Peterson rolled his eyes towards the ceiling. 'For God's sake, Eric! Indulge his curiosity. Then perhaps we can get this meeting over. I've got things to do.'

Eric shrugged. 'First it was the rain – the crop was sodden, so we couldn't take it in. I thought we'd have a dry spell, but we didn't – it rained right in to the winter, so I gave it up. It was rotting in the fields, anyway.'

'And you just left it,' said McGill. 'And it's still there uncut. Is that it?'

'That's right,' said Eric, and added touchily, 'But what's it got to do with you I'm damned if I know.'

McGill speared him with a long stare. 'So you cut down the trees, which is bad enough. Then you leave uncut grass, which is worse. Long, wet grass on a hillside is just about the slipperiest stuff there is. The chances of an avalanche have just gone up considerably.'

Warrick said, 'It was slippery, I know. I tried to get up there during the rain myself. After the third try I gave up.'

'What am I? Some kind of public enemy?' demanded Eric. 'Who the hell is this joker to come with his accusations?'

'I'm not accusing anyone of anything except maybe short-sightedness,' said McGill. 'The first sign of potentially dangerous terrain is a mountain with snow on it, and you have one right on your doorstep but none of you seems to have seen it.'

'Dr McGill is right,' said Ballard.

Eric Peterson lunged to his feet. 'Anyone called Ballard is the last person to accuse me of anything at all,' he said with a jagged edge to his voice. 'Anyone with a yellow . . .'

'That's enough,' cut in Mrs Samson sharply. 'What's past is gone.'

'What's this about?' asked Warrick, looking from Ballard to Eric Peterson. He wore a baffled look, as of a man who feels he is missing the obvious.

Matt Houghton looked bleak. 'It's old history and nothing to do with the subject here.'

McGill stood up. 'Gentlemen, you have my report. It's there on the table before you written up in technical language, and I've explained what it means in words of one syllable. I can do nothing more. I shall leave you to your deliberations.'

'Where are you going?' asked Houghton.

'To do some work.'

'Where can we get hold of you if we need further information?'

'At Mr Ballard's house,' said McGill. 'Or up on the west slope – it needs further investigation. But don't send anyone up there to find me. In fact, no one should be allowed on that slope from now on. It's damned dangerous.'

He left the meeting.

CHAPTER TEN

Ian Ballard swam another length of the pool and then climbed out. He walked to the canvas chair where he had left his towel and began to rub himself down. It was good to relax after spending all day at the Inquiry. He poured himself a beer and checked his watch before slipping it on to his wrist.

Mike McGill came sauntering across the lawn and held out an envelope. 'Business as usual. Old Harrison must have got over his tantrum. This will be your notification to attend; I've had mine.'

Ballard opened the envelope. McGill was right; the letter was from Reed, the Secretary to the Commission. He dropped it on the grass next to his chair, and said, 'So we go on. What comes next in the evidence?'

'The first avalanche, I suppose.' McGill grinned and spread a newspaper before Ballard. 'Eric has got his name in print.'

Ballard looked at the black headline bannered across the front page:

'IGNORANT BLACK MAN' JIBE

He shook his head. 'He's not going to like that.'

McGill chuckled. 'Think he'll come after me with a gun?'

'Eric won't – but Charlie might,' said Ballard soberly. 'He's crazy enough to do it.'

McGill laughed and sat down on the grass. 'Got yourself a lawyer yet?'

'No.'

'You'd better start looking.'

'I've discovered I have an unsuspected talent,' said Ballard. 'I can defend myself very well.'

'You did all right with Turi, and you got Lyall to walk out on a limb before you sawed it off. Not bad going for a novice.'

'Mr Ballard?' Ballard looked up and saw the young man from the hotel office. 'A telegram just came. I thought it might be important so I brought it right out.'

'Thanks.' Ballard ripped open the envelope. 'It's a cablegram from England.' He scanned it rapidly and frowned. 'Now why should . . .?'

'Trouble?'

'Not really.' Ballard handed the cable to McGill. 'Why should a man suddenly fly half way across the world to see me?'

'Who is Stenning?'

'A friend of my grandfather.' Ballard looked at the pool abstractedly.

McGill began calculating. 'He says he's leaving on the night flight. It doesn't really matter whether he comes east or west, it's still about forty hours to Auckland. Then he'll have to catch an internal flight down to here. Say two full days – that means Saturday afternoon.'

'The Commission won't sit on Saturday. I'll meet Stenning at the airport.'

'You'd better have a message awaiting him at Auckland so you can arrange to meet him here.'

Ballard nodded. 'Old Ben said something about Stenning the last time I saw him. He said that if anything were to happen to him or the company then I should get in touch with Stenning. Then he said to forget it because Stenning would get in touch with me fast enough. It seems as though he really meant it.'

'Who is Stenning, apart from being your grandfather's friend?'

'He's a lawyer.'

'Then he's arriving just in time,' said McGill. 'Just the man you need.'

Ballard shook his head. 'He's not the right sort of lawyer. He specializes in taxes.'

'Oh, one of those boys.' McGill chuckled. 'He's probably come to confess all – that he slipped up on sorting out the death duties bit, and instead of three million from the old man you're just going to get three thousand.'

Ballard grinned. 'I'm not going to get three cents. Ben warned me about that. He said that he'd educated me and I'd have to stand on my own two feet as he'd done at my age. I told you that all his money is tied up in some trust or other.' He stretched. 'I'm beginning to feel chilly. Let's go inside.'

'It's warmer in the bar,' agreed McGill.

CHAPTER ELEVEN

The Press gallery was jammed as Harrison led Eric Peterson through his evidence. Dan Edwards had shamelessly bought space for himself by bringing in two cub reporters and then sending them away when the proceedings began. But it was to no avail; protests from other reporters soon led to the seats being occupied, and Edwards was compelled to scrawl his shorthand in as cramped conditions as anyone else.

Harrison made a note on his pad, and raised his eyes. 'So we arrive at the point when Dr McGill left, having delivered his bad news. What happened then, Mr Peterson?'

Eric Peterson shrugged. 'Well, the meeting went on for a long time. In all honesty I have to say that some of us were not convinced of the gravity of the situation. You must remember that this whole thing had been jumped on us suddenly – had taken us by surprise, if you like. After all, if someone steps up to you and says, "The end of the world is at hand!" you're going to need a lot of proof before you believe him.'

'I appreciate your position,' said Harrison. 'Can you give some specific examples of the views of members of the council?'

'Well, my brother argued that, even if McGill was anywhere near right, we didn't want to start a panic. I agreed with that and so did Matt Houghton, the mayor. Phil Warrick didn't seem to have any views at all. He just blew along with the wind and agreed with everybody. Mrs Samson wanted to go all out with preparations for evacuation right there and then.'

'What position did the mine management take?'

'Mr Ballard agreed with Mrs Samson. Mr Quentin said he didn't think there was any danger – he said it was all a lot of hot air. Mr Cameron tended to go along with Mr Ballard.' Peterson clasped his hands before him. 'You must realize that any decision concerning the town had to be made by the council. It wasn't up to the mine management to tell the town what to do. Dr McGill had told us there was no immediate hazard from the west slope, and to some of us there seemed to be no reason for going off half-cocked on a project that might cost the town a lot of money and wasted time.'

'And lose votes if nothing happened,' remarked Edwards cynically.

'Well, as I said, there was a lot of talk and we went round in circles for some time. Eventually Matt Houghton came up with an idea. He said that maybe there was something in what McGill had said, but he'd like a second opinion. He said he'd telephone Christchurch and get some advice.'

'To whom was he going to speak?'

'That was the rub. He didn't know and neither did anyone else. Mr Cameron suggested he talk to someone in the Forestry Department – he said they'd probably know about avalanche conditions. Someone else, I forget who, suggested the Department of Civil Defence. It was decided he'd try both. Mrs Samson said the police should be notified and that was agreed to.'

'Did the mine management make any concrete suggestions?'

'We had the offer of transport – trucks and suchlike. Also bulldozers.'

'Who made that offer?'

Peterson glanced sideways at Ballard. He hesitated, then said, 'I don't remember. It may have been Mr Cameron.'

Ballard smiled thinly.

'And what happened then?'

'The meeting broke up and it was decided we'd meet at eleven the next morning, even though it was Sunday.'

'I see.' Harrison looked around. 'Has anyone any further questions to ask Mr Peterson?'

Smithers raised his hand. 'I represent the Ministry of Civil Defence. Was a telephone call in fact made to the Civil Defence authorities?'

'Not to my knowledge.'

'Why not?'

'I talked with Matt Houghton after the meeting. He was a bit wavery about things. He said he'd do what he always did before making a decision. He said he'd sleep on it.'

'And the police – were they notified?'

'That was a bit difficult. Arthur Pye was away; he was up at the head of the valley investigating a case of sheep worrying.'

'Who is Arthur Pye?'

'Our policeman. Hukahoronui is only a small place – we just had the one policeman.'

'Do you mean to tell me that when you discussed notifying the police it was your intention to tell Constable Pye?' said Smithers incredulously.

'Well, he'd know what to do about telling his superiors,' said Peterson defensively.

'So *nobody* outside Hukahoronui knew of the situation?'

'I suppose that is correct.'

'And in Hukahoronui the knowledge was confined to a handful of people.'

'Yes, sir.'

Smithers consulted his note-pad. 'You say that when it was decided to get a second opinion on Dr McGill's diagnosis of the situation nobody knew whom to consult.' He lifted his head and looked at Peterson with an air of disbelief. 'Did no one on the council read the directives which were sent out by my Ministry?'

'We get a lot of stuff from the Government.' Peterson shrugged. 'I didn't read it all myself.'

'Apparently no one on the council read it.' Smithers took a deep breath. 'Mr Peterson, you were a councillor and a responsible official. Would you not agree that preparations for a crisis in your community were conspicuous by their absence? I am not speaking of avalanches only – we do live in an earthquake prone country, a major reason for the existence of the Ministry of Civil Defence.'

'May I object?' said Lyall quickly.

Harrison looked up from his notes. 'What is your objection?'

'I would like to point out that the township of Hukahoronui was relatively new and the population was largely composed of recent immigrants to the valley. In such a situation the degree of community spirit would naturally be less than in a longer established community.'

'Mr Lyall, is that your objection? You seem to be answering for the witness.'

'It is not my objection, Mr Chairman. My objection is that it is improper for Mr Smithers to ask such a loaded question of Mr Peterson. He is usurping the function of this Commission, which is to decide whether the state of affairs implicit in his question was actually the case.'

'A thin point, but valid nevertheless,' conceded Harrison. 'But it would have come better with the accompanying speech of extenuation. Mr Smithers, your last question was out of order. Have you any further questions?'

'None that I would care to ask this witness,' said Smithers curtly.

'Then you may step down, Mr Peterson, on the understanding that you may be recalled.'

Peterson left the witness chair with an air of relief, and Harrison bent forward to have a word with Reed. He then sat back in his chair, and said, 'Mr Cameron, the engineer of the Hukahoronui Mining Company, has been hospitalized for many months due to the injuries he received in the disaster. However, he has notified the Commission that he feels well enough to give evidence at this time and he is now present. Will you come forward, Mr Cameron?'

There was a low murmur as Cameron limped across the hall leaning heavily on the arm of a male nurse. He had lost a lot of weight and was now almost emaciated; his cheeks were sunken and his hair, pepper and salt at the time of the avalanche, was now quite white. He looked an old man.

He sat in the witness chair and the male nurse drew up another chair behind him. Reed said, 'What is your full name?'

'Joseph McNeil Cameron.'

'And your occupation, Mr Cameron?'

'I was a mining engineer,' said Cameron flatly. 'Specifically for the Hukahoronui Mining Company at the material times under investigation by this Commission.' His voice was strong if slow.

'Mr Cameron,' said Harrison, 'if at any time you feel unable to continue, please do not hesitate to say so.'

'Thank you, Mr Chairman.'

'I understand that you have evidence to give about the events of the evening of the day you had the meeting with the council. That would be the Saturday evening, would it not?'

'Yes, sir,' said Cameron. 'There was a dinner-dance at the Hotel D'Archiac that night. I had invited Mr Ballard and Dr McGill to be my guests. My daughter, Stacey, was also present – she was on vacation from the States at that time and was due to go back the following week. There was a certain amount of table-hopping during the dinner and it was then I learned that the mayor had not made the telephone calls. That, combined with a new and most disturbing report from Dr McGill, worried all of us very much.'

'Could you go into that in more detail?' said Harrison.

'Why, yes. We were just starting dinner . . .'

McGill inspected the menu. 'Colonial goose,' he said. 'That sounds good.'

Ballard chuckled. 'Don't expect poultry.'

'I was going to order that,' said Stacey Cameron. She was a tall, dark girl with typical American svelte good looks. McGill had measured her with a knowledgeable eye and classed her as a long-stemmed American beauty, Californian variety. She said, 'What is it if it isn't a bird?'

'A Texas nightingale isn't a bird, either, honey,' said Cameron. 'It's a donkey. This is a similar New Zealand joke.'

Stacey was horrified. 'You mean it's horse meat?'

'No,' said Ballard. 'It's hogget and stuffing.'

'Now you've lost me,' complained McGill. 'What's hogget?'

'Midway between lamb and mutton. There are millions of sheep in New Zealand and just about as many ways of cooking the animal. Colonial goose is a colonial joke, but it's not bad.'

'A trap for the unwary tourist,' commented McGill. 'Talking of that, when are you going back to the States, Stacey?'

'Just ten days left,' she said with a sigh.

'I've been trying to talk her into staying,' said Cameron.

'Why don't you?' Ballard asked her.

'I'd like to,' she said regretfully. 'If only to look after this crazy man.' She leaned over and patted her father's hand. 'But I have a boss back in San Francisco who's depending on me – I wouldn't want to let him down.'

Cameron said, 'No one is indispensable. How long would it take you to cut free?'

She thought about it. 'Maybe six months.'

'Then what about it?'

'I'll consider it,' she said. 'Really I will.'

Over dinner Cameron yarned about some of the practical difficulties they had run into when getting the mine going. 'The trouble was mainly with the people. The folks around here weren't very enthusiastic at first. They'd got pretty set in their ways and didn't like change. All except old man Peterson, of course, who saw the possibilities.'

'That reminds me,' said McGill. 'What's with the Petersons? And how many of them are there, for God's sake?'

'Three brothers,' said Ballard. 'John, Eric and Charlie. The old man died last year.'

Cameron said, 'John has the brains, Eric has the drive, and Charlie has the muscle and precious little else. If Charlie-boy had twice the brains he has now he'd be a half-wit. The Petersons own the Supermarket and the filling station, they have a half share in this hotel, run a couple of farms – things like that. Charlie wants to develop Huka as a ski resort but he's finding it tough sledding; his brothers don't think the time is ripe for it. Old Peterson saw the possibilities and his boys are carrying on where he left off.'

'You forgot Liz,' said Stacey. 'She's over there – fourth table along.'

Ballard turned his head. He had not seen Liz Peterson since his return to the valley and his image was still of a freckled, gawky girl with pigtails and skinned knees. What he saw was something quite different and he drew in his breath.

Liz Peterson was a rarity – a really beautiful girl whose loveliness did not depend on the adventitious aid of cosmetics. Her beauty lay deeper than the surface of her skin – in the bone structure of her skull, in the sheen of good health and youth, in the smooth and controlled movements of her body. She was beautiful in the way a healthy young animal is beautiful and she had the unconscious arrogance that can be seen in a thoroughbred racehorse or a fine hunting dog.

'Bv God!' he said. 'She's grown up.'

Cameron chuckled. 'It tends to happen.'

'Why haven't I seen her around?'?

'She's been visiting in North Island; just got back this week,' said Cameron. 'She had dinner with us on Monday. Stacey was quite impressed, and it really takes something to impress my girl.'

'I like Liz,' said Stacey. 'She has a mind of her own.'

Ballard looked studiously at his plate. 'Any of the Petersons married yet?'

'John is – and Eric's engaged.'

'Charlie?'

'No – he hasn't had to – not yet; but it's been a close call once or twice from what I hear. As for Liz, she should have been married long ago but Charlie has a way of scaring the young men. He looks after his sister like a hen with one chick.'

McGill said, 'The Petersons don't like you, Ian. What was all that about this morning?'

'An old quarrel,' said Ballard shortly. He glanced at Cameron. 'Know about it, Joe?'

'I've heard,' said Cameron. 'Something about the Ballards cheating the Petersons out of the mine.'

'That's the way the Petersons tell it,' agreed Ballard. 'Not John – he's too sensible; but Eric tends to drive it into the ground a bit. What happened was that my father had a row with my grandfather and emigrated to New Zealand. Although he'd left the family, he was still enough of a Ballard to be interested in gold when he found it on his land. He knew there wasn't enough sign to start a serious operation, the price of gold being what it was, but when he made his will before he joined the army he left the land to my mother, but the mineral rights he left to my grandfather.'

'In spite of the fact that they'd quarrelled?' asked McGill.

'He was a Ballard. What would my mother do with mineral rights? Anyway, after he died my mother had to sell the land – she couldn't farm it herself. She sold most of it – that's the west slope – to old Peterson, who neglected to check if he had the mineral rights. I don't know if he cared about that one way or the other, but when my grandfather bought the rest of the land from my mother – the bit at the bottom of the slope – and started to exploit the mineral rights under Peterson land then all hell broke loose. Accusations of bad faith were tossed around like confetti. The Petersons have always been convinced it was a deep-laid plot on the part of the Ballards. Actually, of course, it was nothing of the kind, but because my name is Ballard I'm stuck with it.'

'When you put it that way it doesn't sound too bad,' said Cameron. 'All the same, I'm not surprised that the Petersons are riled.'

'I don't see why they should be,' said Ballard. 'The only people making a profit out of the mine are the Petersons; the mine brought prosperity to this valley and the Petersons are creaming it off. The Ballards certainly aren't making a profit. You've seen the operating figures, Joe, and you know the company is just breaking even.' He shook his head. 'I don't know what's going to happen if we have to put in extensive avalanche protection. I've been trying to get hold of Crowell all day but he's not available.'

'Who is he?' asked McGill.

'Chairman of the company. He lives in Auckland.'

'I've been thinking of avalanche protection,' said McGill meditatively. 'I've got some figures for you, Joe. When you design the avalanche gallery over the mine portal allow for an impact pressure of ten tons a square foot.'

Cameron flinched. '*That much?*' he asked incredulously.

'I've been talking to people who witnessed the 1943 slide. From all accounts it was an airborne powder avalanche, and so was the 1912 slide, according to Turi Buck. The next may not be any different.'

'Airborne powder! What's that?'

'This is no time for a lecture on avalanche dynamics. All you need to know is that it's fast and it packs a hell of a wallop.'

Ballard said, 'The 1943 avalanche turned a hundred acres of big trees into firewood.'

Cameron put down his fork. 'Now I *know* why you're worried about the town.'

'I wish to hell the council was as worried as I am,' said McGill bleakly.

Cameron looked up. 'Here comes Matt Houghton. If you tell him what you've just told me maybe he'll become as scared as I am.' As Houghton came up, his bald head gleaming, Cameron pulled out a chair. 'Sit down, Matt. What did the Civil Defence people have to say?'

Houghton sat down heavily. 'I haven't had time to talk to them yet. We'll be posting signs on the slope; Bobby Fawcett's scouts are making them and they'll be putting them up tomorrow. Got any stakes we can use, Joe?'

'Sure,' said Cameron, but his voice was abstracted. He was looking at McGill.

Ballard leaned forward. 'What do you mean, Matt – you didn't have time? I thought it was agreed . . .'

Houghton flapped his hands. 'It's *Saturday*, Ian,' he said plaintively, and shrugged. 'And tomorrow is Sunday. We probably won't be able to get through to them until Monday.'

Ballard looked baffled. 'Matt, do you really think that Civil Defence Headquarters closes down at weekends? All you have to do is to lift the bloody telephone.'

'Take it easy, Ian. I have enough trouble with the Petersons. Charlie takes the line that no one can prevent him from walking – or skiing – on his own land.'

'For Christ's sake! Is he out of his mind?'

Houghton sighed. 'You know Charlie. It's that old feud getting in the way.'

'What the hell did I have to do with buying and selling mineral rights? I was only a kid at the time.'

'It's not that; it's the other thing. Charlie *was* Alec's twin, you know.'

'But that was nearly twenty-five years ago.'

'Long memories, Ian; long memories.' Houghton rubbed his jaw. 'That stuff you told us about your training – you know, Johannesburg and Harvard. Eric was inclined to disbelieve you.'

'So he thinks I'm a liar as well as a coward,' said Ballard sourly. 'What does he think it takes to be in charge of a company like this?'

'He did mention a rich grandfather,' said Houghton wryly. He dropped his eyes under Ballard's steady stare. Ballard said, 'I'm expecting a call from old Crowell. You can talk to him if you like. He'll tell you my qualifications.' His voice was chilly.

'Take it easy – I believe you. You've made a success of your life, and that's all that matters.'

'No, it isn't, Matt. What matters is that bloody snow on the slope above this town, and I don't want any ancient history getting in the way. I'm going to make sure the right thing is done, and if the Petersons get in my way I won't go around them – I'll go through them. I'll smash them.'

Houghton gave him a startled look. 'My God, but you've changed!'

'Turi Buck said it first – I've grown up,' said Ballard tiredly.

There was an embarrassed silence at the table. McGill, who had been quietly watchful, said, 'I don't know what that was all about, Mr Houghton, but I can tell you this. The situation is now more serious than that I outlined at our meeting this morning. I've taken more samples from the slope and the stability is deteriorating. I've also been talking to people about previous avalanches, with the result that I've just notified Mr Cameron to prepare for something hitting the mine very hard indeed. I have to tell you that also applies to the town.'

Houghton was affronted. 'Why the hell didn't you talk like that this morning instead of pussyfooting around with scientific quibbles? This morning you said the hazard was potential.'

McGill was exasperated. 'I sometimes wonder if we talk the same language,' he snapped. 'The hazard still is potential and it will be until something happens and then it'll be actual hazard and too goddam late to do anything about it. What do

89

you want me to do? Go up on the slope and trigger it just to prove to you that it can happen?'

Ballard said, 'Go back to your council and tell them to stop playing politics. And tell the Petersons from me that no one votes for dead men.' His voice was like iron. 'You can also tell them that if they don't do something constructive by midday tomorrow I'll go over their heads – I'll call a public meeting and put it to the people direct.'

'And telephone Civil Defence as soon as you can,' added McGill.

Houghton took a deep breath and stood up. His face was red and shiny with sweat. 'I'll do the best I can,' he said, and walked away.

Ballard stared after him. 'I wonder if this is a good time to get drunk?'

CHAPTER TWELVE

'Did Mr Ballard drink heavily that night?' asked Lyall.

Cameron's lips compressed and then he relaxed. 'Not more than most,' he said easily. 'It was a party, you must remember. For instance, he didn't drink as much as me.' As an apparent afterthought he added, 'Or as much as your clients there.'

Lyall said sharply, 'I must protest. The witness cannot be allowed to make gratuitous innuendoes of that nature.'

Harrison was trying unsuccessfully to hide a smile. 'It appears to me that Mr Cameron was merely trying to put Mr Ballard's drinking in the scale of things. Is that not so, Mr Cameron?'

'It was a party in a small town,' said Cameron. 'Sure, there was drinking. Some of the boys from the mine got pretty smashed. Some of the town folk, too. I was a bit rosy myself towards the end. But Mr Ballard was nowhere near drunk. I don't think he's really a drinking man. But he had a few.'

'I think that answers Mr Lyall's question. Go on, Mr Cameron.'

'Well, at about eleven-thirty that night Mr Ballard again tackled the mayor about whether he'd telephoned anybody – Civil Defence or whatever – and Houghton said he hadn't. He said he didn't see that a few hours would make any difference and he wasn't going to make a fool of himself in the middle of the night by ringing up some caretaker and asking him damn silly questions.'

Harrison looked across at Ballard. 'Mr Cameron, it would be improper to ask you why Mr Ballard, at this point, did not make the call himself. Mr Ballard is here to answer for himself, as I am sure he will. But, if there was this urgency, why did *you* not make the call?'

Cameron looked embarrassed. 'We'd been told, quite bluntly, to keep our noses out of town business. And up to that time we thought the call *had* been made. When we found it hadn't we thought the likelihood of getting anyone at Civil Defence who could tell us what we wanted to know was slight. Another thing was that Mr Ballard still hoped to co-operate with the council, and if he made the call they'd think he'd gone over their heads on what they would consider to be town business. Relations between mine and town might be permanently damaged.'

'What did Dr McGill think of this?'

'He wasn't around at the time; he'd gone out to check the weather. But afterwards he said that Mr Ballard was a damned fool.' Cameron scratched his cheek. 'He said I was a damned fool, too.'

'It seems that Dr McGill is the only person to come out of this with any credit,' observed Harrison. 'There appears to have been a lot of buck-passing for reasons which pale into insignificance when one considers the magnitude of the disaster.'

'I agree,' said Cameron frankly. 'But Dr McGill was the only person who had any conception of the magnitude of the trouble which faced us. When he told me to prepare for an impact pressure of ten tons a square foot I thought he was coming it a bit strong. I accepted his reasoning but at the back of my mind I didn't really believe it. I think that Mr Ballard was in the same case, and he and I are technical men.'

'And because the members of the council were not technical men do you think that excuses their dilatory conduct?'

'No,' said Cameron heavily. 'We were all guilty to a greater or lesser degree. It does not excuse our conduct, but it goes a long way towards explaining it.'

Harrison was silent for a long time, then he said gently, 'I'll accept that, Mr Cameron. What happened next?'

'Mr Ballard and I stayed at our table talking and doing a

little drinking. If Mr Ballard did any drinking that night it was then that he did it. He hadn't had more than two drinks up to then.'

Cameron talked with Ballard for some time, maybe twenty minutes, and then they were joined by Stacey Cameron. Ballard cocked an ear towards the dance floor; it was late enough for the jigging rock rhythms to have been replaced by the night-club shuffle. 'Dance?' he suggested.

Stacey grimaced. 'Thanks all the same, but no thanks. I've been danced off my feet tonight.' She sat down and flexed her toes, then looked up at him. 'Liz Peterson wants to know if you think she has smallpox.'

He blinked. 'What!'

'She seems to think that you're ignoring her. She could be right, at that.'

Ballard smiled slightly. 'I'd forgotten she existed until tonight.'

'Well, you know she exists now. Why don't you ask her for a dance? She's sitting this one out.'

Ballard's jaw dropped, and then he smiled. 'Well, for God's sake, why not?' He drained his glass and felt the lump of whisky hit bottom with a thud. 'I'll give it a whirl.' He left, heading for the dance floor.

'Are you crazy?' demanded Cameron. 'Don't you know that Ballard and the Petersons get on like the Hatfields and McCoys? What are you trying to do – start a war?'

'They've got to start talking to each other reasonably sometime,' said Stacey. 'Huka isn't big enough for them to ignore each other forever.'

Cameron looked unconvinced. 'I hope you know what you're doing.'

'Dad, what's all this about an avalanche?'

'What avalanche?'

'Don't talk to me as though I were a half-wit,' said Stacey. 'The avalanche you were discussing over dinner.'

'Oh, that one!' said Cameron with an ill-assumed air of surprise. 'Nothing to it. Just some precautions McGill wants us to take.'

'Precautions,' she said thoughtfully. 'That's not what I understood by the way Ian was reaming out Houghton.' She looked past her father. 'Here's Mike now. How's the weather, Mike?'

'Heavy snow setting in.' McGill checked his watch. 'Nearly midnight. How long do these shindigs go on?'

'The dancing will stop dead on midnight,' said Cameron. 'Very religious guys, these New Zealanders. No dancing on Sunday.'

McGill nodded. 'I won't be sorry to get to bed.' He stretched. 'What did the Civil Defence crowd have to say?'

'Houghton didn't call.'

'He *didn't*!' McGill grabbed Cameron by the arm. 'What have you done about it? Did Ian try?' Cameron shook his head. 'Then he's a goddamned fool – and so are you. Where's the telephone?'

'There's one in the lobby,' said Cameron. 'Look, Mike, there'll be no one there at this time of night qualified to tell you anything.'

'Tell me – hell!' said McGill. 'I'm going to tell them. I'm going to raise the alarm.'

He walked away rapidly with Cameron on his heels. As they skirted the dance floor there was a shout and a sudden disturbance. McGill jerked his head sideways and saw Charlie Peterson with his hand on Ballard's shoulder. 'Just what we need,' he said disgustedly. 'Come on, Joe,' and crossed the floor to where the two men bristled at each other.

Ballard had been dancing with Liz Peterson when he felt the heavy thud of Charlie's meaty hand on his shoulder and felt himself spun round. Charlie's face was sweaty and his eyes were red-rimmed. Alcohol fumes came from him as he whispered hoarsely, 'Stay away from my sister, Ballard.'

Liz's face flamed. 'Charlie, I told you . . .'

'Shut up!' His hand bore heavily on Ballard's shoulder. 'If I catch you with her again I'll break your back.'

'Take your hand off me,' said Ballard.

Some of the ferocity left Charlie and he grinned genially. 'Take it off yourself – if you can.' His thumb ground viciously into the muscle at the top of Ballard's arm.

'Stop this nonsense,' said Liz. 'You get crazier every day.'

Charlie ignored his sister and increased the pressure on Ballard. 'What about it? You won't get into trouble with your momma – she's not here.'

Ballard seemed to droop. His arms hung down in front of him, crossed at the wrists, and suddenly he brought them up sharply, hitting Charlie's arm at the elbow with considerable force and thus breaking free.

Charlie lunged forward but Cameron grabbed one arm and twisted it behind Charlie's back. It was done with expertise and it was evident that Cameron was no stranger to a rough house.

'Break it up,' said McGill. 'This is a dance floor, not a boxing ring.'

Charlie pressed forward again but McGill put his hand flat on Charlie's chest and pushed. 'All right,' said Charlie. 'I'll see you outside when you don't have your friends to help you.'

'Christ, you sound like a schoolboy,' said McGill.

'Let the bastard speak for himself,' said Charlie.

In the distance a voice was raised. 'Is Mr Ballard around? He's wanted on the telephone.'

McGill jerked his head at Ballard. 'Take your call.'

Ballard shrugged his shoulders into his rumpled jacket and nodded briefly. He walked past Charlie without so much as looking at him. Charlie twisted in Cameron's grip and yelled, 'You've not changed, you bastard. You still run scared.'

'What's going on here?' someone demanded.

McGill turned to find Eric Peterson at his elbow. He took his hand off Charlie's chest, and said, 'Your kid brother has gone off his rocker.'

Eric looked at Liz. 'What happened?'

'The same thing that happens every time I get too close to a man,' she said wearily. 'But worse than usual this time.'

Eric said to Charlie coldly, 'I've told you about this before.'

Charlie jerked his arm free of Cameron. 'But it was Ballard!' he pleaded. 'It was Ballard.'

Eric frowned. 'Oh!' But then he said, 'I don't care who it was. You don't make these scenes again.' He paused. 'Not in public.'

McGill caught Cameron's eye and they both moved off in the direction of the lobby and found Ballard at the reception desk. The desk clerk was pointing. 'There's the phone.'

'Who'd be ringing you?' asked McGill.

'Crowell, if I'm lucky.'

'After you with the phone – I want to ring Christchurch.' McGill turned to the desk clerk. 'Have you a Christchurch telephone book?'

Ballard picked up the telephone as McGill flipped through the pages. 'Ballard here.'

A testy voice said, 'I have half a dozen message slips here

asking me to ring you. I've just got in so it had better be important.'

'It is,' said Ballard grimly. 'We're in a bad situation here. We have reason to suppose that the mine – and the town – is in danger of destruction by avalanche.'

There was a blank silence broken only by a surge of music from the dance floor. Crowell said, 'What!'

'An avalanche,' said Ballard. 'We're going to be in dead trouble.'

'Are you serious?'

Ballard put his finger to his other ear to block out the noise of the music. 'Of course I'm serious. I don't joke about things like this. I want you to get on to the Ministry of Civil Defence to let them know about it. We may need help fast.'

'But I don't understand,' said Crowell faintly.

'You don't have to understand,' snapped Ballard. 'Just tell them that the township of Hukahoronui is in danger of being blotted out.'

McGill's finger marked a line in the telephone book. He looked up as someone ran past and saw Charlie Peterson heading for Ballard at a dead run. He dropped the book and jumped after him.

Charlie grabbed Ballard by the shoulder, and Ballard shouted, 'What the hell . . .?'

'I'm going to break you in half,' said Charlie.

Lost in the uproar was a soft rumble of distant thunder. Ballard punched at Charlie, hampered by the telephone he held. From the wildly waving earpiece came the quacking sound of Crowell in Auckland. McGill laid hands on Charlie and hauled him away bodily.

Ballard, breathing heavily, put the telephone to his ear. Crowell said, '. . . going on there? Are you there, Ballard? What's . . .?'

The line went dead.

McGill spun Charlie around and laid him cold with a right cross to the jaw just as all the lights went out.

CHAPTER THIRTEEN

'After the lights went out things got pretty confused,' said Cameron. He half turned in his chair and spoke to the nurse in a low voice. The nurse got up and poured him a glass of water, and when Cameron took it, his hand was shaking.

Harrison watched him carefully. 'You've been giving evidence for quite a long time, Mr Cameron, and I think you should stand down for the moment. Since we are taking evidence chronologically the next witness should naturally be Mr Crowell. Thank you, Mr Cameron.'

'Thank you, sir.' Cameron got to his feet painfully, assisted by the male nurse, and hobbled slowly across the hall.

Reed said, 'Will Mr Crowell come forward?'

A short, stout man got to his feet and walked up to the rostrum with some reluctance. As he sat down he turned his head sideways to look at Rickman, who nodded reassuringly. Reed said, 'What is your full name?'

Crowell licked his lips nervously, and coughed. 'Henry James Crowell.'

'And your occupation. Mr Crowell?'

'I'm the chairman of several companies, including the Hukahoronui Mining Company.'

Harrison said, 'Do you own shares in that company?'

'I have a minority holding, yes.'

'Mr Ballard was the managing director of that company, was he not?'

'Yes.'

'What were his responsibilities?'

Crowell frowned. 'I don't understand the question.'

'Come, Mr Crowell. Surely Mr Ballard had duties which were defined.'

'Of course, sir. He had the normal duties of a managing director – to see to the total interests of the company under the guidance of the board of directors.'

'Which was headed by yourself.'

'That is correct.'

'You have been listening to evidence relating to a telephone call which you made to Mr Ballard. Did you, in fact, make that call?'

'Yes.'

'Why?'

'I had been away from home and arrived back late on the Saturday night. My secretary had left a list of messages from Mr Ballard to the effect that I should contact him. From the number and tenor of these messages I judged the matter to be urgent, so I telephoned him immediately.'

'And what did he say?'

'He said something about an avalanche. I didn't quite understand – he was very indistinct.'

'Didn't you ask him to explain further?'

'Yes.' Crowell's hands twitched. 'There was a lot of noise going on at his end – music and so forth. He wasn't very coherent.'

Harrison regarded him thoughtfully, and then moved his eyes sideways. 'Yes, Mr Smithers?'

'Can the witness state whether or not Mr Ballard asked him to contact the Ministry of Civil Defence to warn them of impending danger at Hukahoronui?'

Harrison's eyes returned to Crowell who wriggled in his seat. 'He did say something along those lines, but there was a lot of noise on the line. A lot of shouting and screaming.' He paused. 'Then I was cut off.'

'What did you do then?' asked Harrison.

'I talked it over with my wife.'

A ripple of amusement passed over the hall. Harrison knocked sharply with his gavel. 'Did you contact the Ministry of Civil Defence?'

Crowell hesitated. 'No, sir.'

'Why not?'

'I thought it was some sort of practical joke. With that music and uproar on the line . . . well, I thought . . .' His voice tailed away.

'You thought Mr Ballard was joking?' queried Harrison.

Both Lyall and Rickman had their hands up. Harrison picked Rickman and nodded. 'Did you think Mr Ballard was drunk?' asked Rickman. Lyall grinned and hauled down his hand.

'I did.'

'When you said that Mr Ballard was incoherent that was what you meant, wasn't it?'

'Yes,' said Crowell. He smiled gratefully at Rickman.

'You must not lead the witness,' said Harrison mildly.

'I'm sorry, Mr Chairman.' Rickman smiled encouragingly at Crowell. 'Who appointed Mr Ballard as managing director?'

'The instruction came from London – from a majority shareholder.'

'You had nothing to do with his appointment, then. Could we say that Mr Ballard was foisted upon you?'

'As a minority shareholder I didn't have much say in the matter.'

'If you had had a say in the matter whom would you have picked as managing director?'

'Mr Dobbs, who was mine manager.'

'And who is now dead.'

Crowell bowed his head and said nothing.

'That is all,' said Rickman.

'What did you think of Mr Ballard when you first met him?' asked Harrison.

Crowell shrugged. 'I thought he was a personable enough young man – perhaps a little too young for the job.'

'Did you suspect him of any proclivities towards drunkenness or practical joking?'

'They did not present themselves – then.'

'But they did eventually? When?'

'On that evening, Mr Chairman.'

Harrison sighed, exasperated at Crowell's woolly-mindedness. 'But we have heard evidence that Mr Ballard was neither drunk nor playing a practical joke. Why should you not believe what he said on that occasion?'

Crowell shook his head unhappily and looked towards Rickman, whose head was down as he busily scanned a sheet of paper. 'I don't know – it was just that it sounded that way.'

'It has been suggested that Mr Ballard was "foisted" upon you.' Harrison uttered the word as though it had a nasty taste. 'Upon his appointment, did you make any complaint of any kind – to anyone?'

'No.'

Harrison shook his head slowly as he regarded this most unsatisfactory witness. 'Very well. I have no further questions.' He looked down from the rostrum. 'Yes, Mr Ballard?'

'I would like to ask some questions.'

'I see that you still have no legal representation. Do you

think that wise? You must have heard the saying that the man who argues his own case has a fool for a lawyer.'

Ballard smiled. 'That may hold good in a law court, but, Mr Chairman, you have repeatedly said that this is not a court of law. I think I am quite capable of asking my own questions.'

Harrison nodded. 'Very well, Mr Ballard.'

Ballard looked at Crowell. 'Mr Crowell, two weeks after the disaster the board suspended me from my duties. Why?'

Rickman's hand shot up. 'Objection! What happened two weeks after the incident does not come within the scope of this inquiry.'

'Mr Rickman has a point,' said Harrison. 'I cannot really see that this is helpful.'

Ballard stood up. 'May I argue the point?'

'Certainly.'

Ballard picked up a note-pad. 'I took notes of your remarks when this inquiry began. You ruled that evidence given here may not be used in a future civil action. It seems to me that this inquiry may be the only public hearing possible.'

He turned a page. 'On the second day Dr McGill said that the death-roll in the disaster was higher than need be. You overruled an objection to that on the grounds that this is not a court of law and the procedure is at your sole discretion.'

He looked up. 'Mr Chairman, this inquiry is being widely reported in the Press, not only in New Zealand but also in the United Kingdom. Regardless of your findings, the public is going to blame someone for those unnecessary deaths. Now, certain imputations have been made about my character, my drinking habits and a supposed propensity for practical joking which, in my own interests, I cannot allow to pass unchallenged. I ask to be allowed to question Mr Crowell about these matters, and the fact that I was suspended from my duties a fortnight after the disaster certainly seems to me to be a legitimate reason for inquiry.'

Harrison conferred briefly with his two assessors, then said, 'It is not the wish of this Commission that a man's reputation be put lightly at stake. You may sit down, Mr Ballard, and continue your questioning of Mr Crowell.'

Rickman said warningly, 'There may be grounds for appeal here, Mr Chairman.'

'There may, indeed,' agreed Harrison tranquilly. 'You will find the procedure set out in the Commissions of Inquiry Act.

Continue, Mr Ballard.'

Ballard sat down. 'Why was I suspended from my duties, Mr Crowell?'

'It was a unanimous decision of the board.'

'That is not exactly answering my question, but we'll let it pass for the moment. You said in evidence that you had nothing to do with my appointment, that you would rather have chosen another man, and that the instructions came from London. Do you usually take your instructions from London, Mr Crowell?'

'Of course not.'

'Then where do you take your instructions from?'

'Why, from . . .' Crowell stopped short. 'I do not take instructions, as you put it. I am chairman of the company.'

'I see. Do you regard yourself as a sort of dictator?'

'That is an insulting question.'

'Maybe you might think so. All the same, I'd like you to answer it.'

'Of course I'm not a dictator.'

'You can't have it both ways,' said Ballard. 'Either you take instructions or you do not. Which is it, Mr Crowell?'

'As chairman I assist the board in making decisions. All decisions are made jointly.'

'A most democratic process,' commented Ballard. 'But the decision to appoint me as managing director was not made jointly by the board, was it, Mr Crowell?'

'The decision need not be unanimous,' said Crowell. 'As you have pointed out, this is a democratic process where the majority rules.'

'But not so democratic as to be a one man, one vote system. Is it not a fact that he who controls most votes controls the company?'

'That is the usual system.'

'And you said in evidence that the instruction to appoint me came from a majority shareholder in London. Is that shareholder a member of the board?'

Crowell twitched nervously. In a low voice he said, 'No, he is not.'

'Then is it not a fact that your board of directors has no real power and is thus a democratic sham? Is it not a fact that the power to control the company lies elsewhere? In the City of London?'

'That is a misreading of the situation,' said Crowell sullenly.

'Let us turn from my appointment to my suspension,' said Ballard. 'Did the instruction to suspend me also come from London?'

'It may have done.'

'Surely you know. You are the chairman of the board.'

'But not concerned with the day to day running of the company.'

'No,' agreed Ballard. 'That was the function of the managing director. You said so yourself in your evidence. Surely you are not suggesting that I suspended myself?'

Dan Edwards could not contain himself. There was a loud snigger from the Press gallery and Harrison looked up, frowning.

'You are being ridiculous,' said Crowell.

Ballard said drily. 'Any ridiculousness inherent in this situation certainly does not emanate from me. There remains one alternative. Are you suggesting that the suspension of the managing director was a minor bit of day to day business that was beneath your notice as chairman?'

'Of course not.'

'Then you will know where the idea of my suspension originated, won't you?'

'Now I come to think of it, the instruction for your suspension did come from London.'

'I see. But that again is not an exact answer to the question. Is it not a fact that you communicated with London because the board is a puppet dancing to strings held in the City of London? Is it not a fact that a suggestion was made – by you – that the company was in danger of being in bad odour because of evidence to be given at this inquiry? And is it not a fact that you intimated that I, as a Johnny-come-lately, was an ideal person to shuffle the responsibilty on to, and that it was then that the instruction was given – from London – that I be suspended?'

'Objection!' cried Rickman. 'Mr Ballard cannot lead the witness in this way.'

'I tend to agree,' said Harrison. 'Such a compendium cannot be permitted, Mr Ballard.'

'I withdraw the question.' Ballard knew, from the rustle in the Press gallery, that he had made his point where it mattered. 'I shall return to the telephone conversation between Mr Crowell and myself. When you were cut off, what did you do? Oh yes; you talked it over with your wife, didn't you?

What was the substance of that conversation?'

'I don't remember.' Crowell added irritably, 'It was late at night and we were both very tired.'

'When you were cut off, did you attempt to replace the call?'

'No.'

'No? Why not?'

'You heard my evidence. I thought you were drunk.'

'How long did you think I'd been drunk, Mr Crowell?' asked Ballard softly.

Crowell looked startled and uncomprehending. 'I don't understand the question.'

'It's quite a simple question. Please answer it.'

'I didn't give it a thought.'

Ballard picked up a sheet of paper. 'You said in evidence that your secretary had left a number of messages from me. You also said that you judged, from the number and tenor of those messages, that the matter was urgent. Did you think I'd been drunk all day? The first call I had was at eleven-thirty that morning.'

'I told you. I didn't give it a thought.'

'Evidently not. So you did not try to call me back?'

'No.'

'And you did not try to communicate with the Ministry of Civil Defence?'

'No.'

'As a matter of interest, Mr Crowell, what *did* you do? After you had discussed it with your wife, I mean.'

'I went to bed.'

'You went to bed,' repeated Ballard slowly. 'Thank you, Mr Crowell. That will be all. He waited until Crowell was rising from the chair and was in a half crouch. 'Oh, there is just one further thing. Did you come forward voluntarily to give evidence here, or were you subpoena'd?'

'I object,' said Rickman. 'That has nothing to do with anything.'

'I agree, Mr Rickman,' said Harrison smoothly. 'This Commission need not be instructed that Mr Crowell was subpoena'd – it already knows.' He ignored the indescribable sound that came from Rickman, and continued blandly, 'And now I think we shall adjourn for lunch.'

CHAPTER FOURTEEN

Over lunch in the restaurant near the Provincial Buildings, McGill said, 'You're doing all right, Ian. You got in some good stuff this morning.'

Ballard poured a glass of water. 'I didn't think Harrison would let me get away with it.'

'Get away with it! God, he compounded with you. He ticked you off when he had to, but he didn't stop you. I thought I'd split a gusset when he brought out the bit that Crowell had been subpoena'd. He agreed with Rickman and harpooned him in the same breath.' McGill paused. 'I don't think Harrison likes Crowell.'

'I don't like him much myself.'

'You're not doing yourself much good with your family. That histrionic speech about the company dancing to strings pulled in the City of London won't go down well with your uncles back home. Where did you learn to pull a trick like that?'

Ballard grinned. 'Watching the Perry Mason Show.' He shrugged. 'It won't make much difference. I've already decided to leave the Ballard Group.'

'After a speech like that you'll have to. I can't see any Ballard company hiring you now. What will you do?'

'Haven't made up my mind yet. Something will turn up.' He frowned. 'I keep wondering what Stenning wants.'

'Do you know him at all?'

'Not well. The old man relied on him a lot, and I know why. He's a tough old bird, about as ruthless as old Ben was himself. Ben told him what he wanted to do, and Stenning figured out a legal way of doing it. He's as sharp as a tack.'

'You say he's old – how old?'

Ballard reflected. 'He'll be pushing seventy now, I suppose. He was much younger than Ben. One of the bright young men that Ben surrounded himself with in the early years.'

'An old guy of seventy flying half way across the world,' mused McGill. 'Could be important, Ian.'

'I can't see how.'

McGill looked up. 'Here comes someone else who is not

doing herself much good with her family.' He stood up. 'Hi, Liz.'

Liz Peterson put her hand on Ballard's shoulder. 'Don't get up, Ian. Hi, Mike.'

McGill drew up a chair for her and then sat down. He put out his hand and rubbed Liz's dog behind the ears. 'Hi, Victor; how's the boy?' The Alsatian lolled his tongue and his tail wagged vigorously.

'I didn't see you at the hearing this morning,' said Ballard.

'I was there. Wouldn't miss it for anything. It's just that I wasn't sitting with the boys. I don't like Lyall – he gives me the cold grues. Where's Joe?'

'Gone back to the hospital. Giving evidence this morning took it out of him.'

Liz tapped on the table. 'My charming brother, Charlie, manufactures the bullets and Lyall fires them.' She burlesqued Lyall's accent. ' "Did Mr Ballard drink heavily that night?" I damn near cheered when Joe fired that right back. It wounded Charlie to the heart.'

'You're not doing yourself much good with them,' warned Ballard.

'To hell with both of them,' she said pleasantly. 'I only stuck around because of Johnnie, and now he's dead I'll be leaving Huka. Maybe I'll be leaving New Zealand.'

'A fine pair you are,' said McGill. 'Don't either of you believe in family ties at all?'

'Not with that pair,' said Liz. 'I nearly gave Charlie a heart attack just now. I said that if anyone implied that Ian was drunk just once more I'd offer my services as your witness. I said that I can tell well enough when the man I'm dancing with is drunk, and that Ian wasn't but that Charlie certainly was.' She laughed. 'I've never seen a man go red and white at the same time.'

'I'd be careful, Liz,' said Ballard soberly. 'Charlie can be violent.'

'Don't I know it! I once had to crown him with a bottle. But I can handle him.'

McGill smiled satirically. 'So unlike the home life of our own dear Queen,' he observed.

Ballard said, 'Thanks for the support, Liz. Ever since the avalanche I've been depressed, but now the depression is lifting. I've made a couple of decisions and now the way ahead seems a lot clearer. You've had a lot to do with it.'

'I bring more than support, sir – I bring information. Rickman and Lyall are cooking up something together. I was driving past the company office just now when they both came out together, laughing fit to bust.'

'Watch it, Ian.' warned McGill. 'It'll be a pincer movement.'

'Thanks, Liz,' said Ballard.

She looked at her watch. 'I think I'll sit with the boys this afternoon. I might learn something more. See you at the hearing.' She stood up. 'Come on Victor.'

As she walked away McGill said, 'The prettiest spy I ever did see.' He finished his coffee and looked around for the waitress. 'We'd better be going, too. By the way, what are these couple of decisions you've made?'

'You've heard one – I'm leaving the Ballard Group.'

'And the other?'

'I'm getting married,' said Ballard placidly.

McGill paused, his wallet half way from his breast pocket. 'Well, congratulations. Who's the lucky girl?'

Ballard dabbed at his mouth with a napkin. 'Liz Peterson – if she'll have me.'

'You must be insane,' said McGill. 'Who'd want Charlie as a brother-in-law?'

CHAPTER FIFTEEN

MacAllister was an electrical engineer, stolid and given to precise answers. When Harrison asked him when the power lines were cut, he answered, 'Two minutes and seven seconds to midnight.'

'How do you know?' asked Professor Rolandson.

'There is a recording device on the circuit breakers. When they kicked out the time was recorded.'

Harrison said, 'What did you do?'

'Established where the break was.'

From Rolandson: 'How?'

'I put a current on the line and measured the resistivity. That gave a rough idea of the distance to the break. I put it as a little short of Hukahoronui.'

'And then?'

'I rang my opposite number in Post Office Telephones and asked if he had the same trouble. He had, and he confirmed my findings. I then sent out an inspection crew.'

'With what result?'

'They rang me nearly two hours later to say that they had found the trouble. They said it was due to a fall of snow. A Post Office crew was also there and my men had used their portable telephone.'

'They just said it was due to a fall of snow?'

'Yes, sir. It didn't seem reasonable to me that a fall of snow could cut the cables so I asked for further information. The entrance to the valley of Hukahoronui is by a cleft or gap, and my men said the gap was filled with snow to a height farther than they could see in the darkness. I know the place, sir, and I asked if the river which runs out of the valley was still flowing. My man said there was a little flow but not very much. I assumed there would be flooding on the other side of the snowfall so I immediately notified the police.'

'Very quick-witted of you,' remarked Harrison. 'But why the police?'

'Standard instructions, sir,' said MacAllister stolidly.

'Did you take further steps?'

'Yes, sir. I went to the scene of the break in the cable. It was snowing quite heavily as I set out and conditions became worse as I proceeded. When I arrived at the break it was snowing very heavily – something like a blizzard. On my truck I had a spotlight but there was too much back reflection from the falling snow to show how high the blockage in the Gap was. I also investigated the flow of the river and found it to be minimal. I judged the situation serious enough to telephone the police again.'

'And what was the reaction from the police?'

'They noted the facts as I gave them, sir.'

'Nothing more?'

'They told me nothing more.'

'You say you could not tell the height of the blockage. Obviously you could not tell the depth – how far back it extended into the Gap?'

'No, sir.'

'Did you take steps to find out?'

'Not at that time. It was snowing heavily and it was dark. To investigate in those conditions would have been most dangerous. I would not climb up there myself, nor would I send anyone else. I judged it better to wait until daylight when we could see what we were doing.'

Harrison looked at Smithers. 'It appears from the evidence of Mr MacAllister that this was the first occasion that anyone outside Hukahoronui had any inkling of trouble.' He switched his gaze to Crowell who was sitting next to Rickman and amended his statement. 'Or anyone who did something constructive about it, that is. Have you any questions, Mr Smithers?'

'No, Mr Chairman. But I think the witness ought to be congratulated on the sensible steps he took – especially his quickness in passing on news of a potentially hazardous situation.'

'I concur.' Harrison turned to MacAllister. 'To what time does your evidence take us?'

'I made the second call to the police at three-thirty on the Sunday morning.'

'Thank you. You may step down, Mr MacAllister, with the knowledge that you have done your duty well.'

MacAllister left the witness chair, and Harrison said, 'I think it is time to get back to what happened in Hukahoronui after the lights were extinguished. We have just heard of a fall of snow which blocked the Hukahoronui Gap. I would like to hear Dr McGill's professional views on that.'

McGill rose, walked to the witness chair, and set his briefcase on the floor. Harrison said, 'You were present in the lobby of the Hotel D'Archiac when the lights went out?'

'Yes, sir. As Mr Cameron said, there was a lot of confusion at that time. Mr Ballard was trying to talk to Mr Crowell and had difficulty in doing so because of the actions of Mr Charles Peterson. I went to his aid and it was about then that the lights went out. Mr Ballard said that the telephone had also gone dead.'

'Did you *hear* the snow falling into the Gap?'

'No. There was too much noise in the hotel.'

'So what happened?'

'The management of the hotel got busy and provided light. There were candles and kerosene lanterns ready for use. I was told that a breakdown of electricity supply was not uncommon, and there had been a similar occurrence only the previous month. Everybody took it as a matter of course. I asked about the dead telephone but no one seemed worried about that, either. The dance was over, anyway, so everybody went home.'

'Including you?'

'Yes. I went home with Mr Ballard and went to bed.'

McGill was woken from a sound sleep by Ballard. He awoke to darkness and automatically flicked at the switch of the bedside lamp, but nothing happened. It was then he remembered about the power failure. Ballard was a deeper shadow in the darkness. McGill said, 'What time is it?'

'Five-thirty. Cameron just rang up with a funny story. It seems that one of his men, Jack Stevens, left early this morning to go to Christchurch to see his mother. He says he can't get out of the valley.'

'Why not?'

'He says the Gap is closed off with snow. He says he can't get through.'

'What sort of car does he have?'

'A Volkswagen.'

'Well, it's not surprising, is it? Look at what happened to those two Americans the other day. Is it still snowing?'

'Very heavily.'

'Well, there you are. It's probably been snowing all night. I couldn't guarantee to get through myself with a Land-Rover.'

'According to Cameron, Jack says it's not like that. He's talking of a wall of snow so high he can't see the top. I told Cameron to bring him here.'

McGill grunted. 'Light that candle on the dressing-table, will you?'

Ten minutes later he was saying, 'You're sure, now. This is not just a deep drift across the road?'

'I've told you it's not,' said Stevens. 'It's a bloody great wall of snow.'

'I think I'd better go and look at it,' said McGill.

Ballard said, 'I'll come with you.' He looked at the telephone and then at Cameron. 'If there's no power how did you manage to ring me?'

Stevens said, 'The exchange has a bank of batteries and an emergency diesel generator to top them up. We're all right for local calls.'

McGill nodded. 'Whatever happened at the Gap must have taken out the electricity cables and the telephone lines both.' He picked up a heavy anorak. 'Let's get going.'

'I'll come, too,' said Cameron.

'No,' said McGill. 'I've just been handed an idea. Do you have diesel generators at the mine?'

'Sure.'

'Then you see that they're in working order. I have a notion that we're going to need power before long.'

'That means me,' said Stevens. 'I'm the mine electrician.' He winked at Cameron. 'Do I get double time for Sunday work?'

Ballard left to put on ski pants and an anorak and then he joined McGill in the garage. He got behind the wheel of the Land-Rover and pushed the self-starter; it whined but the engine did not fire. 'She's cold,' he said as he pushed again. He tried several times but still the engine did not take. 'Confound the bloody thing.'

'Take it easy,' said McGill. 'You've flooded her. Wait a couple of minutes.' He pulled the anorak about him and then put on gloves. 'What's between you and Charlie Peterson? Last night he acted like a bull moose in rutting season.'

'It's an old story,' said Ballard. 'Not worth repeating.'

'I think I'd better know. Look, Ian: the Petersons are forty per cent of the town council and that fool of a mayor, Houghton, will do whatever John Peterson tells him to do.'

'John's all right,' said Ballard.

'Maybe. But Eric is steamed up about the mine and he hates your guts. As for Charlie — I don't know. There seems to be something else sticking in *his* craw. What did you do? Take away his girl or something like that?'

'Of course not.'

'If an old quarrel is getting in the way of co-operation with the council I'd better know about it. Charlie did enough damage last night.'

'It goes back a long way.'

'So tell,' said McGill. 'The snow in the Gap won't go away if what Stevens says is true. We have the time.'

'I never knew my father,' said Ballard. 'I was born in the January of 1939 in England, and I was brought here as a babe in arms. Something else also happened in '39.'

'The war?'

'That's it. My father had split with old Ben and he decided to leave England and farm here. He bought the land and then the war came and he joined the army. He was in the Western Desert with the New Zealand Division and I didn't see him to recognize until he came back in 1943 when I was four years old. My mother wanted him to stay — a lot of the men who came back in '43 refused to return to active service — and there was a bit of a quarrel between him and my mother. In the end it was academic because he was killed in the avalanche here. I saw it happen – and that's all I got to know of my father.'

'Not a lot.'

'No. It hit my mother hard and she turned a bit peculiar. Not that she went round the bend or anything like that. Just peculiar.'

'Neurotic?'

'I suppose you could call it that.'

'What form did it take?'

Ballard stared past the whirling snowflakes eddying in the wind beyond the open garage doors. 'I think you could say she became over-protective as far as I was concerned.'

'Was that what Charlie meant when he said she wouldn't let you out in the snow for fear you'd catch cold?'

'Something like that.'

'He made another crack about you wouldn't go on a slope steeper than a billiard table.'

Ballard sighed. 'That was it. It was made worse because my mother was the schoolteacher here. She tried to run the farm herself but she couldn't, so she sold off most of the land to old Peterson, just keeping the bit the house was on. To earn a living she took the job of schoolmistress. She was qualified for it. But there I was – in the middle. Over-protected and regarded as a teacher's pet into the bargain.'

' "Don't go near the water until you learn how to swim," ' quoted McGill.

'You don't know how true that was, Mike.' There was an edge of bitterness in Ballard's voice. 'Like all kids everywhere we had our swimming hole over by the bluff behind the Petersons' store. All the kids could swim well except me – all I could do was dog-paddle in the shallows and if my mother had known about that she'd have given me hell.'

He took out a packet of cigarettes and offered one to McGill who produced a lighter. Inhaling smoke, he said, 'I was twelve when it happened. It was in the spring and Alec Peterson and I were down by the river. Alec was the fourth of the Peterson brothers. There was a lot of melt water coming down from the mountains – the river was full and flowing fast and the water was bloody cold, but you know what kids are. I dipped in and out of the shallows – more out than in – but Alec went farther out. He was tough for a ten-year-old, and a strong swimmer.'

'Don't tell me,' said McGill. 'He got into trouble.'

'I think he got cramp,' said Ballard. 'Anyway, he let out a yell as he was swept out into the main stream. I knew I wouldn't have a hope in hell of getting him out, but I knew that river. It swirled around the bluff and on the other side there was an eddy where anything floating usually came ashore. It was common knowledge among the kids that it was a good place to collect firewood. So I belted across the bluff, past the Peterson store as fast as I could run.'

He drew on the cigarette in a long inhalation. 'I was right. Alec came inshore and I was able to wade in and grab him. But on his way around the bluff he'd bashed his head on a rock. His skull was cracked and his brains were leaking out and he was stone dead.'

McGill blew out his breath. 'Nasty! But I don't see how you could be blamed for anything.'

'Don't you? Well, I'll tell you. Two other people heard Alec when he yelled but they were too far away to do anything. And they saw me running like hell. Afterwards they said they'd seen me running away and leaving Alec. The two witnesses were Alec's brothers – Charlie and Eric.'

McGill whistled. 'Now I'm beginning to see.'

'They made my life a misery for the next four years. I went through hell, Mike. It wasn't just the Petersons – they set all the other kids against me. Those were the loneliest years I've ever spent. I think I'd have gone nuts if it hadn't been for Turi's son Tawhaki.'

'It must have been tough.'

Ballard nodded. 'Anyway, when I was sixteen years old Ben appeared in the valley as though he'd dropped from the sky. That was when the preliminary exploration was made for the mine. He listened to the local gossip, took one look at me and another at my mother, and then they had a flaming row. He beat her down, of course; very few people could withstand Ben. The upshot of it was that I went back to England with him.'

'And your mother?'

'She stayed on for a few years – until the mine started – then she went back to England, too.'

'And latched on to you again?'

'More or less – but I'd learned the score by then. I'd cut the apron strings.' Ballard flicked his cigarette butt out into the snow.

There was a brief silence before McGill said, 'I still don't get it. Grown men don't behave like Charlie's behaving because of something that happened when they were kids.'

'You don't know Charlie,' said Ballard. 'John's all right and, apart from what he believes about the mine, so is Eric. But for one thing, Charlie and Alec were very close – Alec was Charlie's twin. And for another, while you can't call Charlie retarded, he's never really grown up – he's never matured. Only last night you said he sounded like a schoolboy.'

'Yeah.' McGill stroked the side of his cheek. He had not shaved and it made a scratching sound. 'Anyway, I'm glad you told me. It makes things a lot clearer.'

'But there's nothing much any of us can do about it.' Ballard prodded at the starter again and the engine caught with a steady throb. 'Let's go up to the Gap.'

He drove into town, and as they were passing the Supermarket, McGill pointed to a car just pulling out. 'Looks as though he's leaving, too.'

'That's John Peterson.' Ballard accelerated to get ahead and then waved Peterson down.

As Peterson drew alongside McGill wound down the side window. 'Going far, Mr Peterson?'

John said, 'I've an early business appointment in Christchurch tomorrow, so I thought I'd leave early and get in a couple of rounds of golf there today.' He laughed as he waved at the snow. 'Not much chance of golf here, is there?'

'You may be disappointed,' said McGill. 'Our information is that the Gap is blocked.'

'Blocked? Impossible!'

'We're just going to have a look. Maybe you'd like to tag along behind.'

'All right. But I think you'll find yourself mistaken.'

McGill closed the window. 'As the White Queen said – I can think of six impossible things before breakfast. Carry on, Ian.'

They drove up the road that rose towards the Gap and which paralleled the river. As the headlights' beam swept across the ravine which the river had cut McGill said, 'Jack Stevens could be right. Have you ever seen the river as full as that?'

'I'll tell you when we come to the next bend.' At the next

corner Ballard stopped the car. The beam from the headlights played in calm waters which swirled in smooth eddies. 'I've never seen it so high. The ravine is more than thirty feet deep here.'

'Let's get on.' McGill turned in his seat. 'Peterson is still with us.'

Ballard drove as far as he could until he was stopped by a cliff which suddenly appeared from out the darkness – a cliff which had no right to be there. 'My God!' he said. 'Just look at it!'

McGill opened the door of the car and got out. He walked towards the wall of snow and was silhouetted in the headlights. He prodded at the snow and then looked upwards, shaking his head. With a wave of his hand he gestured for Ballard to join him.

Ballard got out of the car just as John Peterson drew alongside. Together they walked to where McGill was standing and beating his gloved hands together. Peterson looked at the piled snow. 'What caused it?'

McGill said blandly, 'What you are seeing, Mr Peterson, is the end result of an avalanche. Not a big one, but not a small one, either. Nobody will be leaving Hukahoronui for quite some time – at least, not in a car.'

Peterson stared upwards, holding his hand above his head to stop snow driving into his eyes. 'There's a lot of snow there.'

'Avalanches tend to have a lot of snow in them,' said McGill drily. 'If the slope above the town gives way there'll be a hell of a lot more snow than you see here.'

Ballard walked over to one side and looked at the river. 'There'll be floods in the valley if the water keeps backing up.'

'I don't think so,' said McGill. 'The water is deep here and there'll be considerable pressure at the bottom. It will soon drill a hole through this lot – I'd say before the day is over. That will leave a snow bridge over the river, but it won't help any to clear the road.'

He went back to the snow wall and took out a handful of snow and examined it. 'Not too dry but dry enough.'

'What do you mean?' asked Peterson.

'Nothing. Just being technical.' He thrust his hand under Peterson's nose, palm upwards. With the forefinger of his left hand he stirred the snow around. 'Soft, harmless stuff, isn't it?

113

Just like lamb's wool.' His fingers closed on the snow, making a fist. 'There was a man in my line of business called Zdarsky,' he said conversationally. 'He was a pioneer working before the First World War. Zdarsky said, "Snow is not a wolf in sheep's clothing – it is a tiger in lamb's clothing." '

He opened his fist. 'Look at that, Mr Peterson. What is it?' In the palm of his gloved hand lay a lump of hard ice.

'So that was the first avalanche,' said Harrison.

'Yes, sir.'

'And it meant that no vehicles could leave or enter the valley?'

'That is correct.'

'So what happened next?'

McGill said, 'It had been my intention to persuade the town council that the best course of action was to evacuate the population of the valley until the danger had receded. This was now impossible.'

'You say impossible. Surely the obstacle could be climbed.'

'It could be climbed by the fit and active, of course; but what of the elderly, the handicapped and the children? But at least one member of the town council was now convinced that avalanches were something to be reckoned with in Hukaho-ronui. He was now ready to go back to town and throw his full weight into implementing any action I recommended. Mr John Peterson had been the first mayor and his words and actions would count for a lot. We went back to the town to get some action going.'

Harrison nodded and made a note. 'What was the name of the man you quoted to Mr Peterson? How do you spell it?'

'Z-D-A-R-S-K-Y, Matthias Zdarsky. He was an Austrian and an early pioneer in snow studies.' McGill hesitated. 'I have an anecdote which may have some bearing on what I quoted to Mr Peterson.'

'Proceed,' said Harrison. 'As long at it does not take us too far from our purpose here.'

'I don't think it does. A couple of years ago I was in Western Canada as a technical adviser on avalanche protection. There was a cartographic draughtsman who had been given the job of drawing a map of the area showing all the sites of avalanche hazard. It was a long job but he had nearly finished when, one day when he got back from lunch he found that some joker had written in medieval lettering on each avalanche site

114

the words "Here be Tygers," just as on an old map.'

He smiled slightly. 'The draughtsman didn't think much of it as a joke, but the boss of his department took the map, had it framed, and hung it on the wall of his office as a reminder to everyone about avalanche hazard. You see, everyone in the game knows about Matthias Zdarsky and what happened to him.'

'An interesting anecdote,' said Harrison. 'And perfectly relevant. At the risk of wasting more time I would like to know what did happen to Zdarsky.'

'He was in the Austrian army during the First World War. At that time both sides – Austrians and Italians – were using avalanches as weapons in the Dolomites and the Tyrol. It's said that eighty thousand men died in avalanches during the war. In 1916 Zdarsky was going to the rescue of twenty-five Austrian soldiers who had been caught in an avalanche when he himself was caught in one. He was lucky enough to be rescued alive but that's about all you can say. He had eighty broken bones and dislocations, and it was eleven years before he could ski again.'

The hall was hushed. Presently Harrison said, 'Thank you, Dr McGill.' He looked up at the clock. 'I think we will now adjourn for the weekend. This hearing will recommence at ten in the morning on Monday.' He tapped lightly with the gavel 'The hearing is now adjourned.'

CHAPTER SIXTEEN

Next morning Ballard went to the hospital to visit Cameron. He tried to do this as often as possible to keep the old man company and cheer him up. It was a fact that Cameron now *was* an old man; his experience in the avalanche had almost killed both spirit and body. McGill said, 'I'll go to see him tomorrow. I have things to do at Deep Freeze Headquarters.'

'I'll be out that way this afternoon,' said Ballard. 'I'm picking up Stenning at Harewood. Want a lift back?'

'Thanks,' said McGill. 'Ask for me in the office.'

Ballard found Cameron out of bed but in a wheelchair with a blanket tucked around him in spite of the fact that it was a hot day. He was talking to Liz Peterson when Ballard walked into the room. 'Hi!' said Liz. 'I've just been telling Joe how Mike tried to freeze our blood when he gave evidence yesterday.'

'Yes, I think he made Harrison shiver a bit.' Privately he thought it tactless to describe the sufferings of an avalanche victim such as Zdarsky to one who had himself been caught in an avalanche, and he wondered how much Liz had said. 'How are you feeling, Joe?'

'A bit better this morning. I could have stayed yesterday afternoon in spite of my damn fool doctor.'

'You do as he says,' Ballard advised. 'What do you think, Liz?'

'I think Joe should do as he likes. Doctor doesn't always know best.'

Cameron laughed. 'Oh, it's good to have a pretty girl here – especially when she's on my side. But you really shouldn't be here, Liz.' He nodded towards the window. 'You should be out there, enjoying the sunshine. On a tennis court, maybe.'

'I've got plenty of time for tennis, Joe,' she said. 'The rest of my life. Are they looking after you well here?'

'Okay, I guess – but it's just like any other hospital. The food is terrible – they have too many dieticians and too few cooks.'

'We'll have something sent in,' said Ballard. 'Won't we Liz?'

She smiled. 'I'm not bad at home cooking.'

They stayed until Cameron sent them off, saying that young people must have something better to do than to sit around in hospitals. Outside, in the sunshine, Ballard said, 'Doing anything in particular, Liz?'

'Not really.'

'What about having lunch with me?'

She hesitated fractionally, but said, 'I'd like that.'

'We'll go in my car. I'll bring you back on my way to the airport this afternoon. I'm meeting someone.'

'It'll cost you lunch for two. I'll have to bring Victor. I can't leave him in my car.'

'Sure.'

She laughed. 'Love me – love my dog.'

As Ballard started the engine of his car, he said, 'Did you mean what you said yesterday – about leaving New Zealand?'

'I've been thinking about it.'

'Where would you go?'

'England, I suppose – at first anyway. Then perhaps

America. You've travelled around a bit, haven't you? I've always wanted to travel – to see things.'

He drove out of the hospital grounds. 'Yes, I've been places, but they've always been working trips. I'll tell you one thing – I certainly never expected to come back to New Zealand.'

'Then why did you?'

Ballard sighed. 'My grandfather wanted me to. He was a forceful old bird.'

'He *was*! I didn't know he was dead.'

'He died a few days ago.'

'Oh, Ian! I am sorry.'

'So am I, in a way. We didn't always see eye to eye, but I'll miss him. Now that he's gone I won't be staying with the Ballard group. In fact, I've just about made that impossible.'

'It's like Mike says – neither of us get on with our relatives.' Liz laughed. 'I had a row with Charlie last night. Someone saw us in the restaurant yesterday and split to Charlie.'

'Don't get into trouble because of me, Liz.'

'I'm tired of Charlie's tantrums. I'm a grown woman and I'll meet whoever I like. I told him so last night.' She rubbed the side of her face reflectively.

Ballard glanced sideways and caught the action. 'He *hit* you?'

'Not for the first time, but it's going to be the last.' She saw the expression on Ballard's face. 'Not to worry, Ian. I can defend myself. I'm reckoned to be a pretty aggressive tennis player and those smash services develop the muscles.'

'So you hit him back. I doubt if that would make much of an impression on Charlie.'

She grinned impishly. 'I happened to be holding a plateful of spaghetti at the time.' When Ballard burst out laughing she added, 'Eric socked him, too. We're quite a happy family, we Petersons.'

He turned the car into the hotel car park. As they walked into the foyer he said, 'The grub's not bad here; they serve quite a good lunch. But what about a drink first?'

'Something long and cold,' she agreed.

'We'll have it by the pool,' he said. 'This way.' Suddenly he stiffened and halted in his stride.

'What's the matter?'

'The forces are rallying. It's Cousin Francis. Now where the devil did he spring from?'

A youngish man in a business suit stepped in front of them.

'Morning, Ian,' he said, abruptly and unsmilingly.

'Good morning, Frank,' said Ballard. 'Miss Peterson, this is my cousin, Frank Ballard.'

Frank Ballard gave her a curt nod. 'I want to talk to you, Ian.'

'Sure. We're just going to have drinks by the pool. Join us.'

Frank shook his head. 'In private.'

'All right. After lunch, then.'

'No, I haven't the time. I'm catching a plane back to Sydney almost immediately. It'll have to be now.'

'Don't mind me,' said Liz. 'I'll wait for you by the pool. Come on, Victor.' She walked away without waiting for an answer.

Frank said, 'What about your room?'

'All right.' Ballard led the way. They walked in silence until they reached the room. As he closed the door Ballard said, 'What brings you from Australia, Frank?'

Frank swung around. 'You bloody well know what brings me. Why the hell did you put old Crowell through the hoops the way you did yesterday? He was on the phone to me, crying on my shoulder long distance.'

Ian smiled. 'Just trying to elicit a bit of truth.'

There was no answering smile from Frank. 'Now look here, Ian. You're getting the company into a right mess. A fine bloody managing director you are.'

'Aren't you forgetting that Crowell suspended me from duty? Or is what you've just said an offer of the job back?'

'You flaming idiot! The suspension was only until the inquiry was over. If you'd have used your brains and kept quiet everything would have been all right, and you'd be back in the saddle next week. As it is, I'm not so sure. You've been throwing so much mud at the company that I'm not sure you're fit for the position.'

Ian sat on the bed. 'If I'd kept quiet I'd be a dead duck, and you know it. Between the company and the Petersons I wouldn't stand a chance. Did you really think I'd stand still and let you make a patsy out of me?'

'This is a *Ballard* company,' said Frank furiously. 'We take care of our own. Have you no family feeling?'

'You'd take care of me like a fox takes care of a rabbit,' snapped Ian.

'If that's what you think, I'm sorry.' Frank's finger shot out. 'When the inquiry starts again on Monday you'd better keep quiet. No more appeals to the grandstand like those you've been making. If you promise to do that then maybe there'll still be a job for you in the Group. I doubt if I'll be able to swing the managing directorship of Hukahoronui – my old man's hopping mad – but I still think I can guarantee some kind of job.'

'Thanks,' said Ian ironically. 'But I'm underwhelmed by your generosity. 'You know what I think of the Group – I've never made a secret of it.'

'For Christ's sake!' burst out Frank. 'You know how big we are. We just have to pass the word around and you'll never get a job in mining again. Look, you don't even have to *do* anything – just stop asking damn fool questions in public.'

Ian stood up. 'Don't push me, Frank,' he warned.

'I haven't even started yet. For God's sake, be reasonable, Ian. Do you know how much the share price of the company has dropped since yesterday? All this adverse publicity is having an effect even in London. We're dropping money fast.'

'I bleed for you.'

'You know we're going to float a new issue of Hukahoronui shares. What chance do you think we'll have if you continue to hold up the chairman of the board as a bloody fool?'

'The foolishness of Crowell is none of my doing – he's a self-made idiot. That's why you have him there – because he'll jump when he's told. You ought to be getting rid of Crowell, not me.'

'You're impossible,' said Frank disgustedly. 'We're *not* getting rid of you.'

'No,' agreed Ian. 'I'm leaving under my own power, and in my own way. I don't take easily to blackmail, Frank, and the way you're going you're likely to cook your own goose.'

Frank looked up and said sharply, 'What do you mean?'

'Have you considered the composition of the Commission of Inquiry? There's Harrison, the chairman, and his two assessors, both experts in their fields. Rolandson knows about snow, and French is from the Department of Mines. He hasn't said much yet.'

'So?'

'So any more pressure from you and I'll start asking questions about conditions in that mine, and by the time I'm through French will write a report that'll curl your hair – a report that the shareholders won't like at all. Then you'll see something really happen to the share price.'

'You're being really hard-nosed about this, aren't you? Why, Ian?'

'Do you have to ask after what you've been doing? I don't like being manipulated, Frank. I don't like being pushed around. I'm no Crowell. And another thing: the day before I was fired – and let's give it the right name, Frank; none of this bull about suspension – I saw the result of the latest assay. Rich pickings, Frank, my boy; *very* rich pickings. But can you tell me why those results haven't been given to the shareholders?'

'That's none of you bloody business.'

'It might be if I buy some shares. Not that I will, of course. That mine is going to make someone a fortune, but the way you'll set it up I don't think the ordinary shareholders will see much of it.'

'Nobody will make anything if you get on your hind legs and start asking damn fool questions about avalanche defences,' said Frank sourly. 'Good God, do you know how much it will cost us if this bloody Commission goes the wrong way?'

Ian stared at him. 'What do you mean – the wrong way? Were you thinking of *not* putting in avalanche defences?'

'Hell, there's only an avalanche every thirty years or so. By the time the next one comes the mine will be worked out.'

Ian took a deep breath. 'You damned fool! That was when the trees were still on the west slope. Now they're gone there's likely to be a fall in any period of heavy snow.'

'All right.' Frank flapped his hand impatiently. 'We'll reafforest the slope. That'll cost less than the snow rakes your friend McGill wants to have.'

'Frank, do you know how long it takes for a tree to grow? I thought you lot were bad enough but now I know the depth of your greed.' Ballard's voice was hard. 'And I suggest we bring this conversation to a sudden halt.' He crossed to the door and threw it open.

Frank hesitated. 'Think again, Ian.'

Ian jerked his head. 'Out!'

Frank walked forward. 'You'll regret it.'

'How's Uncle Steve?'

'He's not going to like the answer I take back to Sydney.'

'He should have come himself and not sent a half-wit to do his dirty work. He's too intelligent to think threats would have any affect – he'd have tried a bribe, if I know him. Tell him from me that that wouldn't have worked, either. Maybe you'll be able to keep a whole skin that way.'

Frank paused outside the door, and turned. 'You're finished, Ian. I hope you know that.'

Ian closed the door in his face.

As he drove Liz back to the hospital to pick up her car he said, 'Sorry about the gloomy lunch, Liz. I have a few things on my mind.'

'It was a bit glum,' she agreed. 'What's the matter? Trouble with the family? You were all right untill you saw your cousin.'

He did not answer immediately but pulled the car off the road and parked by the kerb. He turned to face her, and said, 'We both seem to have trouble that way. When were you thinking of going to England, Liz?'

'I haven't thought that far ahead.'

'I'll be going as soon as the inquiry is over. Why don't you come with me?'

'My God!' she said. 'Charlie would have kittens. Is this by way of being a proposal, Ian?' She smiled. 'Or do I come as your mistress?'

'That's up to you. You can take it either way.'

Liz laughed. 'Shakespeare didn't write this script. I know we're like the Montagues and Capulets, but Romeo never made an offer like that.' She put her hand on his. 'I like you, Ian, but I'm not sure I love you.'

'That's the problem,' he said. 'We haven't known each other long enough. Just two or three days at Huka, rudely interrupted by a disaster, and a week here. Love doesn't flourish under those conditions, especially when overlooked by brother Charlie.'

'Don't you believe in love at first sight?'

'I do,' said Ballard. 'Evidently you don't. It happened to me at the dance on the night everything started. Look, Liz: when I get on that plane I won't be coming back to New Zealand. I'd hate it like hell if I never saw you again. Maybe you don't love me, but it would be nice if you gave it a fighting chance.'

'Propinquity!' she said. 'A lovely word. Do you think it works?'

'What have you got to lose?'

She looked pensively through the windscreen, staring at nothing. Presently she said, 'If I do go to England with you –

and I'm not saying right now that I will – but if I do there'll be no strings. I'm my own woman, Ian; a very private person. That's something Charlie can never understand. So if I come it will be my choice, and if after a while I leave you, it will be my choice again. Do you understand?'

He nodded. 'I understand.'

'And let me tell you something else, just to clear up something which may have been on your mind. Eric is against the Ballards on principle – it's not just you. But with Charlie it definitely is you. Now, I was only two when Alec died; I never knew him – not to remember. And you were twelve then, and now you're thirty-five. A person at twelve and a person at thirty-five are two different people, not to be confused with each other as Charlie does. I don't know the rights and wrongs of Alec's death – and I don't care. I'll be going to England with a man, not a boy.'

'Thanks,' said Ballard. 'Thanks, Liz.'

'Not that I've said I'm going with you yet,' she warned. 'I'll have to think about it. As to the question you asked – what have I got to lose?' She patted his knee. 'The answer, my dear Ian, is my virginity!'

CHAPTER SEVENTEEN

Ballard dropped Liz at the hospital and went on to Deep Freeze Headquarters. He did not find McGill at the office but finally ran him down at the Officers' Club where he was talking shop. Ballard said, 'I thought I'd pick you up first. Old Stenning will have travelled a long way and he'll be tired, so I thought I wouldn't keep him waiting around.'

'Sure,' said McGill. 'I'll come right along. When is he due in?'

'In fifteen minutes, if the plane's on time.'

They drove to Harewood Airport, two minutes away, and stood chatting on the concourse while they waited. McGill said, 'I've never met a millionaire's lawyer. Will you recognize Stenning when you see him?'

Ballard nodded. 'He's a tall, thin chap with white hair. Looks a bit like Bertrand Russell.'

The aircraft was on time and, as the passengers streamed

through the terminal, Ballard said, 'There he is,' and McGill saw a tall, old man with the face of an ascetic. Ballard stepped forward. 'Good afternoon, Mr Stenning.' They shook hands. 'This is Mike McGill, a friend. He's come to carry the suitcases. I don't think they'll be long in coming.'

Stenning smiled. 'Are you the Dr McGill who has been giving evidence at the Inquiry?'

'Yes, sir.'

'If you're carrying suitcases you've come down in the world.'

'The luggage is coming now,' said Ballard. Stenning pointed out his cases, and Ballard said, 'Let's get this stuff out to the car, Mike.' As they left the terminal he said to Stenning, 'I've booked you a room at the hotel where I'm staying. It's quite comfortable.'

'Just point me towards a bed,' said Stenning. 'I find it difficult to sleep on aircraft. How is the Inquiry going?'

'I've kept the newspapers for you. It's getting good coverage in Christchurch.'

Stenning grunted. 'Good! I've been in aircraft for two days so I've fallen behind with the news. I'm looking forward to discussing the disaster with you, Dr McGill.'

'Any time I'm not in court, Mr Stenning.'

At the hotel McGill tactfully made himself scarce while Ballard showed Stenning his room. Stenning said, 'I'm not as resilient as I used to be, Ian. I'm going to bed. Your grandfather would have said a thing or two about that, were he here. At my age he was an assiduous globe-trotter.' He shook his head. 'I'm sorry he's gone.'

'Yes,' said Ballard. 'So am I.'

Stenning regarded him curiously. 'Are you?' he asked in a sceptical tone. 'If you'd have said the other thing I wouldn't have been surprised – or shocked. Your grandfather was a hard man to get on with. In my opinion he didn't treat you very well.'

Ballard shrugged. 'I'll miss him all the same.'

'So will I, Ian. So will I. Now, if you'll excuse a tired old man . . .'

'Have you eaten? I can get something sent in.'

'No – I just want my bed.'

Ballard indicated a cupboard. 'I laid in some drinks. There's whisky, gin and brandy – with the trimmings.'

'A kindly thought. A whisky before bed will go down very well. I'll see you tomorrow. Ian.'

Ballard left him and found McGill having a beer by the pool. McGill raised an eyebrow. 'Well?'

'Nothing,' said Ballard. 'He didn't say a damned thing.'

McGill frowned. 'I'll tell you something,' he said. 'He sure as hell didn't fly thirteen thousand miles to discuss a disaster with Mike McGill.'

Stenning was absent from breakfast next morning. McGill buttered a slice of toast. 'He doesn't seem to be in much of a hurry. Just like a lawyer; they work to a different sort of time from the rest of us.'

'I had a visit from one of my relatives yesterday,' said Ballard. 'My cousin Frank.' He told McGill what had happened.

McGill whistled. 'You Ballards play rough. Can he do what he threatened to do? Have you blackballed in the industry?'

'I doubt it. He might like to think he can. He could certainly make life bloody difficult.'

'How come Frank was in Sydney? Very convenient, wasn't it?'

'The Ballard Group has interests in many countries, including Australia. It's not unusual to find a member of the family popping up almost anywhere. I think my Uncle Steve, Frank's father, is also in Sydney. That's what Frank implied.'

McGill helped himself to marmalade. 'Goddamn convenient, all the same. Crowell knew they were in Australia because he blew the whistle on you. Frank came running fast enough.'

They talked desultorily until McGill had finished his coffee. 'I'm going to the hospital to see Joe. If Stenning has anything important to say he won't want me around.' He went away leaving Ballard to finish his breakfast alone.

Ballard read the Sunday papers by the pool, concentrating first on the account of the Inquiry. That did not take long, and he went on to the rest of the news which did not take long, either. He felt restless and thought of going to see Liz, but he did not want to leave the hotel without having seen Stenning. He went to his room and put on swimming trunks and worked out his frustration in several lengths of the pool.

It was eleven-thirty before Stenning appeared, carrying several newspaper clippings. 'Good morning, Ian,' he said briskly.

'Did you sleep well?'

'Like a babe. Only to be expected, of course. I had breakfast in my room. Where's Dr McGill?'

'He's gone to see Joe Cameron, the mine engineer. He's still in hospital.'

The clippings fluttered in Stenning's hand. 'So I gathered.' He looked around. 'We could do worse than have a chat here. Very nice place.'

Ballard unfolded another garden chair. 'The town is all right, too. Christchurch prides itself on being more English than England.'

Stenning sat down. 'I'm looking forward to seeing it.' He regarded the clippings, then folded them and put them into his pocket. 'You're having quite a time at this Inquiry. I don't think your family is going to like the things you've been saying.'

'I know they don't like it,' said Ballard. 'I had a visit from Frank yesterday. He wants me to shut up.'

'What did you do?' asked Stenning interestedly.

'I showed him the door.'

Stenning did not comment but he looked pleased in an indefinable way which Ballard could not place. 'You know, I was more than your grandfather's lawyer. I was also his friend.'

'I know he placed a lot of trust in you.'

'Trust,' said Stenning, and smiled. 'Trust – that's what I want to talk about. What do you know about the way your grandfather organized his affairs – I mean his financial affairs?'

'Practically nothing,' said Ballard. 'I knew that he put all, or most, of his money into some kind of trust a few years ago. He made it quite clear that I was not going to inherit, so I didn't take much interest. It was nothing to do with me.'

Stenning nodded. 'Yes, it was a little over seven years ago. Do you know anything about estate duties in the United Kingdom?'

'Death duties? Nothing much.'

'Then I shall enlighten you. A man may give his money away – to his family usually – to a charitable foundation, as Ben did. However, if he dies within seven years of the transaction having taken place then his gift is assessed for estate duty just as if he hadn't made it at all. If he dies after seven years have elapsed then the gift escapes the tax.'

'I had heard about that,' Ballard smiled. 'I didn't worry too much about it, myself. I don't have much to leave, and I've no one to leave it to.'

Stenning shook his head. 'Every man must make provision

for the unknown future,' he said in a lawyerly way. 'Ben died after the seven-year period.'

'Therefore the foundation doesn't have to pay the tax.'

'Precisely. But it was a near-run thing. For one thing, the government changed the law and Ben squeezed in just under the deadline. For another he died just two weeks after the seven years were up. In fact, he nearly didn't make it at all. Do you remember him coming to see you just before you came to New Zealand?'

'Yes. It was when he offered me the job in Hukahoronui.'

'The effort nearly killed him,' said Stenning. 'The next day he took to his bed and never left it again.'

'He sent me his stick,' said Ballard. 'I had a bad leg at the time. He said he wouldn't need the stick again.'

'He didn't.' Stenning looked at the sky contemplatively. 'It was very important to Ben that he should see you at that time. The breaking of your leg was a minor disaster – you couldn't go to see him, so the mountain had to go to Mahomet. It was so important to him that he put at risk a very large sum of money – and more beside.'

Ballard frowned. 'I don't see how it could have been important. All he did was to twist my arm into taking the job at Hukahoronui – and look how that's turned out.' His voice was bitter.

'An avalanche wasn't part of Ben's plans – but it came in useful.' Stenning laughed as he saw the bafflement on Ballard's face. 'You think I'm talking in riddles? Never mind; all will be made clear. Let us look at the charitable foundation. Ben gave it all his personal fortune except what he needed to live on until his death, which wasn't much. Ben was not a man to flaunt prestige symbols; he had no Rolls Royce, for example. His needs were few and his life austere. But the foundation got a lot of money.'

'I could see how it might.'

'It does good work. The money or, rather, the interest on the money, supports several laboratories working mostly in the fields of mining safety and health. Very good and necessary work, indeed.'

'My God!' said Ballard in astonishment. 'Do the trustees know how the Ballard Group works? Every safety regulation is normally bent, or broken if they think they can get away with it. That's like giving with one hand and taking with the other.'

Stenning nodded. 'That perturbed Ben, but there was nothing he could do about it at the time for reasons you shall see. Now let us take a look at the trustees. There are five.' He ticked them off on his fingers. 'There's your uncle Edward, your cousin Frank, Lord Brockhurst, Sir William Bendell and myself. I am the Chairman of the Board of Trustees of the Ballard Foundation.'

'I'm surprised that two of the family are trustees. From what Ben said the last time I saw him he had no great regard for them.'

'Ben made them trustees for tactical reasons. You'll see what I mean when I come to the nub. You're right, of course, in your assessment of Ben's attitude to the family. He had four sons, one of whom died here in New Zealand, and the other three turned out in a way he couldn't stomach. He had no great regard for any of his grandchildren, either, except one.' Stenning jabbed forward a thin forefinger. 'You.'

'He had funny ways of showing it,' said Ballard wryly.

'He'd seen how his sons had turned out and he knew that whatever else he was good at he was not a good father. So he saw to your education and left you strictly alone. He watched you, of course, and he liked what he saw. Now consider – what could Ben do a few years ago when he contemplated what was likely to happen to his personal fortune? He wouldn't give it to his family whom he didn't like, would he?'

'Not on the face of it.'

'No,' said Stenning. 'Anyway, as Ben saw it they already had enough. In all honesty, could he give it to you? How old were you then?'

'Seven years ago? Twenty-eight.'

Stenning leaned back. 'I rather think that when Ben and I first talked about setting this thing up you were twenty-six. Just a fledgling, Ian. Ben couldn't see himself putting so much money and power – and money is power – into the hands of one so young. Besides, he wasn't too sure of you. He thought you were immature for your years. He also thought your mother had something to do with that.'

'I know. He was scathing about her at our last meeting.'

'So he set up the Ballard Foundation. And he had to do two things: he had to make sure that he retained essential control – and he had to live for seven years. He did both. And he watched you like a hawk because he wanted to see how you turned out.'

127

Ballard grimaced. 'Did I come up to expectations?'

'He never found out,' said Stenning. 'He died before the Hukahoronui experiment was completed.'

Ballard stared at him. 'Experiment! What experiment?'

'You were being tested,' said Stenning. 'And this is how it went. You were now thirty-five; you were more than competent at any job you'd been given, and you knew how to handle men. But Ben had a feeling that you have a soft centre and he discovered a way to find out if this was indeed so.' He paused. 'I gather that you and the Peterson family have never got on too well together.'

'An understatement,' said Ballard.

Stenning's face was firm. 'Ben told me that the Petersons had walked all over you when you were a boy. He sent you to Hukahoronui to see if the same thing would happen.'

'Well, I'll be damned!' Ballard was suddenly angry. 'I knew he had a power complex, but who the hell did he think he was? God? And what the devil was it all for?'

'You can't be as naïve as that,' said Stenning. 'Look at the composition of the Board of Trustees.'

'All right; I'm looking. Two Ballards, yourself and two others. What about it?'

'This about it. Old Brockhurst, Billy Bendell and I are all old friends of Ben. We had to have two of the family on the board so they wouldn't smell a rat. If they had suspected what Ben was up to they'd have found a way to shove their oar in and wreck Ben's plan. Any half-way criminal lawyer could have found a way of torpedoing the Foundation before Ben died. But for seven years the three of us have been playing the Ballards on a length of line so the boat wouldn't be rocked. We've been playing along with the two Ballards on the board, only forcing our hand in things which didn't matter too much to them. They think it's going to continue in this way – but it's not.'

'I don't see what this has got to do with me.'

Stenning said evenly, 'Ben wanted you on the Board of Trustees.'

Ballard gaped at him. 'So?'

'So it's arranged like this. The board is self-perpetuating. If a member retires there is a vote to elect his replacement and – this is important – the retiring member has a vote. Brockhurst is nearly eighty and has only held on to please Ben. When he retires you'll have his vote, you'll have Billy Bendell's vote, and you'll have my vote – and that's a majority and there's nothing the Ballards can do about it.'

Ballard was silent for a long time. Presently he said, 'This is all very well, but I'm not an administrator, at least, not of the trustee kind. I suppose there'd be an honorarium, but I have a living to earn. You're offering me a job for a retired business man. I don't want to run a charitable fund, no matter how big.'

Stenning shook his head sadly. 'You still don't get the point. Ben set up the foundation for one reason and one reason only – to prevent his fortune from being dissipated and to keep the Ballard Group intact but out of the hands of his sons.' He took an envelope from his pocket. 'I have here the share quotations of the companies in the Ballard Group as at the middle of last week.'

He extracted a sheet of paper from the envelope. 'It's astonishing what can be put on to a small sheet of paper like this.' He bent his head. 'The total value of the shares is two hundred and thirty-two million pounds. The holdings of the Ballard family – that is your uncles and all your cousins – is about fourteen million pounds. The holding of the Ballard Foundation is forty-one million pounds, and the Foundation is by far the largest shareholder.'

He slipped the paper back into the envelope. 'Ian, whoever can swing most votes on the Board of Trustees controls the Ballard Foundation, and whoever controls the Foundation controls the Ballard Group of companies. For seven years we've been waiting for you to come into your inheritance.'

Ballard felt as though the wind had been knocked from him. He stared blindly into the shimmering pool and knew that the dazzle in his eyes did not come only from the sunlight reflected from water. That wonderful, egotistical, crazy old man! He rubbed his eyes and was aware of wetness. Stenning had been saying something. 'What was that?'

'I said there's a snag,' said Stenning.

'I suppose it's inevitable.'

'Yes.' A fugitive smile chased across Stenning's face. 'Ben knew he was dying. Two days before he died he extracted a promise from me to come out here and see the results of the Hukahoronui experiment – to see if the Petersons were still walking over you. As Ben's friend – and his lawyer – I feel bound to honour his last wish and to do what he would want to do himself were he alive.'

'So it's not settled.'

'I've been reading the newspaper accounts of the Inquiry with great interest. You've been putting up a good fight, Ian, but it seems to me that the Petersons are still walking over you. Ben considered that the man who cannot defend himself is not the man to control the Ballard Group – and I must say I tend to agree with him. The exercise of so much power demands steel in a man.'

'That's the second shock you've handed me today,' said Ballard softly.

'Not that I'm going on newspaper reports,' said Stenning. I'm too much of a lawyer to believe all I read. You'll get a fair judgment, Ian; but out of respect for Ben it must be an honest one.'

'And you are my judge. My sole judge?'

Stenning inclined his head. Ben relied on me a lot, but the last task he set me is the hardest burden I have had to bear. Still, I can't run away from it.'

'No,' said Ballard pensively. 'I don't suppose you can.' He thought of his own eagerness to escape from Hukahoronui when he was a boy of sixteen. The urge to run away from the oppressions of the Petersons had been overwhelming. 'I'd like to go away and think about this for a while.'

'Very understandable,' said Stenning. 'Will I see you at lunch?'

'I don't know.' Ballard stood up and picked up his towel. 'Mike McGill will be around. You can ask him about the avalanche.'

He walked across the lawn to his room.

CHAPTER EIGHTEEN

When, at breakfast the following morning, Stenning announced his intention of attending the Inquiry, Ballard said, 'That might not be easy. There's a great deal of interest and there are queues for the public seats. You can sit with me, if you like.'

'I doubt if that would be advisable,' said Stenning. 'The news of that would get back to your uncles very quickly. But it's all right, Ian. I telephoned Dr Harrison on Saturday before I went to sleep and he has found me a place.' He smiled. 'A courtesy to a visiting lawyer.'

Sharp! thought Ballard. *Very sharp!* He said, 'If you are there at all the news might get back to the family.'

Stenning cut a slice of grilled bacon in two. 'I doubt it. I'm not known in New Zealand and you tell me none of the family is here.'

At ten minutes to ten Ballard was in his seat and running through his notes. He saw Stenning come in preceded by an usher who showed him to a seat in the distinguished visitors' section. Stenning sat down and viewed the hall with interest, and his eyes passed Ballard without a flicker. He produced a notebook and a pen from his briefcase and laid them on the table before him.

As Ballard returned to his notes a shadow fell athwart the table and he looked up to see Rickman. 'May I have a word with you, Mr Ballard?'

Ballard nodded towards the rostrum. 'It will have to be a quick word. We'll be starting soon.'

'This won't take long.' Rickman leaned on the edge of the table and bent down. 'Mr Crowell was most annoyed on Friday at your treatment of him on the witness stand, but he's had the weekend to think it over and now he's in a more considerate frame of mind.'

'I'm glad to hear it,' said Ballard, keeping his face straight.

'You may not know it but Mr Crowell is about to be . . . er

131

. . . translated to a higher station. He is taking the chairmanship of New Zealand Mineral Holdings, the parent company of the Hukahoronui Mining Company. It's been in the wind for quite some time.'

'That will be nice for him.'

'He feels that to do the double job – chairmanship of both companies – would be too much for him. Consequently the chairmanship of the mining company will fall vacant.'

'Interesting,' said Ballard neutrally. He said no more. He wanted Rickman to do the running.

'You know that assays at the mine before the avalanche showed a highly enhanced gold enrichment, and the board decided to float a share issue to capitalize extensive development work. Whoever is appointed chairman will be in a most favourable position. A considerable number of stock options will go with the job – that is, an option to buy so many shares at par.'

'I know what an option is.'

Rickman spread his hands. 'Well, then. When the news of the increased gold values is released the share price will inevitably go up. Anyone with options will be in a position to make a lot of money.'

'Isn't that illegal? Inside deals are frowned on.'

'I assure you that the way it will be done will be perfectly legal,' said Rickman smoothly.

'I'll take your word for that, Mr Rickman. You're the lawyer and I'm not. But I don't see what this has to do with me.'

'As chairman of the parent company, Mr Crowell will have a great deal to say in the appointment of the chairman of the mining company. He feels that you have qualities that make you suitable for the position should you wish to be considered as a candidate.'

'For what consideration?' Ballard asked bluntly.

'Come, now, Mr Ballard. We're both men of the world and we both know what we're talking about.'

'I detect the hand of Uncle Steve,' said Ballard. 'He jerks a string in Sydney and Crowell jumps.' He pointed to the empty witness chair. 'Crowell sat there on Friday and I roasted him to a turn. Now he offers me the chairmanship of the company from which he's just fired me as managing director. What sort of a man does that make Crowell, Mr Rickman?' He shook his head. 'I don't think you can count me in your list of candidates.'

Rickman frowned. 'It's a position few young men would turn down – especially in view of the evidence which may be forthcoming presently at this Inquiry – evidence particularly damaging to yourself. The effect of that evidence *could* be minimized.' He paused. 'Or vice versa.'

'I wouldn't want to be a man of your world, Mr Rickman, or that of Crowell. I'm a plain-speaking man and I'll tell you what I think. First you attempt to bribe me, and now you threaten me. I told Frank Ballard that neither would work. Now I'm telling you the same. Get lost, Mr Rickman.'

Rickman's face darkened. 'If I had a witness to that little speech I'd have you in court for slander.'

'You're making damned sure you don't have a witness,' retorted Ballard. 'Why have you been whispering?'

Rickman made an ejaculation of disgust, turned his back and walked to his seat where he held a rapid conversation with Crowell. Ballard looked at them for a moment and then turned his attention to the seats reserved for witnesses. Mike McGill raised his eyebrows in silent interrogation, and Ballard winked at him.

He had told Mike in confidence why Stenning had flown to New Zealand in such a hurry, and McGill had choked over his beer. 'Two hundred and thirty-two million pounds . . . !' He set down his glass and gazed into space, his lips moving silently. 'That's over six hundred million bucks – even by American standards that's not puny.'

'It's not mine,' said Ballard drily. 'It belongs to the shareholders.'

'That may be, but you'll control it. You'll be able to steer it wherever you like. That's a hell of a lot of power.'

'I'm not a trustee yet. It's Stenning's decision.'

'No, it isn't,' said McGill sharply. 'It's your decision. All you have to do is to steamroller the Petersons. Stenning told you as much. My God, but that grandfather of yours must have been a hellion in his time. He could think up the nicest tricks.'

'Steamroller the Petersons,' repeated Ballard. 'Liz might not think a hell of a lot of that.'

'The world well lost for a woman – is that what you think?' McGill snorted. 'Well, Stenning has made the issue quite clear.

If he'd spelled it out in words of one syllable and had them tattooed on your chest he couldn't have been clearer. You've got to nail the Petersons' hides to the barn door, and you have to do it publicly at the Inquiry. That's your last chance.'

Ballard was acid. 'And just how am I going to do that?'

McGill shrugged. 'I don't know. Up to the time of the first avalanche they were pussyfooting around with local politics and they might come in for a bit of censure on that score. But after that they didn't put a foot wrong. They did all the right things at the right time and they'll get the credit for it. Charlie even volunteered to go on the slope with me after the avalanche when I thought there might be a second fall. That took guts. There's no faulting the Petersons from here on in.'

'So there's no steamroller.'

McGill laughed — a humourless bark. 'Oh, sure there is. There are going to be questions asked about your decision about the mine. Eric made the right suggestion and you turned it down. Over fifty people died, Ian. There's a steamroller, all right; but the Petersons are driving it, and they're going to trundle it right over you.'

CHAPTER NINETEEN

Eric Peterson was giving evidence.

'It must have been somewhere between half past six and seven o'clock on the Sunday morning when my brother, John, came and woke me. With him were Mr Ballard and Dr McGill. They said there'd been an avalanche. At first I didn't believe them. I'd heard nothing, and according to the scare story the town would be blotted out if they were right. But John said the Gap was blocked and that no one could get in or out.'

He shrugged. 'I still didn't really believe it, but John was very convincing. Then he said that if the Gap could be blocked like that then perhaps Dr McGill was right about the danger to the town from the west slope. My brother got busy on the telephone and called an emergency council meeting. It was getting on towards eight o'clock by then and beginning to get light. We held the meeting in the Supermarket.'

There was no cold glare from the overhead fluorescent tubes that Sunday morning. Two oil lamps gave a warmer glow which paled as the sky grew brighter. There was no sunlight yet; the sun had to rise high to clear the eastern slope of the valley and to burn off the mist which hung heavily.

Eric Peterson stoked up the old-fashioned pot-bellied stove with billets of wood, and commented, 'I'm glad we didn't get rid of this relic.' He jerked his thumb towards the back of the store. 'Back there I have two thousand gallons of fuel oil that's good for damn all. The central heating system needs two electric motors to drive it.'

'What's keeping Matt?' asked Mrs Samson fretfully.

'He'll be along,' said John Peterson. 'You know Matt – slow but reliable.'

Eric put the lid back on to the stove. Then there are the fridges and the cold room, all with no power. A good thing this didn't happen in summer.'

'For Christ's sake!' said John irritably. 'Use your bloody brains for once. How in hell could it happen in summer?'

Eric paused in surprise. 'I was forgetting. What I meant was . . .'

'To the devil with what you meant. If you can't talk sense, shut up!'

Tempers were becoming uncertain. McGill said calmly, 'I think we ought to begin without waiting for Mr Houghton. We can fill him in later.'

'No need,' said Phil Warrick. 'He's here now.'

Houghton walked up the aisle towards the group around the stove. 'I know we agreed to meet this morning, but this is beyond a joke. Do you know the time?'

John Peterson raised his hand. 'There's been an avalanche in the Gap, Matt. It's blocked completely. There's so much snow in there you can't see the top.'

'You mean we can't get out?'

'Not in cars,' said McGill.

Houghton looked about uncertainly, and John Peterson said, 'Sit down, Matt. When there's been one avalanche there can be another. I suggest we apologize to Dr McGill and listen to his suggestions.'

'No apology needed – and here's my first suggestion.' McGill surveyed the small group. 'There aren't enough of us here. I

135

want more men brought in; strong men who don't scare easy. And women, too; but no shrinking violets – I want the bossy kind.' Three people started to speak at once and he held up his hand. 'Mrs Samson, will you act as secretary. Take down the names of those who are suggested.'

Eric said, 'There's paper and pencil at the cash desk. I'll get it.'

Ten minutes later McGill said. 'That ought to be enough. Mrs Samson, will you go out immediately, round up all those people and see they get here as soon as possible.'

She got up. 'They'll be here.'

Ballard gave her a note. 'Give that to Joe Cameron. I think you'll find him at the mine, not at his house.'

Mrs Samson left. McGill looked outside at the thin light. 'The first thing that should be done is to let outside know what's happening here. As soon as it gets light enough I want men to climb out; two teams of two men each, for insurance. I'll write letters for them – we don't want the information garbled.'

Ballard said, 'You'll need a secretary for that stuff. You can have Betty from the mine.'

McGill nodded shortly. 'If what comes down the hill is a powder avalanche – which it might be – then this store is going to go.'

'You think it might?' asked Eric.

'I'm certain, now the trees are gone.'

'For God's sake!' snapped Eric. 'Every time I ask a question he blames me for cutting trees.'

McGill hit the side of a display stand with the flat of his hand. It made a noise like a pistol shot and Warrick jumped visibly. 'Now listen to me,' said McGill in a harsh voice. 'We'll all get on better if there are no recriminations. I wasn't blaming anybody; I was just stating the obvious.'

Ballard chipped in, and pointed to the door. 'There'll be a lot of people coming in just now, and we're going to tell them they're facing disaster. They'd better not find out that the town council has had the information for nearly twenty-four hours and has been sitting on it. Got the picture, Eric?'

John's voice was cold. 'I told you once, Eric: if you can't talk sense then shut up.' He nodded to McGill. 'Go on.'

'All right. Accept that this place is likely to go. I want all these shelves stripped and the food taken to a safe place.' His eyes shifted and settled on Phil Warrick. 'Could you organize

136

that, Mr Warrick?'

'Sure,' said Warrick. 'But where's a safe place?'

'Turi Buck's house for a starter – I'll let you know of others later. Begin with staples – leave the chocolate biscuits until last. And if you can find some empty drums you can drain off fuel oil from the tank that Eric mentioned. If we're hit we'll need heat as well as food.'

'Right,' said Warrick with decision. Ballard thought that Warrick was a good man as long as he had to take orders and not give them.

'Don't forget the stock-rooms at the back,' said John Peterson.

Houghton said, 'That's all right for the food, but what about the people? We can't put the whole population in Turi Buck's house. I think we all ought to go up the east slope.'

'That's out for a start,' said McGill. He leaned forward. 'I hope it doesn't happen, Mr Houghton, but if a powder avalanche comes down the west slope it will cross the valley bottom and go clean across the river. I don't know how far it will go up the east slope.' Houghton looked sceptical, and McGill tapped him on the knee. 'It will be moving very fast, Mr Houghton. Not only faster than you can run, but faster than you can drive a car.'

'Is that your guess, McGill?' asked Eric.

'That's my estimate. The snow in the avalanche at the Gap was a bit too dry for my liking. The drier it is the more likely it is to form a powder avalanche, and the drier it is the faster it moves. What's more, the more the temperature drops the drier it will get.' McGill nodded to the window. 'The temperature is dropping very quickly.'

Warrick said, 'If the temperature is dropping what about the mist out there? You'd think it would freeze out of the air.'

McGill frowned, then said, 'Take it from me the temperature is falling. It's dropped a degree and a half since I got up this morning.'

'So where do the people go?' reiterated Houghton.

'We'll know better when I look at the map we had yesterday.' There was a movement at the entrance to the Supermarket, and McGill said to Warrick, 'Go up there and keep those folk corralled for a while. We've got to talk to them all at once. Let me know when they're all here.'

'All right,' said Warrick.

'And don't tell them a damn thing,' said McGill. 'We don't

137

want panic. Just say they'll know everything in – ' He cocked his head and looked past Houghton at John Peterson – 'fifteen minutes.' John nodded.

Warrick went away, and Eric said, 'Of course, there's a perfect place to put the people. 'What about the mine? It's like a bloody big air raid shelter. It's right inside the mountain.'

'Hey, that's a thought!' said Houghton.

'I'm not sure it's a good one.' McGill dropped his chin into his hand. 'The portal is right at the bottom of the slope and any avalanche is going to go right over it.'

'That's all right,' said John Peterson. 'That's why they build snow galleries over roads. I've seen them in Switzerland. The snow goes straight over the top.'

'And if, as you said, most of the snow will go right across the valley, then there'll be no trouble in getting out when it's over,' said Houghton.

'That's when I was talking about a powder avalanche,' said McGill. 'But supposing the temperature starts to rise, then it won't be a powder avalanche. It will be slower and wetter and a hell of a lot of snow will pile up at the bottom of the slope. And that blocks the mine portal. Wet snow sets like concrete after an avalanche.'

'The mine has the equipment,' said John Peterson. 'If they can mine rock, they can mine snow – or ice. They could be out an hour after it's over.'

McGill stared at him. 'I don't think we're on the same wavelength. Do you know how much snow there is on the west slope?'

'I don't suppose I do – not really.'

'Well, I've done some figuring, and my estimate is a million tons – plus.'

Eric burst out laughing, and Houghton said flatly, 'Impossible!'

'What's so goddamn impossible about it? You've got nearly two thousand acres up there covered with over six feet of snow. Ten inches of new-fallen snow equals an inch of rain – but the rain runs off while the snow stays. But that snow up there has been compressed so I reckon you have the equivalent of about eight inches of water lying up there – maybe more. You don't need a goddamn slide rule to work out the weight of that lot. And it's been snowing like crazy for the last thirty-six hours, so I'm likely to be underestimating.'

There was silence. McGill rubbed the side of his jaw with

a rasping sound. 'What do you think, Ian?'

'As far as the mine goes, I'm more worried about the powder avalanche. From what I've seen of your mathematical description of a powder avalanche I'd say you are using fluid dynamics.'

McGill nodded. 'That's right.'

'I thought so. Well, if you have a fluid flowing past the portal at the speeds you've been describing you'll get some weird effects inside the mine. It'll be like blowing across the top of a beer bottle, but more so.'

'Suction,' said McGill. 'Goddamn it – it might pull all the air right out. I hadn't thought of that one.'

'I'll talk to Cameron,' said Ballard. 'Perhaps we can build a baffle or gate of some kind.'

'Let's leave it at that,' said McGill. 'It's something to think of if we run out of other places to go. Let's move on to the next step. Suppose there is an avalanche and someone gets caught. What do we do about it?'

'There won't be much anyone can do,' said Houghton. 'Not from the way you've been talking. They'll be dead.'

'Not necessarily, and it's a defeatist assumption no one must make. Freakish things happen during avalanches. Now, what we've got to get over to these people here is the necessity for speed in rescue once we've been hit. We have to tell them what to do.'

'You have to tell them what to do,' said John Peterson.

'I accept that,' said McGill grimly.

Someone walked along the aisle from the entrance. Ballard turned his head and saw a uniformed policeman walking towards them. A sudden inspiration hit him and he smote McGill on the back. 'Radio!' he said. 'Pye has a transmitter – he must have.'

Arthur Pye stopped. 'Morning, John. What's the trouble? Ma Samson said you wanted to see me on the double.'

Ballard cut in. 'Arthur, you have a radio transmitter, don't you?'

Pye turned. 'Yes, Mr Ballard, normally I do. But not right now. It's been acting up a bit, so it went in for servicing on Friday. I'll have it back tomorrow.'

McGill groaned. 'It's a flaming conspiracy!'

'What's going on?' demanded Pye.

Matt Houghton opened his mouth to speak, but John Peterson put up his hand and explained the problem concisely. Pye regarded McGill with interest. 'This true?'

McGill nodded. 'That's how the power and phone lines were cut. Has anyone else got a transmitter? No radio hams?'

'Not that I know of,' said Pye. 'Maybe one of the scouts. I'll ask Bobby Fawcett.' He turned to John Peterson. 'What's being done about this?'

John indicated the growing crowd at the entrance. 'We're getting together some of the steadier people. I'll tell them the score, and McGill will advise on what to do about it.' He shrugged. 'He's the only one who knows.'

'You'd better do it quickly,' advised Pye. 'They're getting a bit restive.'

John Peterson looked at McGill who nodded. 'Right. Let's get to it.'

McGill said to Ballard, 'Ring up Turi Buck and tell him to prepare to play host to a crowd of kids.' He stood and joined Peterson and Pye. 'We'll be forming an avalanche committee but it's not going to be a talking shop – not if I can help it.'

'It won't be,' promised Pye.

McGill nodded in appreciation. 'You're on it, Mr Pye; and we'd better have a doctor. Now let's go and break the bad news.'

Eric Peterson said, 'So my brother told those people that Mrs Samson had brought in. They didn't believe it at first – not until someone came in from the street and said he couldn't get through the Gap. Even then they took a lot of convincing that the town was in danger.' He shrugged. 'It was just like that first council meeting, but on a bigger scale. Everybody wanted to argue the toss.'

'What time was it then?' asked Harrison.

'Half past eight, going on nine.'

'Then it would be light?'

'Yes and no. In Huka there are mountains on both sides so we don't get direct sunlight until fairly late in the morning. The sky was light enough but there was a thick mist.'

Professor Rolandson held up a finger and Harrison nodded. 'You have said that Dr McGill told you the temperature was falling. And that Mr Warrick queried that because of the mist. I must say I don't understand it myself. I would have thought that, in those conditions, the mist would have frozen out as hoar frost. Was any explanation given for this?'

'None that I heard.'

'And was it still snowing at this time?'

'No, sir, it had stopped. It didn't snow for the rest of that day.'

Rolandson leaned back, and Harrison said, 'How was this situation finally resolved? I mean the convincing of the chosen group.'

'It was Arthur Pye who did it. He listened to the arguments for a while, then jumped in and said it was time to cut the cackle. He was very forceful about it.'

Harrison raised his head and addressed the hall. 'It is a great pity that Constable Pye cannot be here to give evidence. As you may know, he was killed after the avalanche in a most valiant rescue attempt. Yesterday I was informed that Constable Pye and Mr William Quentin, the union representative at the mine, have been posthumously awarded the George Cross by Her Majesty.'

There was a murmur of voices and sporadic clapping which grew quickly into a storm of applause. The Press gallery bubbled and boiled. Harrison let the applause run its course and then tapped on the rostrum. 'Let us get on with the evidence.'

The hall quietened, and Harrison said to Eric Peterson, 'Can you tell us what Mr Ballard was doing at this time?'

'He used the telephone, and then talked to Mr Cameron for a while.'

'He did not participate in any of the arguments?'

'Not then. He took Mr Cameron on one side and they talked together.'

'You did not hear what they said?'

'No, sir.'

Harrison looked at Ballard. 'In view of a certain decision that was made about this time, I would like to hear what was said in that conversation. You are excused, Mr Peterson. Will you step forward, Mr Ballard?'

CHAPTER TWENTY

Ballard was tense. In Hukahoronui he had made a decision, and now he was called upon to justify it. Because of that decision fifty-four people had died who might now be alive and the knowledge lay heavily upon him. He clasped his hands tightly to prevent his fingers trembling.

Harrison said, 'Can you give us the gist of the conversation you had with Mr Cameron at that time?'

Ballard's voice was steady. 'We talked about Mr Eric Peterson's proposal that the mine be used as a shelter. I had already talked with Dr McGill about what to expect of avalanches, and he said that powder avalanches were very fast – anything up to a maximum of two hundred and eighty miles an hour.' He paused. 'That's the translational speed, of course.'

'You mean the general speed of the advancing snow mass?' asked Rolandson.

'Yes. But inside the mass there would be a considerable turbulence, according to Dr McGill. There would be a swirling action resulting in momentary gusts of up to twice the translational speed.'

Rolandson raised his eyebrows. 'You mean there could be gusting at speeds in excess of five hundred miles an hour?'

'So I was informed by Dr McGill.'

'I see your problem. You were afraid of an organ pipe effect as the avalanche swept past the portal of the mine.'

'Yes, sir. The suction would be tremendous.'

'And what of the second type of avalanche?'

'The wet snow avalanche would come down much more slowly – possibly at a speed of thirty to forty miles an hour. As a result of this relatively slow speed it would tend to pile up before the portal, and Dr McGill told me that snow of that nature sets hard into ice immediately. I was faced with the possibility of having several hundred thousand tons of ice of an unknown thickness between hundreds of people in the mine and the outside world. These were the problems discussed by myself and Mr Cameron.'

'And what were Mr Cameron's views?' asked Harrison.

Cameron was pungent. 'Jesus!' he said incredulously. 'You want to put the whole population into a hole in a mountain?'

'It's a shelter.'

'Okay, it's a shelter – I know that – but there are problems. So many problems. I don't know where to start. For instance, when is this disaster supposed to happen?'

'It may never happen.'

'Exactly. So how long are they going to sit in there just waiting? They might stand it a day, but when nothing happens they'll want out. Do you think you can stop them?'

'The town council might.'

Cameron made a hawking sound at the back of his throat which indicated his opinion of the council. 'To tell the truth, I'm not too happy about *anyone* being in the mine if there's going to be a fall. A million tons of snow falling an average vertical height of three thousand feet must set up *some* vibrations.'

Ballard narrowed his eyes. 'What are you getting at, Joe?'

'Well, you know we've been cutting a few corners.'

'I've seen some of the corners that have been cut. In fact, I've written a report for the board. I've not been here long, Joe; not long enough to put things right. I'm telling you now that it's got to stop. Why, in the name of God, did you let them get away with it?'

'I wasn't high man on the totem pole,' snapped Cameron. 'My immediate boss is that spineless lump of jelly, Dobbs – and above him was Fisher with one leg in the grave and incompetent in the first place. And the men were just as bad. That production bonus you've been handing out is goddamn near criminal. The guys are only human and if a shot-firer, say, can earn a fast buck by ignoring a regulation he'll go for the dough every time. And Dobbs looked the other way because he got a piece of the cake, too.'

'And you?'

Cameron looked at the floor. 'And maybe me, too.' He looked up at Ballard challengingly. 'I'm not justifying it. I'm just giving you the facts. I'm not like Dobbs – I didn't do it for the money. I did it for the job, Ian. I had to hold on to the job. This is the last job I'll hold as chief engineer. If I lose it I'll be on the way down – I'll be assistant to some smart young guy who is on his way up – and when you get to my age you can't afford to take chances like that. If I hadn't played along I'd have been fired.'

He laughed humourlessly and tapped Ballard on the chest. 'But don't tell me you haven't had your worries already. I did my best, I tell you I really did, but those business sharks in Auckland are a tight-fisted lot of bastards – all take and no give. I pleaded with Dobbs – I pleaded with Fisher – for more money to go into safety, to go into supporting structures. All I got was the one answer – "Make do." '

Ballard rubbed his eyes. 'All that's water under the bridge. What's worrying you?'

'I'll tell you. If that lot falls off the mountain – wet snow or dry, it doesn't matter – it's going to make a hell of a big thump. Now, maybe we've been interpreting the rules a mite too freely but I wouldn't want to be in there when it happens. I don't think the supporting structures will take it.'

Ballard drew in his breath. 'That's a hot one, Joe. Anyone in the mine now?'

'Sunday maintenance crew. Half a dozen guys. Engineers and electricians.'

Ballard's voice was as cutting as a knife-edge. 'Get them out. Get them out now. And bloody well jump, Joe.'

He turned on his heel and went to the noisy argumentative crowd near the door. Arthur Pye raised his voice in a bull bellow. 'Quiet! Let's hear what McGill has to say about that.'

McGill turned as Ballard arrived at his elbow. 'We've been discussing Eric Peterson's idea of using the mine as a shelter. I think it's not such a bad idea. I think we can discount the suction effect if Joe Cameron can put a stopper at the entrance. And it will easily hold everyone.'

'No,' said Ballard. 'Nobody is going in. I've just ordered the men who are already in the mine to come out.'

There was a babble of voices, cut short again by a blast from Pye. He said, 'Why not, Mr Ballard?'

'Because I don't think it's safe. Mr Cameron has just pointed out that a million tons of snow hitting the valley bottom will make quite an impact. I don't think the mine is safe.'

Pye frowned. 'Not safe?'

'It's my decision, and I've made it,' said Ballard. 'As soon as the men are out I'm having the entrance sealed.'

'Well, that's it,' said McGill. 'No need to argue any more about it.' He looked curiously at Ballard before he turned to Pye. 'I want four men, experienced in the mountains if possible. They'll need ropes and ice-axes, if you have them.'

'Some of the scouts are good climbers.'

'They'll do,' said McGill briefly. 'Where's the secretary you promised me, Ian?'

'And that's how it was,' said Ballard.

Harrison opened his mouth and then closed it. He leaned back and said to the assessor on his left, 'Do you have any questions, Mr French?'

'Indeed I have,' French drew his chair around so that he could get a good view of Ballard. 'You know that I am from the Department of Mines, Mr Ballard?'

'Yes.'

'I have followed your evidence with great care. Are we to believe that you ordered the mine sealed because you thought there would be a danger of tunnel collapse in the event of an avalanche?'

'That is correct.'

'Are you aware that because of the particular nature of this country the mining regulations are framed in such a way as to take account of earthquakes?'

'I am.'

'And so, even if a large quantity of snow did come down the west slope above the mine, there would be little or no damage providing the regulations had been followed. Do you believe that?'

'Yes.'

'And so, by pursuing the course of action which you did, you evidently believed that the regulations, as laid down in law by my department, had not been followed?'

'I believe, with Mr Cameron, that the regulations had been rather too freely interpreted, largely in the interests of economy. It was not a thing I would have relished arguing with an Inspector of Mines, had there been one there.'

'That, Mr Ballard, is a very damaging admission,' said French coldly.

'I admit that, sir.'

'And so, believing this, you had the mine sealed. In the ensuing disaster fifty-four people were killed. After the disaster the mine was unsealed and the supporting structures had, in the event, proved to be equal to the shock. Nothing had collapsed in any part of the mine. If the whole population of Hukahoronui had sheltered in the mine, as was proposed by Mr Eric Peterson, they would have been all safe. What do you say to that, Mr Ballard?'

Ballard looked troubled. 'It has weighed heavily on my mind ever since the avalanche. It is evident that I made the wrong decision, but it is only evident in hindsight. I was there and the decision was up to me, so I made it on the basis of available evidence.' He paused. 'I must add that were I placed in the same position again I would not vary my decision.'

There was an uneasy rustle from the public gallery and the floor creaked. Harrison said gently, 'But the mine *should* have been safe, Mr Ballard.'

'Yes, sir.'

'And it was not?'

'It was not.'

Rolandson leaned forward, his elbows spread wide on the rostrum, and looked across at French. 'Was the mine unsealed by a member of the Inspectorate of Mines, Mr French?'

'Yes, it was.'

'What were his views on the supporting structures that he found?'

'His report was unfavourable,' said French. 'I might add that he made a verbal report to me immediately after his inspection, and his remarks were unprintable.'

Ballard said, 'I made a similar report to the board of the company. I request that it be introduced as evidence.'

Harrison leaned forward. 'Mr Rickman, can that report be produced?'

Rickman conferred in whispers with Crowell for a few minutes, then he looked up. 'I am instructed to inform the Commission that no such report has been received from Mr Ballard.'

Ballard was pale. In a controlled voice he said, 'I can provide the Commission with a copy of that report.'

'With respect, Mr Chairman,' said Rickman. 'The fact that Mr Ballard can provide a copy of a report does not necessarily mean that a report was sent to the board of the company. In point of fact, any report that Mr Ballard may present to the Commission may have been written *post facto*.'

Harrison looked interested. 'Are you seriously suggesting that the report Mr Ballard has offered to me has been fraudulently written after the event?'

'With respect, I am merely pointing out the possibility that it could have been written yesterday.'

'An interesting suggestion, Mr Rickman. What do you think of it, Mr Ballard?'

Ballard looked at Rickman who looked back at him blandly. 'Mr Rickman is imputing that I am a liar.'

'Oh no!' said Rickman with an ingenuous air. 'Only that you very well could be.'

'Mr Rickman is also not improving my present frame of mind,' said Ballard. 'I would delight in answering any questions concerning the safety of the mine from Mr French, from Mr Gunn, who represents the General Mining Union, or from any other interested person.'

The smile disappeared from Rickman's face as Gunn seized upon the offer. 'Mr Ballard, you have said the mine was not safe. Apart from this disputed report, did you mention the matter to anyone else at that time?'

'I did. I talked about it in conversations with Mr Dobbs, Mr Cameron, and Dr McGill, both before and after the avalanche.'

'Had you taken steps to right matters?'

'I wrote the report and was preparing to follow it up.'

'How long was it before the disaster that you took up your position with the company?'

'Six weeks.'

'Only six weeks!' echoed Gunn in well-simulated surprise. 'Then Mr Rickman, or even Mr Lyall, can hardly suggest that you were responsible for the state of affairs in the mine.'

'I had no intention of suggesting it,' said Lyall drily.

Rickman remained silent.

'But someone must have been responsible,' pursued Gunn. 'What, in your opinion, was the reason for this scandalous state of affairs?'

'The mine was teetering on the verge of profitability. If it was not to make an actual loss all margins had to be shaved. Any money that went into the mine went towards productivity – towards profit. Anything that did not conduce towards productivity went to the wall – and that included safety margins.' Ballard moved in his chair and looked towards Rickman. 'Now that a rich vein of conglomerate ore has been struck one hopes that more money will go to safety.'

Rickman leaped to his feet. 'Mr Chairman, I must protest. The witness is giving away the very secrets of the company – secrets he acquired in the course of his duties. Is this the conduct of a responsible managing director?'

Pandemonium broke out in the Press gallery. Lost in the uproar was Ballard's retort, 'Don't you mean ex-managing director?'

CHAPTER TWENTY-ONE

When the Commission of Inquiry reconvened in the afternoon Harrison said acidly, 'I hope we do not have a recurrence of the behaviour which led to the adjournment of this morning's session. Whether Mr Ballard was wise to say what he did is not for me to judge. However, I believe he was goaded into it by the adversary tactics I warned against at the opening of this Inquiry. Mr Rickman, I give you a final warning: you must not be over-zealous in the protection of your client's interest. One more instance like that of this morning and I shall have to ask your client to find someone else to represent him.'

Rickman stood up. 'I apologize to the Commission if I have offended in any way.'

'Your apology is accepted.' Harrison consulted his notes. 'I would like to ask one further question of Mr Ballard. It will not take long and you may keep your seat. Mr Ballard, you say that you consulted with Mr Cameron. I have looked through your evidence most carefully and I find that Mr Dobbs, the mine manager and Mr Cameron's superior, has figured little. Where was Mr Dobbs all this time?'

Ballard hesitated. 'I don't really know. Something seemed to have happened to him.'

Such as?'

'Something psychological, I'd say. He seemed to retreat into himself. He relinquished all his duties into my hands. Naturally I was perturbed about this, so I sent Dr Scott to talk with Mr Dobbs to see if he could discover what was the matter. I think his evidence would be best. I am not a medical authority.'

'Yes, that would be best. I will call him later, if it proves necessary.' Harrison consulted his notes again. 'Dr McGill seems to have effectively taken charge at this time. He was, as it were, the organizing force because only he had any idea of what was to come. I think we had better hear his testimony.'

McGill took his seat, and said immediately, 'I think I can clear up a point that was worrying Professor Rolandson. The mist.'

Rolandson looked up. 'Yes, I'd like to know about that.'

'It worried me, too,' said McGill. 'Although I tried not to

show it. I couldn't see how there could be so much mist in a rapidly falling temperature. It was quite thick – almost to be classified as a fog – and was very troublesome to us. It was only after the avalanche that I got it figured out.'

He knew he would be giving evidence all afternoon so he made himself comfortable in his seat. 'You may remember that the first avalanche blocked the river as well as the road. The river had been frozen, but of course the water flowed freely under the ice. When the river was blocked the water rose and broke the ice. That water was relatively warm and on contact with the cold air produced the mist. It was actually freezing out into frost all the time, but as the water spread over low ground there was a great deal of surface area presented to the air, and mist was being generated faster than it was frozen out.'

'An ingenious theory,' said Rolandson. 'And no doubt correct.'

'As I say, it gave us a great deal of trouble that day. It hampered our operations considerably.'

'What was the prime consideration in your mind?' asked Harrison.

'The safety of the people,' said McGill promptly. 'And I had a great deal of co-operation once the gravity of the situation was made clear. I would like to say now that those who had already realized that gravity gave of their utmost. I would like especially at this time to commend John Peterson.'

Harrison nodded and made a note. 'What steps were taken?'

'It was important to communicate with outside. Two teams were sent to climb out of the valley as soon as light permitted. One team was to climb the avalanche debris blocking the Gap, while the other took a more circuitous route. Once that was set going, I had all the children rounded up and sent to Turi Buck's house which was on the record as being safe. At this time I became worried about the vulnerability of the central, and I – '

'The central?' queried Harrison.

'I'm sorry,' said McGill. 'A transatlantic – or transpacific – confusion. You'd call it the exchange – the telephone exchange. It was right in the open and sure to be hit – and yet we had to have communications. A failure of the telephone system during the organizing period would have made things most difficult. I discussed this with Mr Ballard and Mr Peterson, and one of the mine electricians volunteered to man the board. However,

Mrs Maureen Scanlon, the operator, would not give up the board. She said she would be derelict in duty and refused to leave, She also said that it was her board and that no one else was going to touch it.'

McGill lowered his voice. 'The telephone system worked perfectly all during the organizing period and right up to the time of the avalanche, when the exchange was destroyed and Mrs Scanlon was killed. Mr John Peterson was also killed at that time in an effort to save Mrs Scanlon.'

The silence in the hall was total, and then there came a long, shuddering sigh.

Harrison said quietly, 'You seem to have had your hands very full.'

'Well, Mr Ballard and John Peterson were very able joint chiefs of staff, as you may say. Mr Ballard provided all the resources of the mine and did the organizing from that end, while Mr John Peterson did the same for the town, aided by the other members of the council. The main problem at first was to convince the town people that we were serious, and this is why the telephone system was so important. The council members spoke personally by telephone to every head of household in the valley. For myself, I merely provided overall direction in order to prevent mistakes being made and, after a while, I was able to think of what to do after the avalanche hit.'

Professor Rolandson said, 'How certain were you, at this time, that there would be another avalanche?'

'I was not dealing in certainties but in probabilities. As a scientist I am accustomed to doing this, but it does tend to preclude exactness. Avalanches are notoriously unpredictable. I know of a case in Switzerland where a five-hundred-year-old-building was swept away, thus proving that no avalanche had followed that path for five hundred years. No one could have predicted that. But based upon my investigation of the slope and upon what little theory we have and my own past experience I put the chance of an avalanche at about seventy per cent – and rising as the temperature fell.'

'Would you say rising to eighty per cent?'

'Yes, I'd say that, or even higher.'

'Let me put that in lay terms,' said Rolandson. 'What Dr McGill is saying is that the chance of *not* having an avalanche was the same as throwing a die and showing a six on the first throw. The chances of an avalanche occurring, in his opinion, 'was about four or five to one.'

'Odds that only an inveterate gambler would accept,' commented Harrison. 'I take it that the people were advised to go to safe places. Who determined those places?'

'I did, sir.' McGill hesitated. 'Safety is relative. To tell the truth, I wasn't even too sure of the safety of Turi Buck's house with all the trees gone from the slope. But it was the best we had and that's why we put most of the children there. As for the rest, I looked at the map and as much of the actual ground as I could – the mist made that difficult – and tried to take advantage of topographical features; anything to put something between the people and the snow.' He paused. 'In one case I have to say I made a bad error of judgment.'

'No one can blame you for that,' said Harrison.

'Thank you, sir. The main difficulty was to get the people to move. No one wanted to leave a warm house to stay in the open in the snow, and the thick mist didn't make the prospect more inviting. Constable Pye, a very forceful man, did a lot there.'

'You say there came a time when you were able to think of what to do after the avalanche. What did you mean by that?'

'Speed in rescue after an avalanche is the first essential, but the rescuers must know what they're doing. To find a person buried in snow is exceptionally difficult. Swiss experience shows that it takes a trained team of twenty men twenty hours to thoroughly probe an area of one hectare.'

'A hectare being two-and-a-half acres,' interjected Rolandson.

'Well, we had no trained men and we had no equipment. We couldn't be sure of outside help so we had to improvise with what we had. We stripped TV antennae from the houses; these provided aluminium tubing to make probes for the rescue teams. Mr Cameron, at the mine workshop, made them up into lengths of ten feet. I organized three teams, a total of sixty men, and tried to give a crash course in avalanche rescue.'

'At what time was this?'

McGill shook his head. 'I couldn't say, sir. I was too busy to keep my eye on the time.'

The mist was clammy against the skin. It wreathed in coils as the slight breeze shifted and the range of vision changed sharply. A large group of men, bulky in cold weather clothing, milled about somewhat aimlessly, some stamping their feet to keep warm, others blowing on their fingers and beating their arms across their chests.

'All right, you guys,' yelled McGill. 'Those who have probes step forward and line up.' He inspected them with a critical eye. 'Line up as though you're in the army and on parade – shoulder to shoulder and standing at ease. Feet about ten inches apart.'

The men shuffled about. There was embarrassed laughter as they realized the spectacle they must make. 'There's nothing funny about this,' snapped McGill. 'You other guys gather around and watch.'

He walked forward, holding a ball of string and gave the end to the man on the extreme left of the line. 'Hold that.' He walked along the line, unreeling string, until he was at the extreme right, then he cut the string, and gave it to the man on the end. 'Now, you two guys are the markers. Bend down and stretch that string tight on the snow. Everyone else put the toes of their boots against the string.'

He watched them get into position. 'Right. Now, in front of you is an area in which you think someone is buried, but you don't know exactly where. You put the probe just in front of the toe of your left boot, and push down. You'll hit bottom hereabouts at less than three feet. If there's an avalanche there'll be a hell of a lot more snow than that.'

All the men probed. 'Okay, now you do the same at the toe of your right boot.'

Someone called out. 'How do we know when we've found a body?'

'You'll know,' said McGill. 'It's unmistakable. If you hit a body go easy on the pressure – don't use that probe as a spear. Call your team leader who will mark the spot for the digging team. Right, now you markers take a step forward – not more than a foot – and stretch that string again. All you others put your toes against it and probe again the same way as before.'

He turned to the crowd of watchers. 'You see what they're doing? They're probing every square foot; we call this a fine search, and there's a ninety-five per cent chance of finding a body if there's one there. For a really fine search you probe in front of each boot and then again in the middle. That gives a hundred per cent chance, providing the body isn't deeper than your probe.'

Someone said, 'It's bloody slow, though.'

'Right,' said McGill. 'It's slow. When the next lot of probes comes I'm going to teach you guys coarse probing. There's a thirty per cent chance of missing a body, but it's faster and sometimes speed is more efficient than thoroughness.'

'Here comes Cameron with more probes now,' someone called.

McGill swung around to see the truck coming towards them. As it pulled to a halt he said, 'Okay, get them out of there.'

He pulled out a packet of cigarettes. Cameron got out of the cab and crunched across the snow to take a cigarette from the outheld packet. 'Thanks, Mike. How are you doing?'

McGill looked about to make sure he was out of earshot of the men. 'Not good. You know how long it takes to train the men of the Parsenndienst in Switzerland? And *they* have the equipment.'

'What's that . . . what you said? Some sort of snow rescue service?'

McGill nodded. 'These guys are enthusiastic enough, but when it comes to the crunch they'll not be much use. Some of them might be under the snow, instead of on top where I want them. The rest will be good for nothing.'

'How do you mean?'

'A million tons of snow – or anything else, for that matter – dropping close by takes the pith out of a man.' McGill blew a long plume of smoke. 'It's known as disaster shock. We'll need outside help and we'll need it fast, and I hope to hell they have dogs. A trained dog can find a body in a tenth of the time it takes a twenty-man team. Half the victims of avalanches in Switzerland are found by dogs.'

Cameron turned and watched the line of men probing into the snow. 'Then what are you doing all this for?'

'Just to keep up morale. It helps if they have something to do. How many probes did you bring?'

'Twenty. There'll be another twenty in under an hour.' He looked back at the truck. 'They've unloaded. I'll be on my way.'

'Okay, Joe.' As Cameron drove away McGill stepped forward. 'You guys with the new probes come over here. I'll show you coarse probing.' He paused as a Land-Rover swept up and stopped close by. Two men got out, one of them Ballard. McGill had not seen the other man before.

Ballard hurried over. 'Mike, this is Jack MacAllister. He came over the Gap.'

'We met a couple of your people on top,' said MacAllister. 'They've gone on to get to a telephone. They told us what was happening so I came on down to see for myself.'

'Thank God!' said McGill. It was a cry from the heart. He sized up MacAllister. 'What are the chances of evacuating the valley – all the people?'

MacAllister shook his head. 'Not a chance. It took me all my time getting over. That snow has set solid – it's more like ice now. In places it's a vertical climb. But the telephone boys are trying to get a line over now.'

'That'll be a help,' McGill dropped his cigarette and put his foot on it. 'At least we've got through to outside. Better late than never.'

'They knew last night,' said MacAllister unexpectedly. 'I telephoned the police. There's a whole gang of them on the other side of the Gap right now. They pitched up just as I started to climb.'

'Better and better.' McGill turned to Ballard. 'You know what's been worrying me?'

'What?'

McGill pointed upwards. 'Not being able to see that goddamn slope because of the mist. It's been giving me a real prickly feeling.'

'Hush!' said MacAllister. 'What's that?'

'What's what?'

'Listen!'

There was a faint drone from overhead, growing louder. 'An airplane,' said McGill, straining his eyes against the mist.

'He can't land in this,' said Ballard.

They listened while the aircraft circled overhead but they did not see it. It droned for about ten minutes and then went away, only to return five minutes later.

'And that's it,' said McGill. He put his hands flat on the arms of the witness chair and looked at Harrison. 'That's when the avalanche hit us.'

CHAPTER TWENTY-TWO

Harrison drew in a long breath. 'And so we come to the avalanche itself. It has been suggested in the Press that the sound of that aeroplane, which had been sent to investigate by Civil Defence, was the trigger which set the avalanche in motion. What are your views on that, Dr McGill?'

'That's utter nonsense, sir,' said McGill baldly. 'The idea that sound can trigger an avalanche is a myth, an old wives' tale. In the United States supersonic aircraft studies have been made. Even the high overpressure of two pounds a square foot caused by a military aircraft like the Hustler has had no detectable effect.' He paused. 'But that's in normal use. In Montana experiments were made by F–106 aircraft making aimed dives and pulling out at supersonic speeds. Those did cause avalanche release. But the plane I heard flying over Hukahoronui could not in any way have triggered that avalanche.'

Harrison smiled. 'The pilot of that aircraft will be very glad to hear that. I believe it has been on his conscience.'

'It needn't be,' said McGill. 'That snow was ready to come down, and it came down without his assistance.'

'Thank you, Dr McGill. It appears that the pilot and observer of that aircraft were the only people to see the avalanche as it began to fall. From the depositions I have read it appears that the observer has more to offer in evidence. You are excused, Dr McGill. Please call Flying Officer Hatry.'

Hatry took his seat. He was a fresh-faced young man of about twenty, wearing the uniform of the RNZAF. Reed asked, 'Your name?'

'Charles Howard Hatry.'

'Your occupation?'

'Flying Officer, Royal New Zealand Air Force.'

Harrison said, 'How was it that you came to be flying over Hukahoronui at that time?'

'Orders, sir.'

'And what were your exact orders?'

'To fly to Hukahoronui, and to land if possible. To find out

155

the situation and radio back. I believe the orders originated with Civil Defence. That's what I was told, anyway.'

'Just so. Carry on.'

'Flight-Lieutenant Storey was the pilot and I was the observer. We flew to Hukahoronui from Harewood Airport, here in Christchurch. When we got there we found that landing was out of the question. There was a thick layer of cloud or mist on the valley floor. It would have been pretty dangerous going into that. We radioed this information back to Christchurch and were told to fly around for a while in case the mist lifted.'

'What were weather conditions like – other than the low mist?'

'Very good, sir. The sky was clear and the sun very strong. The clarity of the air was exceptional. Very good for photography. I remember saying to Lieutenant Storey that I thought it would be cold outside. It was that sort of day – crisp and cold.'

'You mentioned photography. Were you instructed to take photographs?'

'Yes, sir. I took two complete spools of the area around the valley – seventy-two exposures in all. These included photographs of the misted area just in case it meant anything. I couldn't understand the mist, sir, because everything else was so clear.'

Harrison shook out some glossy black-and-whites from an envelope. 'And these are the photographs you took?' He began to hold them up one at a time.

Hatry leaned forward. 'Yes, sir, those are the official photographs.'

'I see you took a picture of the snow which blocked the Gap.'

'Yes – we flew low to take that one.'

'You say these are the official photographs. Are we to understand that there are some *unofficial* photographs?'

Hatry shifted in his seat. 'I'm keen on cine-photography and I just happened to have my camera along. It isn't up to much – just eight millimetre. Conditions were so good and the mountains looked so beautiful that I decided to shoot off a reel.'

'And while you were shooting this film the avalanche began and you managed to film it?'

'Some of it, sir.' Hatry paused. 'It's not a very good film, I'm afraid.'

'But when you had it developed you realized its importance and you offered it to this Commission as evidence. It that it?'

'Yes, sir.'

'Well, then, I think the film will be the best evidence available. Please have the screen set up, Mr Reed.'

The hall buzzed with voices as the ushers set up the screen and projector. Curtains were drawn over the windows. In the semi-darkness Harrison said, 'You may begin at any time.'

There was a click and a whirr, and the screen lit up with a series of rapidly flashing letters against a blurred white background. Suddenly a recognizable scene appeared – white mountains and a blue sky. It disappeared to be replaced by a shot of the ground. 'That's the valley,' said Hatry. 'You can see the mist.' He stopped as though conscious of committing *lèse-majesté*. 'I'm sorry, sir.'

'That's all right, Mr Hatry. Make whatever comments you please.'

'There's not much during the first half,' said Hatry. 'Just mountains. Some good views towards Mount Cook.'

The film ran on. It could have been any amateur travelogue – hand held and unsteady. But the tension in the hall grew as the seconds went by and scene followed scene.

Presently Hatry said, 'I think it's coming along about now. I asked Lieutenant Storey to fly north along the Hukahoronui valley.'

'How high were you flying?' asked Rolandson.

'A little over two thousand feet above the valley floor.'

'So that the west slope of the valley actually stretched above you.'

'Yes, sir. Afterwards I found the slope was six thousand feet from crest to valley. Here it is now.'

It was an upward shot showing a little blue sky at the top of the screen, then there were a few scattered rocks jutting up, and then the snow so white as to make the eyes ache which filled the rest of the screen. As an artistic composition it was terrible, but that did not matter.

The scene suddenly jogged and blurred, and then steadied again. 'That's it,' said Hatry. 'That's when it started.'

A faint plume of grey had appeared, a shadow cast by rising snow, which grew larger as it moved down the slope. It disappeared sideways as though the camera had panned away. The next shot was of distant mountains and sky, very wobbly. 'We had trouble in positioning the aircraft,' said Hatry apologetically. 'I suppose we were excited.'

There came another shot of a boiling cloud of whiteness shadowed by grey which plunged down the mountainside, growing in extent continually. Ballard licked dry lips. He had once seen a big oil fire, and watching this growing cloud advancing down the slope reminded him of the billowing clouds of black smoke from that fire, but seen, as it were, on negative film.

Again the scene jerked off the screen and there came a dizzying view of the ground whirling in a spiral. 'I asked Lieutenant Storey to bank,' said Hatry, 'so I could get a good view into the valley. He did it a bit too quickly.'

The camera steadied and it could be seen that the whole of the upper slope was in motion and the line of advance was incredibly fast, even when seen from a distance. Blurred and unsteady though the film was, the sight was impressive.

Suddenly there was a complete change of scene. The moving front of the avalanche was now much farther down the mountain, almost near the bottom, and approaching the bank of mist which covered the valley floor. Hatry said, 'We were flying out of distance. We had to make a quick circuit and come back.'

Something surprising was happening to the mist. Long before the approaching front of snow was near it, the mist was driven back as though an invisible jet was playing on it. It cleared magically and buildings could be seen briefly. Then the snow swept over everything.

The screen flashed blindingly white and there was a flapping sound as the tail of the film was slapped around by the reel of the projector. 'That's when the film ran out,' said Hatry.

'Will someone draw the curtains?' said Harrison. The curtains were drawn open and he waited until the hum of conversation ceased. 'So you took the film. What did you do next?'

'We radioed back, telling what we'd seen.'

'And what was the result of that?'

'They asked us if we could land. I checked with Lieutenant Storey and he said not. There was still some mist about, but that wasn't it. You see, he didn't know *where* to land after the snow had gone over everything. We were then ordered to return to Christchurch.'

'Thank you, Mr Hatry. You may step down.' Harrison looked towards McGill. 'Have you any comments on what you have just seen, Dr McGill? You may answer from where you are sitting.'

'It was most interesting from a professional point of view. If we know the number of frames per second of that film we can measure the speed of the avalanche very accurately and in detail. One of the most interesting features is that it showed something which we have always suspected and, in a sense, knew, but could not prove. Because of the mist we could see that there was an air blast in advance of the moving mass of snow. At a very rough estimate I would put that air blast as moving at something over two hundred miles an hour. Apart from the actual snow impact, such a blast could cause considerable damage. I think the film should be preserved and, indeed, duplicated. I wouldn't mind having a copy of it myself for study.'

'Thank you.' Harrison looked at the clock. 'The time has come for our adjournment. We meet here again at ten o'clock tomorrow morning.'

His gavel tapped on the rostrum.

CHAPTER TWENTY-THREE

McGill joined the throng leaving the hall. Ahead he saw the tall figure of Stenning walking next to Ballard. They were not talking to each other and, once through the doorway, they made off in different directions. He smiled and thought that neither of them was giving the Ballard family any grounds for suspicion.

'Dr McGill!' Someone caught his elbow and he turned to find the Peterson brothers just behind him, first Eric, and then the bulkier figure of Charlie behind. Eric said, 'I'm glad you said what you did about Johnnie. I'd like to thank you for that.'

'No need,' said McGill. 'Credit should be given where it's due.'

'All the same,' said Eric a little awkwardly, 'it was good of you to say so in public – especially when you're on the other side, so to speak.'

'Now hold on a minute,' said McGill sharply. 'I'm a neutral around here – I'm on no one's side. Come to that, I didn't know there were sides. This is an inquiry, not a court battle. Isn't that what Harrison insists?'

Charlie looked unimpressed. 'You're a neutral like I'm the fairy queen. Everybody knows that Ballard and you are in each other's pockets.'

'Shut up, Charlie!' said Eric.

'Why the hell should I? Harrison said he wants the truth to come out – but is it? Look at the evidence this morning. Not nearly enough was made of the fact that Ballard made a bad mistake. Why didn't you prod Lyall into going for him?'

'Oh, Charlie, enough is enough.' Eric looked at McGill and shrugged expressively.

'Not for me it isn't,' said Charlie. 'All I know is that I used to have three brothers and now I've got one – and that bastard killed two of them. What do you want me to do? Stand still while he murders the whole Peterson family?'

'Give it a rest, for Christ's sake!' said Eric exasperatedly.

'Fat chance,' said Charlie, and tapped McGill on the shoulder. 'Now, Dr Neutral McGill – don't tell me you won't be seeing Ballard tonight.'

'I'll be seeing him,' said McGill evenly.

'Well, you tell him what I think. Eric made the suggestion of using the mine as a shelter but Ballard turned him down because the mine wasn't safe. The safety of the mine was Ballard's responsibility – he was in charge, wasn't he? And the mine wasn't safe. In my book that's criminal irresponsibility and I'm going to see he gets nailed for it. You're his friend – you tell him that.' Charlie's voice rose. 'You tell him, if I can't get him for murder I'll get him for manslaughter.'

Eric held his arm. 'Keep your voice down. Don't make one of your bloody scenes in here.'

Charlie shook his arm free. 'Don't tell me what to do.' He stared at McGill with hot eyes. 'And tell that bloody murdering friend of yours to keep out of my way, because if I ever come across him I'll tear him apart piece by piece.'

McGill looked about him. Apart from the three of them the hall was now empty. He said, 'Threats like that are very unwise. Threatening a witness in this Inquiry could get you into trouble.'

'He's right,' said Eric. 'For God's sake, keep your mouth shut. You talk too much – you always have.'

'I'll do more than talk before I'm through.' Charlie's forefinger bored into McGill's chest. 'Tell Ballard that if he so much as looks at Liz again I'll kill the bastard.'

'Take your goddamn hand off me,' said McGill softly.

Eric pulled Charlie away. 'Don't start a fight here, you damned fool.' He shook his head wearily. 'Sorry about that, McGill.'

'Don't apologize for me,' shouted Charlie. 'Christ, Eric, you're as chicken as everybody else. You go arse-creeping to McGill – the high and mighty Dr Know-it-all-McGill – and thank him kindly for putting in a nice word for the Petersons. What the hell is this? Damn it, you know that he and Ballard are running a cover-up operation that makes Watergate sound like a fairy story. What the hell's got into you?'

Eric took a deep breath. 'Charlie, sometimes I think you're going out of your mind. Now will you, for God's sake, shut up? Let's go and have a beer and cool down.' He took Charlie by the arm and steered him towards the door.

Charlie allowed himself to be led away, but twisted his head and shouted to McGill, 'Don't forget to tell Ballard. Tell that son of a bitch I'll have him in jail for ten years.'

At the hotel Stenning went to his room to clean up. The climate was hotter than he was used to and he felt uncomfortably sticky. His suit was too heavy for the New Zealand Summer and he made a mental note to buy a lightweight suit since it seemed that the Inquiry would continue for some time to come.

He felt better after he had bathed and he sat for a while in his dressing-gown while he made notes of the events of the day, amplifying the hasty scrawls he had made during the Inquiry. He shook his head over the evidence and thought that young Ballard was not in a favourable position; the business of the safety of the mine might go heavily against him should someone try to push the point. He thought about it and decided that Rickman would let it lie; he wouldn't want to bring up anything that would reflect on the company. Gunn, the union lawyer had gone out of his way to be kind to Ballard while still sticking his knife into the company. Stenning was surprised that the Petersons' lawyer, Lyall, had not made an issue of it. Perhaps that was to come.

After a while he dressed and went outside to find Ballard sitting at a table near the pool with an extraordinarily beautiful young woman. As he approached, Ballard caught sight of him and stood up. 'Miss Peterson, this is Mr Stenning, a visitor from England.'

Stenning's white eyebrows lifted as he heard the name, but he merely said, 'Good evening, Miss Peterson.'

'Have something cooling,' suggested Ballard.

Stenning sat down. 'That would be most welcome. A gin and tonic, please.'

'I'll get it.' Ballard strode away.

'Didn't I see you at the Huka Inquiry this afternoon?' asked Liz.

'I was there. I'm a lawyer, Miss Peterson. I'm very interested in your ideas of administrative justice here in New Zealand. Dr Harrison was kind enough to provide me with a place.'

She fondled the ears of her dog which sat by her chair. 'What's your impression so far?'

He smiled, and said with a lawyer's caution, 'It's too early to say. I must read a transcript of the early part of the Inquiry. Tell me, are you related in any way to the Peterson family that is involved?'

'Why, yes. Eric and Charlie are my brothers.'

'Ah!' Stenning tried to add things up and failed to find an answer, so he repeated his observation. 'Ah!'

Liz picked up her Cuba Libre and sipped it while regarding him over the rim of the glass. She said, 'Have you known Ian Ballard long?'

'We're fellow guests in the hotel,' he said, blandly avoiding the question. 'Have *you* known him long?'

'All my life – on and off,' she said. 'More off than on. There was a big gap in the middle.' She had noted Stenning's evasiveness and began to wonder just who he was. 'That was when he left for England.'

'Then you must have known him when he was a boy in Hukahoronui.'

'I don't think you need to read a transcript of the Inquiry,' she said, a little tartly. 'That wasn't in evidence today.'

'No,' he agreed. 'I think I read it in a newspaper report.'

Ballard came back and put a frosted glass in front of Stenning. Liz said, 'Mr Stenning is being mysterious.'

'Oh! What about?'

'That's what's mysterious. I don't know.'

Ballard looked at Stenning and raised his eyebrows. Stenning said easily, 'Miss Peterson is a remarkably sharp young lady, but perhaps she sees mysteries where none exist.'

Liz smiled, and said, 'How long have you known Mr Stenning, Ian?'

'Twenty years – or a little under.'

'And you're just good friends,' she suggested. 'And fellow hotel guests, of course.'

'Perhaps I prevaricated, Miss Peterson,' said Stenning. 'But I had my reasons. Perhaps you would be good enough not to mention my name in connection with Mr Ballard.'

'Why should I mention you?'

Stenning picked up his drink. 'It happens. Casual conversations cover a lot of ground.'

Liz turned to Ballard. 'What is all this?'

'It's just that Mr Stenning and I have business which we'd prefer not to parade before other people at this time.'

'Something to do with the Inquiry?'

'Nothing to do with the Inquiry,' he said flatly. He turned to Stenning. 'Talking of the Inquiry, Rickman tried to pull a couple of fast ones this morning before the opening. He came over to me and . . .'

He stopped as Stenning raised his hand and said, 'Am I to take it that you don't mind if Miss Peterson hears about this matter?'

'Why shouldn't she hear it?' asked Ballard in surprise.

Stenning frowned. 'I'm sure I don't know,' he said perplexedly.

'All right, then. First Rickman tried to bribe me, then to blackmail me.' He retailed what Rickman had said.

Stenning grimaced. 'Was there a witness to this interesting conversation?'

'No.'

'A pity. I'd take delight in having the man disbarred.'

Liz laughed. 'You have wonderful friends, Ian. Such nice people.'

'Not nearly as wonderful as the Petersons.' Ballard looked up. 'Here's Mike. What kept you?'

McGill put a glass and a bottle of 'DB' beer on the table. 'A run-in with Liz's charming brothers. Hi, Liz. I won't ask "How's the family?" because I know. Did you enjoy the show,

Mr Stenning? It was a nice movie.'

'It had its moments of drama,' Stenning sat back in his chair and watched Ballard and Liz Peterson with curious eyes.

'What about my brothers?' Liz asked.

McGill filled his glass. 'Eric's all right,' he said, intent on not letting the beer foam over. 'But have you ever wondered about Charlie? If I were a psychiatrist I'd tend to diagnose paranoia.'

'Did he make another of his big scenes?'

'And how!' McGill jerked his head at Ballard. 'He threatened to dismember Ian from limb to limb if he ever meets him.'

'Talk!' said Liz scornfully. 'That's all he ever does.'

'Maybe,' said McGill. 'Ian, if you and this wench are going to consort you'd better wear a blindfold. He said that if you so much as look at Liz he'll kill you.'

Stenning broke in. 'And was there a witness to *this* conversation?'

'Just me and Eric.'

'And he used the word "kill"?'

'The very word.'

Stenning shook his head. Liz said, 'I'll have a talk with Master Charlie. He's got to get in into his thick skull that my life is my own. This time it won't be a plate of spaghetti that I'll crown him with.'

'Liz, be careful,' warned McGill. 'I'm getting the idea that he's genuinely unbalanced. Even Eric thinks he's losing his marbles. It took Eric all his time to hold him in.'

'He's just a big blow-hard,' she said. 'I'll sort him out. But let's not talk about the Petersons – let's not talk at all. How's your tennis, Ian?'

'Not bad,' said Ballard.

She held up her glass. 'Bet you another of these you can't beat me.'

'Done,' he said promptly.

'Let's go,' she said, and stood up.

McGill turned his head and watched them as they walked towards the tennis courts with Victor trotting behind, then he turned back and grinned at Stenning. 'Do you find our conversation stimulating, Mr Stenning?'

'Interesting, to say the least. Miss Peterson is also interesting.'

'An understatement typical of a lawyer.' McGill topped up

his glass. Tell me – If Ian marries a Peterson, does that count in your Peterson Bashing Contest?'

Stenning moved nothing except his eyes which he slanted at McGill. 'So he told you about that. Your question is hard to answer. I doubt if it is what Ben had in mind.'

'But circumstances alter cases.'

Stenning said austerely, 'That truism has no legal validity.'

CHAPTER TWENTY-FOUR

High on the western slope and deep in the snow layer the processes of disaster were well advanced. Destructive metamorphism had long since ceased and constructive metamorphism was well under way. Air, slightly warmed from the ground, rose upwards through the snow laden with water vapour until it reached the impenetrable layer of hoar frost half way through the snow mass. Here it cooled giving up the vapour to create the tapered cup crystals.

By now the cup crystals were large and well formed, some of them being over half an inch in length.

The heavy snow-fall of the past two days had added an increased weight which, operating vertically through gravity against the cup crystals on the slope, had led to a delicately unstable position. A man may take an orange pip, hold it gently between forefinger and thumb, and squeeze ever so gently – and the orange pip will be propelled with considerable velocity. So it was on the western slope. A heavy-footed hawk alighting on the snow could provide that little extra pressure and set the cup crystals in motion.

Something like that did occur and a small slippage started. It was not very much and could have been spanned by a man with outstretched arms. The new-fallen surface snow, very cold, dry and powdery, was lifted a little by the sudden movement and a small white plume arose like a puff of smoke. But underneath chaos had begun. The fragile ice plate of the hoar layer cracked, jostling the cup crystals beneath which began to roll. The delicate bonds which held the snow together sheared, and cracks spread wide, zig-zagging at high speed from the point of original breakage. It was a chain reaction; one event followed another in lightning succession and suddenly a whole section of the snow fifty feet across slumped forward and downward, adding its weight to the untouched snow farther down the slope.

Again the inevitable action and reaction. Event followed on event even faster and presently the whole of the higher slope across a front of a hundred yards was in movement and plunging downwards.

As yet it was not moving very quickly. Five seconds after the first slippage an agile man caught in the open two hundred yards down the slope could have avoided death by running aside not very quickly. The speed of the young avalanche at this time was not much more than ten miles an hour. But the motion and the air resistance caused the light, feathery surface snow to rise and, as the speed increased, more and more of the snow powder became airborne.

The powder mixed turbulently with the air to form essentially a new substance – a gas with a density ten times that of air. This gas, tugged down the slope by the force of gravity, was not checked very much by friction against the ground, unlike the snow in the main avalanche. The gas cloud picked up speed and moved ahead of the main slide. Twenty seconds after the first slippage it was moving at fifty miles an hour, hammering gustily at the snow slope and smashing the delicate balance of forces that held the snow in place.

This was a self-energizing process. More snow was whirled aloft to increase the gas cloud and the avalanche, no longer an infant but lustily growing, fed hungrily on the snow lower down the slope. Already the whole of the upper slope was boiling and seething across a front of four hundred yards, and clouds of snow rose like the thunderheads of a hot summer's day, but incredibly faster.

The avalanche cloud poured down the mountainside even more quickly. At seventy miles an hour it began to pull into itself the surrounding air, thus increasing its volume. Growing thus, it again increased its speed. At a hundred miles an hour the turbulence in its entrails was causing momentary blasts of two hundred miles an hour. At a hundred and thirty miles an hour miniature tornadoes began to form along its edges where it entrained the ambient air; these whirlwinds had internal velocities of more than three hundred miles an hour.

By this time the mature avalanche was encountering air resistance problems. It was moving so fast that the air in front did not have time to get out of the way. The air was compressed and this caused its temperature to rise sharply. Pushed by the heavy avalanche cloud, an air blast began to develop in front of the rapidly moving snow, a travelling shock wave which could destroy a building as effectively as a bomb.

Now fully grown, the avalanche rumbled in its guts like a

flatulent giant. A million tons of snow and a hundred thousand tons of air were on the move, plunging down towards the mists at the bottom of the valley. By the time the mist was reached the avalanche was moving at over two hundred miles an hour with much greater internal gusting. The air blast hit the mist and squirted it aside violently to reveal, only momentarily, a few buildings. A fraction of a second later the main body of the avalanche hit the valley bottom.

The white death had come to Hukahoronui.

*

Dr Robert Scott regarded Harold Dobbs with a professionally clinical eye. Dobbs looked a mess. Apparently he had not shaved for a couple of days and the stubble was dirtily grey on his cheeks and chin. His eyes were bloodshot and red-rimmed and he sullenly refused to meet Scott's gaze. His fingers twitched jerkily in his lap as he sat in the armchair, his face averted.

Scott noted the nearly empty gin bottle and the half full glass on the occasional table by the chair, and said, 'That's the only reason I'm here. Mr Ballard asked me to call in. He's worried that you might be ill.'

'There's nothing wrong with me,' said Dobbs. His voice was so low that Scott had to bend forward and strain his ears to catch the words.

'Are you sure you're the best judge of that? I'm the doctor, you know. What about me opening the little black bag and giving you a check over?'

'Leave me alone!' flared Dobbs in a momentary access of energy. The effort seemed to exhaust him and he relapsed into inanition. 'Go away,' he whispered.

Scott did not go away. Instead he said, 'There must be something wrong, Harry. Why haven't you been working for the past couple of days?'

'My business,' mumbled Dobbs. He picked up the glass and drank.

'Not entirely. The company is entitled to some sort of explanation. After all, you *are* the mine manager. You can't just abdicate without saying anything.'

Dobbs eyed him sullenly. 'What do you want me to say?'

Scott used shock tactics. 'I want you to tell me why you're swinging the bloody lead, and why you're trying to climb into that gin bottle. How many of those have you gone through, anyway?' Dobbs was obstinately silent, and Scott persisted, 'You know what's going on out there, don't you?'

'Let Ian Bloody Ballard handle it,' snarled Dobbs. 'It's what he's paid for.'

'I think that's unreasonable. He's paid to do his own job, not yours as well.' Scott nodded towards the window. 'You should be out there helping Ballard and Joe Cameron. They've got their hands full right now.'

Venom jetted from Dobbs. 'He took my job, didn't he?'

Scott was puzzled. 'I don't know what you mean. He took nothing. What happened was that you stayed at home and cuddled up to a bottle.'

Dobbs flapped his hand; it wobbled loosely at the wrist as though he had no proper control over it. 'I don't mean that – I don't mean manager. The chairman promised me the job. Crowell said I'd go on the board and be managing director when Fisher went. But oh no! Along comes this young Pommy sprout and gets the job because he's called Ballard. As though the Ballards don't have enough money – they've got to take mine.'

Scott opened his mouth and then closed it again as Dobbs continued to speak. He looked pityingly at the older man as he ranted on. The floodgates of resentment had burst open and Dobbs was in full spate. Spittle drooled from the corner of his mouth. 'I'm getting no younger, you know. I've not saved as much as I hoped – those thieves on the stock exchange took a lot of my money. Rogues, the lot of them. I was going to be managing director – Crowell said so. I liked that because I'd have enough to retire on in a few years. Then the Ballard family decided otherwise. They not only took my job but they expect me to serve under a Ballard. Well, they can damn well think again.'

Scott said gently, 'Even so, that's no excuse for pulling out now without a word. Not when there's trouble. You won't be thanked for that.'

'Trouble!' Dobbs ground out the word. 'What does that whippersnapper know about trouble? I was running a mine when he was having his nappies changed!'

'It's not the mine,' said Scott. 'It's the town.'

'A lot of bloody nonsense. The man's an idiot. He's talking of spending millions to stop a few flakes of snow falling off a hillside. Where's the money to come from – I ask you that?

And now he's got everyone running in circles like chickens with their heads cut off. And they tell me he's closed down the mine. Wait until they hear about that in Auckland – to say nothing of London.'

'You seem well informed for one who hasn't been out of the house for a couple of days.'

Dobbs grunted. 'I have my friends. Quentin came in to see what we could do to stop this fool.' He picked up the glass and drank again, then shook his head. 'Quentin knows the score all right but there's nothing he can do. There's nothing any of us can do. It's all cut and dried, I tell you.'

Scott's eyes narrowed. It had not taken him long to come to the conclusion that Dobbs was definitely unbalanced. Resentment had been festering within him and something had happened to cause it to burst out, and he had a good idea of what it was. Deliberately he said. 'Do you think you could have handled the job of managing director?'

Rage burst from Dobbs. 'Of course I could,' he yelled. 'Of course I could have done it.'

Scott stood up. 'Well, it doesn't matter now. I think we'd better get you to a safer place than this. If anything happens out there this house will be one of the first hit.'

'Poppycock!' jeered Dobbs. 'A lot of flaming poppycock! 'I'm not moving and no one can make me.' He grinned, his lips drawn back ferally over his teeth. 'I might move if young Ballard comes here and apologizes for taking my job,' he said sarcastically.

Scott shrugged and picked up his bag. 'Suit yourself.'

'And close the door when you leave,' Dobbs shouted at Scott's back. He wrapped his arms about his thin body. 'I could have done the job,' he said aloud. 'I could have.'

When he heard Scott's car start up he picked up his drink and went to the window. His eyes followed the car until it went out of sight and then he shifted his gaze to the mine buildings. It was difficult to see very far because of the mist, but he could just make out the outline of the office block. He shook his head sorrowfully. 'Closed down!' he whispered. 'All closed down!'

Suddenly the mist cleared as though by magic and he felt a strange vibration through the soles of his feet. The office block, now clearly to be seen, lifted off its foundations and floated through the air towards him. He looked at it, mouth gaping, as it soared right over his house. He actually saw his own desk tumbling out of it before it went out of sight overhead.

Then the window smashed before his eyes and a sliver of glass drove through his throat. He was hurled across the room before the house exploded around him, but of course he did not know that the house was destroyed.

Harry Dobbs was the first man to be killed in Hukahoronui.

As Dr Scott left Dobbs's house he reflected on the strengths and weaknesses of the mind, particularly the weaknesses. Fundamentally a weak man, Dobbs had wanted the managing directorship and had deliberately suppressed the knowledge that he could not really handle it, and that knowledge was a canker inside him like a worm at the core of an apple.

The poor devil, thought Scott as he started his car. *A retreat from reality.*

He drove to the corner and turned, heading into town. he had gone about three hundred yards when he found there seemed to be something wrong with the steering – the car would not answer to the wheel and he had an eerie sensation of floating.

Then he saw, to his astonishment, that the car really was floating and that the wheels were a good three feet from the ground. He had not time even to blink before the car was flipped over on its back and he struck his head against the window plinth and was knocked unconscious.

When he came round he found he was still behind the wheel of the car, and the car was upright and on its four wheels. He lifted his hand and winced as his fingers explored the bump on his head. He looked about him and saw nothing; there was a heavy coating of snow on all the windows and they were opaque.

He got out of the car and stared blankly at what he saw. At first he could not recognize where he was, and when he did recognize his position his mind refused to believe it. A sudden spasm took him and he leaned against the car and vomited.

When he had recovered he looked again at the impossible. The mist was nearly gone and he could see as far as the Gap on the other side of the river. The *other* side. He moistened his lips. 'Right across!' he whispered. 'I've been carried right across the bloody river!'

He looked across the river to where the township of Hukahoronui should have been. There was nothing but a jumble of snow.

Afterwards, quite understandably, he measured the distance he had been taken by the avalanche His car had been carried nearly three-quarters of a mile horizontally, across the river, and lifted nearly three hundred feet vertically to be deposited on its four wheels a fair distance up the east slope. The engine had stopped but when he turned on the ignition it purred away as sweetly as ever.

Dr Robert Scott was caught in the avalanche and freakishly survived. He was lucky.

*

Ralph W. Newman was an American tourist. The 'W' in his name stood for Wilberforce, a fact he did not advertise. He had come to Hukahoronui for the skiing, having been led to believe by a man he had met in Christchurch that the slopes were exceptionally good. They may well have been but it takes more than snow on slopes to make a ski resort, and the essentials in Hukahoronui were lacking. There was no chair-lift, no organization and precious little après-ski conviviality. The two-bit dance they held Saturday nights at the hotel was not much of a substitute.

The man he had met in Christchurch who had told him of the charms of Hukahoronui was Charlie Peterson. Newman judged him to be a con man.

He had come to Hukahoronui for the skiing. He had certainly never expected to find himself in the middle of a line of twenty men, holding a long aluminium pole botched up out of a television antenna, and methodically driving it into the snow at the toe of each boot to the rasped commands of a Canadian scientist. It was all very improbable.

The man next to him nudged him and nodded at McGill. 'That joker would make a bloody good sergeant-major.'

'You're right about that,' said Newman. He felt the probe hit bottom and hauled it out.

'Think he's right about this avalanche?'

'He seems to know what he's doing. I ran across him up on the slope and he had some scientific gear with him. Said it was for testing snow.'

The other man leaned on his probe. 'He seems to know what

he's doing down here, too. I'd never have thought of this way of searching. Come to think of it, the subject never entered my mind until half an hour ago.'

The line of men advanced one foot and Newman set his toes against the tautened string. The string slackened and he drove the probe into the snow again. 'My name's Jack Haslam,' said the man. 'I work at the mine. I'm a stoper.'

Newman didn't know what a stoper was. He said, 'I'm Newman.'

'Where's your friend?'

'Miller? I don't know. He went out early this morning. What's a stoper?'

Haslam grinned. 'The chap at the sharp end of a mine. One of the elite. I get the gold out.'

In went the probes again. Newman grunted. 'If we have to do this for long it's going to be tiring.'

'Listen!' said Haslam. 'I think I hear a plane.'

They stopped and listened to the drone overhead. Soon the whole line of men had stopped and were staring at the greyness above. 'Come on!' called the team leader. 'Haven't you heard a plane before?'

The line moved ahead one foot and twenty probes were raised for driving downwards.

Newman worked methodically. Drive down left . . . haul out . . . drive down right . . . haul out . . . advance one foot . . . drive down left . . . haul out . . . drive down . . .

A sudden yell from McGill stopped him. There was something in the quality of McGill's shout that made the hair prickle at the nape of his neck and caused a sudden hollowness in his belly.

'Take cover!' shouted McGill. 'Take cover right now! You've got less than thirty seconds.'

Newman ran towards the place that had been allotted to him in case of emergency. His boots crunched crisply on the snow as he ran to the cluster of rocks, and he was aware of Haslam at his elbow. McGill was still shouting hoarsely as they reached the rocks.

Haslam grabbed Newman by the arm. 'This way.' He led Newman to a cranny not more than two feet wide and three feet high. 'In here.'

Newman crawled inside and found himself in a small cave. Haslam was breathing heavily when he hauled himself in. Between gasps he said, 'Used to play in here when I was a kid.'

173

Newman grunted. 'Thought you miners all came from outside.' He felt apprehensive. This was a silly time and place for inconsequential conversation.

More men came through the narrow hole until seven of them were jammed in the small cave. It was a tight fit. One of them was Brewer, the team leader, who said, 'Quiet, everyone!'

They heard a distant shouting which suddenly cut off, and then a faint faraway thread of noise difficult to interpret because it was like nothing any of them had heard before. Newman checked his watch. It was dark in the cave but he peered at the luminous second hand as it marched steadily around the dial. 'Must be more than thirty seconds.'

The air quivered imperceptibly and the noise grew a little louder. Suddenly there was a violent howl and air was sucked out of the cave. Newman choked and fought for breath and was thankful that the suction ceased as suddenly as it had begun.

The live rock underneath him quivered and there was a thunderous drumming noise overhead, deafening in its intensity. The air in the cave filled with fine particles of snow which settled everywhere. More and more snow came in and began to build up thickly about the tangle of huddled bodies.

The noise grew louder and Newman thought his eardrums would split.

Someone was shouting. He could not make out the words but, as the sound eased, he knew it was Brewer. 'Keep it out! Keep the bloody snow out!'

The men nearest the entrance scrabbled with their hands but the snow came swirling in faster and faster, much more quickly than they could cope with. 'Cover your mouths,' shouted Brewer, and Newman brought his arm across his face with difficulty because of the restricted space.

He felt the snow build up about him, cold but dry. Finally, what space in the cave not occupied by bodies was filled completely with snow.

The noise stopped.

Newman kept still, breathing deeply and evenly. He wondered how long he could go on breathing like that – he did not know if air could penetrate the snow mass. Presently he sensed someone stirring and he made a tentative movement himself.

He was able to push with his arm and found that by pushing he could compress the snow into a smaller volume and thus make a bigger air space. From what seemed a hundred miles away he heard a faint voice and he stopped moving so that he could listen. 'Can anyone hear me?'

'Yes,' he shouted. 'Who are you?'

'Brewer.'

It seemed pretty silly that you had to shout at the top of your voice to a man not many feet away. 'Newman here,' he yelled. He remembered that Brewer had been nearest to the cave entrance. 'Can you get out?'

There was a pause and presently he heard another voice. 'Anderson here.'

Brewer called, 'Not a chance. There's a lot of snow outside.'

Newman was busy clearing a space. He pushed the powdery snow away, plastering it on the rock wall of the cave. He shouted to tell Brewer what he was doing, and Brewer told everybody else to get busy and do the same. He also asked them to call out their names.

Newman was aware of the dead weight of Haslam next to him. Haslam had not moved or made a sound. He put his hand out and groped for Haslam's face and found his cheek. Still Haslam did not move, so Newman pinched the flesh between thumb and forefinger very sharply. Haslam remained inert.

'There's a guy called Haslam here,' he said. 'He's unconscious.'

Now that there was increased air space there was no need to shout. Brewer said, 'Wait a minute. I'm trying to get my torch from my pocket.' There were gasping sounds in the darkness and the wriggling of contorted bodies, then suddenly a beam of light shot out.

Newman blinked, then turned to Haslam. He moved his hand and pointed. 'Shine that light here.' He bent over Haslam, and Brewer crawled forward with the light. Newman felt for Haslam's wrist pulse but could detect no movement so he leaned down and pressed his ear against Haslam's chest. When he lifted his head he turned towards the light. 'I think the guy's dead.'

'How can he be dead?' demanded Brewer.

'Give me the light.' Newman shone it on Haslam's face which was leaden grey. 'He didn't die of asphyxiation, that's for sure. I've seen that and he's the wrong colour. He'd be purple.'

'There's snow in his mouth,' said Brewer.

'Yeah.' Newman passed back the light and put his finger in

175

Haslam's mouth. 'But not much. Not enough to stop him breathing. Can you guys give me some room? I'm going to try the kiss of life.'

Room was made with difficulty. 'Maybe he died of shock,' someone suggested.

Newman breathed air into Haslam's lungs and then pumped his chest. He kept it up for a long time but Haslam did not react. All that happened was that his body became colder. After fifteen minutes Newman stopped. 'No good. He's gone.' He turned his head to Brewer. 'Better switch off that light. It won't last forever.'

Brewer snapped off the light and there was darkness and silence, each man occupied with his own thoughts. At last Newman said, 'Brewer.'

'Yes?'

'Nobody is going to find us with probes – not in this cave. How much snow do you reckon is out there?'

'Hard to tell.'

'We'd better find out. It looks as though we'll have to save ourselves.' Newman groped about and found Haslam's hat which he placed over the dead man's face. It was a futile but human gesture there in the darkness. He remembered Haslam's last words – *Used to play in here when I was a kid.* It was too goddamn ironic to be true.

There were six men jammed in that narrow cleft in the rock: Newman, Brewer, Anderson, Jenkins, Fowler and Castle.

And the dead man – Haslam.

*

Turi Buck was coping remarkably well with the influx of children. The house under the great rock of Kamakamaru was large – too large now that his family had grown up and gone out into the world – and he welcomed the bustle and clamour. He relished less the glacial eye of Miss Frobisher, the schoolteacher who accompanied the children. There is something about schoolteaching in isolated communities which tends to acidulate the feminine temperament and Miss Frobisher had a high acid content. Turi listened to her comments which tended to a criticism of the civil authorities, the stupidity of men, and other cognate matters. He took her measure and thereafter ignored her.

His daughter-in-law, who was his housekeeper, and his granddaughter were occupied in laying out bedding and allocating quarters for the horde of noisy small fry. This was woman's work and they would brook no interference, so Turi went to the back of the house to see how the emergency generator was to be installed.

Jock McLean, the mechanical engineer from the mine, was a Scot from the Clyde. He tapped the toe of his boot on the level area of concrete where the lines for hanging laundry were suspended from steel poles. 'And how thick is this, Mr Buck?'

'My name is Turi, and the concrete is six inches thick. I laid it myself.'

'Good. We drill four holes for the foundation bolts an' anchor 'em wi' masonry plugs. We don't want this thing shiftin'.'

'How are you going to drill the holes?' queried Turi. 'We have no power.'

McLean jerked his thumb over his shoulder. 'Air compressor wi' an air drill.'

Turi looked down at the concrete and shook his head. 'Not there. Can your drill make holes in rock?'

'Wi' a diamond drill I can go through armour plate.'

Turi pointed. 'Then put the machine over there. Fasten it to the rock.'

McLean stared at the old man, and smiled. 'I think six inches o' concrete should hold her,' he said tolerantly.

'Have you been in an avalanche, Mr McLean?' asked Turi softly.

'People call me Jock.' McLean shook his head. 'We didna' have them in the Gorbals – not when I was a laddie there forty years gone by. Maybe at Aviemore.'

'I have been in an avalanche. I have dug dead bodies from the snow.' Turi nodded his head towards the north. 'Just over there – about two hundred yards away. Put your machine on the rock.'

McLean scratched his head. 'Are they as bad as that?'

'When the avalanche comes it will be worse than anything you have ever known in your life.'

'I doubt it,' said McLean. 'I went ashore at Anzio.'

'I also have been in a war,' said Turi. 'Possibly a worse war than yours. I was in Flanders in 1918. When the avalanche comes it will be worse than that.'

'Aye, well.' McLean looked about. 'We'll have to find a flat bit o' rock an' that willna' be easy.' He strode away, his eyes roving. At last he thumped with his heel. 'It's flat enough here. This'll do.'

Turi walked over and stood on the place which McLean marked. He looked up at Kamakamaru and shook his head. 'This is not the place.'

'An' why not?' demanded McLean.

'In 1912 my father had a workshop here. It was built very strongly because my father believed in building strongly. When the snow came down that winter the workshop vanished. We never found so much as a brick.' He pointed. 'I believe that when the wind comes, followed by the powder, there is an eddy here. This place is not safe.'

'You're a cheery soul,' said McLean. 'What about over there, right under the rock?'

'That would do,' said Turi gravely. 'In 1912 I had some rabbits in a hutch there. The hutch wasn't strongly made because my father didn't make it – I did. But the rabbits were unharmed.'

'Well I'll be damned!' said McLean. 'Let's go an' see what the footin' is like.'

It proved to be satisfactory. Turi said, 'It will be all right here.' He went away, leaving McLean staring after him.

A truckload of canned goods had arrived and there were some drums of fuel oil. Turi showed Len Baxter and Dave Scanlon where to put the oil and then supervised the unloading of the food by some of the older children. After he had done this he went to the back of the house where he found Baxter and Scanlon helping McLean with the generator.

McLean had drilled four holes in the rock and had inserted bolts in the holes, secured by expanding fasteners. Turi marvelled at the speed with which McLean had drilled the holes; evidently McLean had been right to trust his diamond-tipped drill. Now he had erected a tripod and was lowering the generator by means of a block and tackle, while Scanlon and Baxter guided it so that the bolts would enter the holes in the base plate.

At last it was done and McLean grunted with satisfaction. 'Right, boys,' he said, and took four steel nuts from his pocket. 'I can carry on from here.'

Dave Scanlon nodded. 'I'd like to get back. I want a word with Maureen.' The two men went away and presently Turi heard the truck start up and drive away.

Turi's daughter-in-law came out with a laden tray. 'Will you have some tea, Mr McLean? And there are home-made cakes.'

McLean dropped the nuts back into his pocket. 'I'll be glad o' that. Thanks, Mrs . . . Miss . . . er . . .'

'This is Ruihi, my daughter-in-law,' said Turi.

McLean's eyes lit up as he bit into a cake. 'Good,' he said rather indistinctly. 'An old widower like me doesn't often get the chance o' real home cookin'.'

Ruihi smiled at him and went away, leaving the tray, and Turi and McLean spent a few minutes chatting over the tea and cakes. Presently McLean helped himself to a second cup of tea, then waved his arm towards the valley. 'Those dead bodies you were speakin' of a while back – how many were there?'

'Seven,' said Turi. 'A whole family – the Baileys. There was a house there. It was completely destroyed.' He told McLean of how he had helped his father dig.

McLean shook his head. 'Now that's a terrible thing. Not somethin' for a laddie of twelve to be doin'.' He finished the tea and looked at his watch. 'Well, this isna' tyin' down yon generator.' He took the nuts from his pocket and picked up a spanner. 'I'll secure it.'

Turi cocked his head on one side. He had heard a noise and, for a moment, thought it was the aeroplane that had been flying overhead. Then he heard and recognized the eerie bass hum and a higher whistling sound, something he had not heard since 1912.

He grabbed McLean's arm. 'Too late. Into the house – quick.'

McLean resisted. 'What the hell! I've got to – '

Turi hauled at him. 'The snow is coming,' he yelled.

McLean looked at the old man's contorted face and believed him instantly. They both ran to the back door, which Turi immediately slammed closed and locked as soon as they were inside. He took a step forward. 'The children . . .'

McLean saw Turi's mouth opening and closing but he did not hear the end of that sentence because the noise reached a deafening pitch.

Then the avalanche hit.

McLean had heard the barrage which opened the battle of El Alamein and that, in his opinion, had been the ultimate in noise, even exceeding that of the boiler shop where he had been apprenticed on the Clyde. He now knew with a depressing certainty that he had a new measure of the ultimate.

The fundamental note was low cycle, deep in the bass – a sound which grabbed his stomach as though he was being squeezed by a giant hand. He opened his mouth and air was expelled forcibly from his lungs as his diaphragm kicked sickeningly. Superimposed on the bass was a whole series of high-pitched whistles of ear-piercing intensity, tones which collided with each other to produce strange and eerie harmonics. He had the impression that the sound entering his ears was compressing his brain.

The old house quivered on its foundations. The light had suddenly gone as though by an eclipse of the sun, and all he saw through the window in front of him was a dirty grey blur. The house lurched as it received two swift buffets and the windows smashed inwards. He heard no sound of breaking glass.

Fine snow dust jetted into the room through the broken panes as though squirted from a great hose pipe. The dust hit the wall to one side of McLean and sprayed outwards, and then it stopped coming in as suddenly as it had begun. Instead there was an opposite reaction, although not as strong. Air was sucked from the room, taking some of the snow with it.

It seemed to McLean that he had been standing there for an eternity. He was wrong, of course, because, from first to last, the avalanche swept by the rock of Kamakamaru in under twenty seconds. When it was over he stood as still as a statue. He was covered from head to foot with fine snow powder which gave him the appearance of a ghost. There was a ringing sound in his ears and he heard distant cries which seemed to be coming from as far away as the town.

Turi Buck stirred. Slowly he lifted his hands and put them to his ears, and he shook his head as though to assure himself that it would not fall off his trunk. He said, 'It is over.' His voice crashed out unnaturally loudly as it reverberated in the cavities of his skull. He turned his head and looked to McLean, saying again, 'It is over.'

McLean did not move so Turi put out his hand and touched him gently on the arm. A shudder went through McLean and he looked at Turi. His eyes were glazed and staring. Turi said, 'It's finished, Jock.'

McLean saw Turi's lips moving and heard his voice coming as though from a long way off, almost drowned out by the persistent buzzing in his ears. He frowned stiffly and deep cracks appeared in the powdering of snow that covered his lean face, accentuating the grooves that ran from the base of his nose to the corners of his mouth. He swallowed convulsively and his hearing improved. The distant cries he had heard before became louder, shrilling in his ears almost like the noise of the avalanche.

Every child in the house was screaming.

'The children,' said Turi. 'We must see to the children.'

'Yes,' said McLean. His voice came out creakily. He looked down at his hands and saw that he was still holding four steel nuts in his left hand and a spanner in his right hand. He took a deep breath and looked at Turi again. 'You're bleeding,' he said.

The cut on Turi Buck's face, caused by a fragment of flying glass, was the only physical wound suffered by anyone in the house. Psychic wounds were something else again.

Other houses in the valley were not as lucky.

*

Matt Houghton was confident he had nothing to fear from any snow falling down the west slope. His house was built on the other side of the river and a considerable way up the east slope so that it had a commanding view of the valley. The view from his front porch was a source of considerable satisfaction to Matt Houghton and it was his habit, on fine summer days, to sit there and drink beer in the evenings. He had a streak of vanity and, since his election as mayor of Hukahoronui, he liked to think he was overlooking his kingdom. To his mind, the view from the house added two thousand dollars to the value of the property.

Not that he was sitting on his front porch this Sunday morning. For one thing, it was too cold, and for another, the porch was cluttered with hastily packed suitcases brought by his unexpected visitors. His wife, Mamie, was in the kitchen making gallons of tea and cutting piles of sandwiches, and he was playing the genial host.

'It's so very good of you to have us here,' said Mrs Jarvis tremulously. Mrs Jarvis was the oldest person in Hukahoronui. She was eighty-two.

'No need to thank me.' Houghton laughed jovially. 'I'm only doing it to get your vote in the next election.'

She looked at him uncertainly, then said, 'Do you think we're safe here?'

'Of course we're safe,' he assured her. 'This house has been here a long time – second oldest in the valley. It's not been knocked down by an avalanche yet, so I can't see it happening now.'

Sam Critchell, sitting in a big over-stuffed armchair, said, 'You never know. Avalanches can do funny things.'

'What do you know about avalanches, Sam?' Houghton's voice was scornful.

Critchell placidly continued to fill his pipe with liver-spotted hands. 'I've seen a few.'

'Where?'

'At the end of the war I was in the mountains back of Trieste. There were a lot of avalanches that winter. They used the army for rescue work.' He struck a match. 'I saw enough to know that avalanches can be damned unexpected.'

'Well, if I thought this house wasn't safe I wouldn't be here, would I?' demanded Houghton rhetorically.

A long plume of smoke jetted from Critchell's lips. 'Neither would I. All I said is that avalanches can do funny things.'

A tall, stringy woman walked over to Houghton and he took the opportunity to escape this pointless conversation. 'Well, how are things, Mrs Fawcett?' he asked heartily.

Mrs Fawcett carried a clipboard. She was one of the live-wires of the community. She ran the dramatic society with a rod of iron and was the mainspring of the debating society. Her son, Bobby, ran the scout troop. She was bossy and a born organizer and Houghton always had the uneasy feeling that she regarded him with contempt. She consulted the list on the clipboard, and said, 'All here except for Jack Baxter.'

'How many in all?'

'Jack will make twenty-five. With your family there will be twenty-nine of us here.'

Houghton grunted. 'Let's hope the food holds out.'

She gave him the peculiar look she reserved for fools. 'Old people have small appetites,' she said tartly. 'I wonder what's keeping Jack?'

'Who is bringing him?'

'Jim Hatherley.' She held her head on one side and looked up at the ceiling. 'That aeroplane is here again.'

'Doesn't that fool of a pilot know that any sound can start an avalanche?' said Houghton irritably. He left the room, went through the hall and out on to the porch where he stared at the sky. There was nothing to be seen.

He was about to go back inside when Jim Hatherley ran up, somewhat out of breath. 'I've got trouble, Mr Houghton. Jack Baxter slipped on the snow when he was getting out of the car. I'm pretty sure he's bust his leg.'

'Oh, hell!' said Houghton. 'Where is he?'

'Lying by the car just around the corner.'

'Better telephone the doctor; the phone's in the hall. I'll go down and see to Jack.' Houghton paused, biting his lip. He did not like Mrs Fawcett, but she'd know what to do about a broken leg. 'And ask Mrs Fawcett to come out.'

'Okay.' Hatherley went into the house and looked about for Mrs Fawcett. He did not see her but he did see the telephone so he decided to make the call first. He picked up the handset and got Maureen Scanlon at the exchange.

'What number do you want?'

Hatherley said, 'Maureen, this is Jim Hatherley at Matt Houghton's house. Old Jack Baxter took a bad fall and we think he's broken his leg. Do you think you can find Dr Scott?'

There was a pause before she said, 'I'll try.' The line clicked as she broke the connection.

Hatherley tapped on the telephone table as he waited to be put through. He looked about him and saw Mrs Fawcett just entering the hall. He waved her over and rapidly explained what had happened to Baxter. 'Oh, the poor man,' she said. 'I'll go at once.'

She turned, took two steps in the direction of the front door, and died.

When the avalanche hit the valley bottom the dense cloud of snow powder and air ceased to pick up speed but it did not come to a halt at once. The energy it contained had to be dissipated by friction against the ground and the surrounding air and it continued to cross the valley quite rapidly.

It was only when it got to the other side that it really began to slow down. Now it was climbing the east slope gravity was working against it and eventually it came to a halt a hundred yards from the Houghton house and perhaps a hundred feet of vertical distance below it. There was no danger of Matt Houghton's house being overwhelmed with snow.

But the air blast did not stop. It came up the hill from underneath the house moving at about one hundred and fifty miles an hour. It caught under the eaves and ripped off the roof. Because of this the walls were no longer tied together so when the blast slammed at them the house exploded as though hit by a bomb. All who were in the house at that time – twenty-eight people – died. Some were struck by masonry, some were trapped in the wreckage and died of exposure. Two died of heart attacks. Some died immediately while others died in hospital a few days later.

But all in the house died.

Matt Houghton was not in the house, and neither was Jack Baxter. When the house was hit Houghton was bending over Baxter and asking, in what he conceived to be the cool, professional tones of a doctor, where the pain was. He was protected by the car, and the car was protected more by a small hillock hardly more than three feet high which stood between it and the descending hillside. When the air blast roared up the hill and hit the house the car did nothing more than rock heavily on its springs.

Houghton looked up, mystified, but not alarmed. He looked under the car and, finding nothing, he stood up and walked around it. Wind beat at him, the aftermath of the air blast, but it was not so abnormal as to tickle his curiosity. Standing on the other side of the car, he could see into the valley. The curtain of mist had been torn aside and his gaze shifted as he tried to fit what he saw with what he expected.

He shook his head bemusedly and climbed up on to the hillock to get a better view. At first he thought he could not be looking in the right direction so he changed his stance, but that made no difference. His problem was that he could not find the town of which he was mayor.

He rubbed the back of his neck perplexedly and then solved the problem to his own satisfaction. Of course, that was it! There had been a heavy fall of snow during the night and the town was covered in snow. It must have been a heavy snowfall, indeed, to cover the buildings so they could not be seen, but what with that and the mist it was not entirely unexpected.

Baxter moaned behind the car, and Houghton thought it was time to get Mrs Fawcett. He turned, still standing on the hillock, to go up to the house, and then stopped dead. *There was no house!* There was no front porch, no tall stone chimney – nothing! If he had been a little farther up the hill he would have seen the wrecked foundations and the scattered bodies, but from where he stood it was as though the house with the two-thousand dollar view had never existed.

A strangled noise came from him and froth came from his lips. Stiffly he toppled forward and never knew when he hit the ground.

Presently a querulous voice said, 'Matt! Matt? Where is everybody?'

Jack Baxter, his leg broken but untouched by the avalanche, was still very much alive. He did not understand then, or ever after, how lucky he was to have broken his leg at the exact moment he did.

Stacey Cameron took her father's car and drove it to Dr Scott's house which was where he held his surgery. Because she had first-aid training she had volunteered to help on the medical side should such help be necessary, and Scott, being the only doctor, was the hub around which all medical problems revolved. She drew up behind a station wagon which was parked outside Scott's house.

Liz Peterson was there. 'Hi, there,' said Stacey. 'You a volunteer nurse, too?'

'More of an almoner,' said Liz. 'Dr Scott wants us to round up medical supplies. He's had to go because Ballard wants him to look in on Harry Dobbs.'

'Harry?' Stacey shook her head. 'Isn't he at the mine office?'

'No,' said Liz. 'That seems to be the trouble.'

Stacey offered Liz a cigarette. 'Talking about Ian – what exactly happened last night?'

'My idiot brother happened,' said Liz. 'Charlie's a great big pain in the neck.' She accepted a light. 'Tell me, how are things in California?'

Stacey was puzzled. 'What do you mean – how are things?'

'Conditions of living – and working. I'm thinking of leaving here.'

'That's a laugh,' said Stacey. 'I'm thinking of moving in here.'

Liz smiled. 'Perhaps we can do an even swap: jobs, houses – everything.'

'I don't live in a house. I rent an apartment.'

'Any particular reason for burying yourself in a hole like Huka?'

'My father.' Stacey hesitated. 'And other reasons.'

'What's the other reason's name?' asked Liz drily.

'You were dancing with him last night.'

Liz raised her eyebrows. 'And at your invitation, too. I'm not blind or stupid, you know. You were talking to me, and then you went to talk to him. Ian wasn't drunk but he'd had just enough to say, "I'll dance with Liz Peterson and to hell with her quarrelsome brothers." And you gave him the idea. That's a funny way for a girl to act towards her reason.'

'I don't want to appear possessive. At least, not at this delicate stage in our relationship.'

'And what stage is that?'

Stacey smiled. 'The stage at which he hasn't noticed I exist.' She sighed. 'And I only have a few days more.'

'Well, he has a lot on his mind right now. Maybe your chance will come during the avalanche. All you have to do is to be gallantly rescued by Ian Ballard. Then he'll have to marry you – it's as good as making you pregnant, according to all the films I've seen.'

'What do you think of him?'

'A very nice man,' said Liz coolly. 'But I go more for his friend, Mike McGill.' She shook her head. 'There's no joy there.'

'Why not?'

'He says he's been bitten before. His wife divorced him three years ago; she said she couldn't live with a snowman who's never at home. Mike said he couldn't blame her. Who'd want a husband who alternates between the North Pole and the South Pole like a yo-yo?'

Stacey nodded commiseratingly. 'Tell me – what's this quarrel between your brothers and Ian?'

'Too old to bear repeating,' said Liz briefly. She stubbed out her cigarette. 'This isn't stocking up the medical supplies. Let's get busy.'

They drove to the chemist's shop in the main street and Liz got out of the car and tried the door, which proved to be locked. She knocked repeatedly but there was no answer and finally she gave up. 'That bloody fool, Rawson, was told to be here,' she said angrily. 'Why the devil isn't he?'

'Perhaps he's been held up.'

'I'll hold him up when I find him,' said Liz grimly. She looked past Stacey at a truck coming down the street, then stepped forward and waved it down. As it stopped she called, 'Len, have you seen Rawson anywhere?'

Len Baxter shook his head and turned to consult Scanlon. 'Dave says he saw him going into the hotel about half an hour ago.'

'Thanks.' Liz turned to Stacey. 'Let's part him from his beer. Come on.'

In any community there is a sizeable proportion of fools, and a large number of these were congregated together in the Hotel D'Archiac. The philosophy of the management appeared to be 'Business as usual', and perhaps business was better than usual. A rumble of male voices came from the crowded bar and the dining-room was being prepared for lunch as though it was any other Sunday of the year.

Liz saw Eric standing at the entrance to the bar and brought him across the lobby with a jerk of her head. 'What's going on here? Don't these people know what's happening?'

'I've told them and I've told them,' said Eric. 'It doesn't make a blind bit of difference. There are a lot of miners in there being stirred up by Bill Quentin. They seem to be holding a protest meeting about the mine being closed down.'

'It's the first I've heard of it,' said Stacey. 'Dad said nothing about it.'

'Bill Quentin says it's a certainty.'

Liz looked at a waitress carrying a loaded tray of drinks into the dining-room. 'This place should be closed down. Close it, Eric. We do own half the business.'

Eric shrugged. 'You know as well as I do that Johnnie and me are just sleeping partners. We agreed with Weston that we shouldn't interfere with the day-to-day running. I've talked to him, but he says he's staying open.'

'Then he's a damned fool.'

'He's a fool who's coining money.' Eric waved his hand towards the bar. 'Look at it.'

'To the devil with them!' snapped Liz. 'Is Rawson in there?'

'Yes, I saw him talking to – '

'Get him out. I want him to open his shop. We need medical supplies.'

'Okay.' Eric went into the bar and was away a long time. Presently he came back with Rawson, a tall, gaunt man who wore thick-lensed spectacles.

Liz took a step forward and said crisply, 'Mr Rawson, you promised to be at your shop half an hour ago.'

Rawson smiled. 'Do you think this situation is so serious, Miss Peterson?' His tone was of amused tolerance.

Liz took a deep breath and said with iron control, 'Whether it's serious or not, the fact remains that you weren't at your shop as you promised.'

Rawson cast a longing look at the bar. 'Oh, very well,' he said ungraciously. 'I suppose I'd better come.'

'Are you staying here?' Liz asked Eric.

He shook his head. 'I'm going to join Johnnie. This crowd won't be shifted.'

'Do it now,' she advised. 'Come on, Mr Rawson.' As they left the hotel Stacey looked over her shoulder and saw Quentin come out of the bar to join Eric. They seemed to be starting an argument.

When Rawson unlocked his shop he said fussily, 'I don't know that I'm not breaking the law by doing this.'

'Pharmacists are allowed to open on Sunday in emergencies,' said Liz. 'I seem to know more about the law than you do.'

Rawson went inside and snapped a light switch. When nothing happened he said, 'Oh, I forgot. Never mind, I have a few candles at the back.'

Liz said, 'It's light enough without candles. Let's get on with it.'

Rawson went behind the counter and adopted a professional stance. 'Well, ladies,' he said brightly. 'What can I do for you?' Stacey suppressed a smile. She had half-expected him to put on a white coat.

'I have a list,' said Liz, and gave it to him.

Rawson scanned the papers slowly, going with maddening deliberation from one paper to the next. 'My!' he said at last. 'This *is* a lot.'

'Yes,' agreed Liz patiently.

Rawson looked up. 'Who is going to pay for all this?'

Liz looked at him expressionlessly and then glanced at Stacey who stood with open mouth. She leaned over the counter, and said sweetly, 'Would you like payment before or after delivery, Mr Rawson?'

Obtusely, he did not catch the danger underlying her tone. 'Well, this lot will take quite a time to add up.' He chuckled. 'It's a good thing I bought one of those new electronic calculators. It makes things like this so easy, you know.'

Liz slammed her hand on the counter. 'Start producing, Rawson. If you're worried about the money put it on Johnnie's account – or don't you think his credit is good?'

'Oh no, that will be quite all right,' said Rawson hastily. He peered at the list again. 'Right, let's begin. Bandages – ten dozen boxes of two-inch, ten dozen boxes of three-inch, the same of six . . .' He broke off. 'We'll have to go into the stock room for those.'

'Right, let's get into the stock room. Where is it?'

'Wait a minute,' he said. 'There's something not quite right here, Miss Peterson. All this morphine – here on the third page.' He held it out to her. 'I can't really issue that without a prescription. And the quantity!' He shook his head. 'I could lose my licence.'

'If you turn to the last page you'll find Dr Scott's signature.'

'That's not good enough, Miss Peterson. For one thing, page three isn't signed, and for another, it should be done on the prescribed form. The Dangerous Drugs Act is very precise about this kind of thing. This is most irregular and I'm surprised that Dr Scott should have countenanced it.'

'For Christ's sake!' exploded Liz. Rawson was shocked and startled. 'You could be killed at any time and you're worried about names on bloody bits of paper. Now look here: if you don't get moving and produce everything on that list I'll have Arthur Pye confiscate your whole damned stock. He'd do it, too.'

Rawson was affronted. 'You can't threaten me with the police!'

'What do you mean – I can't? I've just done it, haven't I? Stacey, use that telephone and find Arthur Pye.'

Rawson threw up his hands. 'Oh, very well – but I insist on delivering any drugs on the dangerous list to Dr Scott personally.'

'Good!' said Liz briskly. 'That means you'll be helping at last. Where's the stock room?'

Rawson waved. 'That door back there.' As Liz strode towards it he said, 'But it's locked. Can't be too careful about things like that.' He joined her and took a chain from his pocket on the end of which dangled a bunch of keys. He unlocked the door. 'All the bandages are on those shelves to the right. I'll be in the dispensary getting the drugs together.'

The two girls marched past him and he turned, shaking his head at the impetuosity of modern youth. Who would have thought that a nicely brought up girl like Elizabeth Peterson was capable of using language which hitherto he had only associated with bar-rooms?

He went into the dispensary and unlocked the cupboard in

which he kept the registered drugs. He took a box and began filling it with ampoules, keeping careful count and making a note every so often in the Poisons Register. This naturally took up time. He was a most meticulous man.

He was not to know it but the combination of his broken promise and his scrupulosity meant that he was a dead man. If he had been on time at the shop he would have been there when the girls arrived and there would have been no waste of time in extracting him from the hotel bar. His meticulousness in putting everything in the Poisons Register meant that he was still in the dispensary when the avalanche hit.

When the front of the shop caved in, the shock transmitted through the foundations caused a half-gallon bottle to leap off a shelf and fall and smash on the table before him. It was full of hydrochloric acid which splashed all over his face and the front of his body.

Liz Peterson was saved by something which had begun five years earlier. In the winter of that year, which had also been cold, a drop of water had frozen in a minute crack in the concrete which formed the footing of the rear wall of the stock room. The water drop, turning into ice, had expanded and widened the crack. The following year the same thing happened, but with a little more water, and year by year the crack had widened until at this time it constituted a serious danger to the stability of the wall.

Had Rawson known of this he would have had it repaired immediately, being the sort of man he was. But he did not know of it because it was underground. Consequently, when the shock of the avalanche struck, the rear wall constituted a weakness and it gave way easily and without resistance.

Liz was hurled forward against stacked boxes of bandages which cushioned the shock, although the edge of a shelf broke two of her ribs. The whole mass, shelving, boxes and the bodies of Liz and Stacey, was forced against the rear wall which gave immediately, and Liz was precipitated through the air in a tangle of streaming and unwinding bandages.

She fell on to snow, and more snow covered her, holding her body and clamping her arms and legs. She was quite conscious and rational and she wondered if she were about to die. She did not know that Stacey Cameron was in much the same position not more than ten feet away. Both girls lost consciousness at about the same time, roughly one-and-a-half minutes after being buried.

Rawson was also buried about twenty yards away and was dying slowly and quite painfully as the acid ate at his flesh. Fortunately, when he opened his mouth to scream it filled with soft snow and he died mercifully and quickly of asphyxia.

The Hotel D'Archiac, that abode of fools, was speedily demolished. Jeff Weston, the king of fools who had been coining it, was parted from more than his money. Business was so brisk that he had gone behind the bar to help the overworked bartender and when the building was hit he was struck on the head by a bottle of scotch whisky which left the shelf behind him like a projectile.

Most of the men who were drinking in the bar were killed by flying bottles. Behind the bottles came the whole wall and, after that, came the snow which covered everything. They died because they were fools, although a cynic might have said they died of acute alcoholism. But there were no cynics left in Hukahoronui after that Sunday morning.

Those in the dining-room died when the roof fell in. Alice Harper, the waitress who had served McGill with colonial goose on the previous evening, was killed by a heavy suitcase which fell from the bedrooms above. The suitcase belonged to the American, Newman, who had his own troubles at the time.

Newman's room no longer existed as a room and the same applied to the room next door which had been taken by his friend, Miller. Miller was most fortunate to be absent.

Bill Quentin was exceptionally lucky because he had left the hotel with Eric Peterson only moments before the hotel was destroyed. He had gone into the lobby from the bar and found Eric. 'Look here,' he said. 'Does the council know what's going on?'

'About what?'

'About closing the mine.'

'The mine has been closed. Bailard closed it this morning.'

'I don't mean that. I mean closing it permanently.'

Eric shook his head a little wearily. 'No one has said anything to us – yet.'

'Well, aren't you going to do anything about it?'

'What the hell do you expect us to do when we haven't been notified officially? I don't believe it will close.'

Quentin snorted. 'Ballard said it would. He said it at a meeting yesterday. He said the company couldn't afford to spend

191

money on avalanche protection. I think this avalanche scare is a lot of balls. I think the company is trying to weasel out.'

'Weasel out of what? I don't know what you're talking about.' Eric moved towards the door.

'You know what these big companies are like.' Quentin took a couple of steps to keep up with him. 'I hear that Ballard is related to the big boss back in London. Know anything about that?'

'I've heard it.' Eric quickened his pace. 'It's true.'

'I'll bet he's been sent to do the hatchet job. Hey – where are you going?'

'To join Johnnie in the old Fisher house.'

'I think I'll come with you,' said Quentin. 'I think the council ought to know about this. Where's Matt Houghton?'

'At home.'

They stepped off the pavement, and Quentin said, 'That means he's the only sensible man around here. Everybody else is shutting themselves up in holes.'

Eric glanced at him. 'Like me?'

'Don't tell me you believe in Doomsday?'

Eric stopped on the opposite pavement. His back was to the Fisher house and so he did not see his brother run across the road towards the telephone exchange. 'Johnnie's no fool and he believes it,' he said deliberately. 'And I'm beginning to.'

He resumed his stride at a quicker pace and Quentin, a much smaller man, was forced to trot to keep up with him. They entered the house and Eric glanced into the empty room off the hall. 'He'll be in the cellar.'

The two men were just going down the steps into the basement when the house was hit. Eric tumbled the rest of the way and fell on top of young Mary Rees, breaking her leg. Bill Quentin fell on top of Eric and broke Eric's arm. He himself was quite unhurt; he was untouched and inviolate and was not even scratched by the falling rubble of the collapsing house.

*

After shouting his warning, McGill dropped into his own selected shelter, jostled by Ballard. He grabbed the telephone which had been installed by a mine electrician and rang the exchange which was busy. 'For Christ's sake, come on!' he muttered.

He waited for ten seconds which were more like ten minutes

before the operator, Maureen Scanlon, came on the line. He said quickly, 'Plug me into John Peterson, Mrs Scanlon, and then get the hell out of there – fast.'

'I understand,' she said, and the ringing tone came into his ear.

'John Peterson here.'

'McGill. Get your people under cover. She's coming down.'

'What about Maureen Scanlon?'

'I've told her to get out. You can see the exchange from where you are. Keep an eye open for her.'

'Okay,' Peterson slammed down the telephone and snapped at Bobby Fawcett, 'Everyone downstairs. Move it, Bobby.'

Fawcett left the room on the run and Peterson looked out of the window at the telephone exchange up the street. The street was deserted with not a sign of movement. He thumped the table nervously and wondered what to do.

As soon as Mrs Scanlon had put the call through to Peterson she took off the headset, stood up, and lifted her coat from a hook. She knew exactly what to do because Peterson had told her. She was to join him in the old Fisher building, one of the few houses in town which had a basement. She did not bother to put on the coat but had taken only one step to the door when the switchboard buzzed at her. She turned back, plugged in and lifted the headset. 'What number do you want?'

'Maureen, this is Jim Hatherley at Matt Houghton's house. Old Jack Baxter took a bad fall and we think he's broken his leg. Do you think you can find Dr Scott?'

She bit her lip. 'I'll try.' She plugged in a jack and rang Scott's house.

In the Fisher house Peterson made up his mind. He ran from the room and into the hall. A freckled-faced fourteen-year-old girl was standing in the doorway, and he said, 'Into the basement, Mary. On the double.'

The crackle of authority in his voice moved her body without her consciously willing it. But she said, 'Where are you going?'

'To fetch Mrs Scanlon.' He ran out into the street, and Mary Rees went down into the basement to join the others.

Peterson ran up the empty street towards the telephone exchange. He reached the corner where a road ran off to the left towards the mine, cast a hurried glance along it, and skidded to a frantic halt. What he saw was incredible. The mist was gone and he could see as far as the mine, but that was not what held his attention. A building was flying through the air directly at him, disintegrating at it came, and in that split second he recognized the mine office block.

He jumped back and dived behind a concrete wall, landing heavily, and then he twisted over so that he could see. There was a fierce blast of wind in his face and then he saw the office block fall squarely on to the telephone exchange, obliterating it.

The wind gusted at him again and he felt a tremendous pain in his chest. *Heart attack!* he thought dimly, *I'm having a heart attack.* Even while fighting the pain he lost consciousness and died very soon thereafter.

In the basement of the Fisher house Mary Rees added her screams to those of the others as the structure collapsed overhead and something or someone fell on top of her. No one died in the basement but there were several serious injuries, including Mary's broken leg.

*

In the Supermarket Phil Warrick looked about him and said with satisfaction, 'We've just about got it cleared.' He lifted the lid of the stove and dropped in some chunks of wood.

The Reverend Howard Davis, vicar of St Michael's Anglican Church, agreed. 'Just about,' he said. 'This will be the last load.' He wheeled a pushcart before the biscuit counter and began to fill it with packets.

Warrick watched him and grinned. 'McGill said no chocolate biscuits.'

'I don't know what Dr McGill knows about nutrition, but he certainly knows nothing about children,' said Davis with a smile. 'Chocolate biscuits are better than baked beans for keeping up morale.'

Warrick nodded. 'I hope he knows what he's doing about this avalanche. I swear my arms have lengthened two inches because of lugging around all these cases of canned food.' He replaced the lid of the stove.

Davis regarded him with amusement. 'Do you mean you'll feel sorry if there is no avalanche?'

'Oh, you know I don't want an avalanche, but it would be a shame to see all this hard work go for nothing.'

'I don't want an avalanche, either, but there's no harm in being prepared. If John Peterson is willing to have his store looted like this then he must believe McGill, and John is a level-headed man.'

A truck pulled up outside, and two men got out and came into the Supermarket. Warrick said, 'Hi, Len . . . Dave.'

Len Baxter said. 'That plane has come back. It's still floating around up there. Wonder what he wants?'

'He's not going to land,' said Warrick. 'This fog's too thick.'

Davis picked up a coffee-pot and put it on the stove top. 'You'll need something to warm you up.'

Dave Scanlon held out his hands to the stove. He wore a worried look. 'That'll go down well. I'll swear it's getting colder.' He glanced at Davis. 'I'm getting worried about Maureen. Someone said the exchange is too exposed.'

'John Peterson told me he'd look after her,' said Davis. 'I'm sure she'll be all right.' He laid the back of his finger on the coffee-pot to test the heat. 'Won't be long.'

'Got any more oil?' asked Len.

'Two more forty-five-gallon drums,' said Warrick. 'The last I could find. But we must have taken nearly six hundred gallons out of that tank.'

'I was talking to one of the mine engineers up at Turi Buck's place,' said Len. 'He's fixing up a generator there. He said the diesel engine could use fuel oil at a pinch. I never knew that.'

Dave said, 'I think I'll go and check on Maureen after I've had some coffee.'

As Davis picked up a cup, Len Baxter said, 'That reminds me. Does anyone know where my old man is? I've been so busy this morning I've lost track of things.'

'He's gone up to Matt Houghton's house. McGill thought it was one of the safest places in the valley.'

Warrick nodded. 'We discussed that in the council meeting. That and Turi Buck's place are the two oldest houses. The kids have gone to Turi Buck and the old people to Matt's place.'

'Not all the kids,' said Dave. He took a cup of coffee from Davis. 'I saw Mary Rees just now.'

Warrick frowned. 'Where?'

'Here in town. She was standing in the doorway of the old Fisher house.'

'That's all right,' said Davis. 'It has a basement. That's where Maureen will go. John Peterson organized all that.'

'Where will you hide out?' asked Len.

'I will be in the church,' said Davis firmly. His tone rejected any suggestion that he would be hiding anywhere.

Len considered it. 'Not bad,' he commented. 'The church must be the strongest building here. The only one built of stone, anyway.'

Dave Scanlon finished his coffee. 'I'll just pop along and see Maureen, then I'll be back to help you load.' He waved his hand. 'I've never seen the town so deserted, not even on Sunday.'

He turned to go, and froze in mid-stride. 'The mist's go . . .'

The three-ton truck parked outside was picked up bodily and thrown through the plate glass windows of the Supermarket like a monstrous projectile. Even as it came the building was collapsing around them. It had not been built too strongly in the first place and, hit by the giant fist of the avalanche, the showy false front sheared off and fell through the roof.

Suddenly the Reverend Davis found himself floundering in snow. He was dazed, and when he put his hand to his head it came away bloody. He was up to his waist in snow and, to his surprise, in his right hand he still held the coffee-pot. He opened it and looked inside and found it half full of steaming liquid. His head was spinning and hurt when he moved it suddenly. Darkness spiralled before his eyes and everything became dim just before he fell unconscious. The coffee-pot dropped from his hand and fell over on its side, and coffee stained the snow.

Dave Scanlon died instantly. He was hit by the truck and mashed to a bloody pulp. Len Baxter was hit on the head by a falling brick which was driven through the roof from the false front. His body was quickly covered by rubble which, in turn was covered by a rush of snow. He was still alive at that time but he died within a few minutes.

The cast-iron stove was ripped from the concrete plinth to which it was secured by four half-inch bolts. It was driven through the rear wall of the store and hit the fuel oil tank, which ruptured. Phil Warrick went flying after the stove and fell on top of it. He had been stoking it up liberally all morning and it was nearly red hot. The lid came off and a stream of hot embers shot out, igniting the fuel oil which streamed from the tank. Flames ran about and a cloud of black smoke went up, to be shredded immediately by the roaring wind.

The fire could not last long because of the snow which drove over the area, but it lasted long enough to kill Phil Warrick.

196

Embracing the hot stove, he was burned alive under six feet of snow.

*

Joe Cameron, driving the truck back to the mine after delivering the load of snow probes, was caught right in the open. Not for him the eerie sensation of driving a floating car as experienced by Dr Scott. The air blast slammed at the truck broadside on and it rocked violently. The left wheels rose from the ground and the truck went careering along for a few yards on two wheels and it was within a breath of toppling over. Then the wheels came down again with a crunch and Cameron fought to keep control.

After the air blast came the snow cloud of a much denser material. It pounded the side of the truck much more forcibly and this time toppled it over on to its side. The truck did not lie there. Pushed by the snow it began to roll over faster and faster.

In the cab Cameron was getting a mauling. His right foot was trapped between the accelerator and brake pedals; every time the truck rolled the gear lever ground into his stomach as his body flopped helplessly from side to side, and once, when his arm went through the spokes of the driving wheel, a blow on the front axles made the wheel spin and his arm broke with a dry crack which he did not hear.

When the truck finally came to rest it was upside down under fifteen feet of snow. Cameron was also upside down, his head resting against the top of the cab and his foot still trapped. The windscreen was smashed and there was much snow in the cab but enough of an air space left to provide the breath of life for a fairly long time. He was bleeding profusely from a gash on his cheek and the blood stained the snow a bright red.

He was unconscious, but presently he stirred and groaned. As he came round he felt as though he had been through a grinding machine and then stretched on a rack; every part of him ached and there were bits that were very painful. He tried to move his arm and felt the edges of bone grind together at the same time as a hot knife was stuck into his shoulderblade. He did not try to move his arm again.

The danger of death in the snow was very real, but what Cameron did not know was that he was in much more danger of dying by drowning.

First came the air blast and then the heavy hammer fist of the snow cloud. Following these came the sliding surface snow. Not as fast as its predecessors, it moved in a flowing tide inexorably across Hukahoronui. It washed around the church and the spire shuddered; it obliterated the wreckage of the Hotel D'Archiac and swept over the remnants of Mr Rawson's shop; it reached the Supermarket and covered the burned body of Phil Warrick, then it went on across the bluff to the river where it spilled over the edge and filled the river bed with snow.

Across the river its energy was spent and it slowed until it was moving at no more than the speed of a man running fast. A little later, when it encountered the rising ground of the east slope, it stopped entirely having clothed destruction in immaculate whiteness.

The avalanche had finished.

The disaster had not.

*

McGill climbed to the top of a small mound of snow in order to get a good view. He looked down the valley, and said softly, 'Oh my God!'

Most of the town had gone. The only building he could see was the church, which looked as though it had been given a coat of whitewash. Finely powdered snow had been driven into the stonework so that it looked like the ghost of a church. For the rest, there was just a hummocky expanse of snow.

He went back to Ballard and bent over him. 'Come on, Ian. It's over now and we have work to do.'

Ballard raised his head slowly and looked up at McGill. His eyes were dark smudges in a white face and showed no comprehension at all. His lips worked a little before he said, 'What?'

McGill felt compassion because he had a good idea of what had happened to Ballard. His senses had been so assaulted in an unexpected manner that the wits had been driven from him as a soldier might be shell-shocked in an artillery barrage. McGill was not feeling too good himself, but because of his knowledge and experience he had known what would happen and thus armoured had been able to ward off the worst effects.

Ballard was suffering from disaster shock.

McGill shook his head slowly. Compassion was not enough. A lot of people must have died and, if the rest of the survivors were like Ballard, then a lot more would die from want of help. He drew back his arm and slapped Ballard across the face very hard. 'Get up, Ian,' he said harshly. 'Jump to it!'

Slowly Ballard lifted his hand and fingered the red marks on his cheek. He blinked rapidly, weak tears coming to his eyes, and mumbled, 'What did you do that for?'

'You'll get worse than that if you don't get up.' McGill put a crackle in his voice. 'On your feet, man!'

Ballard heaved himself up and McGill led him to the viewpoint. 'Take a look.'

Ballard looked down the valley and his face crumpled. 'Christ!' he breathed. 'There's nothing left.'

'There's plenty left,' contradicted McGill. 'But we have to find it.'

'But what can we do?' said Ballard in despair.

'You can wake up for a start,' said McGill brutally. 'Then we look for the rest of the guys who were around here, and we wake them up. We have to get some sort of organization going.'

Ballard looked once more at the desolation and then stepped down from the mound. He rubbed his stinging cheek, and said, 'Thanks, Mike.'

'Okay,' said McGill. 'You look over there and see who you can find.' He turned his back on Ballard and walked away. Ballard trudged slowly in the direction McGill had indicated. His brain still felt pummelled.

Fifteen minutes later they had grown from two to twenty. One by one the stunned survivors were ruthlessly extracted from the holes where they were hiding, and McGill showed no mercy in the way he handled them. They were all shocked in varying degrees and all showed a marked aversion to looking up at the slope, now visible, from which disaster had come. They stood around apathetically with their backs to the west.

McGill selected the brightest of them and set them searching in their turn and more survivors came to light. In half an hour he was beginning to believe they might stand a chance. He gave one man his notebook and a ball pen and instructed him to take the name of each survivor. 'And ask him who he was standing next to just before he ran for cover. We want to find out who's missing.'

To Ballard he said, 'Take three men and go to Turi Buck's house. Find out how they're shaping.' Others he sent to Matt Houghton's house and he himself set off for the town. His last command was: 'If anyone finds Dr Scott, he's to report to me.'

As it happened, Dr Scott was also on his way to town. He had to cross the river and the bridge had been swept away, but there was no need for a bridge because the river bed was full of snow and he was able to walk across, but with difficulty because the snow was soft. He crossed the river opposite the bluff about where the Supermarket had been and he was still unable to take in the enormity of the disaster. It did not seem either reasonable or possible that the Supermarket should have disappeared.

He trudged through the hampering snow holding his bag, the contents of which were precious. In the distance he saw something black outlined against the prevailing whiteness which, when he came nearer, proved to be a man buried to his waist. Next to him was an overturned coffee-pot.

Scott bent down, turned the man's head and recognized the Reverend Davis. He was alive but his pulse was weak and fluttery. Scott scrabbled at the snow, digging with his gloved hands. The snow was not very compacted and the digging was comparatively easy; within ten minutes Davis was freed and lying on the surface.

As Scott was opening his bag he heard voices in the distance, so he stood up and saw a group of men picking their way over the snow where the town had been. He shouted and waved, and presently they came up to him. The man in the lead was the Canadian, McGill.

'I'm glad you survived, Doctor,' said McGill. 'You're going to be needed. How is he?'

'He'll live,' said Scott. 'He needs to be kept warm. Hot soup would help.'

'He'll have it if Turi Buck's house held up. The church is still standing so we'll use that as a base. Better take him there.' McGill looked down at Davis and noted the clerical collar. 'Seems appropriate. As for heat, he'll have that if we have to burn all the pews.'

Scott looked around. 'What a hell of a mess.'

McGill turned to MacAllister, the man from the power

station. 'Mac, you take a couple of guys and go to the Gap. If anyone is coming over tell them we need help real bad. But we need trained help – men who know about snow rescue. We don't want a lot of amateurs lousing the place up.'

MacAllister nodded and turned away. McGill said, 'And, Mac, if there are trained snow dogs in New Zealand we need those, too.'

'Right,' said MacAllister, and selected his men.

Others helped pick up Davis, and McGill led the way to the church.

Turi Buck had left McLean when the engineer was still in a shocked stupor. He went to the source of the screaming, taking with him a jar of barley sugar which he found in the kitchen. It took him a long time to subdue the terrified children, but presently he was helped by Ruihi.

'The barley sugar is good,' she said. 'But hot, sweet cocoa would be better.' She went into the kitchen and had to remake the fire which had been extinguished, and when she lit the fire the kitchen filled with smoke because the flue was choked with snow.

Miss Frobisher was of no use at all. She was curled into a foetal ball and whimpered from time to time. Turi ignored her and directed his attention to the children.

McLean looked down at the spanner in his hand and frowned. Slowly his mind began to work. *Why am I holding this spanner?* he asked himself, and the answer came creaking into his mind. *The generator!*

He moved stiffly towards the door and opened it. A light breeze came into the room, whirling up the powdered snow on the floor. He stepped outside and looked towards the rock of Kamakamaru and crinkled his eyes in disbelief. The generator stood where he had left it, even though it had not been bolted down. *Thank God!* he thought. *What's good for rabbits is good for generators.*

But the portable air compressor he had used to drive the drill had vanished, and he remembered it had stood on the place on the rock where he had first proposed to put the generator. He walked forward past a tree which had been sheared at a height of ten feet. He stopped and grunted in his throat as he saw the drill. The air hose which had connected it to the compressor had snapped and now swayed in the breeze; the drill itself was driven deep into the trunk of the tree as though it had been flung like a giant dart.

When Ballard and his team arrived at the house he was thankful to hear the voices and even laughter. Children are resilient, and, once the shock had worn off, they became excited, even over-excited. He went inside and saw Turi sitting in a big armchair surrounded by a flock of children and looking somewhat like a biblical patriarch. 'Thank God!' he said. 'Are you all right, Turi?'

'We're all fine.' Turi nodded across the room to where Ruihi was supporting Miss Frobisher and administering tea. 'She was shaken up a bit.'

From behind the house came a whine which settled into a steady throb. Startled, Ballard said, 'What's that?'

'I think Jock McLean will be testing the generator.' Turi stood up. 'Would you like some tea?' he asked, as politely as though they were ordinary guests visiting his home.

Ballard nodded dumbly. Turi sent one of the older children into the kitchen with instructions to bring back tea and sandwiches. Then he said, 'What happened to the town?'

'Turi, there is no town.'

'Gone?'

'I saw nothing standing except the church.'

'And the people?'

Ballard shook his head. 'I don't know. Mike is there now.'

'I will come to help search,' said Turi. 'After you have refreshed yourselves.'

Presently the tea and sandwiches arrived and Ballard ate as hungrily as though he had not eaten for a week. The hot tea was welcome, too, especially as Turi had laced it liberally with brandy.

When he had finished he idly picked up the telephone and held it to his ear. All he got was silence. As he cradled it he said, 'Communications – that's what we're going to need. There was some food supposed to come here, Turi.'

'It came. We have plenty of food.'

'We'll take some back to town. It will be a load to carry but we'll have to manage.'

'Ruihi said, 'The car's in the garage, isn't it?'

Ballard sat upright. 'You have a *car*?'

'It's not much of a car,' said Turi. 'But it goes.'

Ballard thought of the soft snow which covered Hukahoronui and thought that perhaps the car was not such a good idea after all; but he went out to have a look at it. It proved to be an elderly Australian Holden station-wagon and he ignored it because the Massey-Ferguson tractor standing next to it looked to be worth its weight in diamond-studded platinum. Fifteen minutes later it was loaded with canned goods and on its way to town, towing an improvised sledge.

When Ballard arrived at the church he found more people than he had expected, with McGill at an improvised desk by the altar, the centre of a growing organization. In one corner Scott was very busy, aided by three women. Most of his patients had broken bones and two men were breaking up a pew to make splints. Ballard saw that Eric Peterson was in line for attention, so he strode over to him. 'Is Liz all right?'

Eric's face was white and drawn. 'I don't know. She and that American girl were at Rawson's shop, I think, when we were hit.' His eyes were bleak. 'The shop's gone – not there at all.' There was hysteria in his voice.'

'You have your arm fixed,' said Ballard. 'I'll check.'

He went over to McGill. 'Turi's place is okay,' he said. 'Everyone is fine there. They've got a generator working and I have a load of food outside – with a tractor. You'd better take charge of that.'

McGill gave a long sigh 'Thank God the kids are safe.' He nodded. 'Good work, Ian. That tractor will be useful.' Ballard turned away and McGill said, 'Where are you going?'

'To look for Liz and Stacey. They were in the chemist's shop.'

'You'll do nothing of the kind,' snapped McGill. 'I don't want any half-assed rescue attempts.'

'But – '

'But nothing. If you go tramping out there you'll ruin the scent for a dog, and a dog can do better work than a hundred men. That's why everybody is being kept in this church – for a time, at least. If you have information about where people were when we were hit, take it to Arthur Pye over there. He's our Bureau of Missing Persons.'

Ballard was about to reply hotly but someone pushed past him and he recognized Dickinson who worked at the mine. Dickinson said quickly, 'I've just come from Houghton's house and it's like a bloody butcher's shop up there. I think

203

some of the people are still alive, though. I reckon we need Dr Scott.'

McGill raised his voice. 'Dr Scott, will you come here?'

Scott finished knotting an improvised bandage and walked across. McGill said to Dickinson, 'Carry on.'

'The house looks as though it blew apart,' said Dickinson. 'I found Jack Baxter and Matt Houghton outside the house. Jack's as chirpy as a cricket, but his leg's broken. There's something funny about Matt; he can hardly speak and he's paralysed all down one side.'

'Could be a stroke,' said Scott.

'I put them both in a car and brought them down as far as I could. I didn't dare cross the river on that soft snow so I left them on the other side.'

'And the house?'

'Oh, it's bloody awful in there. I didn't stop to count the bodies but there seemed to be hundreds. Some of them are still alive, I do know that.'

'What sort of injuries?' asked Scott. 'I'll need to know what to take.'

McGill grinned mirthlessly. 'You've not got much. Better take the lot.'

'Turi brought a first-aid kit from the house,' said Ballard.

Scott said, 'That I can use.'

They had not been conscious of the distant vibration in the air but now it burst upon them with a bellow. Ballard jerked and ducked his head, thinking it was another avalanche about to hit them but McGill looked up at the roof. 'A plane – and a goddamn big one!'

He got to his feet and ran to the church door, followed by the others. The aircraft had gone down the valley and was now banking and turning to come back. As it came closer they saw it was a big transport marked with United States Navy insignia.

A ragged cheer broke out and there was a beatific smile on McGill's face. 'A Navy Hercules from Harewood,' he said. 'The Marines have arrived in the nick of time.'

The Hercules finished its turn and steadied at a lower altitude, flying straight down the valley. From its stern black specks dropped and then the parachutes opened and blossomed like multi-coloured flowers. McGill counted: '. . . seven . . . eight . . . nine . . . ten. And those are just the experts we need.'

CHAPTER TWENTY-FIVE

John Reed, Secretary to the Commission, poised his pen expectantly. 'Your full name, please?'

'Jesse Willard Rusch.' The tall, squarely-built man with the decidedly unfashionable crewcut had a strong American accent.

'And your occupation, Mr Rusch?'

'By rank I am a Lieutenant-Commander in the United States Navy. By occupation I am, at present, Supply Officer to Antarctic Development Squadron Six. It's the outfit that does all the flying in the Antarctic in support of our Operation Deep Freeze.'

'Thank you,' said Reed.

Harrison regarded the American with interest. 'I understand that you were the first man trained in snow rescue to arrive in Hukahoronui after the avalanche.'

'I understand that, too, sir. But there were five of us. My feet happened to hit the ground first.'

'But you were the leader.'

'Yes, sir.'

'Can you tell us the chain of circumstances which took you there?'

'Yes, sir. I understand that your Civil Defence people put in a request to Commander Lindsey, the officer commanding our Advanced Base here in Christchurch. Because the request concerned snow rescue and because I am Supply Officer to VXE-6 – that's the squadron – he dumped the job in my lap.'

Harrison stared at the ceiling and the notion crossed his mind that Americans were strange people. 'I don't quite see the connection,' he said. 'What has snow rescue to do with you being Supply Officer? I take it that a Supply Officer is of the nature of a quartermaster.'

'Sort of,' said Rusch. 'I'll have to explain. There's always a lot to do in the Antarctic; there are usually more jobs than bodies, so it becomes normal for a man to wear two hats, as it were. It has become a tradition, a much prized tradition, that the Supply Officer of VXE-6 doubles up on rescue and is automatically in command of any rescue operations in the field, particularly those involving air transport.'

'I see. That explains it, then.'

'I ought to say that we are all trained parachutists. We do our parachute training at Lakehurst, New Jersey, and our field rescue training in the region of Mount Erebus in the Antarctic. Our training there is done with experienced instructors drawn from the Federated Mountain Clubs of New Zealand.' Rusch paused. 'So when a New Zealander makes a request we jump to it fast.'

'You have made yourself very clear.'

'Thank you, sir. At the time of the request, which was in mid-winter, the staff of our Advanced Headquarters here was run down. Flights to the ice – to the Antarctic – are not routine at that time of the year and any flights are for emergencies, or perhaps experimental reasons. We normally have twelve men tapped for rescue – all volunteers, I might add – but at that time only myself and four others were available.'

Harrison made a note. 'Have you ever run short of volunteers?'

'Rusch shook his head. 'Not to my knowledge, sir.'

'Interesting. Please proceed.'

'We were briefed, together with the aircrew, and the aircraft was loaded with our equipment which is prepacked ready for instant use. The standard operating procedure is that a team of four men jump with one packed sled. However, in view of the briefing and the possible conditions at our destination I loaded extra sleds. We jumped with five men and five sleds and landed in Hukahoronui at 12.56 hours. To the best of my knowledge that was fifty-five minutes after the disaster.' Rusch smiled. 'Imagine my feelings when the first man to greet me turned out to be someone I already knew from the Antarctic – Dr McGill.'

Rusch smothered his parachute and snapped the quick release button. He pushed back his face mask and checked the others as they came down, then turned to meet the group of men who were stumbling towards him across the snow. Arms akimbo, he stared incredulously at the man in the lead. 'Well, I'll be a son of a bitch!' he said. As McGill approached Rusch stepped forward. 'Dr McGill, I presume.'

'Good morning, Lieutenant-Commander.' McGill rubbed

his eyes tiredly. 'Or is it afternoon?'

'It's afternoon, and it doesn't look too good to me. Where's the town?'

'You're looking at it.'

Rusch looked about him and whistled softly. 'You've cut yourself a slice of trouble, Mike. Are you in charge here?'

'I guess I am.'

'No!' Ballard came forward, his hand gripping Eric Peterson's good arm. 'This is Eric Peterson, a town councillor – the only one around. He represents the civil authority.'

Rusch gave McGill a quizzical glance, then shook Peterson's left hand a little awkwardly. 'We could have met in better circumstances, Mr Peterson.'

Peterson was taken wrong-footed. 'Me!' he said to Ballard. 'What about Matt Houghton?'

'He seems to have had a stroke.'

Peterson's face worked. 'Well, now,' he said indistinctly, and indicated his right arm. 'I can't fly fast on a broken wing. You'd better be co-opted, Ian. You and McGill.'

'Right!' Ballard turned to Rusch. 'We need medical supplies.'

'Those we've got.' Rusch swung around and yelled, 'Hey, Chief, I want the medical sled – on the double.'

Ballard said, 'Dr Scott, you take charge of that, and make all necessary arrangements. What about communications, Lieutenant . . . er . . .?'

'Rusch. Lieutenant-Commander Rusch. We have five walkie-talkies, so we can set up a network. There's a bigger transmitter in one of the sleds for outside communication. We ought to be able to raise Chi-Chi . . . Christchurch, that is.'

'That had better go to the church,' Ballard decided. 'That's our headquarters. I'd like to talk to somebody at Civil Defence as soon as possible.' He paused. 'By the way, I'm Ian Ballard. Let's get busy.'

On the way back to the church McGill fell in step with Ballard. 'What did Turi feed you on at the house? Raw meat?'

'Someone must take charge of administration and it's not going to be you. You know about snow rescue, so get to it. But before you go let me have a list of what you need so I can make sense when I talk to Christchurch.'

'Okay.' They walked a few more paces, and McGill said, 'What was the idea of pushing Peterson forward like that?

He's as much use as a fifth wheel.'

'Strategy. He abdicated – didn't you hear him? I knew it would happen. Look, Mike: I'm a trained administrator and I'd be wasted doing anything else. You're a snowman and you'd be wasted doing anything else. Let's get our priorities right.'

'Makes sense.' McGill grinned. 'And legal, too. We're now town councillors, you and me both.'

They went into the church. Rusch stopped just inside and frowned as he surveyed the scene. Worse than a war.'

The pews were full of white-faced, lethargic men and women with lustreless eyes. They sat or lay in abandoned attitudes, still and silent, gazing back in horror at the closeness of death, Only a few of them moved and, of those, only a scant half-dozen were attempting to help the others.

McGill said, 'You're not going to get much help from this lot. They've been hit badly by disaster shock.'

'Blankets,' said Ballard. 'We'll need blankets. Come up to the office.' He led the way to the desk that McGill had set up, and sat behind it. 'Right, Mike. What else do we need?'

'Trained rescue men – in quantity. They can come in by helicopter and light planes equipped with skis. And they can get these people out on the return trip.'

'We've got some helos at Harewood,' said Rusch. 'We've been stripping down for winter maintenance but I know that four are serviceable.'

'We need rescue dogs, too,' said McGill.

'I don't think so,' said Rusch. 'There are none in the country as far as I know. I could be wrong, though. Try Mount Cook and Coronet Peak.'

Ballard nodded. Those were popular skiing and climbing areas. 'There should be trained men there, too.'

Rusch said, 'Your doctor has gone to a house the other side of the valley. One of my guys has gone with him. I'll leave another here to help with the radio, and then he can help with the injured here. We're not exactly medicos but we can set bones. The rest of us will take a general look at the situation and set out a plan.'

Ballard raised his voice. 'Arthur, come here for a minute.'

Arthur Pye, who was trying to question one of the sur-vivors and not getting very far, straightened up and walked to the desk. His face was haggard and his movements stiff, but there was that spark of intelligence and comprehension in his eyes which was missing from most of the others.

Ballard said, 'What's the score, Arthur? How many missing?'

'God, I don't know.' Pye wiped his face with a big hand. 'How could anyone know?'

'Then make a guess. I have to tell Christchurch something.'

'It's bloody hard getting anything out of anybody.' Pye hesitated. 'All right - say three hundred and fifty.'

Rusch stiffened. *That many!*

Pye waved his hand. 'You've seen the town – or what's left of it. They're still drifting in, one or two at a time. I reckon the final tally will be very much less.'

McGill said, 'The ones who are coming in now are the lucky ones. There'll be others who are buried.'

'Come on, Mike,' said Rusch. 'Let's start looking. Our radio man is fixing up the transmitter, Mr Ballard. If you want to contact me use his walkie-talkie.'

Rusch and McGill left the church and Ballard looked up at Pye. 'Are you sure about the number?'

'Of course I'm not sure,' said Pye wearily. 'But it's about that. I think John Peterson bought it. Mary Rees says she saw him run out into the street just before the avalanche hit.'

One of the Americans walked up the central aisle unreeling wire from a drum. He stopped in front of the desk and said, 'CPO Laird, sir. I've got the radio set up outside; it's better there because of the antenna. But I have a portable handset you can use here. It's two-way – you use it like an ordinary telephone.' He put the handset on the desk and plugged it in.

Ballard looked down at the telephone. 'Who will I be talking to?'

'Communications centre, Operation Deep Freeze. I've just been talking to them.'

Ballard took a deep breath and stretched out his hand. 'Hello, this is Ballard in Hukahoronui. Can you put me through to Civil Defence Headquarters? It's in the Reserve Bank Building, Hereford Str – '

A calm voice cut in. 'No need for that, Mr Ballard. They're on the line now.'

CHAPTER TWENTY-SIX

Rusch, McGill and two of the American servicemen crunched across the snow over the desolation that was Hukahoronui. McGill took off his glove and bent to feel the texture of the snow. 'It's hardening,' he said, and straightened up. 'I was training some guys in snow rescue before we got hit. I said then they'd be no good, and I was right. You know what's worrying me right now?'

'What?' asked Rusch.

'We're going to get a lot of people flying in here if Ballard does his stuff – maybe several hundreds.' McGill nodded to the west slope. 'I'm worried that she'll come down again. That would really compound this disaster.'

'Is it likely?'

'There's still a lot of snow up there, so I think only half of it came down, sliding on a hoar frost surface. I'd like to take a look.'

The man behind Rusch touched his arm. 'Sir.'

'What is it, Cotton?'

'Look at that dog, sir. It's sniffing at something in the snow.'

They looked to where Cotton pointed and saw an Alsatian pawing at the snow and whining. 'Maybe it's not trained,' said McGill. 'But it's the best we've got.'

As they approached, the dog looked up at them and wagged its tail – and then scraped at the snow with its forepaw. 'Good dog,' said Rusch. 'Cotton, use that shovel.'

Cotton found the body beneath three feet of snow and Rusch checked the pulse. 'This one is gone. Let's get him out.'

They pulled the body from the snow and Rusch's breath hissed from his lips. 'What in the name of God happened to his face? Do you know him, Mike?'

'His wife wouldn't know him,' said McGill bleakly. His face was pale.

The dog wagged its tail happily and trotted off across the snow, where it stopped and began to sniff and scratch again. 'Cotton, you're now the dog handler,' said Rusch. 'Harris, round up some able-bodied men and dig wherever that German shepherd scratches.'

McGill heard the familiar sound of skis hissing on snow and turned to see two men approaching. They stopped and the one in the lead pushed up his goggles. 'What can I do to help?' said Charlie Peterson.

McGill looked down at Charlie's feet. 'You can lend me your skis for a start. I'm going up the mountain.'

Miller pushed forward from behind Charlie and stared down at the body. 'Christ!' he said. 'What happened to him?' A retching sound came from him and he turned and vomited helplessly.

The body did not seem to worry Charlie. He looked down, and said, 'It's Rawson. What happened to him?'

'How do you know who it is?' asked Rusch. 'The guy's got no face.'

Charlie pointed. 'He lost the first joint of the little finger of his left hand.' He looked up at McGill. 'Take Miller's skis. I'll come with you.'

'That slope's not the safest place in the world, Charlie.'

Charlie grinned crookedly. 'You can get killed crossing the road. I said that before, didn't I?'

McGill gave Charlie a level stare, then made up his mind. 'Okay. Help me get them off him. He's in no condition to do it himself.'

Five minutes later Rusch watched them go. He looked up at the slope and frowned. It wasn't a job he would fancy doing. 'Sir!' called Cotton urgently. 'We've got another one – alive and female.'

Rusch strode over. 'Be careful with that shovel, Harris. Cotton, bring up that empty sled.'

The limp body of Liz Peterson was lifted on to the sled and covered warmly with a blanket. Rusch looked down at her. 'Lovely girl,' he commented. 'Take her to the church. We've just started to earn our pay.'

The Canterbury Provincial Chamber was very quiet as Lieutenant-Commander Rusch gave his evidence, although there had been a shocked whisper as he described the finding of Rawson's body.

'The dog was a big help in that first hour, sir,' said Rusch. 'He found three victims, two of whom were alive. But then he lost interest. I think he was tired – the snow was very deep and hard to get through, and maybe his scent was failing. He wasn't a trained animal, anyway.'

'Did you find out whom the dog belonged to?' asked Harrison.

'His name was Victor and he belonged to the Scanlon family. There were no survivors from the Scanlon family.'

'I hope Victor has found a good home.'

'I believe he has, sir. Miss Peterson is looking after him.'

Harrison looked across the room towards the Petersons' table. He smiled at Liz Peterson and nodded. 'Most appropriate,' he commented. He consulted his watch. 'Our next evidence deals with the activities of the Civil Defence authorities. As it is getting late in the afternoon this hearing will adjourn until ten o'clock tomorrow morning.'

He turned to Rusch. 'Thank you, Lieutenant-Commander. It only remains for me to thank you and your comrades for a job well done.'

The hard-bitten Rusch actually blushed.

CHAPTER TWENTY-SEVEN

'Listening to that evidence gave me a cold grue all over again,' said McGill. 'I was too busy at the time to think about it much, but when you get it all laid out then it really hits you.'

'A terrible experience,' said Stenning.

They were standing at the desk in the hotel waiting for the receptionist to finish telephoning. 'Where is Ian?' asked Stenning.

'Gone off somewhere with Liz,' McGill smiled. 'Have you come up with an answer to the question I asked? What happens if Ian marries her?'

Stenning shook his head. 'That will take a great deal of thought.'

The receptionist came off the telephone and took keys from a board. 'Mr Stenning. Dr McGill. There's a letter for you, Dr McGill.'

'Thank you.' McGill tossed the letter lightly in his hand. 'Care to join me in a drink?'

'I think not,' said Stenning. 'I think I'll take a short nap.'

Stenning went to his room and McGill went into the bar. He ordered a drink and then opened the letter. As he unfolded the sheets a cheque slipped out and fluttered to the bar counter. He picked it up, glanced at it, and his eyes widened as he saw the amount it was made out for. He laid down the cheque and his brows drew together as he read the first page of the letter. He flipped over the sheet and read absorbedly, the drink untasted at his elbow. He arrived at the final page then, turning back to the beginning, he read it all through again. Then he sat on the bar stool and looked ahead of him broodingly, which unnerved the bar-tender who happened to be at the focus of his blank stare.

'Anything wrong with your drink, sir?'

'What?' McGill roused himself. 'No, give me another – and make it a double.' He picked up the glass and swallowed the neat scotch in one gulp.

When Ballard arrived McGill was waiting for him and steered him into the bar. McGill crooked his finger at the bartender. 'Two more doubles. We're celebrating, Ian.'

'What's there to celebrate?'

'Guess what I've got in my pocket?'

'How could I possibly guess?' Ballard looked at McGill closely. 'Mike, are you drunk? You look like a boiled owl.'

'In my pocket,' said McGill seriously. 'In my pocket I have a steamroller. It arrived air mail from Los Angeles.' He took the letter from his breast pocket and waved it under Ballard's nose. 'Read it, my friend. Read it and weep. I don't feel like cheering even though it's the saving of you.'

'I think you *are* drunk.' Ballard took the envelope and opened it. He glanced at the cheque and said, 'What the hell is this? A bribe?'

'Read,' urged McGill.

Ballard started to read the first page and then, frowning, glanced at the bottom of the last page to find that the letter was from the American, Miller. Its contents were appalling.

'Dear Dr McGill,

'I have been wanting to write this letter for a long time but I have been putting it off because I guess I was scared. What happened has been on my conscience ever since the avalanche which caused so many deaths, including that of my good friend, Ralph Newman. A friend sent me newspaper clips about the inquiry into the Hukahoronui disaster. On reading the clips I relived that terrible experience and I know I have to speak up. I am having this letter notarized so that it may be used in evidence if you think it necessary, but I send it to you in the hope that you will not think it necessary. I leave it to your good judgment.

'Early on the morning of that dreadful Sunday I went skiing with Charlie Peterson. There was a mist in the valley but he said there would be sun on the higher slopes. I was a bit nervous because I had heard talk of avalanches at the hotel, but Charlie laughed at me and said that someone was pulling my leg. We went up into the hills at the head of the valley and did some skiing but the slopes were not very good there, and Charlie suggested that we go to the slopes nearer Hukahoronui. This we did.

'We finally arrived at the top of the west slope above the town and we saw a sign there saying that no skiing was allowed. I wanted to turn around and go another way, but Charlie said the land was Peterson land and that no one could stop him from doing what he wanted on his own land. He said all this talk of avalanches was nonsense and there had never been one in Hukahoronui. He laughed when he said the sign had been put up by boy scouts and it was just about their mark.

'We had quite an argument up there on the mountain. I said the scouts must have been told to put the sign there and I guessed it was you who had told them. I said that maybe you were right about the danger of an avalanche. Charlie just stood there laughing and there was something funny about him right at that time. He said that an avalanche might be a good thing and anything that could get rid of Mr Ballard couldn't be all bad.

'He went on about Ballard for quite a while, a lot of real wild talk. He said that Ballard had killed his brother and stolen the mine from his father and that it was about time someone stopped him from stealing the whole of Hukahoronui. He ranted on like this for maybe five minutes, then he said the mine wouldn't do Ballard much good if it wasn't there.

'I told him he was talking crazy and asked him how he could make a whole gold mine disappear. Suddenly he shouted, "I'll show you!" and took off down the hill. He wasn't going very fast and he kept jumping up and down very heavily. I went after him to try to stop him, but suddenly there was a crackling noise like French fries in the pan and Charlie gave a shout. I stopped and saw him jumping sideways up the hill.

'Nothing seemed to happen at first and then I saw the snow cracking where Charlie had been. A lot of cracks zigzagged very fast and a bit of snow went up into the air. Then the slide started. Charlie and I were safe because we were above the fall. We just stood there and watched it happen and I've never seen a more awful sight.

'We watched it go down into the mist over the town and I started to cry. I'm not ashamed of that. Charlie shook me and said I was a crybaby. He said to keep my mouth shut. He said if I told anybody about it he would kill me. I believed him when he said that – he was crazy enough for anything.

'I asked him what we were going to do and he said we were going into town to see what had happened. He said it was just a lot of feathery stuff that had gone and it had probably just given the people a good scare, though he hoped it had done for the mine. He laughed as he said that. So we went into the town and saw the dreadful thing that had happened.

'Then Charlie threatened me again. He said that if I as much as blinked an eyelid in his direction the world would not be big enough; he would search me out and find me wherever I was.

'As God is my witness this is the truth of what happened that Sunday morning. I am deeply ashamed of my silence and I hope this letter will go towards making amends. I suppose there will be a public fund for the families of the victims because there usually is. I enclose a check for $10,000. This is nearly all my savings and I cannot afford more.'

Ballard looked up. 'For God's sake!'

'It's like holding an unexploded bomb, isn't it?'

'But we can't use *this*.'

'Why not? Stenning would just love you.'

'To hell with Stenning. I wouldn't do that to anybody. Besides . . .'

His voice tailed away, and McGill said, 'Lover's Lane must run straight and narrow? Ian, you have the Ballard Trust right in the palm of your hand.'

Ballard stared at the drink in front of him. He put his hand out, but only to push it away in a rejecting gesture. He turned to McGill. 'Mike, tell me something and tell me honestly. Before the avalanche we were making every preparation possible. We *expected* an avalanche, didn't we? Does this really make any difference?' He tapped for emphasis on the bar counter and, as the bar-tender came running, he shook his head violently in negation. 'You exonerated the pilot of that plane – you said the snow was ready to come down. Do you still believe that?'

McGill sighed. 'Yes, I still believe it.'

'Then we don't use this.'

'You're too gentlemanly for your own good, Ian. This is a tough world we live in.'

'I wouldn't want to live in the kind of world where I'd use this letter.'

'It won't wash,' said McGill flatly. 'I know what you're thinking. If this letter is produced you can say goodbye to Liz. But it's not good enough. That son of a bitch killed fifty-four people. If Miller had claimed it was accidental I might have gone along, but he says Charlie did it deliberately. You can't suppress it.'

'What do I do, Mike?'

'There's nothing for you to do. It's my responsibility. The letter is addressed to me.' He took it from Ballard's fingers, replaced it in the envelope, and put it back in his pocket.

'Liz will never believe I didn't go along with you,' said Ballard gloomily.

McGill shrugged. 'Probably not.' He picked up his glass. 'Come to think of it, I don't think I'd like you as much if you'd grabbed the chance of hammering the Petersons with eager cries. You're a silly bastard, but I still love you.' He raised the glass in a toast. 'Here's to chivalry – still alive and living in Christchurch.'

'I still think you're drunk.'

'That I am, and I'm going to get a hell of a lot drunker – if only to forget how many shits there are in this world.' He drained his glass and set it down with a thump.

'When are you going to give the letter to Harrison?'

'Tomorrow, of course.'

'Hold off for a bit,' said Ballard urgently. 'I'd like to get straightened out with Liz first. I wouldn't want her to get this slammed at her cold at the Inquiry.'

McGill pondered. 'Okay, I'll save it for twenty-four hours.'

'Thanks.' Ballard pushed his untasted drink before McGill. 'If you're insistent on getting drunk there's my contribution.'

McGill twisted on his stool and watched Ballard walk out of the bar, then he turned back to the hovering bar-tender. 'Two more doubles.'

'Then the gentleman is coming back?'

'No, he's not coming back,' said McGill absently. 'But you're right about one thing. He *is* a gentleman – and there are damned few of them around these days.'

Ballard and Stenning dined together that night. Ballard was abstracted and in no mood for small talk. Stenning noted this and was quiet, but over coffee he asked, 'Ian, what is your relationship with Miss Peterson?'

Ballard jerked his head, a little startled by the intrusive question. 'I don't see that's any of your business.'

'Don't you?' Stenning stirred his coffee. 'You forget the matter of the Ballard Trust. It is still very much on *my* mind.'

'I don't see what Liz has to do with it.' His lip curled. 'Don't tell me you want me to walk over her, too.'

'I don't want you to do anything you don't wish to.'

'You'd better not try,' said Ballard.

'Yet I have to interpret Ben's wishes, and it's much more difficult than I anticipated. Ben didn't tell me about Liz Peterson.'

'The old man didn't think much of women,' remarked Ballard. 'He lived for business, and for him women had no place in business so consequently they didn't exist. He didn't tell you about Liz because, to him, she was a nonentity.'

'You understand Ben better than I thought.' Stenning paused with his coffee cup in mid-air, then set it down gently. 'Yes, that is certainly something to be taken into consideration.'

'I don't know what you're talking about.'

'It depends on your relationship with Miss Peterson. It was something McGill asked me – he wanted to know, if you married her, whether it would have any effect in the "Peterson Bashing Contest", as he called it.'

'And what answer did you give him?'

'A dusty one,' said Stenning. 'I had to think about it.'

Ballard leaned forward. 'Let me tell you something,' he said in a low, but intense, voice. 'Ben thought he was God. He

217

manipulated me, and he's been manipulating the family through the Trust. Now that's all right if it's just in the course of business, but if the old bastard is going to control my private life from beyond the grave, then that's another thing.'

Stenning nodded. 'Your analysis of Ben's attitude towards women has proved quite illuminating. I think you are quite right when you say that Ben didn't mention Miss Peterson because he discounted her completely. This, therefore, has a strong bearing on how I intend to interpret his wishes. The conclusion I have come to is this: you may marry or you may not – you may even marry Miss Peterson or you may not. Whatever you do will have no bearing on my decision regarding your suitability as a trustee. If Ben discounted Miss Peterson, then so shall I.'

'Thanks,' said Ballard hollowly.

'Of course, the problem still remains with the Peterson brothers.'

'Thanks again,' said Ballard. 'For nothing. Do you really believe that if I walk over the Petersons, as you so delicately put it, I would stand a chance with Liz? God knows she doesn't get on with her brothers, but she wouldn't be the woman I think she is, the woman I want to marry, if she didn't have some family loyalty.'

'Yes, you would appear to have quite a problem.'

Ballard stood up. 'Then to hell with you, Mr Stenning.' He threw down his napkin. 'And to hell with the Ballard Trust.'

Stenning watched him walk away, his face expressionless. He lifted the cup to his lips and found the coffee cold, so he called for another cup.

CHAPTER TWENTY-EIGHT

Witness after witness passed before Harrison and his assessors, their actions minutely scrutinized, their utterances tested; a long parade of townsfolk, policemen, mountain rangers, doctors, engineers, scientists, soldiers and civil defence workers. Dan Edwards, wearied in the Press gallery, said to Dalwood, 'I think the old bastard is hoping for a new job when he dies – he's understudying the Recording Angel.'

There was a movement in the valley. At first there was just a handful of rescuers but the number swelled hour by hour, brought in by helicopter and ski plane. The mountain rangers came from Mount Cook, from Coronet Peak, from Mount Egmont, from Tongariro – men knowledgeable and skilled in their trade of snow rescue. Doctors came in Air Force and US Navy helicopters, which took out the children and the badly injured.

The mass of snow which blocked the Gap was attacked fiercely. Steps were cut and guide ropes laid so that within hours it was possible for any moderately active person to enter or leave the valley. This was done by volunteers from the mountain clubs who had come in dozens at a time to the place of disaster, many of them flying from as far as North Island.

These men knew what to do and, once in the valley, they formed teams to probe the snow, at first working under the general direction of Jesse Rusch. They were aided by a force of police and an even larger detachment of troops. Even so, they were not too many; the area to be patiently probed, foot by foot, was over four hundred acres.

At first Ballard acted as co-ordinator, but he was glad to be relieved by a professional civil defence man flown in from Christchurch. He stayed on to help Arthur Pye. The identification of the survivors and the dead and the listing of those still missing was work in which local knowledge was vital. There was pain in his eyes as he saw the name of Stacey Cameron on the list of the dead.

He said, 'Any news of Joe Cameron?'

Pye shook his head. 'Not a sign of him. He must be buried out there somewhere. They've found Dobbs dead. Funny thing about that: the chap who dug him out said that Dobbs had cut his throat. The body was drained of blood.' He rubbed his eyes. 'God, but I'm tired.'

'Take a break, Arthur,' said Ballard. 'Get something to eat and have a nap. I can carry on.'

'If I went to sleep now I feel as though I'd never wake up again.' Pye rose from his chair and stretched. 'I'll take a walk outside. The fresh air might do me some good.'

Ballard checked to find if he was needed and then walked over to a pew where Liz Peterson was lying swathed in blankets. Her face was deathly pale and she still appeared to be dazed. He knelt beside her, and said, 'How are you feeling, Liz?'

'A bit better now.'

'Have you had some soup?'

She nodded and moistened her lips. 'Have you found Johnnie yet?'

He hesitated, wondering whether to tell her or not. She had to know sooner or later, so he said gently, 'He's dead, Liz.' She closed her eyes and sighed. 'He died well. Young Mary Rees says he was trying to get Mrs Scanlon out of the exchange when it happened.'

Liz opened her eyes. 'And Stacey?'

Ballard shook his head.

'But she was with me – she was standing right next to me. How can she be dead when I'm not?'

'You were lucky. You were one of the first to be found. Stacey was only a few feet from you but nobody knew that. When there were enough men to make a proper search it was too late for Stacey. And Joe is still missing.'

'Poor Stacey. She was on holiday, you know.'

'I know.'

'She thought a lot of you, Ian.'

'Did she?'

'More than you know.' Liz leaned up on one elbow. 'I've seen Eric, but where's Charlie?'

'He's all right. Take it easy, Liz. He volunteered to go up the mountain with Mike. Mike is afraid there'll be another fall so he's gone to check.'

'Oh my God!' said Liz. 'It would be terrible if it happened

again.' She began to shiver uncontrollably.

'Don't worry. Mike wouldn't be on the mountain if he thought it was that dangerous. It's just a normal precaution, that's all.' He put his hands on her shoulders and pressed her back, then tucked the blankets closer about her. 'I think you'll be going out on the next flight.' He looked towards his work table. 'I must leave now, but I'll see you before you go.'

He went back to the table where Bill Quentin was standing. 'I hope it's good news, Bill.'

Quentin nodded. 'Mrs Haslam – they've just got her out. She's still alive but in pretty bad shape. The doctor said she'll be all right, though.'

Ballard crossed her name off one list and added it to another. 'Any news of her husband yet?'

'Not a thing.' Quentin hesitated. 'I made a damn fool of myself before the avalanche, Mr Ballard. I'm sorry about that.'

Ballard looked up. 'Not to worry, Bill. I've made some monumental bloody mistakes in my time, too. And while we're about it, my name is Ian. Those who have gone through this lot together are entitled to be on first name terms.'

Quentin swallowed. 'Thanks. I'll be getting back.'

'Bring good news.'

Miller wandered up. His face was pasty white and his eyes looked like two burnt holes in a blanket. 'Any news of Ralph Newman yet?'

'I'm sorry, Mr Miller. Nothing yet.'

Miller moved away again, mumbling to himself as he went. He had been asking that same question at ten minute intervals.

Ballard looked down at his lists. The papers were dog-eared and the lists confused, with many scribbles and rough erasures. He took fresh paper and began to transcribe them anew in alphabetical order, a tedious and mundane but necessary task.

Brewer, Anderson, Jenkins, Newman, Castle, Fowler – and Haslam; seven men – one dead – locked in a cave by snow and ice. They had no key.

'It's cold enough to freeze the balls off a brass monkey,' said Anderson.

Newman did not reply. It was the eighth time Anderson had uttered that conversational gem and it did not improve on rehearing. He pulled his anorak closer about his body and tried to control his fits of shivering.

'How long has it been?' asked Brewer.

Newman peered at his watch. 'Nearly six hours.'

There was a spasm of coughing from Jenkins. He spluttered a while before he brought it under control, then he gasped, 'Where are they? Where the devil are they?'

Newman said into the darkness, 'Brewer?'

'Yes?'

'What about another try?'

'It's bloody useless. You dig into the snow and it falls in from the top. You could get trapped that way.'

'Is that light still working?' For answer Brewer switched it on and there was a feeble glimmer. 'What if I tried?'

'It's too bloody dangerous.'

Newman shivered violently. 'I'd still like to try.'

'You're safer here in the cave. They'll be coming for us pretty soon.'

'If there's anyone left up there. Like to bet on it, Brewer?'

'I'm not a rich Yank,' said Brewer. 'I don't have the money to bet with.'

'Just your life,' said Newman. 'If we stay here we'll die anyway.'

'Shut up!' shouted Jenkins. 'You flaming well shut up!'

'Yes,' said Brewer. 'That kind of talk's no good.' He paused. 'Let's have another sing-song.'

'Singing won't get us out, either,' said Newman. 'We've got to work at it. We can't rely on anyone digging down to us. Who would know where to look?'

'Jenkins is right,' said Brewer sharply. 'If you can't be more cheerful you'd better keep quiet.'

Newman sighed. *What's the use?* he thought. Something occurred to him, and he said urgently, 'Sound off!'

'What's that?'

'Call out your names. I haven't heard Fowler or Castle for a long time.'

Castle said, 'Fowler's asleep.'

'Then you'd better wake him up before he dies.' Newman was boiling with frustration. 'Brewer, how much snow above us, do you think?'

'Too bloody much.'

'It might be only ten feet – it could be six feet. That's nothing.'

'For the last time,' said Brewer. 'Shut your big mouth.'

Newman stirred and inadvertently put his hand on Haslam's face, knocking the hat aside. It was icy cold.

Newman was wrong.

The cave was in a jumble of big rocks, the debris of long-gone glaciation. The rock immediately above the cave was a big one, more than sixty feet high, which was why the place had been chosen as offering good shelter from the avalanche. It was reckoned that, when the snow came, it would pour over the top of the rock and anything at the bottom would be relatively sheltered.

And so it was – but the hollow in front of the rock had filled with snow as a housewife fills a cup with flour. The snow was level with the top of the rock. Newman was entirely wrong. The depth of snow above the cave entrance was not ten feet, or an optimistic six feet.

It was sixty feet.

Cameron shouted.

He had been shouting for a long time and all he had achieved was a sore throat and a hoarse voice. The truck rested upside down and he was still trapped with his foot jammed in the pedals. He had tried to release it but the pain caused by his movements soon made him stop. Consequently he, like the truck, was still upside down and he had the eerie impression that his head was bulging with the pressure of blood.

He also had a headache of such intensity that it nauseated him.

He shouted again. Even to him it sounded weak and when he stared at the snow through the shattered windscreen, which was feebly illuminated by the last glimmer of the roof light, he knew that the sound was being absorbed by that cotton-wool whiteness. For the tenth time he decided to stop shouting in order to conserve his strength. He knew he would break that promise to himself; the idea that someone might be quite close and not know he was there was too frightening. But he did stop shouting for a while.

He wondered how much snow there was above him. Three feet? Six feet? Ten feet? There was no way of knowing. He thought he detected a little stuffiness in the air of the cab, and that made him afraid. It would be hell to die slowly of lack of

223

oxygen. With his technician's mind he began to make calculations of the probable permeability of snow with regard to air, but his mind was confused in any case, he did not know enough about the variables. *McGill would know,* he thought dimly.

There was something else Cameron did not know, and it was better for him that he should not. The truck was upside down in the river bed, and the snow which had dammed the flow of water was being eaten into upstream of him. Slowly but inexorably the river was coming to him.

*

High on the west slope McGill paused for breath and leaned on his ski-poles. 'This'll do,' he said. 'We'll test it here.'

Charlie Peterson stared down the slope. 'Lots of activity down there.'

McGill watched another helicopter land. 'Yes, they're coming in faster.' He glanced at Charlie. 'We want no bouncing about. Try to imagine you're walking on custard and don't want to break the skin.'

'I'll be light-footed,' said Charlie, and laughed. 'I never thought I'd ever try to imitate a bloody ballet dancer.'

McGill grunted and looked along the line of the slope. 'Your brother told me he grew a hay crop here. Did you have cattle grazing?'

'Hell, no! It's too steep. You'd have to breed your cows with short legs on one side and long legs on the other.'

'That figures,' said McGill. 'Professor Roget was right about his cow test.'

'What sort of test is that?'

'It was in the early days of skiing in Switzerland. Someone asked Roget how to tell if a slope was safe for skiing. He said you had to think like a cow, and if you reckoned you'd be uncomfortable grazing then the slope wasn't safe.'

'I reckon we'll lose a lot of stock.' Charlie pointed up the valley. 'There's bad flooding up there on the farm.'

'The river is blocked, but it'll soon clear.' McGill turned his ski-pole over. 'This is eyeball science,' he said wryly. 'I lost my kit.' He pushed the stick into the snow, keeping up a steady pressure. When it hit bottom he marked the depth with his thumb and withdrew the stick. 'Under three feet – that's not too bad.' He looked down at the hole he had made. 'I wish to hell I knew what was down there.'

'Why don't we dig and find out?'

'That's just what I'm going to do. Charlie, you stand up-slope from me about ten yards away. Keep your eyes on me. If anything gives then mark the place where you last saw me.'

'Hey, you don't think . . .?'

'Just a precaution,' said McGill reassuringly. He jerked his thumb towards the valley. 'If I thought what I'm doing would cause any more damage down there I wouldn't be doing it.'

Charlie climbed up the slope and turned to watch McGill, who started to excavate a hole. His movements were gentle but he worked quickly, piling the snow up-slope of the hole. Finally he thrust his arm down as far as it would go and came up clutching some brown strands. 'Long grass. That's not too good.'

He straightened. 'We'll go across diagonally and upwards, making a hole every hundred yards.' He shaded his eyes from the sun and pointed. 'I have a good idea that the avalanche broke up there by those exposed rocks. I'd like to have a look at the place.'

Charlie's eyes followed the direction of McGill's pointing arm. 'Is that necessary?'

'Not strictly necessary but I'd still like to see it.' He grinned. 'It's about six holes away. Come on, Charlie.'

They went on, making their way across and up the slope. When they had gone a hundred yards McGill stopped and dug another hole, then they went on again. For the first time Charlie showed signs of nervousness. 'You really think this is safe?'

'As safe as crossing the road,' said McGill sardonically.

'A pal of mine was killed in Auckland crossing a road.'

McGill dug another hole. Charlie said, 'What's the verdict?'

'Same diagnosis. Not too much snow but slippery underneath. If it went now it wouldn't do too much damage, but I hope to hell we don't get more snow before we're finished down there.'

They toiled higher. Charlie watched McGill digging and then looked upwards over his shoulder towards the rocks where McGill thought the avalanche had begun. They were about two hundred yards away. His gaze returned to McGill and he called out, 'What makes it slippery?'

'The grass.'

'I think we should get off the slope.'

'That's what we're doing,' said McGill equably. 'Not far to go now. Just as far as those rocks.' He straightened his bent body. 'I don't think we'll do any more digging. We'll head straight up.'

'I don't think that's a good idea,' said Charlie. His voice was edgy.

'What's the matter with you?' asked McGill. 'Why the sudden jitters?'

'I don't like standing out here. I saw what happened before.'

An aircraft went overhead very low and McGill looked up and saw the white blur of a face behind a window. Whoever it was seemed to be taking photographs. He shook his head and looked again at Charlie. 'It's quite safe,' he said. 'Take my word for it.'

There was a splintering noise from the valley behind him and he turned around. 'What was that?'

Charlie stared. 'I don't know. It's too far away to see.'

On the white floor of the valley the black specks which were men began to converge on one point like ants intent on dismembering a dead beetle. McGill could not see what was at the focal point. He said, 'Something odd seems to have happened. Are your eyes any better than mine, Charlie? Where are they all heading?'

Charlie shaded his eyes. 'Can't tell.'

They watched for a while but could not distinguish the cause of the sudden activity. At last McGill said, 'Well, let's get on.' Charlie did not move. He was standing very still, looking down into the valley. 'Snap out of it, Charlie.'

'Oh, Christ!' said Charlie. 'Look!'

McGill turned. In the valley there was a blossom of red fire which expanded as they watched, and a coil of oily black smoke grew upwards like a giant tree making an ugly stain in the air.

Breath whistled from McGill. 'What the hell was that?' he said as the sound of the explosion reached them. 'Let's get down there.'

'Sure thing,' said Charlie.

CHAPTER TWENTY-NINE

Jesse Rusch was going towards the church but turned aside sharply as someone yelled, 'I've found someone.' He ran towards the group of men who had broken their line, put aside the probes, and taken up spades. He stood on one side and watched them dig carefully, and had to smile as someone else said disgustedly, 'It's a flaming cow.'

Flaming it certainly was not. One of the men pushed at a hoof and the leg was seen to be as stiff as a rod. Rusch stepped forward. 'Dig it out, anyway.'

A man turned around. 'Why? It's a waste of time.'

'Because there might be someone under the cow,' said Rusch patiently. 'That's why.' It was a possibility but privately he thought it unlikely, so he said, 'Three men to the cow – the rest can carry on probing.'

The men dropped their spades and picked up the probes with alacrity, leaving the man who had queried the utility of digging out the cow alone with his spade. He stared at his mates in disgust, and said, 'Hey, the man said three.'

He turned and saw a group of men standing twenty yards away, their hands in their pockets. 'You lot,' he called. 'Come and give me a hand.'

They stared at him with blank eyes, then turned their backs on him and shuffled away slowly. The man flung down his shovel. 'God Almighty!' he said passionately. 'I've flown four hundred miles to help these bastards, and the bloody lead-swingers won't even help themselves.'

'Leave them be,' said Rusch quietly. 'They're not themselves. Regard them as dead men, if that's any help. Pick up your spade and get on with it. If you want help, ask your team leader.'

The man blew out his cheeks expressively, the picked up his spade and dug it viciously into the snow. Rusch watched him for ten seconds, then turned aside and went on his way.

Just outside the church he encountered a helicopter pilot from VXE-6 called Harry Baker, and he saw at once that Baker was angry, so steamed up that he should have melted the snow for yards around. He cut in before Baker opened his mouth and said quietly, 'When you tell me what's bugging you keep it soft.'

Baker jerked his thumb at the sky. 'Some goddamn maniac buzzed me up there as I was coming in. He was taking photographs.' His voice was choked with rage.

Rucsh shrugged philosophically. 'I guess those are the Press boys. They'll be chartering planes and coming in like locusts from here on in.'

'Jesse, up there it's already becoming more crowded than Times Square,' said Baker earnestly. 'If it gets any worse there'll be trouble.'

Rusch nodded. 'All right, Harry. I'll see the Civil Defence people here and see what we can do about tightening up air control. If necessary, I'll insist on grounding all unauthorized flights. In the meantime keep your cool.'

He went into the church, where he nodded to Ballard who was talking to a woman lying on a bench, and went up to the altar to speak to the Civil Defence Local Co-ordinator.

Ballard said, 'I'm sorry, Liz. I know I promised you an early flight out but there are people in worse shape than you. Mrs Haslam, for instance, needs hospital attention badly – and there are some kids, too.'

'That's all right. I'm feeling much better now. Is Charlie still up there with Mike?'

'Yes.'

She looked worried. 'I hope they're safe. I don't like them being up there.'

'Mike knows what he's doing,' said Ballard.

The stretcher bearing Mrs Haslam was being loaded into the helicopter by Arthur Pye and Bill Quentin. She moaned, and said feebly, 'Where's Jack? I want my Jack.'

Pye said, 'You'll be seeing him soon, Mrs Haslam,' not knowing whether he was a liar or not.

Harry Baker adjusted his helmet and said to the ground controller, 'When I take off I want this crowd to stand back. They were pushing a bit too close last time.' He jerked his thumb at the sky. 'It's bad enough being crowded up there.'

The ground controller nodded. 'I'll shoo them away.' He looked towards the helicopter and saw Pye and Quentin walking away and, beyond them, the loadmaster closing the sliding door. The loadmaster waved, and he said, 'That's the last one. You can take off now.' Baker climbed up into the cockpit, and the ground controller shouted, 'All right, stand back, everybody. Get well away. Come on, now.'

Baker said to his co-pilot. 'Let's get this thing off the ground. We have time for three more trips before nightfall.'

Pye and Quentin walked with the rest, shepherded by the ground controller. The engine of the helicopter fired and the rotors began to move. It looked ungainly as it rose from the ground, gathering vertical speed. Quentin was not watching when the crash happened, but Pye saw it. The helicopter rose directly into the path of a low flying light plane which appeared from nowhere and struck it in the rear. There was a splintering crash and, locked together, the two machines dropped straight into the snow.

Everyone began to run and Pye and Quentin were in the lead. Pye heaved on the sliding door of the helicopter but it had warped and would not budge. 'Give me a hand, Bill,' he panted, and Quentin also heaved at the door which slid half open creakingly and then jammed.

Immediately inside was the loadmaster whose helmet had saved him from being knocked totally unconscious. He was shaking his head groggily as Pye grabbed him by the arm and hauled him out bodily. Pye then climbed inside with Quentin just behind him.

Two children were strapped into a seat, their bodies lolling forward and supported only by the straps. Pye did not know whether they were living or dead as he fumbled at the straps, and he had no time to find out. He freed the first and passed her back to Quentin, and then tackled the second, a boy. From far away he heard a bellow from the ground controller – 'You guys in there had better be quick. She might go up.'

He freed the boy who was passed out to fall into waiting hands, then he said to Quentin, 'I'll have to go back there to get behind the stretcher. You take this end.'

There were two stretchers and when Pye looked at one of them he saw there was no use in doing anything about that one. The man lying in it had his head at a totally impossible angle and Pye judged, in that hasty glance, that his neck was broken. He turned to the other stretcher and heard Mrs Haslam say, 'Is that you, Jack?' Her eyes stared at him unwinkingly.

'Yes, that's right. I've come to take you home.' His fingernails tore and his fingers bled as he worked frantically at the straps which secured the stretcher. He got one loose and turned to find that Quentin had released the other. 'Right. Take it gently.' He bent forward and said to Mrs Haslam reassuringly, 'We'll soon have you out of here.'

It was at that moment the petrol ignited. He saw a white flash and felt searing heat, and when he inhaled his next breath he drew flaming petrol vapour into his lungs. He felt no pain and was dead before he knew it, and so was Bill Quentin, Mrs Haslam, Harry Baker and his co-pilot, whom nobody had seen on the ground in Hukahoronui.

There was no sound in the inquiry room other than the creaking of the old kauri floor. Harrison said into the silence, 'A public inquiry has already been held into the reasons for this air crash. It was held by the inspector of Air Accidents as was his statutory duty. Its findings will be incorporated into the findings of this inquiry. However I propose to say a few words on the subject now.'

His voice was even and his demeanour grave. 'Lieutenant-Commander Rusch has already given evidence that the dead helicopter pilot had complained of the hazardous nature of the flying conditions and the reasons for the hazards. Even at the moment of the crash Lieutenant-Commander Rusch was talking to the authorities at Harewood Airport and you have heard, from his evidence and that of others, that he was most forthright, and indeed, aggressive in reinforcing the strictures of his fellow officer.

'At the time of the crash it was assumed that the aircraft which was the cause of this accident had been chartered by a newspaper. In actual fact, it turned out to be an official flight made by a junior minister of the Government who was intent on finding the extent of the disaster area at Hukahoronui. Regardless of whether the flight was official or unofficial, it is evident that there was a grave breakdown of communication between the Ministry of Civil Defence and the civil and military air authorities, leading to what might be construed as criminal negligence.'

He looked up at the Press gallery with cold eyes, and Dan Edwards twitched in his seat. 'I might add that the Press acted most irresponsibly in their flights over the disaster area. While a reporter may think he has a duty to get at the facts, he has a higher duty to the community than to the newspaper which employs him. While I understand that certain civil air pilots have been reprimanded and suitably punished by the withdrawal of their flying licences, I regret that a similar punishment cannot legally be meted out to those who so irresponsibly chartered the aircraft and gave the orders.'

He switched his attention to Smithers. 'And I hope the Ministry of Civil Defence is reviewing its procedures immediately and not waiting for the findings of this Commission to be published. There could be a similar disaster tomorrow, Mr Smithers.'

He did not wait to hear anything Smithers might have to say, but tapped with his gavel. 'We stand adjourned until ten a.m. tomorrow.'

CHAPTER THIRTY

As Ballard left the hall he saw McGill talking to a bespectacled, middle-aged man whom he had previously noticed in the front rank of the Press gallery. When he approached he heard McGill say, 'I'd be much obliged if you could get them for me.'

Dan Edwards scratched the side of his jaw. 'Tit for tat,' he said. 'If there's a story in it I want an exclusive.' He smiled. 'It's all right for old Harrison to act pontifical, but I'm still a newspaperman.'

'If there's a story you'll have it first,' promised McGill. 'Even Harrison would agree that this is in the public interest.'

'When do you want them?'

'Yesterday – but today will have to do. Can I meet you in your office in half an hour?'

Edwards grimaced. 'I was looking forward to a beer, but I suppose that can wait.'

'If I find what I'm looking for I'll buy you a case of beer.'

Edwards said, 'I'll hold you to that,' and went away.

Ballard said, 'What's all that about, Mike?'

'Just checking on something – professional stuff. Seen Liz yet?'

'No. I'm meeting her later.'

'Don't waste time,' advised McGill. 'The balloon goes up

231

tomorrow. If Harrison knew I was sitting on this he'd ream me out for sure.' He looked past Ballard. 'Ah, there's the guy I want to see.' He walked away with Flying Officer Hatry, talking fast and making gestures with his hands. Ballard looked after him curiously, then shrugged and went to get his car.

He had missed Liz at lunch-time – she had left quickly with Eric and Charlie – and she had not appeared for the afternoon session. During the mid-afternoon recess he had telephoned her at her hotel and asked to see her. 'You'd better not come here,' she had said. 'Charlie wouldn't like it. I'll come to your hotel after dinner. What about nine o'clock?'

At the hotel he avoided Stenning by the simple expedient of staying in his room. In view of what had happened the previous night he had no wish for further conversation with Stenning. He whiled away the time by reading a novel which bored him, and his thoughts went skittering away from the narrative which should have held his attention.

He wondered where McGill was and what he was doing. He thought of how he was going to break the news to Liz – that was going to be damned difficult. How do you tell the woman you love that her brother is – to all intents and purposes – a multiple murderer?

He had dinner in his room. At nine-fifteen he was pacing the floor and, at nine-thirty, when Liz still had not shown up, he contemplated telephoning her again. At nine-forty the telephone rang and he grabbed it.

'Ballard.'

'A guest for you, Mr Ballard.'

'I'll be right there.'

He went to the reception desk where the clerk said, 'In the lounge, Mr Ballard.'

Ballard walked into the hotel lounge and looked about. In a corner he saw Stenning reading a newspaper but there was no sign of Liz. From behind him a voice said, 'I'll bet you didn't expect *me*, Ballard.'

He turned and saw Charlie Peterson. 'Where's Liz?' he demanded.

Charlie swayed slightly on his feet. His face was reddened and covered with a film of sweat, and a tic worked convulsively under his left eye. 'She won't be here,' he said. 'I've made sure of that. I've told you before – stay away from my sister, you bastard.'

232

'What have you done with her?'

'She's got nothing to do with you – now or at any other time. You must be either stupid or deaf. Didn't McGill pass on my message?'

'He did.' Ballard contemplated Charlie for a long moment, then said, 'I asked Liz to come here because I had something important to tell her. Since she isn't here I'll tell you.'

'I have no interest in anything you have to say.' Charlie looked about the lounge. 'If we were anywhere else I'd break your bloody back. You're always careful never to be alone, aren't you?'

'You'd better listen, Charlie; it's for your own good. And you'd better sit down while you hear it, before you fall down.'

Something in Ballard's tone of voice caught Charlie's attention. He narrowed his eyes, and said, 'All right, say your piece.' He flopped down heavily on to a settee.

As Ballard sat down he saw Stenning looking across at them wearing a puzzled expression. He ignored Stenning and turned to Charlie. 'You're in trouble – bad trouble.'

Charlie grinned humourlessly. '*I'm* in trouble! Wait until you hear what's in store for you.'

'We know what went on on top of the west slope before the avalanche. We know what you did, Charlie.'

The grin disappeared from Charlie's face. 'I wasn't on the west slope and no one can say I was. Who says I was?'

'Miller says so,' said Ballard quietly. 'We have a letter.'

'He's a liar,' said Charlie tautly.

Ballard shrugged. 'What reason has he for lying? What reason has he for sending ten thousand dollars to the Disaster Fund? You tell me.'

'Where is this letter? I want to see it.'

'You'll see it. It will be given to Harrison tomorrow morning.'

Charlie swallowed. 'And what the hell am I supposed to have done? Tell me because I don't know.'

Ballard looked at him steadily. 'He says you deliberately started the avalanche.'

The tic on Charlie's face twitched. 'Lies!' he shouted. 'He's a bloody liar!'

'Keep your voice down,' said Ballard.

'Keep my voice down!' said Charlie in suppressed fury. 'I'm accused of murder and you tell me to keep my voice down!'

All the same he spoke more softly and looked quickly about the lounge.

'Now listen to me. I asked Liz here so I could break it to her gently so she wouldn't hear it for the first time in open court tomorrow. I don't know how you've prevented her from coming here, but since you're here I decided to tell you. I'm giving you a chance, Charlie.'

'What chance?' he asked in a grating voice.

'Miller may be a liar or he may not. But whichever he is I'm giving you the chance to get on your hind legs tomorrow as soon as the session starts and get in your version to Harrison before the letter is produced. And don't think I'm doing it for you. I'm doing this for Liz.'

'Some chance,' sneered Charlie. 'You cooked up this, Ballard; you and McGill between you.'

'I know the truth of that,' said Ballard quietly. 'And so, I think, do you. And another thing – I don't know how you stopped Liz coming here but if you've hurt her you'll be responsible to me.'

Charlie stood up suddenly. 'You bloody bastard, no one is responsible for Liz *except* me, and no pommy son of a bitch is going to get near her least of all anyone called Ballard.' He looked around the crowded lounge and then jabbed out his finger. 'I tell you, if I catch you anywhere I can get at you, you'll wish you'd never heard of the Peterson family.' He turned on his heel abruptly and walked from the lounge.

'I almost wish that now,' said Ballard softly, and turned his head to look across at Stenning who looked back at him with an expressionless face.

McGill worked late that night, mostly in a photographic dark-room at Deep Freeze Advanced Headquarters. It was finicky and exacting work, involving fine measurement, but he was greatly helped by a US Navy photographer. Even so, it was long after midnight before he finished and all he had to show was an envelope containing some eight by ten glossies and a few transparencies.

He drove back to the hotel and parked his car in its slot next to Ballard's car and got out, taking the envelope with him.

He turned to go into the hotel, and then hesitated before walking around to look at Ballard's car. It was empty and the door was locked. He shrugged and was about to turn away

234

again when he heard a thread of a sound so weak it would have been obscured had he moved his feet on the gravel. He stood very still and listened, straining his ears, but heard no more.

He walked to the other side of Ballard's car and stepped on something soft and yielding in the darkness. He stepped back and flicked on his cigarette lighter and peered downwards, then he drew in his breath sharply and, turning on his heel, he ran to the hotel entrance as fast as he could.

The night porter looked up in alarm as McGill burst into the foyer and skidded to a halt. 'Phone for a doctor and an ambulance,' said McGill breathlessly. 'There's a seriously injured man in the car park.' The porter was immobile with early morning stupidity, and McGill yelled, 'Move, man!'

The porter jerked and reached for the telephone and a minute later McGill was hammering on Stenning's door. 'Who is it?' Stenning's voice was muffled and sleepy.

'McGill. Open up.'

Presently Stenning opened the door. His white hair was tousled and his eyes still sleep-filled, and he was knotting the cord of a dressing-gown about his waist. 'What is it?'

McGill was curt. 'You'd better come with me and see the result of your goddamn meddling.'

'And what do you mean by that?' Stenning was coming awake quickly.

'You'll see. Come on. It's not far so you needn't dress.'

'Slippers,' said Stenning. 'I'll need slippers.' He went back into the room and reappeared seconds later.

As they went through the foyer McGill called out, 'What about that doctor?'

'On his way with the ambulance,' said the porter.

'Can you turn on the lights in the car park?'

'Yes, sir.' He turned and opened a door behind him and snapped switches. 'A car accident?'

McGill didn't answer that one. 'You'd better rouse the manager. Come on, Stenning.'

They hastened across the car park which was now brightly lit. Stenning said, 'Someone hurt?'

'Ian – and he's hurt bad. Over here.'

A startled exclamation was torn from Stenning as he looked down at the bloody body of Ballard. 'Oh my God! What happened?'

'It was no car accident, that's for sure.' McGill took Bal-

235

lard's wrist, ignoring the blood. 'I think he's still alive – I'm not sure. Where's that goddamn doctor?'

'What do you mean – it isn't a car accident? It looks bad enough to be one.'

'How in hell could he be hit by a car here?' McGill waved. 'The space between these cars is only three feet.'

'He could have crawled in here.'

'Then where's the trail of blood he left?' McGill stood up. 'What you're looking at, Stenning, is a man who has almost been beaten to death – and I'm not sure about almost. It's what happens when a man gets *walked over,* Stenning.' His voice was harsh and accusing.

Stenning's face was white. McGill said in a shaky voice, 'You sit in your plush offices in the City of London and you manipulate men, and you set up what you call *experiments,* for God's sake, and you talk of people being walked over.' His finger stabbed down at Ballard's body. 'This is the reality, Stenning. Look at it, damn you!'

Stenning swallowed and his Adam's apple bobbed up and down in his skinny throat. 'There was no intention of . . .'

'No intention of murder?' McGill laughed and it was an ugly sound in the quiet night. 'What the hell else do you expect to happen when you interfere with a maniac like Charlie Peterson?'

Stenning was a lawyer and his mind worked on tracks as precise as a railway engine. 'I saw Charlie Peterson and Ballard in the hotel tonight. They had a long conversation and it wasn't amiable – but that's not proof of anything.' He turned his head and looked at McGill. 'Do you *know* it was Peterson?'

'Yes,' said McGill bluntly.

'How do you know?'

McGill paused. He suddenly realized he was still holding the envelope of photographs. He looked at it for a moment and his mind worked fast. 'I know,' he said, lying deliberately. 'I know because Ian told me before he passed out.'

In the distance a siren wailed as the ambulance approached.

CHAPTER THIRTY-ONE

At ten o'clock Harrison walked into the hall and sat on the rostrum flanked by Rolandson and French. He waited until the rustling had stopped, then said, 'I have to report that Mr Ian Ballard was seriously injured in a car accident in the early hours of this morning and is at present in Princess Margaret Hospital. He is in a coma and Dr McGill is, quite understandably, with him.'

There was a surge of noise. In the Press gallery Dan Edwards frowned, and said, 'Damn! I wonder if that affects the story?'

'What story?' asked Dalwood.

'Oh, nothing. Just something I was getting a line on.' He nudged Dalwood. 'Look at Charlie Peterson. He's laughing fit to bust a gut.'

Harrison tapped with his gavel to restore order. 'We are now at a stage of the Inquiry when the evidence of Mr Ballard and Dr McGill is not absolutely essential, so there is no need to adjourn. Call the first witness, Mr Reed.'

Twenty-four hours after the avalanche the number of those still missing had been cut down to twenty-one. All the others had been accounted for – dead and alive. Ballard said glumly, 'There's still no sign of Joe Cameron.'

Jesse Rusch said, 'A friend of yours?'

'I suppose so. I hadn't known him long. I don't suppose there's much hope for him now, but perhaps it's better that way. His daughter was killed.'

'There've been too many people killed here,' said Rusch, thinking of Baker. 'And some of those deaths were unnecessary.'

'All of them were,' said Ballard bleakly.

Turi Buck came up and silently held out a piece of paper. Ballard took it, then looked up. 'The Marshall family, all four of them?'

'We've just dug out the house – or what's left of it.'

'Dead! All of them?'

'Yes.' Turi went away, his back bent.

Ballard made four violent slash marks on the list before him. 'Seventeen.'

'We'll be able to get bulldozers in this afternoon,' said Rusch. 'That should speed things up.'

'And it could be dangerous,' said Ballard. 'A bulldozer blade could chop a man in half.'

'We'll be careful,' said Rusch. 'We'll be real careful. But speed is important now. If anyone buried is still alive now they can't last much longer.' By the tone of his voice he doubted if anyone could possibly be still alive.

Cameron was almost totally exhausted. He had been asleep or perhaps unconscious – it did not matter which – but now he was awake again. His whole body was racked with pain and the fierce headache was still with him. He had been sick during the night and had been afraid of choking on his own vomit, but he had managed to twist his head to one side and so had not suffered that particularly ugly death. Also during the night he had uncontrollably voided both urine and faeces and now the stench of himself sickened him.

He became aware of a sound and, at first, thought it was human and his hopes rose. It sounded as though someone was chuckling quietly. Cameron called weakly and then listened as the distant laughter went on. He thought he was going mad – who would be laughing in the middle of a snowdrift?

His senses swam and he passed out for a few minutes. When he awoke again he heard the sound but it had subtly changed. It was now more of a gurgle than a laugh or a chuckle, a sound such as might be made by a contented baby in its cot. After listening for a long time he knew what it was and again became afraid. He was listening to the sound of water.

Presently he was aware that his head was becoming wet. A trickle of water had entered the cab and swirled about his scalp as he hung there suspended upside down, and now he knew that he would drown. Not much water need come in to cover his mouth and nose – no more than six inches.

On the surface two young men were piloting a bulldozer through the hummocky snow alongside the river. The driver was John Skinner, a construction worker from Auckland; he was also a member of the Alpine Sports Club. His companion was a university lecturer and a member of the Canterbury

University Ski Club called Roger Halliwell. Skinner stopped the bulldozer by the river, and said, 'The flooding upstream will stop as soon as the river clears that snow away.'

'I hear a lot of cattle were drowned,' said Halliwell.

'No people, though. That bloody avalanche must have been bad enough without the risk of drowning.' Skinner looked around. 'Now where was it that the Yank wanted us to dig?'

A section of snow in the river bed slumped as it was under-cut by water and Halliwell looked at it idly. Then he said, 'I think I saw something down there.'

'What?'

'I don't know. Something dark. It was round.'

'A boulder, maybe.'

'Perhaps.' Halliwell frowned. 'I'm going to have a look.'

He dropped from the bulldozer and walked to the edge of the river and then put his foot delicately on to the snow. It was soft but bore his weight without him sinking too much. He walked on slowly, lifting each leg high. As he progressed the snow became more slushy because it had been penetrated by the river water, and suddenly he sank up to his waist. He had a nightmare vision of going right down, but he found himself standing on something.

He put his hand down into the snow and encountered a shape which he explored. It was a wheel with a tyre on it. 'There's a car in here,' he yelled.

Skinner jumped down and unclipped a wire rope from the rear of the bulldozer. There was a big snap-shackle on each end, one of which he clipped to a stout bar on the bulldozer. 'Can you catch this?' He whirled the other end of the rope around his head.

He missed on his first cast, but Halliwell caught it the second time. There was some difficulty in finding somewhere to attach the shackle. Halliwell knew it had to be an integral part of the chassis of the buried vehicle and he groped around in the snow for some time quite unsuccessfully.

In the cab Cameron was close to drowning. The water covered his nose even though he withdrew his head into his shoulders like a tortoise trying to retreat into its shell. There was only a matter of an inch to go before it covered his mouth. While he could do so he took a deep breath.

The truck lurched and water washed over his head. When the movement had finished Cameron's head was completely under water and he battled to keep his breath. The truck moved again, this time upwards, and Cameron screamed at the pain and thought his back was being broken. The bulldozer hauled the truck bodily from the river bed and on to the bank where it lay on its side.

Halliwell ran up to it. 'There's someone in here,' he said in wonder. 'And he's alive, by God!'

Within the hour Cameron was in a helicopter on his way to Christchurch. But he was a badly broken man.

Newman was unlucky.

All night he had been digging upwards in total darkness. He had to dig a hole at least two feet in diameter to accommodate the shoulders of a broad man. There had also to be steps cut in the side where he could stand. For digging he used whatever came to hand. His most useful tool was a ballpoint pen which he jabbed repeatedly into the snow above him, breaking it out, chunk by chunk. Often the snow dropped into his eyes, but that did not matter because it was dark anyway. Twice he dropped the pen and that did matter because he had to go down and grope with gloved hands until he found it. He lost time there.

In one sense he was lucky. He did not know how far he had to dig and had he known it was as much as sixty feet it is doubtful if he would have ever begun. But during the time he was under the snow it had begun to settle and compact as the air was squeezed out of it. While this made it a harder material to penetrate it also meant that it lessened the distance he had to dig to a little over fifty feet.

He dug alone because the others in the cave had lapsed into total apathy.

Fifty-two hours after the avalanche the sky was darkening and Sam Foster, a Ranger from Tongariro, debated with himself whether or not it was worth while having his team continue the search. There were still a few men missing but it was inconceivable that any would be alive even if found. Perhaps it would be better to call off the search until the morrow.

He strode into a gently sloping cup-shaped hollow and was somewhere in the middle of it when the snow gave under his feet. Newman had dug to within a foot of the surface, and when Foster's weight broke through one of Foster's boots slammed into his head. He fell down the hole he had made. It was not a long fall because the bottom of the hole was packed with the debris of his digging. But it was enough to break his neck.

The others, of course, were rescued, excepting Haslam who was dead already. Newman was the last person to die in the valley. The last person to die as a result of the disaster at Hukahoronui was Mrs Jarvis, the oldest inhabitant, who lingered tenaciously in hospital for a week before she succumbed.

There was a second avalanche on the west slope of Hukahoronui that year but it happened in the spring thaw. There was nobody there to kill.

CHAPTER THIRTY-TWO

At three-thirty in the afternoon McGill parked his car and hurried across Durham Street towards the Provincial Government Buildings. Instead of going into the chamber where the hearing was being held, he went upstairs to the entrance to the Press gallery and had a word with the usher. Presently Dan Edwards came out to see him.

'I keep my promises,' said McGill. 'You've got your story.' He gave Edwards an envelope. 'A photostat of a letter which is self-explanatory and some photographs which I'll explain to the Chairman. What's going on down there now?'

'Harrison is winding things up. A pathologist is giving medical evidence.' Edwards paused, his thumb beneath the flap of the envelope. 'Talking of that – how's Ballard?'

'In a bad way.'

'These bloody hit-and-run drivers.' He saw McGill's look of surprise, and said, 'One of the boys checked at the hotel. It was obviously hit and run, wasn't it?' He regarded McGill closely. 'Or am I missing something?'

McGill poked his finger at the envelope. 'You're missing your story.'

Edwards pulled out the copy of the letter and scanned it. His jaw dropped. 'Jesus! Is this straight up?'

'I'll be giving the original to Harrison in less than five minutes.'

'Thanks, McGill. Maybe I'll give *you* a case of beer.' He went back into the Press gallery and found a young reporter.

'Take this back to the office. Give it to the editor – in no one else's hands, understand. Off with you.'

He regained his seat and Dalwood said curiously, 'Anything doing?'

Edwards grinned broadly and nodded down into the hall. 'The fireworks are due to start any minute.'

McGill walked across the vestibule, past the two policemen standing outside the chamber, and went inside. Harrison turned his head, and said to the witness, 'Excuse me, Dr Cross. Good afternoon, Dr McGill. How is Mr Ballard?'

'He's still unconscious, Mr Chairman.'

'I'm sorry to hear it. It's good of you to return, but not really necessary under the circumstances.'

'I think my return was very necessary, Mr Chairman. I am in possession of fresh evidence.'

'Indeed? Step forward, Dr McGill. You are excused for the moment, Dr Cross.'

The pathologist stepped down and McGill stood before the rostrum. He took an envelope from his pocket. 'I received this letter and discussed the contents with Mr Ballard. We both agreed that it was too important to conceal even though it could destroy a man's reputation.'

He handed the letter to Harrison who opened it and began to read. It took him a long time and the lines of his face deepened as he read. At last he raised his head, and said, 'I see. Yes, it would have been wrong to withhold this.' He looked at the letter again. 'I see that each page is signed and countersigned, and has the seal of a notary public. Would that be the American equivalent of our own Commissioner for Oaths?'

'It is almost the exact equivalent, Mr Chairman.'

Harrison's eyes roved about the room. 'Mr Lyall, would you mind stepping over here?'

Lyall looked surprised, but said, 'Not at all, Mr Chairman.' He got up and walked over to stand next to McGill.

Harrison said in a low voice, 'This concerns one of your clients. I think you'd better read it.' He held out the letter.

A few minutes later Lyall said nervously, 'I don't really know what to say, Mr Chairman.' His face was pale. 'I feel inclined to withdraw from this case.'

'Do you?' Harrison's voice was grim. 'This is not a *case*, Mr Lyall; it is a Commission of Inquiry. Apart from that, I doubt if anyone would respect a lawyer who deserted his client when

242

things became hard.'

Red spots burned in Lyall's cheeks. 'Very well,' he said abruptly. 'But is it admissible evidence?'

'That is something which I and the assessors will have to decide,' said Harrison heavily. He took the letter from Lyall and passed it to Rolandson.

McGill said, 'I have other supporting evidence.'

'No evidence can be brought to support this letter if the letter itself is not admissible,' said Lyall. 'And if you admit the letter there will certainly be grounds for appeal.'

'There'll be no appeal,' said McGill. 'And you know it.'

'You are not here to argue a lawyer's case, Dr McGill,' said Harrison in tones of freezing rebuke. He turned to Rolandson. 'What do you think?'

'I think it's appalling,' snapped Rolandson.

'I mean, is it admissible?'

'Let me read it all.' Presently Rolandson said, 'It has been witnessed under oath. It is admissible.'

Harrison gave the letter to French, who read it and soon looked as though there was a bad smell under his nose. He tossed the letter down. 'Certainly admissible.'

'I think so, too. I'm sorry, Mr Lyall.' Harrison passed the letter to the Secretary to the Commission. 'Read that aloud, Mr Reed.' He paused as though confused by the homonyms he had uttered.

Reed scanned the letter and then began, 'This is a letter from a Mr George Albert Miller of Riverside, California, and is addressed to Dr Michael McGill.'

He read the letter slowly and in an even tone which contrasted oddly with the events Miller described. When he had finished he said flatly, 'Each page is signed by Mr Miller and countersigned by Carl Risinger. Each page is impressed with the seal of a notary public.'

The silence in the hall was total and seemed to last forever. It was as though time had stopped. There was a strange movement as people twisted in their seats to look in one direction. It was as though Charlie Peterson had developed a new form of attractive force – all eyes turned towards him like compass needles towards a magnet.

He was sitting slumped in his chair, his face white and his eyes staring. Next to him Eric had withdrawn and was looking at Charlie with a baffled expression. Liz was sitting upright, her hands in her lap, and staring rigidly ahead. Her brow was contracted and her lips compressed. She was very angry.

Charlie's eyes flickered from side to side and he became aware that everyone was watching him in silence. He jumped to his feet. 'It's a lie!' he shouted. 'Miller is a liar. He started the avalanche, not me.'

The silence broke and a wave of sound washed around Charlie. Harrison hammered with his gavel furiously. With difficulty he achieved order and said icily, 'Any more disturbance and I will adjourn this session.' He looked at Charlie with cold eyes. 'You will sit down, Mr Peterson.'

Charlie's right hand stabbed out, pointing at Harrison and McGill's eyes narrowed as he observed the strip of sticking-plaster which decorated his knuckles. 'Aren't you going to hear me?' Charlie yelled. 'You were ready enough to hear Ballard when his reputation was at stake.'

Harrison turned to Lyall. 'You must control your client, Mr Lyall. Either he sits down or he leaves – by force, if necessary.'

Lyall called out, 'Sit down, Charlie. You're paying me to handle this.'

'And you're not doing too well,' grumbled Charlie. But he sat down and Eric whispered to him furiously.

Lyall said, 'I must formally protest against the admission of this unsubstantiated letter as evidence. It attacks my client's reputation seriously and, in my opinion, unjustifiably. Mr Miller is not available for my cross-examination and I must protest. Further, I give formal warning that a motion of appeal will be entered immediately.'

Harrison said calmly, 'As I remarked to Mr Rickman earlier in these proceedings, you will find the necessary procedure set out in the Act of Parliament which governs the holding of Commissions of Inquiry. Dr McGill, you mentioned that you have other evidence. Is this evidence in support of Mr Miller's allegations?'

'Yes, sir.'

'Then we will hear it.'

'Objection!'

'Overruled, Mr Lyall.'

'It is photographic evidence, Mr Chairman,' said McGill. 'I have taken the liberty of having the equipment made available. I would like to operate it myself.'

Harrison nodded abruptly. 'See to it, Mr Reed.'

In the few minutes it took for the apparatus to be set up,

noise again swelled in the hall. Dalwood said to Edwards, 'You knew what was coming, you old fox.' He was still scribbling furiously.

Edwards offered him a self-satisfied grin. 'My boss will be remaking the front page right now. We've got a photocopy of Miller's letter.'

'How the hell did you get that?'

'McGill wanted something from us.' He nodded down at the hall. 'You'll see.'

Harrison called for silence and the hall quietened quickly. 'Proceed, Dr McGill.'

McGill stood next to a cine projector. 'I have here the original film taken of the avalanche by Flying Officer Hatry. The film he submitted to the Commission was a copy; the original is a better print. I don't think that Flying Officer Hatry should be censured for this, either by this Commission or by his superiors in the Air Force. For a keen photographer to part with an original would be a highly unnatural act.'

He switched on the projector. 'I will show only that portion of the film which is relevant.'

An unsteady picture appeared on the screen, the whiteness of snow and a few scattered rocks with blue-sky beyond. A plume, as of smoke, arose and McGill switched off the projector to freeze the action. He stepped forward with a pointer in his hand.

'As you can see, the avalanche started here, just by these rocks. It was daytime and the sun was shining in a clear sky. Under those conditions rock and snow take up heat in a different way; the rock warms more quickly, and this difference may set up stresses in the snow just enough to upset an already critical balance of forces. That was my assumption when I first saw this film.'

He switched off the cine projector. 'I have here a greatly enlarged portion of that scene which I am going to put in this special projector. It is called a comparator.' He switched it on. 'The degree of enlargement is such that the image is very grainy, but it will suffice for our purposes.'

Again McGill went to the screen with the pointer. 'Here are the rocks and there is the plume of snow powder which is the start of the avalanche. This photograph is from a frame of the film which we will call frame one. The next slide you will see is a similar shot but taken thirty-six frames later. That is, there is a two-second difference between the taking of the two photographs.' He went back to the comparator and inserted the second slide.

'There is not much difference, as you can see. The plume of snow powder is marginally greater.' He paused. 'But if we alternate the slides rapidly, as this machine is designed to do, you will see something curious.'

The image on the screen began to flicker rapidly and the snow plume oscillated. McGill used his pointer. 'Two of what I thought to be rocks – those two specks there – are obviously moving. This one at the top does not move very much in the two-second interval, but the one beneath moves a fair distance upwards. I submit that the speck at the top is Mr Miller, and the one beneath is Peterson climbing up to him after the avalanche was triggered.'

The increased sound in the hall was almost like the growl of a wild beast, and Harrison's gavel slammed down. 'I must protest again,' said Lyall. 'Two grainy images on a film which cannot even be seen to be men! What sort of evidence is this? They could very well be flaws in the film.'

'I have not yet finished,' said McGill quietly.

'Neither have I,' retorted Lyall. 'I would like to talk to you in private, Mr Chairman.'

Harrison listened to the roil of noise in the hall. 'I think if you keep your voice down you'll be private enough here.'

'I must object,' said Lyall intensely. 'Dr McGill has been giving evidence about something he could not possibly know – evidence that reflects upon my client. He has stated flatly in this room that one of those specks on the film is Charlie Peterson. Further, he has also stated that the lower of those specks *is* Mr Peterson and that he started the avalanche. Can he prove this?'

'Well, Dr McGill?' said Harrison.

McGill was silent for a moment. 'No,' he admitted.

'Assuming, for the sake of theoretical argument, that those specks are men,' said Lyall. 'They could be anyone, and nothing to do with my client.'

'Now wait a minute,' said McGill. 'Charlie just said that Miller started the avalanche. If he knows that, then it means he was there. And we have Miller's sworn evidence.'

'I'm quite capable of drawing my own conclusions,' said Harrison. 'I suggest you confine your evidence to that which you know, Dr McGill.'

Lyall said, 'As I see it, it's Miller's word against that of my client. And Miller isn't here to cross-examine.'

'What would he gain by accusing Charlie!' asked McGill. 'He'd have done better for himself by keeping his mouth shut. As it is, he's out ten thousand dollars.'

'That's enough,' said Harrison sharply. 'As I said before, you're not here to argue a lawyer's case, Dr McGill. Now you say you have more evidence?'

'Yes, sir.'

'Photographic?'

'That and my own testimony.'

'Then I suggest we proceed.' Harrison again hammered with his gavel until he succeeded in achieving silence. He waited until the silence was absolute, then said quietly, 'Dr McGill, you may continue.'

McGill returned to the projector. 'After the avalanche I went up on the west slope to see if there was further hazard. As it turned out, the hazard was minimal in the immediate future. Charlie Peterson volunteered to accompany me. We made an examination of the slope and Mr Peterson was very cool and showed no sign of nerves. It was only after I had indicated my intention to examine the site where the avalanche had begun that he showed signs of nervousness. At the time I put this down to a natural fear of being in a potentially hazardous situation.

'As we went up the mountain his nervousness increased rapidly and he suggested we go down. We were not far from the site which I wished to examine so I ignored his suggestion. In the event we never reached the site. There was the air accident in the valley and we went down the slope immediately.'

'Interesting,' said Harrison. 'But I don't see the point.'

'This is the point,' said McGill. 'While we were on the slope an aircraft flew over us at very low altitude and I saw someone taking photographs. I discovered afterwards that the plane had been chartered by a newspaper here in Christchurch. I went to the newspaper office last night and went through all the photographs that had been taken. Here are some of them.'

The projector clicked and flashed again, and a black-and-white photograph appeared on the screen. McGill said, 'In the bottom right-hand corner you can see Peterson and me.

In the top left corner you see exposed rocks. By the rocks there are ski tracks here – and here. I think that Peterson didn't want me to see those tracks; that's why he was nervous.'

'An unwarranted suggestion,' snapped Lyall.

McGill ignored him, and put another picture on the screen. 'Here is an enlargement of the breakaway point of the avalanche. There is a ski track going into it, and this ragged line, and another here, is where a man jumped up the slope. It had been snowing heavily that night, and all these tracks could only have been made on the morning of the avalanche.'

He switched off the projector. 'I further state on oath that the first time I saw Miller and Peterson on that Sunday they were both on skis.'

The dark room exploded. 'Lights!' shouted Harrison. 'Turn on the lights!'

An electrolier sparked into brilliance, and then sunlight flooded the room as an usher pulled aside a curtain. Charlie was on his feet. 'Damn you!' he yelled, pointing at McGill.

'Shut up, Charlie!' called Lyall sharply, but he was too late.

'Damn you all!' cried Charlie. 'It was Ballard who killed my brother – everyone knows that. Nobody would have died if they'd gone into the mine as Eric wanted. And Alec wouldn't have drowned if it hadn't been for Ballard. He's a bloody murderer, I tell you!' Froth flecked his lips. 'He started the avalanche – him and Miller between them.'

Lyall sagged and McGill heard him say, 'He's crazy!'

Charlie's throat worked convulsively. 'Ballard didn't like Huka or anyone in it.' He threw his arms wide. 'He wanted to *destroy* it – and he. *did*. Most of all, he didn't like us Peter-sons. He killed two of us – and he made a whore out of my sister.' His arm swung around and pointed to Liz.

Harrison's gavel cracked sharply, and he said, 'Dr Cross, is there anything you can do?'

Eric grabbed Charlie's arm, but Charlie tossed him aside effortlessly. 'And McGill was in on the whole thing and I'm going to kill the bastard!' He plunged across the hall towards McGill but before he could reach him Eric had recovered and was on his back.

'Let me go,' he screamed. 'Let me get at him!' Again he broke Eric's grip and started again for McGill, but this time several men had moved in to subdue him. There was a brief flurry and then Charlie broke loose and ran sideways and made for the door. It opened before he got there and he ran into the arms of two policemen. They both put an armlock on him and he was marched out of sight.

Harrison thumped his gavel in vain. Into the uproar he said quietly, 'This hearing is adjourned.'

CHAPTER THIRTY-THREE

Half an hour later McGill, still in the hall, was beseiged by reporters. 'No comment,' he kept repeating. 'I said all I had to say when I gave my evidence. There's nothing more.'

He broke free, went into the first room he saw and slammed the door behind him. He turned and saw Harrison and Stenning. 'Sorry, but do you mind if I take refuge for a few minutes. Those reporters are driving me crazy.'

'Not at all,' said Harrison. 'You've caused quite a stir, Dr McGill.'

McGill grimaced. 'Not as much as Charlie. How is he?'

'Dr Cross put him under sedation.' He paused. 'I think there's a case for a court order for psychiatric treatment.' Harrison recollected his manners. 'Oh, this is Mr Stenning, a visitor from England. He's here to see how we conduct our administrative justice. I've been telling him that not all our Inquiries are so rowdy. I don't think he believes me.'

'I'm acquainted with Mr Stenning,' said McGill. 'We stay at the same hotel.'

Harrison picked up his briefcase. 'I think it will be safe to leave by the back way, gentlemen.'

Stenning said, 'Could I have a word with you, Dr McGill?'
'Of course.'

'Feel free to use this office,' said Harrison. 'Will you attend the Inquiry tomorrow, Mr Stenning?'

'I think not. I have urgent business in England. I assure you it has been most interesting.'

'Well, then, we'll say goodbye now.' They shook hands.

When Stenning and McGill were alone Stenning remarked, 'Harrison was wrong – that letter was not admissible because Miller was not there to be cross-examined. I think the Inquiry will be adjourned while Harrison takes legal advice. It shows the inadvisability of setting a layman to do a lawyer's job.'

McGill shrugged. 'Does it matter now? We've seen that Charlie is as crazy as a loon.'

Stenning regarded him speculatively. 'You said in your evidence that Ian had agreed that the letter should be produced.'

'That's right.'

'Strange. At the end of our last conversation Ian told me to go to hell. He also consigned the Ballard Trust to the same destination. He must have changed his mind. It would be interesting to know exactly when he changed it.'

'I think he changed it when Charlie Peterson started beating the hell out of him.'

'You think it *was* Peterson?'

'For God's sake! Don't you? You've just seen Charlie in action. He tossed Eric around as though he was a rag doll, and Eric's no midget. And I got a good look at his hands this afternoon. His knuckles were pretty raw.'

'Is that the only reason you think it was Peterson? I have to be sure, Dr McGill.'

'Of course not,' said McGill, lying bravely with a frank open face. 'Ian told me himself when I found him in the car park. He said, and I remember his exact words, "It was Charlie, use the letter and smash him." Then he passed out.'

'I see.' Stenning smiled, and said obliquely, 'I think Ian is lucky to have you for a friend.'

'I'd do the same for anyone who was getting the raw end of a deal, Mr Stenning. He was getting it from both sides, you know. Your hands are not entirely clean in this matter.'

Abruptly he turned his back on Stenning and left the room. He crossed the Provincial Chamber, now deserted, and went into the vestibule where he ran straight into Liz Peterson. She lifted her hand and slapped his face with all the force she could muster, which was considerable.

His head rocked sideways and he grabbed her wrist. 'Steady, Liz.'

'How could you?' she said passionately. 'How could you do that to Charlie?'

'Someone had to stop him.'

'But not like that. You needn't have crucified him in public.'

'How would you suggest? He was mad, Liz; he was going insane. Even Eric thought so. Eric told him outright he was losing his mind. He was eaten up by guilt and he wanted to pour it all out on Ian.'

'Ian!' Liz said contemptuously. 'That man wanted to marry me. I never want to see him again. He could have suppressed that letter.'

'He wanted to,' said McGill. 'But I talked him out of it. It would have been a fool thing to do. He was supposed to see you last night. Did he?'

She shook her head. 'Charlie played one of his tricks. He got me into his car on some excuse and then drove me out of town going like a maniac.' She stopped as she realized what she had just said and then swallowed. 'Anyway, he dumped me on a country road and just drove away. It was nearly midnight when I got back into town. I phoned Ian but he wasn't in. I thought I'd see him this morning but he had the accident.'

'Did Charlie know you were going to see Ian?'

'Not unless Eric told him.'

'So you told Eric, and Eric mentioned it to Charlie. That was a fool thing to do.' He took her arm. 'You need talking to, my girl, and you'd better have a drink while you listen.'

Five minutes later at a discreet table in a hotel lounge McGill said, 'It's a bit of a convoluted story. When Miller's letter came, Ian read it and asked me just one question. He wanted to know if the avalanche would have happened anyway, regardless of what Charlie had done. I had to say that it would have come down. It was only a matter of time, Liz.'

He picked up his drink and stared at it. 'Once Ian heard that he wanted me to suppress the letter. I talked him out of that, but then he said he wanted to clear things with you.'

'And I didn't turn up,' Liz said dully.

'The next time I saw him he was a hospital case, and I was lying like a flat fish to a man called Stenning – you've met him.'

'What's he got to do with it?'

McGill told her about old Ben Ballard, the Ballard Trust and the task that had been laid upon Stenning. It took quite a while. He wound up by saying, 'Even when Ian knew about Miller's letter he told Stenning to go to hell. Stenning just told me that.'

'He was prepared to give all that up?' said Liz slowly.

'Not because he didn't want to hurt Charlie, but because he didn't want to hurt you. Don't blame Ian for anything. Anyway, it doesn't matter any more. Stenning has evidence that

Ian did walk over the Petersons in the end. He might suspect a fiddle but he can't prove it, and because he's a lawyer he'll accept it.' McGill smiled. 'From something he said just now I rather think he likes it this way.'

'Aren't you cheating Stenning?' asked Liz with a half smile.

'Not really. I think old Ben was wrong. He said a man must have steel in him to run the Ballard Group but I think there are enough men of steel around – too many, perhaps. They're going out of fashion. What the Group needs now is a man-manager, an administrator, a diplomat – and Ian is all of those. And if he needs any steel he'll have it if he has a Peterson next to him.'

'Oh, Mike, do you think . . .?' Liz put her hand on McGill's and her eyes were bright with unshed tears. 'I'm torn, Mike. The police have taken Charlie away because of the avalanche and . . .'

'No!' said McGill sharply. 'Not because of the avalanche. That hasn't been proved – and may never be.'

'Then why?'

'Ian intended to meet you last night but, instead, he got Charlie. Stenning saw them at the hotel. And Charlie beat Ian half to death in the car park, probably when he was on his way to look for you. There was no car accident. The police were waiting to arrest Charlie for assault as soon as he came out of the hall.'

Liz was as pale as she had been when McGill had first seen her in the church after the avalanche. He said gently, 'He had to be stopped, Liz. I've often wondered what would have happened if he and I had gone that extra two hundred feet up the west slope after the avalanche and I'd seen those ski tracks. I think, maybe, there'd have been another avalanche victim. He's strong enough to have torn me in half. He had to be stopped and I took the quickest way I knew.'

Liz sighed shudderingly. 'I knew he was violent and had his strange ways, and I knew they were becoming worse. But not as bad as this. What will become of him, Mike?'

'He'll be all right. There'll be people to look after him. I don't think he'll stand trial for anything. He's beyond that, Liz – way beyond. You saw him this afternoon – you know what I mean. Harrison said as much, too.'

She nodded. 'So it's all over.'

'It's over,' he agreed. 'My masters want me to go south to

he ice. They've put up a geodesic dome at the South Pole –
Buckminster Fuller strikes again – and they want a snowman
o check the foundations.'

McGill leaned back in his chair and picked up his glass. He
said casually, 'Ian is in the Princess Margaret Hospital –
third floor. The Ward Sister is a tough old bird called Quayle
but if you say you are Ian's fiancée she might let you . . .'

He became aware he was talking to thin air. 'Hey, you
haven't finished your drink!'

But Liz was halfway across the room on her way, and
beside her Victor trotted, his tail waving in a proud plume.

Desmond Bagley

– a master of suspense –

'I've read all Bagley's books and he's marvellous,
the best.' *Alistair MacLean*

FONTANA PAPERBACKS

Geoffrey Jenkins

Geoffrey Jenkins writes of adventure on land and at sea in some of the most exciting thrillers ever written.

'Geoffrey Jenkins has the touch that creates villains and heroes – and even icy heroines – with a few vivid words.' *Liverpool Post*

'A style which combines the best of Nevile Shute and Ian Fleming.' *Books and Bookmen*

SOUTHTRAP
A BRIDGE OF MAGPIES
FIREPRINT
HUNTER-KILLER
A RAVEL OF WATERS
THE UNRIPE GOLD
A GRUE OF ICE
THE WATERING PLACE OF GOOD PEACE
IN HARM'S WAY

FONTANA PAPERBACKS

Fontana Paperbacks: Fiction

Fontana is a leading paperback publisher of fiction.
Below are some recent titles.

- ☐ ULTIMATE PRIZES Susan Howarth £3.99
- ☐ THE CLONING OF JOANNA MAY Fay Weldon £3.50
- ☐ HOME RUN Gerald Seymour £3.99
- ☐ HOT TYPE Kristy Daniels £3.99
- ☐ BLACK RAIN Masuji Ibuse £3.99
- ☐ HOSTAGE TOWER John Denis £2.99
- ☐ PHOTO FINISH Ngaio Marsh £2.99

You can buy Fontana paperbacks at your local bookshop or newsagent. Or you can order them from Fontana Paperbacks, Cash Sales Department, Box 29, Douglas, Isle of Man. Please send a cheque, postal or money order (not currency) worth the purchase price plus 22p per book for postage (maximum postage required is £3.00 for orders within the UK).

NAME (Block letters)_____

ADDRESS_____

_____